SEKANDAR'S VECTOR

A PARADIGM SHIFT IN UNDERLYING HUMAN ASSUMPTIONS OF VIOLENCE

ALEXANDER GOODMAN

Sekandar's Vector
© 2018 Alexander Goodman

ISBN 978-0-646-99160-3

A catalogue record for this book is available from the National Library of Australia

Published by Alexander Goodman
Cover design by Baron Design, Canberra

DEDICATION

In loving memory of

Barbara

**I will always be grateful
that you nurtured the seed**

For Karen

CONTENTS

Title
Dedication
Preface

1
Home – Farewell

Narrators
Narrator - Prime Narrator

Emanation - Departure – Arrival

2
Symposium
Violence - War - Kin - Virus - Gaia – Panthea

3
Intercession
Divination - Encounter - Enquiry - Elucidation –
Assignment

4
Subterfuge - Invitations - La Visite – Warriwul
Interlude

5
Conversion - Submission - Pedagogy – Media
Interlude

6
Amerigo
Hollywood - Pentagon - Mesoamerica – Eigenstate -
Poverty

Preface

In 1964 when I was thirteen years of age and living in Katoomba NSW, I dreamt that I would bring to the world something important, maybe epochal. I had no idea what that would be. I just knew it would be. My dream was so vivid, so translucent that I could not forget it. I could not deny it. There are moments in our lives that move us so profoundly, so deeply within that we subconsciously refresh those life changing, life making moments every following day of our lives. My dream of long ago, was one such moment for me.

It occurred to me all those years ago, that there seemed to be a general acceptance that violence was an inherent characteristic in human behaviour. I questioned that. I still do. I didn't accept that it is inevitable. I still don't. I believed that a paradigm shift was required. It still is. The 'epochal something' that I would bring to the world, was right there. Not only that a paradigm shift is required, but also that it is inevitable.

What a pretentious notion! - Yes, you might rightly say so - and yet, my dream is being realised through *Sekandar's Vector*. The theme of my novel is: 'The antithesis of the quintessential human doctrine that you can solve all your problems by using violence, by being violent.'

Sekandar, who is from elsewhere in the Milky Way Galaxy, arrives on Earth with a mission: 'To effect a paradigm shift in underlying human assumptions of violence.'

There are many characters. The main ones are Sekandar the alien who is the initiator of the paradigm shift, and Karen Krause the leader of his team of humans empowered to work with him to effect the change.

All the characters in Sekandar's Vector are fictional; resemblances to real people, living or deceased, are unintended or coincidental. Beliefs, statements and assertions expressed in the story are of the characters; they are not necessarily mine.

The word vector means: 'a variable quantity that can be resolved into components.' This is sure to arouse curiosity.

The two principal characters, Sekandar and Karen Krause came to me in 1969 when I was living in Kogarah, a suburb of Sydney NSW. Names of other characters have come to me since then. Sekandar (Sekundah) is an eastern form of 'Alexander.' Varia is the Latin neuter of 'varius' (various) and also means 'exquisite' in another context. Jiemba, means 'laughing star' in the Wiradjuri language of Australian aborigines. It alludes to the morning star, the planet Venus, and serves a particular purpose in the story.

Imago (Imargo) the estate in Germany of Karen Krause is an important location at different junctures in the book. Imago, is from the Latin *imago* meaning image. In psychoanalysis the principle meaning of 'imago' is: an idealized image of someone or something - a paradigm. I also used this word to arouse curiosity.

The various settings are mostly on Earth, on most continents; locations in Australia feature. Some locations are elsewhere in the Milky Way Galaxy; the story begins and ends on Sekandar's home planet Terra Dyad that orbits its star, Filo. Terra is Latin, meaning 'earth.' Dyad (dye-add) meaning 'something that consists of two elements or parts,' is from the Greek 'duas' meaning 'two.' Is Terra Dyad an esoteric anomaly? Filo (Feelo) means 'friend.'

Writing Sekandar's Vector has been a profound experiential journey; one that I was compelled to take. Some say I am a wordy wizard. Words aplenty I have penned and said of many things, and yet each word in perfect position etched in time has been insufficient, until now.

Humankind is amazingly enigmatic; mysterious and difficult to interpret or understand. Perhaps that is our greatest strength as a species, or is it?

I appreciate the Universe as the totality of being, expressed in numerous magnificent ways; overwhelming in its power, beauty and fundamental mystery that compels the deepest reverence and wonder.

I look to each day afresh - for it is life, the very gift of the Universe. In its short course dwell all the translucent truths of our existence, and as life passes through diffusely I endeavour to see it all with clarity.

The bliss of knowing life and of being saturated in its splendour are but moments in time; moments of yesterday's dream - vivid memories in mind. I encourage you to look well to this day therefore, for yesterday is only a dream, and tomorrow is merely a vision. Today well-lived makes yesterday, and a vision of hope for every tomorrow.

Whether or not Sekandar's Vector is epochal it remains a vision of hope for every tomorrow.

Alexander
2018

1

Home

The air was still. Sekandar strolled slowly from his
house into his extensive tranquil garden, which is adorned
with a variety of indigenous shrubs and trees framing the
manicured lawns of Paralía, his private estate. He paused
briefly and glanced at Filo, the star that his home planet
Terra Dyad orbits. The star was sinking slowly below the
horizon, ushering another long summer twilight that he
always enjoyed. The warmth of the star that had warmly
bathed his world in its light for another day, gradually
gave way to a subtle cooling breeze; a mere zephyr drifting
inland from the sea close by. Soon the first stars in the
night sky will be visible. He knows every one of them;
not only their names but also their properties and their
respective places in the galaxy. He sat in his favourite
garden recliner, where he has often found himself in recent
days, and pondered the future.

He sat still for a minute or two without another thought
then formed his characteristic smile when he returned to
the moment; a smile with smiling eyes included. This is
his last evening at home with his family before he sets off
on another mission. Time with them is precious; there is
never enough of it, and he will cherish every minute of this
evening with them. Tomorrow he is to present himself to
the Galactic Council to be formally conferred with a mission
that he has been preparing for a long time. He has been on
other missions but he is especially looking forward to this
one.

The twilight was fading as the last quivering rays of light
were being swallowed by the encroaching darkness of night,
and the first stars bravely flickered to life. As he watched
the light disappear the thought occurred to him that the
star of his home-world is similar to that of the star in his
mission brief. That is another GV2 - a dwarf yellow star.
The subject planet of that star orbits at a distance similar
to that of his home-world, and it is of similar size. Of course
he knows all that and he also knows that the subject of

his mission is the dominant intelligent species that inhabit that planet; a species he has studied closely for most of his professional life. In many ways he knows them better than they know themselves yet he has never stood before one of their kind. He soon will.

Sekandar's mind was drifting nearer to that other home-world as Varia, his partner of thirty-four years approached. Speaking softly she said, "Sekandar, the meal is served and is ready to be eaten."

He eased back to the moment and stood slowly, then stroked her long gold-tinted platinum blonde hair as he embraced her and kissed her gently. Holding her hand, together they stepped the few paces to the meal table set outside under the open sky and took their places there. Varia and the children, Zane and Aedon had been busy all afternoon preparing this meal to share with Sekandar. There was no demarcation about meal preparation in their household but on this occasion Varia insisted that she and the children would prepare something special. That they did. The meal was of dishes and drinks native to their home planet; all the courses were Sekandar's favourites. During the meal there was lots of animated and jovial talk between each member of the family, about happenings in their daily lives; exactly as one would expect of a happy, close and loving family.

A couple of hours elapsed as they enjoyed the meal and the company of each other. When everyone was satiated and the chatter had subsided Varia, who was sitting next to Sekandar, put her hand in his. Peering into his eyes she looked deep within his soul, and whispered. "Are you ready for your mission Sekandar?"

He had never seen her so earnest in her enquiry; she had similarly enquired before each of his missions but this time he sensed her deeper concern. Almost half the time of their partnership they had been apart. Sekandar's missions had taken him to many locations across the galaxy. He never worried about her when he was away. She is a competent woman with an air of self-assurance and independence about her that attracted him all those years ago, and still does. Of course those are but two attributes of her character that attracts him. He loves everything about her, and frequently tells her so. Thirtyfour years has not diminished their love for each other. On the cusp of another separation he knows that she doesn't want him to leave, but that she will let him go. In the event that he didn't return from this mission Sekandar knew that she would not just be a survivor without him, she would continue to flourish in her profession as the highly regarded Master of Ethics at the Terranian Institute for Education, an institution that had contributed to The Whole, well beyond the expectation of anyone.

"Yes, my dear Varia I am ready," responded Sekandar confidently.

That wasn't enough for her. She had discussed the mission at length with him and she knows that this one is very different. She knows that the risks are much more evident than with his previous missions. She also knows that his upcoming mission is profoundly important.

Looking directly into her dark blue eyes Sekandar strove to reassure her. "You and I know that the success of my mission this time will produce the greatest change in the galaxy that we will see in our lifetimes. The current phase of our ascendancy of the galaxy will soon be complete because of the change. Current indications from our risk assessment team are that there is a 0.97 probability we will witness the culmination and completion of the change well within a human generation. There is also a plausible probability that we may well succeed much sooner. The risks associated with this mission are far greater than anything I have had to deal with previously, and the team has accounted for every possible contingency. I have complete confidence in my ability, and believe that I will succeed. I am mindful that the Council would not have chosen me if there was any doubt about that."

He didn't need to say more. Varia had maintained her direct eye contact with Sekandar as he reassured her. She closed her eyes, leaned forward and kissed him, slowly, gently.

Holding him in her embrace she said, "Sekandar, I love you with all my heart and with all my soul. I always have and always will. I accept that the Council has chosen the right person for this crucial mission. I know it too. Although we will maintain contact when you are away, I will be longing for your safe return, and to hold you close again." Sekandar kissed her, again.

They stayed in their embrace briefly, being interrupted by two somewhat excited, very hopeful children.

"Can we have an ice cream Papa?" pleaded Aedon. "We have cleared away the dishes and you said this morning before you left for work that you would let us have an ice cream. It's not too late. Can we please, please?"

His smiled. Having turned to the children, he now kept that pose and turning his head to look at Varia he said, "Well now let me see. Mama, have these children been good *all* day?"

Varia replied, "I cannot say for certain, Papa. They haven't been within my line-of-sight all day but when they have been they have been almost angelic, anticipating our time together this evening. Perhaps you would do well to enquire of the children themselves?"

The children remained silent, trying desperately hard to look like angels; well at least what they thought angels might look like. Sekandar held out both hands in a gesture inviting his children to embrace him. Giggling, they did so. He turned them 'round quickly and marched them just as quickly into the house, inviting Mama to join them.

Standing on one side of the kitchen bench, with the other three on the other side, Papa enquired, "Which flavour will we have tonight?" "Chocolate!" pleaded Zane. "Strawberry!" pleaded Aedon.

"Choices, choices." said Papa, frowning. "How will I decide? Mama, this is too hard for me to decide. Can you decide for us?"

Standing erect and with her arms folded she replied authoritatively, "Yes, certainly. In my official capacity as decider of the ice cream flavours it is my pleasure to inform you that we each shall have our own choice of flavour tonight."

Giggles all 'round, was the best way to greet the news. Papa obtained the sugar cones, assembled the ice cream in them, and distributed them. Mama and Papa chose Papa's famous homemade rich caramel sauce, as a topping. Yum!

When the children were all cleaned up and ready for bed, Sekandar gathered his family in the lounge room. Snuggling up to his partner as they lounged on the sofa, and facing the children opposite he began.

"Thank you for a wonderful evening! The meal you prepared was excellent. Of course the best part of that was the ice cream," he declared, smiling characteristically. "And, the *real* best part of the evening was that I shared it all with you. Just being with you and Mama is what matters and means the most to me. I love you to bits. Tomorrow I am going away again. I will be home again soon. Promise me that you will work hard in school, completing all your assignments. And, promise me that you will remember that it is not only your responsibility to contribute to The Whole, but it is also your duty."

The children knew what The Whole meant, and they responded, "Yes, Papa we promise and we will be dutiful." Sekandar smiled then commanded, "Good, now off to bed with you! Good night, sleep well, dream sweet."

The children simultaneously jumped to their feet, flung themselves with a hug and a kiss at Papa and Mama in turn, then scurried off to their bedrooms - giggling as they went.

Sekandar, still snuggling up to Varia said, "You are raising our children just right." Quickly, and persuasively she responded, "Sekandar, we are, we are!" He nodded.

Varia stood up and looking down at Sekandar with a glint in her eye she whispered, "You have a big day tomorrow, all your provisions are packed and ready. You need to come to bed with me, now!" He obeyed, taking the hand she offered, and she led him to their bedroom. She gave him a night to remember, the perfect end to his last full day at home, for a while.

Farewell

As Varia was getting the children ready for another school day, and herself for another day at the Institute, Sekandar checked his provisions one last time; it's an age-old habit occasionally justified. Even accounting for Sekandar's species' advanced development, things that shouldn't be left out sometimes were. This time everything is in order. "Breakfast is ready!" the children called out.

They had earnestly requested to prepare this one; because it is special. Varia had earlier informed them of the importance of their Father's mission. The family seated themselves ready for breakfast around the small meal table, and before they started eating Sekandar indicated for each of them to hold hands.

In a gentle tone he devoutly said, "Let us remember our appreciation for the Universe, its power, beauty and mystery calling for our deepest reverence and wonder. And for our individual places in it, as integral elements of The Whole. We are truly thankful for this food, its bounty. And for the highest expressions of its creation, including our family."

Smiling, and addressing his children he added, "My dear Zane and Aedon, I will be home again soon, and look forward to another meal with you. In the meantime, look after your mother and each other. Now, let's eat."

Breakfast proceeded silently at first, then with happy animated talk about the busy day ahead. Everyone assisted in clearing away the breakfast utensils then each went about their final preparations before setting off into their day.

Sekandar stood with Varia by the front door of their residence, waving as Zane and Aedon boarded the electro-magnetic taxi assigned to take them to school. The taxi lifted vertically from the street and floated into its assigned skyway then was quickly out of sight.

Holding hands they admired the sky that carried a smattering of small cumulus clouds, not enough to inhibit the early morning warm rays of Filo. It was going to be another beautiful summer day, one that Sekandar would not see into night as he did yesterday. Still in human form, adopted by the family for the preceding twentyfour hours and now to say goodbye, Sekandar and Varia held each other close for what seemed like minutes.

Widening their embrace and looking directly into each other's eyes, they simultaneously said, "I love you to bits!" chuckling adoringly as the words were leaving their lips.

Varia said, "Peace be with you, Sekandar. I await your return." The slight hint of a sullen frown briefly formed on Varia's brow as she spoke. Sekandar unconsciously registered that and didn't respond.

Stepping away a pace or two he mentally programmed the co-ordinates of the Galactic Council building and waved goodbye. Becoming a kind of misty iridescent shimmer he dematerialised into the incorporeal and was teleported to the Galactic Council where his human form rematerialised.

As that happened he momentarily mused about the advanced development of mentally integrated algorithms that would enable those of his species to teleport themselves across the Galaxy; the capability to teleport had so far been limited to the atmospheric proximity of terrestrial bodies. He looked forward to that because as part of his contribution to The Whole he has been a contributor to its development.

Sekandar rematerialised at the foot of the steps to the main entrance to the Galactic Council building. Obtaining his bearings he instinctively looked about himself then up at the building. It is an unassuming yet distinctive building, set in wooded parkland atop a small rise in the central district of the city. It is not a huge presumptuous edifice dwarfing everything around it such as those he had seen on other worlds.

He remained on the spot for a minute or so and slowly turned full circle as he surveyed the city, very much alive for him. It seemed to be organically glistening under the brightness of the late summer morning. It is his birthplace, and an enchanting pulsating entity full of the wonder of his youth, the adventures of his early adulthood, the challenges and triumphs of his professional career, and his courtship and all those magical years of happiness with Varia.

Events of those times flashed vividly through his mind as he turned full circle again before slowly scaling the steps to front door. He smiled characteristically then entered the building, walking apace to the Prime Narrator's rooms. Nearing them, he stopped, turned and walked slowly in the direction his own rooms; his office where he had worked on the project.

There was no need for him to be early and so he took the opportunity to still his mind a while, and then to peruse certain items in his project files. The files are not in physical form, rather they reside with The Whole which will instantly deliver to his mind any specific item he requests.

Narrators

Narrator

Sitting in his office before his appointment with the Prime Narrator, Sekandar found himself drifting back in his thoughts, back as far as he could recall. He wondered why he was reminiscing again so soon after doing just that as he stood on the Galactic Council steps only moments before.

"Memories," he said to himself. "That is what remains with the passage of time." He knows he is blessed to have such fond memories of a happy childhood at Epitome, his family's residence that was home for him, his parents and his three siblings. In his formative years, anniversary celebrations with his extended family of aunts, uncles, cousins, nieces and nephews were special occasions too. He remembered his formal education years where he formed friendships that remain with him.

With fingers interlocked his hands smoothed his hair as they slipped to the back of his head. He spread his elbows, sighed and said, "Yes, Memories. These are what we take with us wherever we go." He smiled his characteristic smile.

His thoughts returned to the present, and to his human visual aspect. On his home world Sekandar is rather inconspicuous, mainly due to his typically Terranian plain and functional clothing. Even so his overall clothed appearance is distinctive. His forthcoming mission however will require him to be dressed quite differently. In consultation with Varia he has given that some thought. She has advised him, appropriately.

Sekandar's thoughts then dwelt a moment or two on his chosen human form. It is not an atypical choice among Terranians, although it is not particularly common either. He is about 1.8 metres tall. His build is average and he weighs about 90 kilograms. His eyes are dark hazel, and they appear translucent in the sunlight and under certain artificial lighting.

Hair, eye and skin colour chosen by Terranians is fairly evenly apportioned between the same assortments found among humans. Sekandar's hair is dark blonde with splashes of dark auburn here and there and his complexion is of a subtle lucent light olive-coloured hue, an unusual combination along with his sparkling dark hazel eyes. He wondered whether he would be conspicuous in a crowd of another species, particularly a species he has not yet seen in person.

His thoughts returned to the present, and to perusal of his project files. They detail everything about his team. Members of his team were chosen in collaboration with the Galactic Council, and in consultation with The Whole. The selection process is impossible to explain to a human.

Sekandar was chosen to lead the team for a number of reasons, his exceptional intellect being one of the principal determinants. That was evident at an early age. Upon completion of his formal education he was subsequently chosen to form and lead the team, whose mission will produce a fundamental change within the Galaxy, securing his species' ascendancy of it.

His leadership of the team requires him to be a Narrator of the Council. Given any definition that may make sense to a human, Narrators are not politicians; not that politicians per se make any sense to humans. 'Narrator of the Galactic Council' is a respected role among Terranians, and also among other intelligent species within the Terranian galactic hegemony established millennia ago.

Different roles are assumed by Narrators, each of them carry responsibility, obligation and duty. Since becoming a Narrator, Sekandar has been on numerous missions throughout the Galaxy. His exploits have enabled him to amass an extensive knowledge about the Galaxy and beyond; of things previously unknown or not well understood. His knowledge is incorporated into The Whole. His achievements have identified him not just as a Terranian with an exceptional intellect but also as one who is acutely insightful and wise.

Prime Narrator

Iskandar, Prime Narrator of the Galactic Council was pacing, a habit of his during thought. Not that pacing helped, he is not a worrier, he just liked to pace. Indeed some of his fellow Narrators have often referred to him as 'Iskandar the pacer.' A reference not intended to be emphatic, but more as an identifier.

Iskandar has been Prime Narrator since his late adolescent years. Although it is an honoured and highly esteemed and respected position it is a role which is neither hereditary nor hierarchical. Rather, it is more like a convenience to initiate narration between members of the Council. There are no hierarchies with his species. They were relegated to history millennia ago, having been deemed more harmful than useful. His species achieves everything co-operatively, not competitively. He is relaxed about his meeting with Sekandar.

He has requested that Narrator Sekandar attends the Council in human form; Sekandar's mission requires it. Sekandar had done so many times before, and indeed also for his last day at home together with his family. Assuming human form is a preference for their species anyway, and the form particularly liked by all. Iskandar didn't yet understand why that is so, neither did anyone else. The origin of his species has been shrouded in mysterious stories of antiquity. His species' normal form is without apparent material substance. It has been so for

millennia, although not initially so. He is an individual of
an incorporeal species able to assume any material form
that suits any purpose.

Together with all the members of the Council, each
contributing valuable insight and wisdom to the plan of
action, Iskandar had been working with Sekandar for a very
long time on strategies for the forthcoming mission. Today
he will be formally conferring Sekandar with the mission.
This would seem to be a mere formality; a remnant of
protocol passed down from ancient times, yet it enables
him to articulate the plan in essence, bestow the aneling of
the Council, and then to bid farewell to Sekandar who will
be acting as representative not only of the Galactic Council
but also of The Whole.

As if telepathically recognising him, the doors to
Iskandar's private rooms opened automatically as Sekandar
confidently approached them; these doors opened only to
authorised persons. He walked through the doorway and
greeted the Prime Narrator with his outstretched right
hand. "Good morning Prime Narrator."

No etiquette was needed. In the scheme of things they
were equals. Iskandar responded, "Good morning Narrator
Sekandar. Thank you for being on time. Indeed not just
for you but for us all the time has arrived, if I may put it
that way. Before we enter the Council Chamber I want to
congratulate you on your dedication and proficiency as
you prepared for this mission. Every Narrator lauds your
inclusive bearing throughout the planning and preparation
process. Your example is exemplary."

Sekandar was not expecting that. Had he switched
on his telepathic facility he would have read the Prime
Narrator's thoughts but he had been switched off since
yesterday, the start of his last day with his family. Iskandar
was aware of that. Sekandar's response to the praise was a
simple "Thank you, Prime Narrator." Iskandar added, "It is
appropriate and well deserved praise."

Iskandar paused a moment then drew closer to
Sekandar. "Before we go to the Council Chamber there
is something I have to inform you about. Our security
surveillance recently detected a series of signals emanating

from an unidentified source in a sector in the Galaxy just beyond our quadrant. The signals which have been at various frequencies are aimed directly at Terra Dyad, and have been repeated at irregular intervals. At this stage we don't know if the signals are random or specific. As I speak, we are working to identify the source and whether there is a specific target on our planet. I am informing you because we are also factoring in potential inferences to your mission, and we will keep you informed of our analysis. I will now install in you a secure channel for this purpose."

Iskandar gently placed each of his middle fingers onto Sekandar's corresponding left and right temples. He pressed lightly then withdrew. Concerned, Sekandar enquired, "You have given me the most secure channel. Is that necessary?"

"It may be. The importance of your mission requires it," Iskandar replied prosaically.

"I understand, Prime Narrator," Sekandar formally acknowledged.

With a deliberate change in tone, Iskandar commanded, "Come, our fellow Narrators await. Remember to switch on your telepathy channel before we enter the Council Chamber; as usual every Narrator will be telepathic in session."

They left the Prime Narrator's room immediately then briskly proceeded to the Council Chamber, just a short distance through the hallowed halls of the Galactic Council building. Time enough for Sekandar to look around this place of governance that had been standing for almost a millennium. He had been within its walls on many occasions and knew it well. On this occasion he found himself being a bit reflective of those occasions and of this place, and wondering if he would perceive it all differently when he returned from his mission. Iskandar read those thoughts and telepathically said, "All will be well, Sekandar."

Emanation

Their walk through the corridors to the Council Chamber was relatively short. There were no attendants at the doors to the chamber. None were required or needed; the entire building was shielded from any external probe or assault. The huge doors opened as they approached, recognising them as with the doors to the Prime Narrator's room. They entered the large high-vaulted chamber, and the several hundred Narrators assembled therein rose to their feet in unison. Iskandar has requested that every Narrator attending this session of the Council assume human form. Not a word was spoken, neither audibly nor telepathically.

Iskandar and Sekandar approached the steps to the central dais, mounted them then positioned themselves centrally upon the dais where they turned and stood together facing the assembled Narrators. Thunderous applause erupted as soon as they turned to face the audience.

When the applause had subsided to distinct silence the Prime Narrator said, "This Extraordinary Meeting of the Galactic Council is now in session. Please be seated."

Iskandar waited until the audience settled then began. "My fellow Narrators, there are two items of business in this session of the Galactic Council. Let us deal with the first." He paused briefly as he drew breath, then said, "Teleportation has until now been limited to terrestrial proximity. For the last hundred years The Whole has contributed to the development of the necessary algorithms for our incorporeal species to use mentally integrated capability to teleport ourselves across the Galaxy. The ability to do so is now ready for implementation."

Iskandar continued, "Narrators of the Galactic Council please stand." In unison the assembled Narrators rose to their feet. In a gentle yet authoritative tone he devoutly said, "Let us remember our appreciation for the Universe, its power, beauty and mystery calling for our deepest reverence and wonder. And for our individual places in it, as integral elements of The Whole. We are truly thankful for the existence our species, the highest expression of its creation, and for the privilege of our leadership of the Galaxy." In unison everyone repeated, "We are truly thankful."

Prime Narrator Iskandar symbolically raised his hands, palms up and held out at chest height before him. Everyone followed his lead. The lighting in the Council Chamber was just bright enough for everyone to be easily seen. There was a soft spotlight upon the two on the dais. All the lights dimmed further to a softness as all hands were raised. Each individual Narrator dematerialised into the incorporeal, each becoming a kind of misty iridescent shimmer, coloured in the full spectrum of white light that glowed softly then coalesced into a whole and slowly brightened slightly. There was no sound. The Whole remained so for two minutes exactly before separating into individual shimmers again, and then coalescing and rematerialising into individual human forms. Everyone returned to their places, and stood as before.

Iskandar said, "So be it." In unison everyone repeated, "So be it." Satisfaction with the installation of the new capability was clearly evidenced by the distinct murmur rippling excitedly across the assembly.

Facing the assembled Narrators, Iskandar said, "The second and ultimate item of this session of the Galactic Council will now be carried out."

Befitting his assumed human form he took a deep breath again and said, "The Galactic Council has been convened to formally confer upon Sekandar his mission. We know that the success of his mission will produce the greatest change in the Galaxy that we will see in our lifetimes. Our ascendancy of the galaxy will progress because of The Change. There is a reasonable probability that we will witness the culmination within a few years. The risks associated with his mission are far greater than anything we have had to deal with previously, and we have accounted for every possible contingency. We, the Galactic Council have complete confidence in his ability, and believe that he will succeed. We have no doubt about that."

Turning to face Sekandar, and looking directly into his eyes, Prime Narrator Iskandar confidently and with a voice of profound authority said, "We formally confer upon you, Narrator Sekandar the mission to effect the change; the paradigm shift in underlying human assumptions of violence."

Iskandar raised his hands again, palms up and held out at chest height before him. Everyone followed his lead. As before, all the lights dimmed to a softness as all hands were raised. Each individual Narrator dematerialised and then rematerialised as they had done previously, and they returned to their places, where they stood as before.

Iskandar said, "So be it. It is done." In unison everyone repeated, "So be it. It is done." The effect of the process upon Sekandar was as an aneling by The Whole.

Sekandar stepped forward and addressed the full complement of the Galactic Council one last time before his departure.

"My fellow Narrators. Our ascendancy of the galaxy is progressing to plan. Our new capability will complement our others. We will ensure that we use all our capabilities for the benefit of The Whole. The task of my mission, to effect The Change, - the paradigm shift in underlying human assumptions of violence, will be accomplished. I will be in constant communication with The Whole, and as is the usual custom I will submit my formal report to the Council upon my return."

He then stepped back a pace as Iskandar raised his right hand waving it in farewell, every Narrator rose to their feet again and said, "Farewell, Narrator Sekandar. We look forward to your safe return to Terra Dyad. Peace be with you."

The Prime Narrator then said, "This session of the Galactic Council is closed." He remained standing as the Narrators filed out of the chamber, in no particular order, each going about their business. Iskandar and Sekandar waited until everyone had departed. They then walked out together, and directly to the steps of the Galactic Council building. They shook hands and separated. Sekandar retained his human form. The Prime Narrator re-entered the Council building, and may or may not have done likewise.

Departure

Sekandar's mission requires him in human form, and so he chose to travel to his destination by the old way. The 'old way' utilises physical transporters; ground cars, aerial craft and spaceships. He rather enjoys these forms of transportation. They help him to feel more human. He didn't need to go from there to there to there to get to the interstellar ship. Indeed, given that dematerialised teleportation was no longer limited to terrestrial proximity, he could have chosen different options. He could have dematerialised and transported himself directly to the Terrestrial Space Port, board his interstellar ship then lift off electro-magnetically from there and proceed directly to the programmed orbit at his destination, or he could have teleported himself directly to his destination! He said to himself, "It's fun doing it this way."

He hailed a taxi that floated down towards him in its electro-magnetic field from its aerial road, one of many aerial commuter routes across the planet. The taxi had no driver, unless you could call the computer the driver, drew near to him at his level, a door opened, he stepped in and sat down. Sekandar didn't have to instruct the taxi to take him to the Terrestrial Space Port, he just thought it. He knew he wouldn't be able to do that on the planet of his destination. Transportation would seem comparatively primitive there. Somehow the thought of that caused a sense of excitement to stir within.

Enroute to the Terrestrial Space Port, Sekandar now fully equipped and prepared for his mission, had a few minutes to savour a final appreciation of his home planet. Those thoughts were telepathically read by Varia who responded with a telepathic hug and a kiss.

"You spoil me! Thank you," he replied. He could feel her release her mind. His characteristic smile had just formed when he acknowledged a telepathic link with the Prime Narrator.

Iskandar said, "Isn't it good that the feeling of excitement is still an essential part of the makeup of our species? We feel and share your excitement Narrator Sekandar, and we temper it as we ponder the importance of your mission."

"Thank you Prime Narrator," replied Sekandar. No sooner had those communications transpired when his taxi came gently to a standstill. It had taken him to the Terrestrial Space Port. The door opened, he stepped out, and unhurried he proceeded to check in for the shuttle which was waiting to take him to his interstellar ship docked at the Interstellar Interchange Port.

It was just before dusk when the shuttle taxied to its position for lift-off. The electro-magnetic shuttle lift-off was smooth, and then ascending the flight at first was not quite as smooth due to some barely perceptible turbulence created by summer storms raging nearby. Orbit launch altitude was reached quickly after circling out north-eastward, then back over the coastline in a course bound for the Interstellar Interchange Port. The flight attendants served a light snack that was all too small. He hadn't eaten since breakfast with his family, and he was feeling hungry after the momentous session at the Galactic Council. He smiled as he thought about what he had just experienced, and he was feeling more humanlike with each passing minute. And so he should, his destination is planet Earth, in the Orion Spur of the Galaxy.

The orbiting Interstellar Interchange Port was displayed on the viewer. Shortly before the shuttle docked, the port loomed large. Transfer from the shuttle to the interstellar ship was quicker than he expected; efficiency of transportation systems was constantly improving. The seamless silvery skin of the ship shimmered briefly and as the outline of a door was evident. The door became transparent as Sekandar walked through it. Now that he was on board, he took the time to familiarise himself with his new personal interstellar space cruiser, constructed and commissioned specifically for this particular mission.

His ship is not large, it doesn't need to be. Even so it is about twenty metres long and five metres in girth, at the widest point. It is a variant of the latest class of small personal electro-magnetic space cruisers. It is sleek, clad in shimmering silvery metal and fully automated; 'automated' meaning a perpetual telepathic link between Sekandar and the ship's computers, enabling constant communication regulating everything from plotting and navigating the ship's course to maintenance of the on-board environment, and constant contact with Terra Dyad, and with The Whole.

Sekandar perused the control station before him that consisted of nothing more than an array of Terranian symbols on a panel on the wall. Assuming control as he focused his mind, the ship became an extension of himself with The Whole. The electro-magnetic motors started and the ship silently cruised at an accelerated pace to its programmed co-ordinates just beyond the plane of Terra Dyad's solar system in preparation for the first hyper-jump on his trip to his destination.

The trip to Earth proceeded effortlessly as the ship first cruised at sub-parsec speed then negotiated a series of jumps through hyperspace across the Galaxy. It was over in what would have seemed to a human an inordinately short duration.

When the ship arrived from hyperspace at the outer reaches of Earth's solar system, Sekandar decided to have a look around. In preparation for his mission to Earth he had previously been within the plane of its solar system, and this time he wanted to see whether any other interstellar travellers were in the vicinity; none were detected, although there was evidence that there had been recent visitors. He then took his time to marvel at this solar system that he had studied closely, and he wondered about its familiarity. The electromagnetic motors silently impelled the ship towards Earth where Sekandar piloted it into a low orbit around the planet. Preparations for the final leg of his journey were underway.

Transfer to his personal pod seemed effortless, almost like a habit; he had done it often on missions elsewhere in the Galaxy. This time he paused a moment to look down at this little world so many parsecs from his own. He smiled and his eyes gleamed as he scanned the world below, indicating his confidence in this particular mission; he knew it would be special.

There was a faint click as his pod detached from the interstellar ship and it electro-magnetically descended slowly towards the thin layer of grey-white cirrus clouds below, automatically seeking and finding its programmed path to its landing site.

The landing was gentle and silent, of course. He had arrived. Nobody noticed his arrival; nobody could have noticed, the orbiting interstellar ship and his pod were cloaked from any form of detection by humans, or any other intelligent being for that matter.

Arrival

He landed in a Wald, a forest. Well, it had the appearance of a forest but actually it was part of a large metropolitan parkland; one of several which surround Berlin. Before leaving the orbiting interstellar ship Sekandar had dressed himself in attire that would be in keeping with current dress standards on Earth. He stepped from the shuttle onto recently manicured green grass lightly strewn with fallen autumn leaves in various hues. He marvelled at the scene before him and was overcome with a sense of serenity, akin to coming home. The fresh air, the aromas, the trees, the grass. Although he had learned about it all during his research of Earth, he never imagined it to be so like this; like his home planet.

He gathered his provisions from the cloaked pod then telepathically signalled to the orbiting interstellar ship to retrieve it, to ensure there was no possibility of it being stumbled upon by an unsuspecting human. He would have it sent to him whenever and wherever he needed it. There was no sound of course as the pod electro-magnetically lifted off, gently rustling leaves on the nearby trees as it rose higher and higher, then accelerating exponentially until it slowed again nearing its destination where his pod reattached to the interstellar ship. If the ship was in the atmosphere, a faint click would have been heard externally.

Sekandar now had some time to get acquainted with Earth before his planned rendezvous in the evening, time to feel what it is to be a human on Earth. He ambled out from the clearing in the grove of trees where his pod landed, and noticed there were a few people around. A few were strolling. A few were sitting on benches looking intently at some kind of hand held device that they manipulated or talked into; they must be the communication devices he had read about. Here and there were cuddling couples. Varia came to mind; the very thought of her automatically established contact. "Varia would like it here," he thought to himself. "I think I would," she telepathically replied. Nobody in his vicinity noticed him. That he wanted, to maintain anonymity for now.

He could see vehicles moving along a street just a short distance away. These he knew to be a common mode of ground transport on Earth; interesting ground cars moving on wheels carrying no more than a few humans, one of them apparently being in control of the vehicle. Small transporters on his home world were fully automated and electro-magnetic; no need for wheels or controllers. Another thought: "What did humans call them? Ah yes, cars ... and ... drivers!" He was looking forward to riding in the wheeled ground cars, and told himself that he must drive one too. Maybe that would be fun.

Dishevelled. Unkempt. The words came to mind as a bent figure of a man nearby uttered something in a husky voice, almost inaudible. Sekandar approached him and enquired, "What was that you said?"

The man looked up at him and said, "Alms for the poor?"

Sekandar took a step back returning a quizzical look at the bent figure, as he sought to recall and find in his own memory the meaning of 'alms.' In the time it took him to scan the man's brain, discovering that his current circumstance resulted from a relatively short series of events following the untimely death of his family, Sekandar said, "Come with me, I will give you alms."

The bent figure straightened a bit, and clearly stunned by the command responded in a less husky voice, "Thank you ... Sir."

Taking the man with him, they reached the pavement beside the road he had seen earlier and hailed a taxi; he recalled that human practice from his memory too. As they got into the taxi Sekandar requested the driver, "Please take us to the nearest good hotel."

It was a short ride; being in the city there were several hotels from which to choose. "This one has a good reputation. I recommend it," the driver said as he pulled into the kerb. Sekandar paid the driver and they got out; he could produce any currency as needed, at will.

Escorting the man into the hotel Sekandar said to him, "Sit here and wait."

Remaining within sight of the man he approached the reception counter, booked a room then returned to take the man with him and they followed the porter who escorted them to their room. Sekandar tipped the porter; another human practice, and entered the room ushering the man ahead of him. The man was stunned by the speed with which everything had happened, and was obviously frightened. Placing a hand on his shoulder Sekandar gently coaxed him to sit in a chair, and said, "Do not be afraid. Everything will be fine. Now, look at me."

Sekandar looked into the man's eyes and probed his mind. Soothing it as he did so he asked, "What is your name?"

"Niko ... Nikolei. Why did you bring me here?" the man replied feebly.

Sekandar responded, "I am Sekandar. I brought you here to get you back on your feet. Now, go and take a shower, have a shave, comb you hair and when you have dried yourself off I will give you clean clothes that you will put on. Do you understand me?" Niko nodded then sheepishly shuffled off to the shower.

Having been cleaned up and dressed in clean clothes that Sekandar had procured with the assistance of the concierge, Niko found himself with Sekandar back in the lobby. Sekandar called the concierge over to speak with them. "Nikolei, I want to introduce you to Justin Tyme the concierge of this hotel. Mr Tyme is hiring you as his doorman. Please thank him for his kindness."

With a short preceding unintelligible stutter Nico mumbled, "Thank you Mr Tyme."

The concierge said, "It is a pleasure to have you join our team, and just in time too because our doorman retired yesterday, after many years of faithful service to our hotel. I have been looking without success for a replacement. Your impeccable references sealed the job for you," declared the concierge. Speechless, Niko raised his eyebrows as he turned his head to peer wide-eyed with incredulity at Sekandar who presented an open hand horizontally raised in response.

After he had ensured that a guest he had been attending to was escorted to his waiting taxi, the concierge requested that Niko should speak further with him, about his quarters and other matters. Niko responded with a mumbled 'yes sir,' then turned to face Sekandar and asked, "What can I say?"

Sekandar telepathically replied, "All you need to say is 'thank you.' Those two words will see you rise, in a few short years to be the owner of this hotel, and of the hotel chain itself. When that happens remember to reward the concierge, your new employer, Justin Tyme."

Having by then made his way with Niko to the sidewalk, Sekandar hailed a taxi which pulled into the kerb. He said, "I will not forget you Nikolei." Just as Niko was about to say thank you, Sekandar got into the taxi which drove off and was quickly out of sight. Before re-entering the hotel for his orientation with his new employer Niko briefly looked skyward and said, "Thank you. I will never forget you either, Sekandar."

Sekandar was feeling more human, and Earth was beginning to feel more familiar, as he cruised in his taxi along the inter-city motorway. Somehow, that was no surprise to him. He felt comfortable on Earth. 'Why?' he thought to himself.

Riding along he was not conscience of his surroundings, rather he was meditative. As if to reorient himself he ticked off a 'list' in his mind: "I have come from far away to fulfil my mission that I have known since my early years. Humans don't yet know that. In the fullness of time they will, and they will thank me for the change I make in the human paradigm. My arrival on Earth is the culmination of years of study and preparation undertaken at the behest of the Galactic Council. I have their sanction. My mission is not difficult to accomplish, it just takes time. Why did I do that? .. Nikolei." The name stuck.

The taxi arrived at its destination, he paid the fare and got out. His mission had begun. "But what was that occurrence with Nikolei all about?" he thought. "That wasn't planned." The name stuck ... Nikolei. He gave that thought to The Whole, for assessment ... investigation, and then he entered the symposium venue. Sekandar's attendance at the symposium was planned.

2

Symposium

Dr. Karen Krause is attending a symposium. It is one of a series of symposia that have been scheduled over the next few years; these arranged by the Society for Human Development.

The principal topic for discussion at this symposium is aimed at finding answers to the perennial questions: 'Why do humans have a propensity to slide into violence, believing that any problem can be solved that way, and how can this be reversed?' The quest for answers has been relentless. Karen is attending the symposium with what she thinks is an answer, one that she is keeping to herself, for now.

It is a full program. She knows the speakers, and their topics. The sessions will be protracted with speaker after speaker iterating and reiterating their particular hypotheses. She is at this symposium with a purpose. She will be listening carefully for the slightest hint that at least one speaker might know what she knows.

Dr. Ezekiel Eisner, professor of astronomy and cosmology opened the symposium. Following the expected introduction he then proceeded with curious remarks:

"What are the different forms of violence? There is a myriad of definitions which all constitute a violation of human rights and includes physical, sexual, psychological, emotional; financial and material abuse; abandonment; neglect; and serious loss of dignity and respect, and of course war."

"We are attending this symposium eager to discover reasonable answers about the role of violence in our world, and how we can mitigate then ultimately banish it. In this quest let us strive for the mind of a beginner, and a broad forensic approach to our knowledge of the issue. My hope is that the payoff will be the 'electricity' that lights up our lives to a non-violent future."

"We live in an electric world. We find electricity indispensable. Electricity courses invisibly in the darkness over great distances along thin power lines. The universe does the same since all matter is electrical. Yet until recently astronomy was stuck in the past, unable to see that stars are as electric lights strung along invisible cosmic power lines that are detectable by their magnetic fields and radio noise."

"Why were discoveries of the reign of electro-magnetic activity among the stars ignored for so long? The answer may be found in the inertia of prior beliefs and the failure of our educational institutions. We humans are better storytellers than scientists. We see the universe through the filter of tales we are told in childhood and our education systems reward those who can best repeat them."

"Dissent is discouraged so that many of the brightest intellects become bored and drop out. Until now the history of science has been sanitized to ignore the great controversies of the past which were generally acquired by accreditation. History shows that entrenched paradigms resist extraordinary disproof."

"It may be that there is a similarity between those issues of cosmology and the issues that are the subject of this symposium. Let the symposium begin. Our first speaker is …"

On her tablet Karen took notes of each speaker's presentation.

Violence

One of the many violent circumstances that could be included in this symposium is violence against children, which includes physical and psychological violence, but also neglect and exploitation. This is the first topic on the program. Behavioural scientist, Dr. Lilly Ruhr asked, "How can we prevent violence against children?"

Responses from the delegates defined two distinct types of violence experienced by children up to 18 years of age. They are: child maltreatment by parents and caregivers in children aged 0-14, and violence occurring in community settings among adolescents aged 15-18 years. After several minutes of discussion it was generally agreed that these different types of violence can be prevented by addressing the underlying causes and risk factors specific to each type.

Dr. Ruhr pointed out that all violence against children and especially child maltreatment occurring in the first decade of life is both a problem in itself and a major risk factor for other forms of violence and health problems through a person's life.

The delegates agreed that continuing data collection and information related to violence against children, violence prevention policies and programs, and systems for the provision of appropriate medical emergency trauma care, will result in a fall in violence against children.

Karen knew this would ease the problem but she sensed that there is another solution. She kept that to herself, for now.

The program moved on to other domestic violence issues. Dr. Ruhr lamented that the conversation about domestic violence leaves us to ask: "Will the conversation somehow lead to less domestic violence in the future or excluding that, will it lead to more help for its victims?"

One delegate claimed that incidents of reported domestic violence have fallen according to the best available evidence but we know there is much more to do. According to studies one in four women say they have been victims of domestic violence. Even though that number may fall over time, millions of women will be victims.

To get a sense of what the next steps should be Dr. Ruhr informed the symposium that she had canvassed researchers and advocates, with expertise spanning psychology, sociology, and law enforcement.

While there wasn't complete consensus, five ideas kept coming up over and over again. First, keep trying prevention programs, scale up the most promising, and study how well they work; many researchers believe the best way to deter abuse is to stop people from becoming abusers in the first place. Several approaches have shown promise.

Secondly, make penalties for domestic violence consistent and firm. Thirdly, increase funding for support services. Many working in the field say that the demand for services far exceeds the supply. Fourthly, change the way courts handle cases involving domestic violence. Divorces frequently involve allegations of domestic violence but judicial systems would not necessarily handle the issues separately, with one judge presiding over the divorce, and another hearing the criminal domestic violence case. This was tough on the victims, who had to deal with multiple sets of legal proceedings, each with a different process. Finally, help women to be economically independent.

The delegates agreed that the suggestions highlighted should be addressed.

A law professor among the delegates, Dr. Amne Tahir stated: "So many women stay in destructive relationships because if they leave they will be homeless with their children or they can't support themselves and their children. Of course policy changes that tend to help women financially make a difference too."

War

The program moved on to the question: Is war in our genes? Mathematician, Dr. Miri Tschkenov pointed out that many people have asserted that war is encoded within our biological make-up. That mankind has plagued itself with war since the beginning of functioning societies and will continue to in the future. He also pointed out that others have asserted that violence within humans can be thought of as somewhat instinctive, just like many other animals. He said that yet others cited the old supposition that natural selection has separated the weak from the fit, affecting evolution in all species. He challenged the common claim that natural selection is considered 'survival of the fittest' and declared that the alleged dictum, 'What better way to find the strongest of a group?' indicates a poor understanding of the evolutionary process.

The next speaker was Dr. Valentine Plessis, an anthropologist who had studied the tribal people of South America. She believed that these people were in a constant state of war, causing extreme aggression. Though she claimed she had recorded sufficient data to surmise that humans may have acquired genetic coding for war, other contributors at the symposium still felt that such an assumption still needed to be tested further.

The question of whether warfare is encoded in our genes, or appeared as a result of civilisation, has long fascinated anyone trying to come to grips with human society. Might a willingness to fight neighbouring groups have provided our ancestors with an evolutionary advantage? With conflicts raging across the globe, these questions have implications for understanding our past, and perhaps our future as well.

Anthropologists, whose knowledge of so-called traditional societies could provide clues as to how our ancestors behaved, also took sides in the debate. Some researchers concluded that warfare is only an invention which had not existed before civilisation, others reported that among some tribal groups fighting and raids on enemy villages were commonplace. Both of these conclusions were criticised in the discussion among symposium delegates. The first: for overlooking widespread evidence of violence and the second for inappropriately using societies of small-scale farmers as a proxy for prehistoric hunter-gatherers. A claim that humans in primitive societies have long been in a state of chronic warfare was hotly disputed.

Of course, any traditional society that anthropologists choose to study has still been exposed to outside influences. And, they differ vastly from one another, not least in their participation in warfare but early accounts suggest that lethal aggression did exist between some hunter-gatherer groups before their contact with other societies. It's difficult to conclude that prehistory was free from intergroup aggression. Military historians and evolutionary psychologists have long argued that warfare existed before the agricultural revolution.

Delegates supporting this hypothesis also claimed that violence has decreased over the centuries. This may seem difficult to believe given the gloomy headline news that prevails. Maybe this view of history at least suggests hope for the future, they suggested.

Karen said to herself, "Maybe it does." Within herself she senses a very different scenario.

Dr. Plessis pointed out that philosophers have had different visions of prehistory. Some saw humanity's earliest days as being dominated by fear and warfare, whereas others thought that without the influence of civilisation, humans would be at peace and in harmony with nature. The debate about that continues to this day. Without a time machine, researchers examining warfare in prehistory largely rely on archaeology, primatology and anthropology.

The mention of 'time machine' resonated with Karen, and she wondered why.

Dr. Plessis's concluding remarks informed delegates that the evidence of warfare becomes clearer in the archaeological record after the beginning of the agricultural revolution around 10,000 years ago, when humanity moved from hunting and gathering to farming settlements. War may have existed before then, but there are few remains from the early days of Homo Sapiens, and causes of death can be extremely difficult to ascertain from skeletons. This means that the archaeology remains inconclusive.

Kin

Dr. Plessis suggested that if humans look to their closest animal relatives, we can learn that violent tendencies hit both extremes. Chimpanzees are known as having a type of warfare, whereas bonobos who are just as closely related to humans as chimps are, have a high tendency for love making instead. Some in the audience awoke from their germinal slumber at that comment.

When it was discovered that chimpanzees make war, the world was shocked. A group in Tanzania were observed beating members of a rival community to death, before taking over the defeated group's territory. Despite attempts to dispute the original findings, similar patterns of behaviour were later discovered in other groups, and evidence for warfare in one of our closest relatives became indisputable.

However, bonobos share as much DNA with us as chimps do, and are overall more peaceful, despite some anecdotal reports of aggression between groups. This is partly attributed to differences in the two species' social systems. Bonobos' societies are female-dominated, which perhaps keeps male aggression in check, whereas chimpanzees' social hierarchy is male-dominated.

How did our last common ancestor behave? Were they like bellicose chimpanzees or peaceful bonobos? Although parallels between all three species are fascinating, using them to answer this question is difficult, as ultimately each followed its own evolutionary pathway. But chimps demonstrate that war without civilisation does exist in a species similar to our own. Similarities can also be seen between chimpanzee and human hunter-gatherer warfare. In both species, an imbalance of power and risk-averse tactics are often a feature of attacks: a group of chimpanzees will assault a lone rival, and hunter-gatherer groups avoid pitched battles in favour of guerrilla warfare and ambushes.

Some delegates inferred that no scientific conclusions can be made about warfare being encoded in human genes. Violence has definitely evolved with our species, but many other factors come into play when tendencies for war are being discussed. Cultural factors make warfare much more prevalent in some societies than others. Humans are all born with violence written somewhere in their genetic makeup, as shown with the classic fight or flight response. The extent to which humans take their violence sometimes does lead to war, but not all humans are the same in the way they would handle situations.

Throughout human history war has constantly been a huge topic. Violent outbursts, shooting sprees in large cities and genocide have shown the savage capabilities that we humans have. One delegate pointed out that science will continue to try to understand why tragic events happen but to some extent not all things can be explained with science, and warfare seems to be one of those things.

Karen thought this was perhaps a provocative suggestion, knowing that the scientific approach is to constantly observe what is, develop hypotheses based on observations then to test the hypotheses. Tests proving hypotheses result in theories. Speculations are not theories.

Virus

Virologist, Dr. Yang Meixa suggested that warring or violent behaviour is not innate to human nature, that war is a problem that has a solution we haven't found yet, just like cancer.

Karen listened closely to this speaker, wondering, "Will there be another speculation here or maybe a hypothesis?"

Dr. Meixa claimed that there is evidence to suggest that war is neither a biological impulse nor an economic imperative. So what are the other factors that can explain the emergence and recurrence of war? Pointing to the work of several anthropologists the speaker indicated that they all shared the belief that war is a cultural innovation. The suggestion being that war emerged sometime in human prehistory and began to spread like a virus.

To illustrate how war is a culturally infectious virus Dr. Meixa put it this way, "Imagine your neighbour is a violent aggressor who is out to get your land, even if that means your blood with it. You on the other hand are a person who wants peace. You would have few options but to embrace the ways of war for defence. So, essentially your neighbour has infected you with war."

To explain the significance of this she continued with the line of reasoning suggesting that society is now a very civilized place. This apparent assertion drew a burst of laughter from the audience. Unperturbed, Dr. Meixa continued and said, "Survival violence is not at the forefront of everyone's mind everywhere. Thus it would be reasonable to expect the propagation of the war virus to slow down."

Dr. Meixa's little treatise ignited animated discussion among the delegates. Some arguing exactly that point, noting that it is unthinkable for many countries in this era to go to war but that in previous eras expansionist ambitions by these same countries and fear of their deadly neighbours led to devastating world wars. Though only time will tell, it is possible that through cooperation and diplomacy countries like those will have cured their war virus permanently.

Karen knew that she must arrange a private conversation with this speaker; what was her name again? Finding it on the symposium program she noted her name and contact details.

It had been a long day already. Most of this stuff she had heard before. She came to the symposium with a purpose; to look for the slightest hint that one speaker might know what she knows. Well, she found a few that might have an inkling. Although she eagerly wanted to contact them she hoped that the final speaker might offer more hope, more certainty that she was not alone with what she knew.

Gaia

Karen knew a lot about Professor Dr. James Lynne. He had previously been a proponent of the Gaia hypothesis, also known as the Gaia principle named after Gaia the ancient Greek goddess of the Earth. He was a member of a group of academics and others who propose that organisms interact with their inorganic surroundings on Earth to form a synergistic self-regulating, complex system that helps to maintain and perpetuate the conditions for life on the planet.

Karen thought this was a curious interest for a professor of political science. Her intrigue encouraged her to read extensively about this hypothesis. She knew that topics of interest in this idea include how the biosphere and the evolution of life forms affect the stability of global temperature, ocean salinity, oxygen in the atmosphere, the maintenance of a hydrosphere of liquid water and other environmental variables that affect the habitability of Earth.

The hypothesis was initially criticised for being teleological and contradicting principles of natural selection, but later refinements resulted in ideas framed by the Gaia hypothesis being used in fields such as Earth system science, biogeochemistry, systems ecology, and geophysiology. Even so, the Gaia hypothesis continues to attract criticism, and several delegates made it clear that they consider it to be only weakly supported by, or at odds with the available evidence.

Professor Lynne had also previously adopted the Gaia philosophy, a broadly inclusive term for related concepts that living organisms on a planet will affect the nature of their environment in order to make the environment more suitable for life. This set of hypotheses holds that all organisms on a life-giving planet regulate the biosphere in such a way as to promote its habitability. As a concept Gaia philosophy draws a connection between the survivability of a species, hence its evolutionary course, and its usefulness to the survival of other species.

Through her research she had learned that Gaianism describes a philosophy or 'philosophical determinism,' an ethical worldview which, though not necessarily religious, implies a transpersonal 'devotion' to earth as a 'super-organism.'

Karen was aware that Lynne, although he was not a vocal adherent of Gaianism; an earth-centered philosophical, holistic, and spiritual viewpoint that shares expressions with various religions, he did think this was a matter worth closer investigation in pursuit of solutions to human propensity to use violence, believing it may reveal solutions. He reiterated that thought in his presentation at this symposium.

Panthea

James Lynne was not finished yet and now turned his attention to Pantheism. From his viewpoint as a political scientist, his research into the role of violence among us lead him to conclude that the pantheists' perspective has merit worth further analysis.

Summarising the Statement of Principles of the World Pantheist Movement he noted that Pantheists:

- revere and celebrate the Universe as the totality of being;

- believe that all matter, energy, and life are an interconnected unity of which we are an inseparable part;

- acknowledge that we are an integral part of Nature, which we cherish, revere and preserve in all its magnificent beauty and diversity, and that all humans are equal centres of awareness of the Universe and Nature, and all deserve a life of equal dignity and mutual respect;

- believe that there is a single kind of substance, energy or matter, which is vibrant and infinitely creative in all its forms, and that body and mind are indivisibly united;

- see death as the return to nature of our elements, and the end of our existence as individuals, body and mind being indivisibly united;

- honour reality, and keep their minds open to the evidence of the senses and of the unending quest of science for deeper understanding;

- believe that every individual has direct access through perception, emotion and meditation to ultimate reality, which is the Universe and Nature;

- they uphold the separation of religion and state, and the universal human right of freedom of religion.

"Some of these principles," said Lynne, "are the essence of what inspires me to seek a more inclusive, peaceable approach to the science of politics and of being political. Thereby ultimately influencing bodies politic to assertively resist the temptation to propose the use of violence in every circumstance and deliberation. I will submit them to the next plenary session of the Society for Human Development, in the hope that these or similar ideals will be incorporated into the society's charter."

Karen was impressed, and she also sensed a barely perceptible vibration in the air about her. "What was that?" she asked herself as she reflexively glanced at the person sitting to her left.

As Lynne was concluding his session a few delegates began in dribs and drabs to file out of the room. The symposium was concluding anyway. Karen closed her device, secure in the knowledge that her notes were automatically transferred to her private secure data cloud.

Again, she knew that she must arrange a private conversation with James Lynne, before the next session of the Society for Human Development. She had also noted the names and contacts of the other speakers; those not members of the Society.

Dr Ezekiel Eisner came to the lectern and said, "Touching on my opening comments, we have attended this symposium eager to discover reasonable answers about the role of violence in our world. Maybe I should have said 'plausible.' I feel that we may have some answers coming from this symposium. In our quest let us continue to strive for the mind of a beginner, and a broad forensic approach to our knowledge of the issue. Ultimately the payoff will be the 'electricity' that lights up our lives to a non-violent future. Thank you all for your attendance, and thank you to our session leaders and contributors."

He named the session leaders, calling them individually to the dais to receive the traditional tokens of appreciation and concluding applause. Finishing up he said, "Our next symposium will be ..." He gave the date, venue and location then said, "Good night to you, and safe travels."

3

Intercession

Divination

Karen glanced to her left again. Sitting beside her during the symposium was the stranger who asked, as delegates were filing into the room before proceedings got underway at the symposium, if he may sit with her. Offering a peculiar smile he engaged momentarily with her glance, stood up and turned away from her to join the shuffle of delegates leaving. She remembered that he had not introduced himself, and he hadn't taken any notes. Those thoughts stayed with her as she too joined the exiting shuffle.

In the venue's lobby inexplicably she found herself looking for the stranger. She couldn't see him in the crowd now filing outside. She hailed the concierge for her coat and her car, turned to leave, and there he stood. Wearing that peculiar smile, a smile with smiling eyes included that seemed to characterise him, he was looking straight at her.

Approaching him she said, "Where are you staying?"

"I am with you," he answered in a gentle, calm voice.

A fog enveloped her mind, numbing it and without thought she said, "Yes, of course."

With no further word between them they made their way to her waiting car. She opened the door and got in. He got in the other side. She drove off, not aware that she had not followed up her list of 'must see' symposium presenters.

From the symposium venue she drove through the city streets to the Autobahn and entered it. After driving several kilometres on the Autobahn she exited and proceeded along Landstraßen to her country estate. She had been travelling as though on autopilot for several kilometres, all the while with no word between herself and the stranger. As they neared her estate her mind that had somehow been unable to assume a fully conscious presence partially lifted from its slumber and without clear conscious thought she asked the stranger, "Who are you?"

He didn't answer her question and said, in a gentle calm voice, "The others will be with us soon after we arrive."

The fog still enveloped her mind and she was again disinclined to question him further. She continued driving. She perceived that she was alert enough to do that competently, although that didn't matter because the car's computer would take over if she failed to stay focused.

They arrived at her country estate and entered between the intricate stonework pillars supporting a wrought iron arch over the gateway bearing the name Imago. The long driveway majestically wound its way through a series of heavily wooded undulations and manicured grassed clearings to the front entrance of the house.

As she drove slowly the fog on her mind seemed to be gradually lifting again, and she looked up momentarily at the mid-autumn bright full moon, then back to the driveway that was now gently draped in a thin blue cool mist sparkling in the moonlight. She sensed that she was about to encounter something of great importance. She had sensed that earlier in a recent dream; as though it was a divination.

The house came into view; a large two-storey country house, with an attic under the roofline, in a rather typical German style expressing the wealth of its owner. Karen's valet was waiting before the entrance as she gently brought the car to a standstill in the driveway. He approached the passenger's door. Opening it wide he said as the stranger alighted, "Welcome to Imago." Quickly moving to the driver's door he opened it and said, "Welcome home Dr. Krause." He closed the car door behind her then escorted her and her guest to the front door.

The stranger paused and turned. He smiled, and looking up at the full moon he said in that yet gentle calm voice, "It has begun." Karen returned his words with no more than a contemplative smile. The valet opened the front door and they entered. He followed and ushered them into the drawing room, then closed the door behind her leaving the doctor and the stranger alone.

They stood there, looking directly into each other's eyes. She felt no sense of fear; rather it was a sense of embrace. She felt comfortable in the stranger's presence. Her mind was now clear of the fog she had experienced earlier and she was yet disinclined to speak. Without a blink he maintained direct eye contact, so direct that she felt that his mind was penetrating her being. It was. He telepathically revealed himself as Sekandar who came to her in a dream she had some time ago. Karen smiled.

Sekandar said, "I will speak in terms that you will understand. You know why am I am here." Karen returned a reflexive affirmative nod. In her dream he had telepathically informed her of his mission and of his impending arrival. She knew there was a rightness about the encounter, and yet she didn't understand why that was so.

He continued, "The others will join us soon, and before they do I can now enlighten you further. From the earliest awakening of human beings as an intelligent species we have observed your development. Your species is relatively quick to acquire technological skills and employ them for corporeal comfort or material advancement, and slow to acquire and develop the advanced inter-personal and social abilities that would enable Humankind to set out on a pathway to join us in our peaceful ascendancy of the Galaxy."

Maintaining direct eye contact Karen listened intently as he continued.

"It has been a long, arduous and painful journey for human beings. In your species' primordial past your ancestors took a wrong turn in their development when they acquired some false ideas about who they were. One of those was that the way to effect control of activity in groups was to create hierarchies, giving some or one at the apex the power to control, direct and influence everyone else in the hierarchy. That led to inappropriate, unwanted intrusion in the lives of everyone. Over millennia this created a genetic defect establishing the generic propensity in human beings to use violence to solve their problems. With the authority vested in me by the Galactic Council I am here to correct the anomaly." He paused, took her hand and said, "I have chosen you to effect the change."

Karen was not perturbed by Sekandar's explanation, and neither by his physical contact. Despite not yet knowing why, his explanation and contact had a rightness about it. Turning to Karen he said, "Dr. Krause your team has arrived." He let go of her hand.

At that moment 'the others' arrived at Imago. They were: Doctors Lilly Ruhr, Guy de Villiers, Amne Tahir, Miri Tschekov, Valentine Plessis, Ezekiel Eisner, Yang Meixa, James Lynne; journalists Rey Gibbs and Layne Bauer, and politicians Jorie Barak and Jiemba an Australian aborigine. The valet opened the front door as one after another the group entered the house. He gathered coats and scarves from each person, and issued each of them with house shoes. Absorbed in thought with the fact of being involuntarily led to Karen's estate, the group exchanged glances with one another, but no words. The valet ushered them to the drawing room door. He entered and said, "Dr. Krause, your guests have arrived. Shall I usher them in?"

"Yes, of course. Thank you Giles," she replied reflexively.

As her 'guests' entered the room she was conscious that she was asking herself, "Has Sekandar chosen me or is he directing me?"

Sekandar's telepathic answer was immediate. "Karen, I have chosen you to effect the change based on my comprehensive understanding of your advanced intellect and natural inquisitive perceptions about your species' underlying assumptions of violence, and I have chosen your team who will work with you. Welcome your team Dr. Krause."

Encounter

The valet opened the door and the team filed into the room. As they entered they were in subdued discussion with one another, about why they were here, that gradually abated as they entered the room. Karen welcomed each person in the customary manner. The valet offered drinks which some accepted. Silence befell the assembled who now stood in an informal array and all eyes turned to Sekandar, yet the stranger to each of them but Karen. The fog that enveloped Karen's mind, was now enveloping the minds of the rest of the group.

James Lynne in softened voice broke the silence asking Sekandar, "I know everyone else here, and you are?"

Sekandar did not answer James' question, and said. "It is good to meet you Dr. Lynne. Dr. Krause has invited you here to prepare you for your assignments."

James was untypically disinclined to pursue his original question to the stranger, and he slipped a question to Karen, "What assignment is that Karen?"

Karen casually deflected his question, "My dear James it is so good to see you again, and you look so well. By the way, your presentation today was typically thorough and thought provoking, just as I would expect from you." He tilted his head to the side in response. Karen added, "I want to talk with you later about that."

James did not react; his mind was still enveloped in a fog. The other guests remained silent and still, almost as though they were frozen in time.

Karen turned to Sekandar, seeking direction from him. He gave her what she sought. Wearing his characteristic smile he dropped his head slightly then raised it again to look directly into her eyes. The gaze was but momentary, that was all he needed. She then turned again to face James Lynne, and she lifted the fog from his mind, then from the rest of the group.

James twitched to life then asked, "Karen, I sensed today as the symposium was winding up, that there is something you want of me. Is that so? "Yes, James I have a very important assignment for you." Having lifted the freeze from the others she secured their attention then added, "And for all of you too."

Sekandar stood back a bit and remained absolutely still as Karen acquired a measure of control over the minds of her team. She began, "You know why you are here." There were nods of agreement and muted utterances of 'yes we do' from some individual members of the group; in their dreams before his arrival Sekandar had informed them of their inclusion in an important assignment with Dr. Krause.

She continued, "I will now enlighten you further. You have been invited here to be informed that we have been assigned a mission to correct an anomaly that occurred in the primordial past of our ancestors. We will be reversing the mindset of humans to pursue the propensity to use violence to solve problems. This will be done by effecting a change to a defective gene in every human being."

Pointing upward toward the night sky visible through one of the tall windows of the room she continued, "The ultimate destiny of Humankind is out there, among the stars of our galaxy. The correction of the anomaly will enable humankind to set out on a pathway that will lead us to take our place among others in the peaceful ascendancy of the Galaxy."

There were various expressions of what might described as muted amazement and muffled astonishment. Karen continued. "Although it has been a long, arduous and painful journey Humankind over many millennia, successful completion of our mission will not take a long time. It may be exacting, there are minds out there that are bound to resist the change, and for a short time that will be emotionally painful for them. There is an old human saying that 'old habits die hard,' and in this case nobody will die and nobody will suffer enduring pain due to the correction of the anomaly."

She stopped speaking. In the absolute silence that ensued all eyes were on her, she turned again to Sekandar in a telepathic exchange that was indistinguishable to an authoritative supplication, a definitive invocation that issued in a precise course of action. She turned to face the team and asked each individual member in turn, "Do you understand me?" They replied, affirmatively nodding. They were of one mind.

There had been no uninvited influence by Sekandar upon the minds of the individual team members. He chose each of them for their intellect, and knew in advance that they would apply their intellect to Karen's proposition, and accept the assignment. The course of action given to her in his telepathic exchange included the opportunity for each member to put their questions to him.

Enquiry

James Lynne again broke the silence, and turning to Sekandar he asked, "Who are you? What are you? Where do you come from?"

This time Sekandar answered freely and openly. "Thank you Dr. Lynne for your questions." Addressing the group, he continued, "You will know me as Sekandar. I come from far away, across the Galaxy that you know as The Milky Way. We named the Galaxy Kala-Ge. That is a name that might sound familiar to some of you, and to you in particular Jiemba, and to James. My home planet is known as Terra Dyad. We call ourselves Terranians. My world is not confined to that one planet. Rather it is the Galaxy itself."

"I stand before you in human form. My normal form is without material substance as you know it, although originally our form was what you would know as humanoid, like you. Over millennia we have become an incorporeal species. Some of you may interpret that as 'spiritual.' That is a close approximation but not definitive. In the fullness of time and when the time is right you will come to understand the nature of our being. We are able to assume any material form that suits our purpose. We prefer humanoid form and you may be pleased to know that we particularly like to appear as humans, and often do. Why we do is a mystery to us that may be resolved as a result of this mission. The origin of my species is believed to be elsewhere in Kala-Ge. Whether there is a connection with the origins of human beings is yet to be resolved." Guy de Villiers stirred, with obvious apprehension. The thought of a spiritual being intrigued him and he was compelled to ask, "Sekandar, may we see your incorporeal form?"

Sekandar slowly drew near to Guy and looked directly into his eyes. "Dr. de Villiers, why do you ask me to appear to you in my incorporeal form?" Guy hesitated, his eyes narrowed then widened. Drawing very close to Sekandar he asked, "Are you the one we have been expecting?"

As a theologian he couldn't have asked a more direct question than that. Absolute silence again befell the gathering, so silent that a dropped feather gently landing on the floor would have been clearly audible. Although it was only seconds the silence seemed to reverberate for minutes then Sekandar answered Guy's penetrating question. "Yes, and no," he said. "Yes, you have been expecting me because I came to you in your dreams, and I led you here to meet with Dr. Krause and her team. And no, I am not the one you are otherwise been expecting."

Guy stepped back gradually disengaging eye contact with Sekandar, apparently satisfied with the unequivocal answer, yet pondering the mystery of it and feeling a little perplexed. Sekandar's human form remained, for now.

Jiemba began to intone in his native Australian aboriginal dialect. Sekandar turned to face him and waited patiently for him to finish. Jiemba's intonation was but a few minutes, and when he had finished he looked deeply into Sekandar's eyes and said, "My people know you. The dreamtime of my people speak of a traveller who appears in the western sky just after the sun sinks below the land, and then again just before the sun comes from the land to light the sky again in the morning. His name is my name too; Jiemba - the laughing star. He is laughing because he is happy when he is shining, because when he is shining he heralds the sunset and the dawn."

Sekandar responded with his characteristic smile, then said, "Jiemba, your dreamtime story describes an element of the eternal flow of the Galaxy, and of the Universe. Your people are of country, and one day country will be not just the land where your people stand and the sky where Jiemba is, it will be The Whole. When that day comes Jiemba the laughing star will be even happier, and you will be too."

Jiemba's eyes gleamed. Having an import beyond ordinary understanding not apparent to the senses nor obvious to intelligence he said, "Jiemba will be with The

Whole." He stepped back, apparently satisfied with this new dreaming, yet feeling pensive; thoughtful yet not sad.

The valet entered the room and, directing everyone to the dining room, he said "Dinner will now be served."

As they made their way around the large elliptical dining table Karen implored everyone to be seated. Sekandar remained standing and stood by his chair at the foot of the table expectantly but patiently waiting until everyone was seated. He then sat down and proceeded to taste the food on the plate before him. "Hmm, nice," he thought. Anticipating more questions he said, "Now is the time for anyone else to ask me your question. Please, I want you too. After we have eaten Karen will prepare you for your assignments."

Miri Tschekov and Ezekiel Eisner looked at each other. Aware that they each had similar questions to ask, Ezekiel signalled to Miri to go first.

Miri said, "Sekandar, I am a mathematician. Ezekiel is an astronomer, cosmologist and physicist. In our respective disciplines there are speculative mathematicians who call themselves physicists. We call them SMs. They insist that the universe is mathematical, in the sense that every elementary particle of it is a part of a mathematical whole. Physicists have given the properties of particles names such as electric charge, spin, lepton number and so on but the SMs say those are simply words to describe purely mathematical properties. The SMs say the same goes for the spaces that the particles are in, which also have mathematical properties. Why am I saying this to you? Your knowledge of the universe must surely surpass that of anyone on Earth." Sekandar smiled. "If I may continue, at least for the benefit of everyone else here." Sekandar nodded his approval.

Miri continued, "Ezekiel and I don't agree with everything these so-called physicists assert. SMs assert that the universe is mathematical, meaning that all of its properties are mathematical. So, we say that all you need to do to falsify this is to find a single property that isn't mathematical. SMs argue that breakthroughs in physics have undermined all such claims of such properties."

He looked over to Ezekiel as he said, "However, we have found properties that aren't mathematical, and therefore 'all such claims have not been undermined." Returning to Sekandar he said, "The SMs claim optimistically that consciousness will one day be understood as a form of matter. We say that when they made that claim they demonstrated their ability to be unlimited in their imagination. Indeed we are undertaking a comprehensive analysis of their mathematics to reveal the fundamental role of imagination in their claims." Sekandar smiled.

Miri returned a smile then continued, "We agree with the SMs that when our human imagination first got off the ground and started deciphering the mysteries of space that it was done with mental power. Yes, and we say that it was not exclusively mathematical. As scientists we need to be careful not to imagine the mathematics and so convince ourselves that our mathematics proves the hypotheses." He took a breath and asked, "Sekandar, can you enlighten us on the veracity of our observations?"

Sekandar responded, "Dr. Tschekov, let us first hear what Dr. Eisner has to say on this perspective."

Ezekiel began, "Thank you Sekandar. Miri elucidated our observation admirably. The only way I can add to that is to give my perception of the bind that SMs have put themselves in. Miri and I agree that mathematics doesn't even pretend to explain things. It merely affirms that if you accept some things such as axioms and a logic then some other things follow. Put that together with some modelling tying mathematical symbols to reality, which you also have to assume, and you can link certain measures in reality to other measures. Some people will accept that as an explanation, but others will say it explains nothing."

Ezekiel continued energetically, "Some people of faith will claim to have ultimate explanations, that have nothing to do with mathematics, and others will claim these are mere delusions, superstitions. I would suggest true mathematics does not even want to participate in such debates. Of course not. Indeed, Gödels 'incompleteness theorem' proves that mathematics can't even explain or prove all of itself. Which is to say, there are mathematical qualities which cannot be mathematically proven." The team chuckled with him.

He added, "On a related Computer Science note, which some view as a branch of if not a superset of mathematics, you can't use computer science nor mathematics to prove that a program will end in finite time or whether it will run forever. This is one example of many that mathematics, as we understand and define it, is incapable of adequately and fully addressing everything."

With a serious note in his voice Ezekiel explicated, "Miri and I take a scientific approach to our work, i.e., we constantly observe what is, develop hypotheses based on our observations. We then test the hypotheses. Tests proving our hypotheses result in theories that explain some things and encourage more observation. We also apply a scientific approach to the tests." Looking around the group and gauging reactions agreeing with that, he continued.

"Others here have questions to ask of Sekandar, so I won't elaborate on that now. I can say that my work leads me to conclude that we live in an electric universe. Yet, as I said in my opening remarks at the symposium, until recently astronomy was stuck in the past, unable to see that stars are as electric lights strung along invisible cosmic power lines that are detectable by their magnetic fields and radio noise. Discoveries of the ascendance of electro-magnetic activity among the stars was ignored by SMs because of the bind they put themselves in, limiting observation to their mathematics rather than observing what is." Ezekiel paused, then asked Sekandar, "Can you verify for us the veracity of our observations?"

Sekandar's characteristic smile returned. He said, "You are on the right track, and heading in the right direction. I encourage you to be mindful that every investigative discipline devised by your species is adept at finding elements of truth within. Your challenge is to find them. In time, you will. You will soon learn that your observations have a bearing on the tasks at hand for Humankind following The Change." Doctors Ezekiel Eisner and Miri Tschekov just looked at each other each with a brief sideways tilt of their heads, and grinned.

Elucidation

"That's all very informative but there are questions to be answered!" demanded the young journalist Layne Bauer, who had been somewhat dispassionate 'til now. Facing Sekandar she said, "You have told us what you will do and why, but the obvious questions that will be raised in the minds of my colleagues by what they will perceive as your audacious statements are these: Why intervene, why now, and how?"

Before Sekandar could respond and answer Layne's questions, Rey Gibbs the other journalist vigorously interjected, "Yes, and they are likely to ask, 'Who do you think you are that you come here and tell us we got it all wrong, and that you're going to fix it?' And I know that some of my colleagues would add: It just may be that we like it on our Earth just the way we are, and you can mind your own business and go back to your little Terra Dyad!"

Karen stood up and was about to indicate her concern about Rey's inferred antagonism. Sekandar raised a hand gesturing her to remain silent. She resumed her seat.

Addressing the two journalists he said, "Layne, let me respond to your concern after I first clarify something for you. The 'why' of what *you* will do has been clearly enunciated. Does my emphasis on the word 'you' clarify your understanding?"

Conceding the error of her statement, Layne quietly replied, "Yes of course it does."

Sekandar continued, "Rey, without doubt some of your colleagues will aggressively dismiss me just as you state. That is their disposition founded firmly in their training as journalists, prone to pursue the negative; a programmed reflexive response to the stimulus presented to them. They will also seek to dismiss my apparent interference in human affairs; this is perhaps a more human reaction." Rey squinted but didn't respond otherwise.

Sekandar smiled and continued, "Layne and Rey, your questions are entirely pertinent. Let me answer your question 'why intervene?' The ultimate destiny of Humankind is out there, among the stars of our Galaxy.

You have dreamt about your destiny since your emergence as an intelligent species. Your destiny will be realised. Humans are relatively quick to acquire technological skills and employ them for advancement but slow to acquire and develop advanced inter-personal and social abilities. It has been a long, arduous and painful journey. Way back in your species' primordial past your ancestors took a wrong turn in their development when they acquired some false ideas about who they are."

Layne laughed, and asked, "May I quote you on that, or is it off the record?"

Sekandar clearly enjoying her cheekiness replied, "Absolutely not. Everything I say here is on the record." Layne clenched her fist and jubilantly punched the air. Sekandar drew near to her and whispered, "Layne, I can easily say that now because I know that when you have received the power to effect The Change in those around you, you will know not to report me to world. You will instead inform the world about how The Change will positively affect the future of Humankind." He stepped back and asked her, "Say so if you understand me."

Hearing the authority in his voice, Layne answered assuredly, "Yes I do."

Sekandar smiled characteristically and continued with his answer to Layne's 'why' question. "One of those false ideas acquired by your ancestors was that the way to effect control of activity in groups was to create hierarchies, giving some or one at the apex the power to control, direct and influence everyone else in the hierarchy. Over millennia that lead to inappropriate unwanted intrusion in the lives of everyone, and to the use of violence as a means to dominating hierarchies generically. The correction of the anomaly will reverse the human mindset to pursue the propensity to use violence to solve problems. The effect of the change will enable Humankind to set out on a pathway that will lead you to take your place with us in our peaceful ascendancy of the Galaxy. We look forward to embracing you into that."

"'Why now?' From the earliest awakening of humans as an intelligent species we have observed your development.

Technological advancement of your species is on the verge of exponential development that will propel you beyond your solar system and out into the Galaxy. Now is the time to effect a change in your genetic makeup that will ensure the replacement of your propensity to use violence to solve problems, with an inherently peaceful and co-operative disposition with each other and with those you encounter beyond. I am here to facilitate the change now that would otherwise have taken many more generations."

"'How will I intervene?' It is not about me as an individual. I am part of The Whole. You will learn all about that in the fullness of time. At this stage of your journey it is about 'the whole' of humankind. As individuals you will be reversing the mindset of humans by modifying a group of genes. Please so say if you understand me." The two journalists said nothing more. Somehow, they couldn't.

Looking at Karen, he continued, "I have given Dr. Krause the power to effect the change in each one of you, and each of you will be given the power to effect the change in those whom you encounter when you go about your lives."

Gathering everyone's attention with his penetrating eyes as he scanned them Sekandar said, "You will now be changed. In time, when the whole of humankind has been changed, your species will be ready to follow your path to take your rightful place with us in our ascendancy of the Galaxy."

Guy de Villiers felt compelled to speak again, and assuming a spokesperson-like demeanour asked the obvious question.

"Sekandar, It seems to me that you are expecting us to concede that your proposal is tenable, and undeniably so. What would you do if we don't concede?"

For the second time since they met, Sekandar slowly drew near to Guy and looked directly into his eyes. "Dr. de Villiers, do you accept that my proposal is undeniably tenable?"

Guy did not answer. He was not deterred and repeated his question, "Sekandar, what would you do if we don't concede?"

Of course, Sekandar was not deterred either and said, "Dr. De Villiers, if you do not agree with my proposal I will erase from your mind any memory of our meeting, you will be taken safely to your home, you will never remember anything about me or Karen and her team, and I will find a person to take your place. Say so, if you understand me." Guy did not respond to Sekandar's self-assured authoritative directness.

Taking a step closer Sekandar continued, "May I refer to you by your first name?"

"Certainly." Guy replied.

Taking a step back, Sekandar continued. "Thank you. Guy, you have not been chosen at random to be in this team. Neither has anyone else. We, that is the Galactic Council's team for this project, have been studying you for several years. The project itself has been developing for many years. You fulfil all the criteria, making you the right person to take your place in the team to effect this most important change for the benefit of your species. We know you so well that we know you will 'concede,' as you put it. Your participation in this project will ultimately enlighten you to the point where your long-held desire for a closer understanding of what you perceive as 'the divine' will be truly realised."

Sekandar again drew near to Guy. With his penetrating eyes he engaged him to his core, and whispered, "Guy, the light shines in the darkness, and the darkness will not quench it." Guy didn't respond. His mind was in a whirl. Sekandar stepped back, waited for Guy to settle and asked the question again, "Guy, do you accept that my proposal is undeniably tenable?" Sekandar released his penetrating visual contact.

Guy took his time to answer. Taking his eyes from Sekandar he looked up, seeking a prayerful acceptance - a blessing that he truly is 'called' to the role. Sekandar did not hurry Guy nor intervene, neither verbally nor telepathically in Guy's supplication. Reconnecting his eyes with Sekandar, Guy's answer came with outstretched hands. Sekandar gently took them - then Guy, with rising emotion in his voice said, "I think you know me better than

I know myself. I am compelled to trust you. I concede that your proposal is undeniably tenable."

Sekandar embraced Guy, and telepathically said to him in private, "Thank you Guy. The fundamental importance of your role will soon be revealed to you." They each released their embrace.

Sekandar telepathically sought and acknowledged the concession of everyone else, then said aloud, "I thank you all for your trust in me and your acceptance of your assignment to the task."

Assignment

Sekandar asked Karen to call for Giles the valet to join them. Giles soon entered the room. Sekandar then took a step back and Karen stepped forward turning to face the group. With her right elbow bent, her forearm inclined toward the group assembled and the palm of her raised right hand held vertically, Karen said, "With the authority vested in me by the Galactic Council, through Sekandar its appointed emissary I effect The Change is each one of you, and confer the power to effect The Change in those whom you encounter."

As she uttered the words, Sekandar caused the room lights to dim. In the softened light a warm gentle draft was felt. Sekandar dematerialised into the incorporeal, becoming a kind of misty iridescent shimmer that glowed softly then slowly brightened into the full spectrum of white light. There was no sound. He remained so for two minutes exactly before coalescing and rematerialising into his human form. The team members were awestruck. Astonishment and surprise overcame them. Guy, who was awed more than the others, almost dropped to his knees - almost; Giles had moved quickly to hold him up and he regained his composure. Karen then said, "So be it." In unison everyone repeated, "So be it."

Sekandar again stood beside Karen, and said, "The power conferred upon you all includes the ability to effect the genetic change as I described. It also gives you telepathic capability to enable you at any time to confer with one another, with Karen and with me, wherever any one of us are in the world. You will know when you need to communicate. I will be in perpetual telepathic surveillance of each of you to ensure your safety, and to intervene for that reason should your safety be compromised." He then added, "The Whole is with you."

Karen stepped forward again, and said, "Go about your work. Peace be with you." Sekandar repeated, "Peace be with you."

Giles opened the dining room doors and stood aside as the team walked out. Their departure was not quite as nonchalant as it was when they arrived. Karen shook the hand of each of her team members in turn as she wished them safe travels. The valet ushered everyone to their cars, and re-entered the house when the last one had driven away.

Closing the door Giles turned 'round, finding Karen and Sekandar standing right there facing him. Karen gestured for Giles to turn again and re-open the door. She and Sekandar stepped outside and onto the circular driveway by the front steps. Giles re-entered the house and closed the door behind him, leaving it unlocked. As he was doing so he said to Sekandar, "Good night, Sir." With his characteristic smile Sekandar responded, "Good night, Giles. Peace be with you." Giles returned his smile, a knowing smile.

Sekandar took Karen's hands in his as his eyes turned skyward with her to look up at the full moon, now overhead in the clear stillness of the mid-autumn night sky. Lowering his eyes and still holding her hands he looked deeply into her eyes. She was transfixed as again his eyes penetrated her being. Sekandar then dematerialised into the incorporeal, becoming a misty iridescent shimmer that glowed softly then slowly brightened as he immersed himself entirely into her body, to give her a very special gift. It was an adjustment to her genetic code enabling her to temporarily assume the incorporeal state of his species, specifically allowing him at his behest to teleport her to him only; she will be given permanent capability later.

The adjustment process was brief. When he retrieved himself from within her being and had rematerialised, he slowly released her hands from his, and facing her he said, "Come to me when I call for you."

Taking his hand again in hers she replied, "I will come to you when you call for me."

Sekandar let go of her hand, took a backward pace and said, "The Whole is with you, Karen." Again he dematerialised; a touch brighter this time, and coloured in the full spectrum of white light which then faded to invisibility. There was no sound. He was gone.

Dr. Karen Krause had not just been changed genetically, but also in other ways as a person. She was not her former self. As she stood there on the driveway before the house on her estate Imago, the realisation of the power and capability that had been bestowed upon her caused her to ponder the enormity of the task before her and her team.

A snowflake landing on her cheek brought her back from her thoughts. She must have been standing there for some time; the previously bright full moon above was now partially hidden from view by snow clouds that were gradually curtaining the sky, shrouding the stars as the curtain of clouds was being drawn. The stillness had given way to a chilly zephyr, wanting to be more than that. A first few fluttering snowflakes soon became more numerous, settling gently in her hair and on her shoulders. It was time to go inside. As she opened the door she heard Sekandar softly say telepathically, "Gute Nacht Karen, schlaf schön." She smiled.

4

Subterfuge

Kitty Kalinski was engrossed with her friend Zed, on the chatline. Just a few days to go before the mid-winter school holidays, and there was lots of planning to do; or should that be 'scheming?' I mean, a girl can't just sit and twiddle her thumbs when there is so much fun to be had during the holidays.

Zed really likes Kitty. Not that that matters to her. She sees him more as a co-conspirator than a boyfriend. Zed can live with that, for now. He is biding his time, reasoning that: "Her intellect will eventually get the better of her as she 'matures,' and then she will see me differently." Right now Zed is happy that Kitty agreed with his suggested escapades and outings over the holidays. For both of them right now it is a matter of convincing their parents to agree. That may mean a certain measure of tact, bluff and subterfuge. The pair decided that Kitty is the one to be the chief 'negotiator,' but it also meant that Zed has to do his bit too.

Professor Dr. Ezekiel Eisner was not home in Berlin all that often. His profession as a prominent astronomer and cosmologist kept him away from home most of the time. It just so happened that he is home at the moment; good news for Zed who would otherwise have to deal with his Mum, not something he particularly wanted. In his mind Dad is a bit more malleable but since he arrived home from his last away Zed thought he was 'different,' yes somehow different. "Maybe he isn't quite so malleable," the thought plagued him as he entered his Father's study.

"Hi Dad, how's it going?" enquired Zed.

"It's going ok thanks son. How's school? Holidays soon, isn't it?" Ezekiel responded as he looked up, not entirely disengaging from his desk strewn with papers; a usual state.

Ignoring the 'how's school,' Zed went on, "Yep, school holidays start at the end of this week. Hey Dad, I just wanted to let you know that I invited my friend Kitty over tonight. Is that ok?"

The name 'Kitty' caused Ezekiel to pay attention now to Zed. "Kitty, she's General Kalinski's daughter, isn't she?"

"Yes Dad, she is," replied Zed quickly. Wanting to have his Father focus on the matter at hand, he continued with his request, "Is it ok for Kitty to come over tonight?"

Ezekiel ignored Zed's question, and enquired, "Do you know if the General is in town?"

"What? What does that have to do with Kitty coming over tonight?" exclaimed Zed.

"Oh, oh, I just wondered if you knew whether her Father was at home," replied Ezekiel, hiding his furtive interrogation.

Zed, not suspecting any such thing replied, "No I don't know, but Kitty said her Dad would be back home this weekend. She said he's been in Washington; some secret stuff I guess."

This response really got Ezekiel's attention, and he responded with a reflexive probe, "Secret stuff, what do you mean?"

Zed responded blandly, "I dunno, it's all hush, hush. I mean Kitty doesn't say anything about that."

"Interesting," thought Ezekiel. "Hmm. Yes sure Kitty can come over tonight. Is her Mum dropping her off and picking her up later?"

"Yeah, she is. Thanks Dad." Zed silently celebrated his thinly disguised glee as he left the study.

Zed sent a text to Kitty, plainly indicating that all was going to plan. He waited for what seemed like an eternity for the doorbell to 'announce' her arrival. Well, it was all of twenty minutes, an eternity when you're wanting things to go right - right? It rang! He stealthy 'raced' to answer the door. Opening it wide he... he stood there aghast! At first he didn't notice Kitty. All he saw was her Father, the General! Zed opened his mouth and no words came forth.

Kitty, tout de suite, rescued her stunned friend, and said, "Hi Zed, may we come in?"

Not quite recovering from the shock, Zed gestured for Kitty and her Father to enter. Kitty continued with her rescue and said, "Dad arrived home early and wanted to bring me over; gives us a chance on the way to catch up, and he'd like to meet your Dad. Is he still here?"

"Yes, yes he is here. I'll ask him to come..," said Zed, almost spluttering. Escorting his 'guests' to the sitting room Zed said, "Please have a seat." He scurried off to retrieve his Father. Zed, trying to regain his composure, knocked on the study door and sidled in as he heard his Father say 'enter.' "Kitty is here Dad, and she brought her Father along."

Ezekiel, was pacing and reading a paper he held. Not wanting to appear surprised he casually dropped the paper on his desk and said, "She brought her Father? Oh, that's handy, I was hoping to talk with him. Show them in."

Zed fetched Kitty and her Father, ushering them to the study and followed them in. "Good evening Dr. Eisner, I'd like to introduce you to my Father," Kitty said as they entered, handing over to her Father who began,

"It's a pleasure to meet you Dr. Eisner. I have been meaning to meet you for some time, and my work has prevented that. Military duties, you know."

"It's a pleasure to meet you General Kalinski," Ezekiel responded. My son mentioned that his girlfriend's Father is a General. That piqued my interest. I was in the military myself, national service some years ago."

Facing Zed and Kitty, Ezekiel intimated, "And it's lovely to see you again Kitty. You must tell me about the plans you and Zed have made for the school holidays."

"What?" Thought Kitty. "Does he know about that already? He must be spying on us. I wonder how much else he knows!"

Gesturing Kitty and Zed toward the door, Ezekiel continued, "Tell me later. You can leave me with your Father. You and Zed must have lots to talk about." She smiled took Zed's hand and led the way taking him out with her.

Once they were away from the study and out of earshot, Kitty whispered, "Your Dad's a spy. How could he have known that we have been planning things, have you been blabbing?"

Zed reassured her, "Of course not. What do take me for Kitty? He's probably just interested."

She puffed a little exasperation. "Girlfriend! Did you put that idea into his head too?"

"Well, you are," responded Zed positively.

With a mischievous glint in her eye she took Zed's hand then disappeared with him down the hallway and into his bedroom, as she muttered, "I'll deal with you, Mister."

"Call me Ezekiel, I think we can be on a first name basis. We may have to be, it looks like those two will be around together," continued Ezekiel, as soon as the kids had left the room.

The General agreed, "Yes, they seem to be getting on well. By the way, my first name is Scott but privately I'm known as Kal; shortened from Kalinski, it's my nickname that's been with me since my high school days. Please, call me Kal." Ezekiel nodded assent.

Kal continued, coming straight to the point, "I understand that you recently attended a symposium here in Berlin, something to do with research into the issue of violence in the world at-large; I read the media reports."

"Yes, indeed I did. I was the facilitator on the day; opened and closed the event." Replied Ezekiel.

Kal enquired, "Dr. Krause attended the symposium, didn't she?"

"Yes, she did. Do you know her?" Ezekiel enquired, hoping to draw the General on his real interest in Karen.

"No, not personally but perhaps academically. I studied at Westpoint you know. Her early papers on the issue of violence were the subject of some of my university coursework in psychology; perspectives of 'violence' were included in some course units."

Ezekiel, felt free to probe knowing he had lured the fox from his lair, "Is there something in particular that you would like to know, Kal?"

"Well, yes there is Ezekiel. I acknowledge that you and Dr. Krause as academics share an interest in the subject of the recent symposium, and I would like to know whether she has asked you to participate in … let's say a scientific study of the issue."

Aha! Ezekiel knew that this may be an opportunity to effect a change - maybe not yet. Obviously the General is here to gather information. Managing to maintain the unexpected advantage his manoeuvre presented he replied, "Yes, I guess you could say she did, although it's not an exclusively scientific study. My colleagues who attended the symposium tend to have a scientific bent and they are sure to see merit in that approach. Dr. Krause commissioned me, along with others to undertake an important task."

"And what is that?" Kal asked, clearly surprised by Ezekiel's open response. "To ascertain whether a paradigm shift in inherent human assumptions of violence is attainable," Ezekiel replied. Smothering his little deviation from the truth, he continued, "It looks like it will become a valuable resource for a whole raft of people dealing with the ravages of violence in our communities. In any event, the project is in its infancy. Do you want to participate?"

Surprised by the invitation Kal reacted clumsily, "No, no I just wondered."

Ezekiel nudged, "Wonder no more Kal. I can arrange an appointment with Karen for you. I'd love to tag along - could be interesting."

Even with his extensive interrogatory experience Kal stumbled. "Well, maybe, if that's not imposing."

"Of course not. I'm, sure Karen would be intrigued with another perspective, and a military one at that! I'll get some appointment opportunities, you choose one and we'll go from there. Agreed?" Ezekiel chortled within, feeling he had scored an important victory.

"Agreed," chuckled Kal within, feeling likewise.

"Now, let's fetch those kids and we can have a light supper together, and they can tell us both about their 'schemes' for the holidays. Good idea?" Ezekiel enquired in a chirpy lilt.

"That's a great idea," responded Kal anticipating a playful negotiation with the kids, and maybe another opportunity to glean some more information about the important task that the esteemed Dr. Karen Krause had commissioned.

Over supper two men helped two teenagers to believe that their schemes for the school holidays had been duly approved by 'the proper authority.' And, Ezekiel Eisner ensured that three human beings had been changed. Later that night two conversations occurred, one via secure intercom and the other telepathically.

Invitations

Jorie Barak, Cabinet Minister and senior member of the Knesset, the national legislature of Israel, is talking with Jiemba, Senator from Australia. Jiemba, an Australian aborigine and member of an Australian Senate delegation is in Tel Aviv at the invitation of the Israeli government, promoting 'cultural ties' between Australia and Israel.

That convenience enables him with Jiemba to telepathically formulate 'conversion' plans, and a plan to meet with Jorie Barak later in Australia.

"Do you have private access to the Australian Prime Minister?" Jorie asked Jiemba.

"All I have to do is ask for a private conversation, and I will have it," Jiemba emphatically replied. "Have you converted your Prime Minister?" Jiemba enquired.

"That will be done when Cabinet meets tomorrow," Jorie replied then continued, "Now, to the attending delegates here. As we discussed earlier, I will convert those from Africa and South America, and you those from India and South East Asia. Maybe we're getting ahead of ourselves but a plan is better than none. Don't you agree?"

Jiemba formed a curious smile and replied, "Nothing ever goes to plan Jorie. Then again, you and I are used to that in our profession."

The morning session for delegates concluded and everyone randomly filed out of the meeting room and into the adjoining dining room where lunch was to be served. There is ample time to mingle over pre-lunch drinks.

With hand out-stretched Jorie greeted a delegate. "I am Jorie Barak, Cabinet Minister of the Knesset," pointing to his name tag. "Welcome to Israel!" and, looking at the delegate's name tag, he added, "Let me get you a drink, Natália Rivero."

"Thank you Mr Barak, just water," replied Natália.

Jorie signalled a waiter circulating and procured a glass of water and handed it to her. "Call me Jorie, please" he insisted. Accepting the glass Natália replied, "Thank you Jorie. I'm Natália, call me Natália," she politely enjoined.

"What cultural ties do you want to foster between our countries, Natália?" enquired Jorie.

"I am the Head of Cultural Affairs at the Itamaraty - the Brazilian Foreign Affairs Ministry," she replied. "Due to other engagements the Minister is unable to attend the sessions here in Tel Aviv, and requested that I represent him. In that capacity one of the many areas that interests me is folk dances, indigenous dances in particular. Aiming to establishing enduring ties we are organising an interchange program between various national groups, and we have also planned a festival of indigenous dance. Everyone from around the world will be invited. You are most welcome to be our guest at the inaugural festival which is scheduled for mid-Autumn next year; you will have a formal invitation soon. Can you come?" Out it gushed.

"Why, thank you Natália. I will have my secretary check my calendar, and if I am free I would be delighted to come," Jorie answered, confidently sensing further 'conversion' opportunities at such an event.

"Excellent! By the way Jorie, do you dance?" Natália quickly added.

"Ah, not these days but I did a bit in my high school years," Jorie responded nervously.

"That's ok. We can get your feet moving again and your renew your rhythm!" Natália declared.

Jorie, trying to look pleased with her enthusiasm replied, "Sounds like fun. I will look out for the invitation." Wanting to extricate himself from Natália, Jorie encouraged her to mingle, "We'd better move on, others to meet ...," and he turned away, to greet another delegate.

He didn't have to seek another delegate to talk with. One was right there facing him, as he turned. "Hello, my name is Shaka Ndaba. I noticed your name on the program, you are a Cabinet Minister here?"

"Hello, yes I am" replied Jorie, surprised by Shaka's big voice accompanied his big white teeth which seemed to want to devour him.

"May I speak with you Mr Barak?" asked Shaka, in quieter voice.

"Certainly. What is it you wish to talk about Mr Ndaba?" enquired Jorie.

"It will seem forward of me but I want to invite you to Zululand, well actually to KwaZulu-Natal. It's a province of South Africa. I am a developer there" declared Shaka assertively.

"Really, what do you develop Mr Ndaba?" Jorie responded.

"Ah, you pick me up on that pretty quick, don't you? That's fair enough. I develop new towns and suburbs in South Africa, mainly in KwaZulu-Natal my home province. Not just physical infrastructure such as roads, civic facilities, utilities, commercial precincts and so on but also 'spiritual' infrastructure. My current project is Inkululeko, a new town." Shaka replied.

Perplexed by the term, Jorie asked, "Spiritual infrastructure? I have never heard the expression. What do you mean?"

Pleased that his term drew Jorie's question, "It's an 'umbrella' term I invented covering everything in civic, public, and personal realms including political and spiritual expression."

"Goodness me," responded Jorie, as his jaw briefly dropped. "Do you own all that?"

"Absolutely not, Mr Barak. I just develop all that. Ownership of everything is given to the people, over time as each project is completed," came Shaka's emphatic response.

"It's a kind of Kibbutz?" Jorie questioned dubiously.

Shaka answered firmly, "No, no. I make my money through a perpetual municipal levy; a very small amount for each defined piece of property. Let's go no further into that right now. I invite you, as a politician to visit a few of my towns. I want you to give me your assessment of the political arrangements that are developing in them. It's an outsider's point of view that I need to assist me to evaluate my own perceptions, and then to devise guidance strategies that I can employ. Will you seriously consider my invitation?"

Jorie peered at Shaka for a moment or two thinking, "This man is either mad or a genius. Maybe a mad genius would be a better description or maybe he is just mad." He then answered, "I will consider your invitation Mr Ndaba."

"Thank you Mr Barak. I will appreciate your acceptance in due course. Let's say some time in the next month? You will be contacted." Shaka said insistently. He then turned and walked away.

Jorie Barak stood motionless, his mind in a whirl. 'Who was that man?' he thought, feeling rather befuddled by the encounter with Mr Ndaba of KwaZulu-Natal.

He came back to the now when a voice said, "Mr Barak, I have a message for you." It was an attendant of the 'cultural ties' function who spoke then handed Jorie a folded piece of paper. He took it, opened it and saw that it was from Jiemba.

The note read: 'Forgive me Jorie for not having the opportunity to personally inform you that I have been called back to Australia. There is some kind of political crisis brewing back home. I have to leave straight away. I will contact you as soon as practicable. Please destroy this note.' Jorie understood that kind of situation. He was not perturbed, although he wondered why Jiemba had not communicated his news telepathically, and why he had requested that his note be destroyed.

His thoughts went back to the strange Mr Shaka Ndaba. "I wonder why he was so insistent about my acceptance of his invitation." Jorie Barak didn't recall having lunch or talking with other delegates. The afternoon came and went. So did dinner. And, two human beings had been changed. Later that night three conversations occurred, two via secure intercom and the other telepathically.

La Visite

She is taking a vacances that has been planned for a long time. It is an unusual place to visit one's mother but also fortuitous. "How long is it since I've seen Mum?" thinks Valentine Plessis as she walks along the concourse towards customs.

The flight from Paris was worthy of no comment really, uneventful and incident free as usual. She is grateful for that but this is India, a totally different place, and an entirely different experience to Europe were she has spent most but not all of her professional life.

"This way please," says a young customs officer directing her to a 'search' bench. "Just my luck," huffs Valentine to herself. "Is everything alright?" she enquires.

"Yes, ma'am. It's just a routine check. Your Passport please." Taking it the customs officer commands, "Look directly at me Miss Plessis, I need to see your face clearly." Valentine obliges.

The officer maintained her eye contact and spoke into her lapel mic uttering something unintelligible. Valentine understands very little of Hindi; she hadn't a clue about what was being said. Presumably to listen to the voice in her earpiece, the officer paused a few times. Valentine waited. The officer smiled as she maintained eye contact with Valentine. The 'mic' conversation ended.

Abruptly the officer said, "Thank you ma'am everything is in order." She waved impatiently for Valentine to move on. With the search bench ever further behind her as she looked straight ahead and walked away in quickening steps the customs officer nodded to another officer, directing him to follow her. Valentine didn't notice that but she did notice the car that followed the taxi she took from the airport.

Valentine had never previously been to the house she stood before. It looked rather more upmarket than she expected. Checking the note re the address that she had made on her mobile 'phone she gave a little blithe shrug of her shoulders, approached the door and pressed the button on the adjacent intercom. "Hello, is this the residence of Madam Simone Plessis?" she enquired.

"Please identify yourself," came the politely spoken reply from a woman speaking in an accent with obvious contrived Indian intonation.

"I am Mademoiselle Valentine Plessis. Is this the residence of my Mother, Madam Simone Plessis?" No immediate reply was forthcoming. Valentine waited. She noticed that the car that had followed her taxi and had parked opposite the house, had now disappeared. She wondered why, and made a mental note.

It must have been at least a couple of minutes since she enquired when, without any indication that the door would be opened it was flung wide open. A woman lunged at her, throwing her arms around her and kissing her cheeks in the customary French welcoming way. "Mon cher Valentine! Comme c'est génial de vous voir, entrez, entrez," cascaded the words in obvious glee.

Stumbling over the threshold as she felt herself being pushed into the house, Valentine gathered herself and only then was she able to look at the woman. It was her Mother. In the hustle she hadn't recognised her. "Bonjour maman comment vas-tu?" She squeezed those few words out, then...

"Quelle surprise pour vous voir..," her Mum continued, only to have Valentine interrupt her.

"Mum it's ok, we can speak English. You need the practise now that you have English speaking house staff." Her Mother shrugged dismissively.

Valentine continued, "It's good to see you again Mum, and you look so well."

"Yes, yes I am well, and I am so happy that you can stay over with me. Come, I'll show you to your room, there you can freshen up and we will then have lunch together," her Mum responded excitedly. Valentine followed the attending servant. Simone, still excited scurried to the kitchen.

The house staff prepared a colourful varied salad lunch which was served in the atrium shaded from the hot Indian sun of early afternoon by abundant overhead greenery.

Mid-way through lunch Valentine, who had been doing most of the listening in conversation, looked up and lowered her lunch-laden fork when a man entered the atrium, approached her Mum from behind and placed a hand on her shoulder as he leant to kiss the top of her head, then said, "Good afternoon my sweet Simone," then looking up at Valentine, "You must be Valentine."

Simone slipped her hand into the hand on her shoulder and said as she looked up into the face above, "Ah, Jules. I was expecting you later. How did your meeting go?"

Lifting his eyes from Simone to Valentine, Jules said, "Postponed I'm afraid, leaving me free to come and meet your beautiful daughter."

Valentine responded silently with questioning raised eyebrows at her Mother.

"Mon cher Valentine, this is my friend Jules Béraud," and turning to Jules she said, "Jules, this is my beautiful daughter Valentine."

With a look seeking an explanation, she peered at her Mother. Detecting his French accent and trying not to appear too surprised Valentine responded, "Good afternoon, Monsieur Béraud."

Le Monsieur noticed Valentine's peering look at her Mother. He replied with an almost seedy expression, "Good afternoon to you, Mademoiselle."

Simone fluttered with an awkward explanation. "We ... we have been friends for some time ... We met at a reception for the new American ambassador to India. Jules is an advisor to the ambassador you know. Well, no of course you don't ... didn't ... you know what I mean."

Ignoring her Mother's discomfort at not informing her daughter earlier, Valentine enquired of Jules, "That must be an interesting job Jules. May I call you Jules?"

Jules assented then tried to steer her away from further enquiry down that line, "But of course, no need to be formal ... and what brings you to India? Are you just visiting your Mother?"

"I am here to visit a colleague who is a visiting Fellow at Delhi University, we are planning an anthropology project in South America, and of course I would not fail to visit my Mother while I am here in India."

Steering the conversation back to Jules, Valentine didn't miss a beat and asked, "You are wearing a military uniform. Are you a military advisor?"

"Yes, I guess you could say that," Jules replied, reluctantly.

Wanting to direct the conversation Simone interrupted, "Jules and I have been invited to attend a dinner tomorrow night at the Indian Prime Minister's residence; visiting politicians from somewhere or other. Would you join us? I'm sure Jules can get you in ... and don't worry about clothes. I can arrange something nice for you."

Sensing an opportunity to effect the change to a wider more influential group, Valentine replied, "I'm booked with my colleague in the morning, and then for lunch. After that I'm free. Sounds wonderful, thank you."

'Dr. Valentine Plessis effects the change across India!' Valentine imagined a news headline as she alighted from the limo that had driven her, her Mother and her 'boyfriend' from her Mother's residence to this. This is something else. The Indian Prime Minister's residence Panchavati, a complex of office-cum-residence zone and security establishments, including one occupied by the Special Protection Group. It is not what Valentine imagined. She dispensed with the news headline, and allowed herself to be escorted into the resplendently decorated building before her, and then into a lavishly appointed function room set out in a manner that shouted 'tax-payer funded,' where she and her chaperones were announced as they entered.

The dinner was as she expected. The food was excellent and impeccably presented. Any wine requested was available, including the very best champagne; French of course. There were formal speeches by those 'visiting politicians from somewhere or other,' as Simone had said earlier. That was followed by mingling before everyone was asked to be seated again for dessert.

The conversation during 'mingling' and as they were seated, was mostly trivial, or maybe it was encoded diplomatic jargon. Valentine didn't know whether or not it was anything other than trivial small talk. She had no way of knowing either way, and then one guest caused her to think differently. Jules Béraud, 'military advisor' seemed to be an aberration. So thought Valentine and she felt that there was something about him that just didn't fit. She wondered why her Mother had not mentioned him previously, and now here she was being drawn into a curious conversation with him.

"I understand that you recently attended a symposium in Berlin, something to do with research into the issue of violence in the world at-large; I read the media reports. Is that a subject that usually interests anthropologists?" Jules enquired.

Valentine was intrigued by his question, so she just told him straight. "I was a presenter at the symposium on violence; no doubt you noticed that in the media reports. Yes, many things that relate to various aspects of humans within past and present societies interests anthropologists. In social and cultural anthropology, my particular field of expertise - if I may say so, we anthropologists study the norms and values of societies, and not surprisingly the role of violence is an element that is of particular interest in that context. Does the issue of violence in the world interest you Jules?"

"Yes of course it does, I am a military officer. Dealing with violence comes with the job. That may sound crude but that's how it is. Do you mind if I ask you a question?" Responded Jules.

"Another question? Very well, what is it you wish to ask me?" replied Valentine.

"I have heard that Professor Karen Krause who attended the symposium has set up some sort of focus group. Has she asked you to join her group?" Jules asked directly.

"Really, where did you hear that?" Valentine replied, questioning his interrogation.

With crude condescension Jules responded, "I am so sorry Valentine. I should not have been uncouth with you. What I would really like to know is whether Professor Krause might allow me to join her group?"

"Why not ask her yourself?" Responded Valentine, unfazed by his clumsy tat.

"Yes of course. I will ask her." Jules responded, quieted by her tact.

There was a moment of silence, enough for Valentine to telepathically seek advice from Karen on what she should do next. She was readied, and made her move.

"In answer to your question Jules, yes Professor Krause did ask me to join her group, and I did, gladly." That got his undivided attention, just what she needed. He engaged eye contact with her. Conversation between them ended.

In the limo that took them back to Simone's house after the function, Jules was quiet and said nothing. When the car pulled up at the house all three alighted.

"Jules, you have been very quiet since dessert was served this evening. Did it disagree with you? Are you ok?" enquired Simone, concerned.

"I'm sorry, I do feel a bit queasy ... It's not the food ... I just have a lot ... on my mind." Jules replied, with a distant look on his face. As soon as they were inside the house Jules shakily said, "Would you please excuse me ladies? ... I think I need an early night ... I have an early start tomorrow." And he left the foyer and went straight to the bedroom.

Raising their eyebrows Simone and Valentine watched him depart then turned their heads to look at each other. Simone said, "What has gotten into him?"

Valentine naughtily replied, "Mum, he is a man. Since when did you ever know why men do anything? No, don't answer that!" They laughed themselves silly about that, said goodnight to each other then went to their respective rooms.

Valentine was very pleased with herself, knowing that two more human beings had been changed. Later that night two conversations took place one via secure telecom and the other telepathically.

Warriwul

Jiemba hoped that Jorie Barak received the note he left for him in Tel Aviv, and he wondered why news of his recall to Australia had not been communicated telepathically. Jiemba also hoped that Jorie had detected a hint of external mental interference, as he himself had. Jiemba was right on both counts. Sekandar made sure of that; he had mentally intervened to ensure that Jorie's safety was not compromised.

Jiemba's flight from Sydney to Canberra touched down on time. After retrieving his luggage he was ushered by his senior advisor to his waiting official car.

"Did you have a good flight Senator?" enquired Minarmatari, the advisor.

"Yes, it was fine thanks Min," replied Jiemba; Min, being Jorie's preferred abbreviation of his advisor's name. "Why have I been recalled? What is the crisis here?

Min dutifully explained. "There has been an incident that has left your Mother in what seems to be a trance. In accordance with your directive, that I must not contact you about personal matters when you are away from Australia, I kept this news from you until now, and used the 'political crisis' decoy; useful on this occasion. I hoped you didn't mind."

Jorie replied, "Yes, thank you Min. I don't mind. Well done. Have you been able to find out anything more?"

Min elaborated. "Yes, we have spoken individually with those who were with her before your Mother acquired her trance-like condition. Each gave us the same or similar story; that one night they saw 'strange lights in the sky.' And, that the lights 'descended from Jiemba,' i.e., the planet Venus, and that the lights 'enveloped' your Mother for quite some time before ascending and returning to Jiemba. Yes, I know it sounds improbable but the witnesses have been emphatic about what they saw. We have detained them so as to prevent the story from becoming well known in the district. Somehow we have managed to hide the incident from the local journalists and from National News Media networks."

"Incredible it may be but we need to check this out. I think I know what has happened. When can you get me to her?" Jiemba asked.

"We can go there immediately Senator. I have arranged transport," replied Min. Without delay Min escorted Jiemba to a chartered jet standing by ready to fly them to the township of Parkes in the Central West, a region of New South Wales; use of a government aircraft was not considered because that may have aroused unwanted curiosity.

As they walked quickly to their waiting aircraft, Min said, "I will brief you further Senator, when we are airborne." They boarded, the aircraft taxied and it took off. When cruising altitude was attained, so as to ensure they were out of reach of long range eavesdroppers, Min continued his briefing. "Good, now I can continue. Senator, I know an astrophysicist who works with the optical telescope at Siding Spring Observatory and the radio telescope at Parkes Observatory. We have known each other since high school. We get together regularly, as good friends do, so I called him to ask if he had observed any unusual cosmic activity recently. That wasn't an unusual question to ask of him because he knows of my interest in his work." Min paused, and ensuring that he had eye contact with Jiemba he delivered the news. "Senator, according to my friend something very odd occurred on the night in question."

"Go on, go on." Jiemba implored Min, as his eyes widened.

Min continued, "My friend said that he and his team observed what they think may have been an intense electric plasma bolt that lasted a matter of seconds. It occurred in the celestial vicinity of Venus and simultaneously in the terrestrial vicinity of the co-ordinates of your Mother's location. Of course, my friend doesn't know about the incident with your Mother. He gave me the co-ordinates anyway because he said they may interest me. He impressed upon me that he told me on the understanding that although their observation has been properly logged, it was still undergoing extensive analysis. Only after that has been completed, i.e., when everything has been checked and rechecked, will a hypothesis be formulated. Even after all that, the observation won't make to the News Media for quite some time yet."

Jiemba did not seem in the least alarmed with Min's revelation. Rather, he smiled and said, "I think I know what has happened Min but I can't tell you, yet." Feeling the aircraft begin its descent he added, "That was a quick flight - our descent has begun. We will soon be in Parkes, and I want to see my Mum." Jiemba laughed. Min smiled and frowned at the same time. "By the way, I want to speak to your astrophysicist friend too."

Jiemba and Min made their way to the waiting taxi that Min had arranged. As they boarded Min said, "We're in luck Senator, my friend is working tonight at The Dish."

"Ah yes, The Dish. I saw the movie. The Dish is the popular name of the Parkes radio telescope," said Jiemba.

Min added, "You know, it has been in service since 1961. Josh, my friend i.e., Dr. Joshua Barak ..."

"Did you say Barak?" Jiemba interjected.

"Yes, he ..." Min got no further with his sentence.

Jiemba's face beamed, and he was nodding his head affirmatively as he interjected again. "This will be interesting Min. I think your friend Josh is the son of someone I know, a colleague you might say ... Yes." Min was curious. Jiemba continued, "We will speak with Dr. Barak first but my mind is preoccupied with everything else about this fascinating 'incident' with my Mum. We'll see her as soon as we have can ... How far is it to the telescope?"

"It's only a half hour drive Senator, North of here," Min replied.

Jiemba looked out through the rear window and said. "Good. I think we aren't being followed. We can relax. We have time to talk about other things."

Winter nights in the Central West of New South Wales are often cloudless; this night was so, and with a new moon. On dark nights like this the stars of The Milky Way are brighter to the naked eye than as seen from densely populated regions; there being no urban light pollution here. For Jiemba, in spite of his concern for his Mother and the as yet unresolved issues surrounding the incident, this night was ideal for beginning a new Dreaming for his people. Starting that process with the genetic change of his long-time friend and faithful advisor as they were travelling in the taxi, was a special moment. More than that, knowing that his friend welcomed it, it was enriching.

Min took his genetic change in his stride and was ready to do his bit to effect The Change for others. He listened with an open heart and a keen intellect to Jiemba's story about Sekandar, Karen and the rest of the team. "What happens next, Senator?"

"Min, to you I am Jiemba, okay? Call me Senator only in the company of my colleagues in politics or in public," implored Jiemba.

"Of course," Min agreeably acquiesced. Jiemba nodded his approval.

"Min, I sense that we will witness something wonderful tonight." The driver stopped the taxi at the base of The Dish. Jiemba and Min alighted to be met by Dr. Joshua Barak. Having genetically adjusted the taxi driver enroute, Jiemba requested him to join them. The driver obliged. Jiemba asked him, "By the way, what is your name?"

The driver replied, "Warrin, Sir."

Ever inquisitive, Jiemba said, "Aha, that's a name from the Sydney region. One day you must tell me about your tribal heritage." Jiemba's interest drew a smile from Warrin.

Josh greeted his friend first, then the Senator and Warrin. "Welcome gentlemen to the CSIRO Parkes Observatory. Come, I have something I know you will be eager to see." He lead them quickly to an inconspicuous door in the circular base of the facility, they entered and scaled the stairs to the operations room on the upper level. "Please be seated," he said, pointing to chairs arranged in an array facing the workstation.

Seating himself he turned to his computer and manipulated the keyboard, quickly resulting in the display of an image on a large overhead monitor. Turning to face the group he paused, smiled and said, "Gentlemen, before I explain that image to you it is important that you know that my father has been in contact with me. I know about Sekandar and The Change, and I willingly accepted the adjustment myself." This news was calmly accepted by Jiemba. Josh continued. "I assume Min has told you that I am an astrophysicist. Well yes ... I like to see myself as a cosmologist. Not in the mould you may be familiar with. I am a member of an organisation dedicated to bringing astrophysics back into the fold of true science. We can discuss that later. Oh, by the way, please call me Josh. All my friends do."

Pointing to the image on the monitor he said, "Isn't that wonderful? It is a plasma surge that occurred in very close proximity to Earth, so close in fact that we are sure it touched Earth. Knowing what I know about Sekandar, it seems to me that this occurrence has a particular meaning or purpose attached to it. What do you think Senator?"

Jiemba beamed. The question was unanswered. Turning to face the stairwell behind him he said, "Josh, I think we have a visitor." Heads turned to see an aboriginal woman standing at the top of the stairwell. She did not speak, and gestured for the four to follow her. They did. The woman lead them outside, walked beyond the edge of The Dish above them, and pointed to the Milky Way shining brightly in all its magnificent splendour across the clear night sky.

All eyes followed her pointing finger, and she said, "Warriwul! Warriwul is calling us. We must go there, we must go now."

Walking to her Jiemba held her other hand and, as everyone maintained their gaze upon the Milky Way, in their own language he said, "I know it too my Mother. That is why I am here with my friends. Come, let us sit a while and dream." She lowered her upward gaze to peer into Jiemba's eyes, and he beseeched her, "Tell me what Warriwul said to you."

Myaree returned her gaze to the sky. Jiemba let her be for a moment, and asked the group to sit down on the grass in a close circle facing each other. He said to them, "This is Myaree, my mother." Placing a finger to his lips he said, "Shh. Myaree will speak now."

Myaree began to intone in her native Australian aboriginal dialect. Jiemba joined in. Of course, it was unintelligible to everyone except Myaree and son but it was mesmerising in its effect. After several minutes, the pair stood up and raised their arms to Warriwul. The others reflexively stood with them. Shortly after, the intonation ceased. The group remained standing as silence enveloped them. The wonder and mystery that dwells with the awe-inspiring Milky Way held them in its spell.

The air entertained a hint of coolness. A gentle breeze was freshening. The air warmed slightly and began to swirl with an embracing vigour around the group. In their midst the moon-less darkness gradually gave way to a kind of misty iridescent shimmer that glowed softly at first then brightened and coalesced into a human form.

"Welcome, Sekandar." Jiemba said as he stepped forward to embrace the visitor. The rest of the group stood with eyes wide open in amazement, except Myaree. She began to intone again.

Sekandar approached her, took both her hands in his and spoke to her in her own language. "It is wonderful to see you again, Myaree. Warriwul has sent me to you again. This time, to tell you that you will soon be with us all in country with him." Tears of joy welled in Jiemba's eyes and Myaree could hardly contain herself.

"When will we be together with Warriwul, Sekandar?" Myaree pressed him.

"Your son has work to do. When that is done we will then go together. Warriwul is patient. There is no hurry." Sekandar's gentle reassurance immediately relieved her barely veiled anxiety, and she sank into her son's waiting arms. "Jiemba will be with you a while now. He has lots of news for you." Jiemba lead his mother away into the moonless darkness, to sit with her, to comfort her, and to share all his news with her.

Not having understood a word that was said between the three, Josh couldn't wait any longer and asked Sekandar, "There's no point me asking what all that was about, but I have lots of questions for you."

"You certainly do, Dr. Barak! Let's go inside. The night is getting cooler." Sekandar placed his hands on the shoulders of Josh and the taxi driver, and they re-entered the telescope tower.

Coffee all 'round was made, and Josh started with his questions for Sekandar. "What did the plasma surge have to do with what I have just witnessed?"

"Josh, it was an anomaly, a deviation in electrical activity within the solar system that appeared to you here on Earth to be coming from the celestial position of Venus, whereas it actually originated on Jupiter. You would have figured that out soon enough. The plasma surge served to condition Myaree's mind to know that I would be returning to her. And, before you get too excited about that. Let me say that, yes it was rather dramatic; we Terranians are not averse to some fun. And, yes it could have led to undesirable consequences, except that I knew you would be on duty. Need I explain more?"

Josh wasn't about to give in. "Well, yes you do. If that was an anomaly, how could you predict that?"

Sekandar took another sip of his coffee and said, "All will be revealed, in the fullness of time Dr Barak." Josh narrowed his eyes and peered into Sekandar's alien eyes. Warrin took another sip of coffee.

Interlude

"Der Sommer in Berlin kann sehr schön sein, Dr. Krause," said Giles as he approached Karen, who was sitting alone by a small shaded table in her panoptic estate garden. With a tray in hand he was carrying on it glasses and a pitcher of iced lemon barley water, an old favourite that Karen remembered from her childhood holidays in Australia with her mother's family. He placed them on the table. "Your refreshments Ma'am."

Karen acknowledged, "Thank you Giles. Yes indeed, summertime is beautiful here on the estate, when it isn't raining. This season is warmer than usual. I love it like this. I hope I am not disrupting your duties Giles. I would like you to sit with me a while, and enjoy a drink. This perennial favourite quenches best when the weather is hot, like today."

With a nod, Giles acknowledged her request and sat down. They then switched to converse telepathically. Giles enquired, "Is there something in particular that you wish to discuss Ma'am?"

Karen responded, "Please use my first name Giles. We have known each other for many years, and our relationship has gone beyond being my valet. We are associates now," Karen insisted.

Giles acquiesced, "Yes, Ma'am ... I mean Karen. It will take me some time to get used to that but I'm sure I will."

With that matter dealt with, Karen continued, "Good. First let me say that I am very pleased that Sekandar invited you to join the team. I would have requested it anyway. You, like me will now be aware that he is much more astute than anyone might discern, and he sees abilities in you that will be invaluable to us all. I think his discernment is right."

Giles smiled and Karen continued, "You will also be aware that Sekandar has shielded the entire estate from any form of electronic and photographic surveillance, and he requested that we converse telepathically on matters of the project just to be sure that our conversations are not detected." She looked 'round about, then continued. "Have you noticed any activity on the perimeter that deviates from normal goings-on since I have been away?"

Giles replied, "Sekandar's astuteness was noticeable to me from our first meeting, and I noticed that he had shielded the estate. And yes, there has been a great deal of unusual activity on the perimeter; people with cameras and gadgets. I expected that and therefore I patrol every day. It is worth noting that no unauthorised persons have attempted to enter the estate. I must say that their concealment of themselves and their gear has not been too clever. Then again, I was trained to notice things; Special Services you know."

Karen smiled and said approvingly, "Yes, I know, Giles. And by the way," she added, gesturing as she quoted, "Sekandar informed me that the shield 'informs' him of any surveillance irregularity, and he 'deals with it.' I have asked him to show you how he does. He said he will 'in the fullness of time,' and 'when the time is right.' That causes me to think that he may have more control over the project than any of us can discern."

Giles nodded, then said, "I have lots to do as your valet Karen. Is there any other project matter that you wish to talk about, and as I am still your valet is there anything else I may assist you with?"

Karen replied, "Thank you Giles. That is all for now." Giles departed, walking slowly towards the house.

No sooner had Giles returned to the house when Sekandar materialised to stand before Karen, and said, "Guten Tag Karen. Wie geht's dir Heute?"

"Mir geht's sehr gut, Sekandar. Und du?" replied Karen.

"Ich auch. Danke dir," replied Sekandar, smiling characteristically as he sat on the chair vacated by Giles.

Telepathically he said, "It's so good to see you again Karen. To be able to see you with human eyes is an ability I never tire of, and it is always a pleasure to see you."

Smiling, and with a hint of a blush, Karen responded, "Thank you Sekandar." She then asked, "What is your assessment of our progress?"

Sekandar replied, "The change is progressing quicker than I had anticipated. My analysis confirms the success of an additional capability I have given the team, i.e., to transfer adjustments automatically, first from team members and then by and from those they have adjusted. I now expect the paradigm shift to be accomplished somewhat sooner than the development team on Terra Dyad initially calculated. Just how much sooner I will know when I have completed further analysis of the applicable implemented algorithms, enabling me to calculate the exponential effect. Another notable observation is that Giles is doing an excellent job here at Imago. He vindicates my choice. He has secured the estate and effectively each team member visiting here. The security of the team elsewhere is on my watch, of course."

Karen said supportively, "That is good news indeed." She added, "You know that I have known Giles for many years, and no doubt you have noticed that I sense another purpose for your inclusion of him in the team. Can you enlighten me about that?"

"Right there is one reason why I chose you Karen; your powers of observation. Yes, I have another purpose for Giles, a very important one. I can't go into that right now, apart from assuring you that his task will imperil neither him, nor you. Neither will Imago be put at risk. I assure you that when the time is right I will enlighten you. Please keep your thoughts about this to yourself." Sekandar bade her.

Pausing before her response, Karen placed her hand on Sekandar's hand, "It must be a very important task. Inform me when you are ready to." He lightly squeezed her hand.

"We have work to do." Karen said smartly, as she released her hand from his.

"Yes, indeed we do," acknowledged Sekandar, adding, "I will be in Europe a while longer. Guy may need my assistance. Then ... well, you know anyway,"

Karen enquired, "When will I see you again Sekandar?"

"Even though the nature of my mission necessitates my presence in multiple places, almost simultaneously, I will come to you when you call for me." Sekandar reassured her.

Taking his hand in hers they stood up together and she replied, "I too will come to you when you call for me." Sekandar let go her hand, took a step back and said, "Peace be with you, Karen." He dematerialised, and was gone.

5

Conversion

Guy de Villiers is casting his mind back, a long way back to the earliest memories of his childhood. His was a difficult one. His mother, a woman with obvious creative artistic ability died relatively young. His Father was highly intelligent; in his teens he was Dux of his school. Unfortunately his father's will was broken by the refusal of his guardian Aunt to allow him to take up a scholarship that would have enabled him to matriculate to university. It was a classic case of misguided economic choice by his Aunt who insisted that he get a job. Times back then were hard. Guy's father's Aunt was unable or unwilling to perceive the potential benefits that would accrue when he graduated from university.

Guy didn't know his paternal Grandparents and had only vague memories of his maternal Grandfather. He had fond memories of his Step-grandmother. However he did very well in school. He probably saw it as a place of refuge where he could escape tensions at home. The result of taking that refuge was that he achieved high marks in every grade, enabling him to go to university where he studied a range of varied subjects. Those lead him to study divinity. Submersing himself in that discipline he excelled and was awarded his doctorate. His Father would have been pleased.

His academic achievement could easily be the envy of any similarly disadvantaged kid, and his career a classic tale with rags-to-riches potential. A perception like that meant nothing to Guy. His positive mindset enabled him to excel in track and field events, especially long distance running. And, he had dedicated his life to serving his Lord, fulfilling his 'calling' in teaching theology. He had been doing that for nearly twenty years.

So, back to the here and now. Professor Guy de Villiers, Doctor of Divinity, chosen with others by an alien to change the course of human history. Who could ever have imagined this? Certainly not himself. Reflecting again on the enormity of it, he knew that his decision to yield to Sekandar's profound intervention in human affairs was the right one. He knew that only good would result from the intervention; to change the human paradigm from a propensity to solve problems by using violence, to a co-operative endeavour for the benefit of The Whole. Yet, he wondered why God had apparently not revealed this part of his plan earlier. Why had there been no prophecy of the arrival of Sekandar? He has been asking himself frequently, "Have you missed something Guy?"

He knows that the answers to his self-questioning will come, in the fullness of time. Answers always come, not always as expected or wanted but they do come. He just hoped he would not have to wait much longer. Guy's wait would soon be over.

Today, there is a seminar to attend of clerics from every diverse Christian denomination or 'faith', and he is ready with his scheduled presentation; not surprisingly and maybe not coincidentally it is related to issues of violence. His turn to speak arrived, he was introduced, and he stepped up onto the low-level dais and walked a few paces to the lectern.

He looked out at the faces. Some were familiar, some not. He rubbed his nose; an old habit of his, and then began his speech. "My fellow brethren, as you can see on the agenda I am here to talk about the issue of violence in our culture. I could give you an in-depth treatise about violence in a broad cultural context. I won't. The issue of violence in our culture is what interests me; i.e., the culture of our religion. The religion we have built over millennia, around what we call 'our faith,' has produced some of the most violent episodes in human history. The ancient texts of the Bible, acknowledged to be the basis of our religion are riddled with assertions and attitudes of violence and violent behaviour. We all know that. Paradoxically those same texts exude a compassionate love for us all that we have come to know as the true nature of God." Guy's introduction induced some quizzical raised eyebrows and a muffled 'humph' here and there among the brethren.

Guy continued. "It seems to me that our interpretations over those millennia of divine revelation inculcate a much more oracular response in us than God requires. I have come to understand that God doesn't demand of me that I shove my beliefs, interpretations and perceptions of The Word or The Bible, down the throat of anyone; that being the main criticism of those who have been the object of 'the proselytiser.' Rather, I know that he calls for me so that I draw closer to him, and that he forgives me when I fail. The way I live my life advocates The Word better than anything else. When I want to see my perception of a true Christian, I look for someone whose treatment of others is based on love, and who inwardly strives to improve him or herself; not the other way around." Yet more humphs; this was a rather staid group of clergy.

"Let me get back to the matter of 'faith.' We count ourselves as 'learned' and we see that it is easy for those who are not of our faith to bait us into 'logical flaws' surrounding our faith. My simple yet unequivocal point about that is that faith isn't about believing something we know to be false, as for example an atheist would assert, rather it is believing in something we can't prove to be true. The corollary being that it is easy to tear down any belief system but virtually impossible to tear down faith. For example, try asking an atheist scientist about the origins of the 'focused matter' that gave rise to what produced what they believe was the 'big bang' and he or she will either provide a faith-based answer; 'it was always there,' confess total ignorance or worse still they will fall back on their 'proof;' 'mathemagic,' as one physicist describes their mathematics. A friend of mine too has some enlightening thoughts about all that."

"Whether you or I alienate some fellow Christians with our particular understanding of our faith is a non-issue; it is not the subject of popular vote, it is a personal faith. We believe Jesus is our personal role model, and that at the same time he is God. Realising the simplicity of that, I am more concerned that I do my best to love God with all my heart and to love you and my neighbours because that's what he told me to do." The raised eyebrows of some of the assembled brethren were exchanged for muted affirmative utterances."

"I'm sure you would agree that we have no problem with scientists explaining natural phenomena, as long as they don't try to use their understanding of how things work to justify a belief that God doesn't exist. Not only has science disproven many 'facts' that we the faithful claim to be true but science has also disproven many 'facts' that scientists themselves have claimed are true.

"That brings me to the issue of violence. Statistically we know that most, but not all scientists are atheists or agnostics. It is obvious to me that arrogance is one of the biggest issues standing in the way of any civil discussion between them and 'believers in the faith.' From my viewpoint arrogance is our most serious manifestation of violence. All too often we adopt an arrogant stance. I believe we need to eradicate arrogance from any defence of our faith. How do we do that?" Silence descended. Guy reiterated, "Seriously my brethren, how do we do that?"

At first the silence lingered, then one of the brethren stood up. This was the moment Guy had been waiting for. Just as he anticipated, the first to react to his appeal came from his old friend from his theological college.

"My dear Guy ..." Dr Thaddeus Theophanous always addressed his 'old friend Guy' that way, "Please enlighten us as to why you are creating an issue about your notion of violence around your obvious use of the generic notion of arrogance among the faithful. Are we not here to discuss the issue of violence in the community at large?"

"My dear Thaddeus, we are the community at large. We are in the perfect position to set the example for others to follow. When we put our case we can do it with humility, and not arrogance. I believe that when we do that we are truly behaving as vessels for God to do his will."

"The writer of the Gospel put it so well. You will recall that Jesus, when he used that wonderful hyperbole of the camel through the eye of the needle, he was unequivocal in his answer to the question as to who can be saved. Jesus' answer is the basis of the gospel, i.e., 'With man this is impossible, but not with God; all things are possible with God.' As Jesus said. And to emphasise the lesson, 'we are saved through God's gifts of grace, mercy, and faith' as Paul said. And again, 'nothing we do earns salvation for us.' It is 'the poor in spirit,' those who recognize their spiritual poverty and their inability to do anything to justify themselves to God, who 'inherit the kingdom of God' as Jesus said. The materially rich person so often is blind to spiritual poverty because of his or her pride in accomplishments that leads them to being contended with the wealth ensuing from acquired accreditations. The consequence is that a person in that position is as likely to humble him or herself before God 'as a camel is to crawl through the eye of a needle.' We ...”

Thaddeus interrupted, and stood up again. “My dear Guy,” he said it this time with a pronounced emphasis that gave no doubt about his disdain, “That's a nice little sermon but you are waffling! Get to the point you really want to make. There are others of us here who are waiting to have their turn.”

“Be patient Thaddeus ... Let me finish. We need to remind ourselves that our role in the ascendancy of God's Kingdom is to be faithful to our calling, not arrogant about it. In an 'earthly' or 'pragmatic' sense, if you will, striving for ascendancy in all areas of life is a ceaseless and difficult journey. Good reputations can be both a propellant and a tether. This is what Jesus meant when he talked about a rich man reaching the kingdom of God being harder than a camel passing through the eye of a needle. He didn't mean riches were bad, nor did he say it was impossible. The lesson was simple: when you have more to lose, you'll have a harder time ascending. I reiterate, the key is to be faithful to our calling and rely on the surety of our faith, and not to be arrogant about it. Discarding arrogance for some of us may be too much to lose. Indeed in order to eradicate all forms of violence, not just arrogance we all have something to lose.” Some of the brethren were very uncomfortable.

“This brings me to what I believe is the solution to the eradication of arrogance from any defence of our faith.” Guy paused, drew a deep breath and said, “My fellow

Christians, we have to change the genetic makeup of all Humankind."

Thaddeus jumped to this feet. There was no 'my dear' this time. There was just scarcely muted rage, building to an inevitable crescendo. "Dr de Villiers, that statement is the last of a succession of irritations that leads me to a loss of patience bringing me to the realisation that I can no longer accept your absurd gibberish. Changing our genetic makeup. Indeed. Are you mad? What you say is tantamount to heresy. No, it is blasphemy!"

By the time Thaddeus had all but uttered those accusative words, half the assembled brethren were already on their feet demanding Guy to recant his words. The seminar was in uproar. The scene was getting hostile as emotions erupted. Guy was gesturing for everyone to calm down, and he was trying to speak ... and then ... the room suddenly fell silent. Absolutely silent.

In the silence the lighting dimmed slightly. From the back of the room a man surrounded by a faint aura slowly approached the dais, stepped up onto it and turned to face the audience. All eyes were upon him as. With great difficulty Thaddeus spluttered, "Who are you?" His question echoed in the prevailing silence. He was unable to say more. His was the only voice to be heard; all the others were stilled.

Sekandar gestured to Thaddeus to draw near. "Thaddeus, you will know me as Sekandar. Guy is a member of a team conferred with a mission to effect a change to the human genome that will eradicate the propensity of your species to solve your problems by using violence in any form."

Sekandar allowed only Thaddeus to speak, and for the assembled brethren only to hear everything said. "Obviously I should have said 'what are you?' Are you an angel sent to us by God? If not, are you a ... a demon, and ... and have you possessed Guy?" Thaddeus asked with anxious trepidation.

Holding his hands wide before him with open palms, Sekandar answered. "Do not be afraid, Thaddeus. No, I am not an angel or a demon, and I have not possessed Guy. He is the same Guy you have always known, except that his genes have already been changed, and with his consent the power to effect the change in the human genome has been conferred upon him. As for me, I am the emissary of the Galactic Council sent by them to fulfil this mission. Guy is perfectly able to effect the change without my assistance. I have intervened only because emotions among you here turned hostile, and I am pledged to keep him from harm. Is there anything else you would like to ask me?"

Thaddeus stood there, his mouth wide open in wonder and awe. Sekandar turned to Guy who spoke. "My dear Thaddeus. We have known each other for many years. I know that you have trusted my assessments on many theological issues. Let me assure you I have given a great deal of thought to Sekandar's proposition, and I have concluded that it is right, it is good for humanity. Would you now trust me to allow Sekandar to explain the proposition?"

Thaddeus, whose eyes were fixed upon Sekandar, turned them to Guy and said, "Why do I sense that I am compelled to comply with your appeal?"

"Because deep within you know it is right, my friend." Guy replied.

Thaddeus returned his gaze to Sekandar, and said "What do you have to tell me?" What followed the question happened so fast that in outward appearance nothing changed, save a glint in Thaddeus' eyes that reflected profound understanding, trust and acceptance. Inwardly everything had changed.

Thaddeus smiled, as he embraced Sekandar. After a few moments Sekandar gently prised open his embrace, maintained direct eye contact with him and said, "Welcome, my brother to the new paradigm."

He stepped away as Guy embraced Thaddeus, his old friend. Sekandar reanimated the brethren who then thronged the trio. Sekandar gently made space for himself, Thaddeus and Guy to stand with everyone gathered around them. Having the undivided attention of the brethren he said, as he laid his hands on the shoulders of the two old friends, "This is a new beginning for you all. Maintain your faith as you know it. Love each other in the way you know. Soon you will learn a new perspective of 'ascendancy,' where we are together as one."

Lowering his arms from the shoulders of the two, Sekandar stood clear of everyone. The aura that had surrounded him since his entrance among the brethren glowed brighter, emanating the full spectrum of white light which then faded to invisibility. He had dematerialised into the incorporeal. There was no sound. He was gone.

Submission

Amne Tahir was born into a devout Muslim family, adhering to the five pillars of Islam. His religion and his knowledge of the law in all religious and international jurisdictions have led him to his inclusion in the small team of people that is turning the world on its head. He has been profoundly contemplative about the apparent paradox between The Change and his religion and he knows that Sekandar's intervention in human affairs will change it at its very core; submission to the message of The Prophet.

Violence pervades every aspect of human life. Not only does the pervasion include all forms of psychological and physical violence, but also neglect, exploitation and coercion in all its hideous forms. Amne recalled the prophet's frequent use of coercion, and of violent words and acts, and he pondered what he was up against. He knows there are several references in his religion to the use of sanctioned violence perpetuating a legacy of violent intolerance. He is fully aware that some Muslims of his own generation have chosen to believe in the literal currency of ancient fiats condoning coercion and violence. He knows that that has caused suffering and death on a massive scale; just as in ancient times. He is also aware that most Muslims of his generation do not openly condone it but that privately they may.

Amne attended his local mosque which was filled with his fellow brethren, there for daily prayers. It was a particularly large congregation, as several members were preparing for their pilgrimage to Mecca. On his entry to the mosque Amne was addressed in the usual manner with greetings of 'peace, mercy and the blessing of Allah be upon you,' and he replied with the usual 'and upon you be peace.' At this point everything proceeded as usual but he was circumspect about what might follow after prayers. He knew that any verbal dissent, however subtle might be interpreted as pernicious in the uncompromising ambience of the mosque. Consequently, after telepathic consultation with Karen and Sekandar an unobtrusive strategy avoiding any unpleasant reaction was devised.

Following prayers, a friend approached him and said, "Amne, my old friend I need to talk with you. Come away from here to where we can talk in private." His friend led him to his car and indicated that he get in. Nothing was said as his friend drove them to his residence where he entered the house with him. As soon as the door was closed behind them his friend said, "It's safe here, we can talk. Do you have any idea what happened back there at the mosque?"

Amne smiled in response and said reassuringly to his friend, "Yes, I do Sadiq. Will you allow me to explain?"

Bewildered, Amne's friend almost choked on his words as he requested, "I think you'd better explain, because a voice in my head told me to bring you here without delay to do just that. What is going on?"

Amne placed a hand on his friend's shoulder and said, "Sadiq my dear friend, let's sit down. This will not be easy for you." Bleary-eyed, his mental perception dulled by what had happened to him, Sadiq sat down under Amne's gentle persuasion.

Lifting his hand from Sadiq's shoulder, Amne began. "You did not imagine the voice in your head. It was real. It was the voice of someone you will soon meet. He has chosen you to fulfil a very special task. A task that I know you will fulfil far better than anyone else I know in our brotherhood. Before I ask him to meet you, please let me elaborate. Some time ago I was chosen to be a member of a small team of men and women who were given the power to remove from the genome of individuals the human propensity to use violence to solve problems. The genetic code of you and everyone attending mosque today has been changed. I did that. As a consequence every individual in the world of Islam will soon be changed. It is important that you know that this change is not happening exclusively in the Islamic world but to every human being, regardless of religious persuasion. Everything has changed in the world. Nothing will ever be the same."

Sadiq wanted to stand but Amne returned his hand to his friend's shoulder, gently persuading him to remain seated. "Is this person you want me to meet a prophet?" Sadiq asked directly.

"No, he is not." Amne answered unequivocally, and gesturing for his friend to stand he looked directly into his eyes and said, "It is time my friend for you to meet the person whose voice you heard in your head." Amne moved Sadiq clear of the chair in which he had been seated. "Stand here with me, I will call him."

Sadiq felt a gentle draft that seemed to be freshening, then warming. The draft began to swirl with an embracing vigour around the two of them. Amne was relaxed, Sadiq was transfixed. In their midst the swirling draft gradually gave way to a kind of misty iridescent shimmer that glowed softly at first brightened into the full spectrum of white light and then coalesced into a human form.

Amne extended his hand in greeting. "Welcome Sekandar, I am pleased to introduce you to my dear friend Sadiq." Sadiq promptly closed his eyes and fell to his knees. Sekandar and Amne smiled, then together they eased him back onto his feet. Sekandar gently stroked Sadiq's brow, slowly bringing him to open his eyes.

As Sadiq's eyes opened Sekandar said as he extended his hand in greeting, "It is a pleasure to meet you, Sadiq. I am Sekandar. I am the person who spoke to you in your mind. Welcome, to the new paradigm."

"Amne was right, this is not easy for me," Sadiq said as he cautiously shook Sekandar's hand. "What are you? What do you want of me? Why did Amne say you have chosen me to fulfil a very special task, a task that he knows I will fulfil far better than anyone else he knows in our brotherhood? And what is the task anyway? What is this really all about?"

Patiently Sekandar requested, "May we sit down? I will answer your questions and explain everything."

Pointing to the sofa, Sadiq replied, "Yes of course, please sit here,"

Sekandar engaged direct eye contact with Sadiq and said, "I am Sekandar a Narrator of the Galactic Council that convenes on Terra Dyad my home planet, out there among the stars of the Galaxy. I have come to Earth with a mission to effect a paradigm shift in underlying human assumptions of violence. The change will be achieved by a modification of the human genome, as Amne has said. His genes have been changed and so have yours. The genetic code of you and everyone attending mosque today has been changed. What I want of you is this: you have been given the power to make the same change in others as has been done for you, and your contact with those among your brethren who have been radicalised will facilitate a rapid change among them."

Sadiq responded. "I'm trying to get a handle on all this. It is overwhelming on one hand and extraordinarily intrusive on the other. I am wondering why I should not perceive your obvious intervention in human affairs as yet another attempt to undermine the true religion of Islam. One thought says that I have never seen such arrogance, and yet what you have done to me moves me to see the relevance of what you are doing. The dichotomy is confusing me. Yes, this is not easy for me. You see, from the point of view of Islam, religious pluralism is simply incorrect because we have clear proof that Islam is the true religion and that the other religions cannot be on par with it. Also, given that the Noble Qur'an has not been tampered with, and that Islam is the final and conclusive religion, it effectively amounts to the abrogation of the religions predating or postdating it."

Sekandar extended his right arm, turned the palm of his hand upward and said, "Sadiq, this is not about religion.

In answer to your question 'what is this really all about?' it is about the future of Humankind. It is about your species fulfilling your primordial dream to go out into the Galaxy. The change is required to enable Humankind to ultimately join us in our ascendancy of the Galaxy. We do not exclude anyone."

Sadiq responded. "Sekandar, Islam says God is great, God is omnipotent, God is almighty, and God is the creator of the entire universe. If the world wants to have peace, then it has to accept Islamic rule."

Sekandar replied, "Sadiq, it is not about submission or surrender to anyone or anything, anywhere." Knowing that Sadiq genuinely needed a richer, deeper insight Sekandar engaged even closer with his eyes, and with profound assurance he telepathically said to him, "I have something very special to share with you. Something that will enlighten you and wipe away the torment of your confusion."

Externally there was no apparent deviation in Sadiq's persona. Within, there was yet another change in him; this one was very deep within his soul. Holding him at arm's length Sekandar asked, "Can you feel the difference?"

Sadiq was smiling, broadly. "Yes, yes I can. I can. It is whole. It is magnificent!"

Sekandar drew Amne near and they both said, "Yes indeed it is, Sadiq. It is whole, it is The Whole. Welcome home."

For the first time in a long time, Sadiq felt a tear slip joyfully from his eyes. "Why me?" he asked of his of his long-time friend, now his 'brother' with The Whole.

Amne, embraced his friend, and said as he released, "We have known each other since our childhood. We schooled together, we studied at university together. We have matured together as our families shared so many wonderful moments of our lives. You were the obvious choice for the task you have now been given. Sekandar and I know that with ease you will effect the change in those of your extended family who have been radicalised."

"Yes, I understand." Sadiq turned to Sekandar. "Why did you not intervene sooner? So much suffering would have been avoided."

Sekandar embraced him, and as he released he said, "Humankind has been on a long journey. It belongs to you and yours. It is a journey you had to take. We did not intervene sooner because the time was not yet right. Humankind is on the verge of exponential development that will propel you beyond your solar system and out into the Galaxy. In order for you to join us there, now is the time to effect a change in your makeup that will ensure the replacement of your propensity to use violence to solve problems, with an inherently peaceful and co-operative disposition with each other and with those you encounter beyond. The fullness of time has come. You, Sadiq have been chosen because of your strength of character. At heart, you are a good man."

Sadiq replied, "Thank you both, for your compliments. I will gladly fulfil my task. I feel as though a longing that has been deep within me all my life has now been satisfied."

Taking Sadiq's hands in his Sekandar reaffirmed, "In part it has, and in the fullness of time it will be fully satisfied as you take your place with The Whole." Turning then to Amne he said, "Amne and I must leave you now. Communication between us will be maintained, as you are now aware. Peace be with you, Sadiq." Sadiq escorted them to the front door of his residence, and waved goodbye as they drove away. When they were out of sight Sadiq fell to the floor in the doorway, and prayed.

Pedagogy

Not only is Dr. Karen Krause the leader of the team to effect the change in the human genome, but she is also Professor of Psychology in the Education & Psychology Department at Freie Universität Berlin. Today she is speaking to a cohort of freshmen. This a task she loves to do. She has been known to say that it keeps her grounded. She has not met this particular group of students; it is their first day together in their psychology course. They have not yet been genetically 'changed,' and that is just how she wants it to be, for now.

She started this class with the same question that she asks every year. It's not what the freshmen are expecting. She stood well away from the doors and waited for everyone to enter the lecture theatre. She then entered, gracefully descended the steps down to the dais, elegantly stepped onto it, stood behind the lectern and with a presence all her own she turned to face the class and said, "Good morning, class. Welcome to your first academic year in psychology. I expect that you have read 'Psychology 101' - everyone seems to know about. Does anyone have a question?"

The reaction was the same as usual; bemused glances to neighbouring students, raised eyebrows, giggles, and even a few titters from those students who were already nervous on their first day in class.

Karen waited, not long. About a third the way from the back, and a few seats from the left side of the theatre a young man slowly rose to his feet.

"Dr. Krause, why did you chose to become a psychologist, and why did you select developmental psychology in particular?" he asked.

Delighted with the fairly quick response, Karen said, "Wow! Two questions. Excellent. Thank you. What is your name?"

"Martin... Martin Klug, Dr. Krause," answered the young man.

"Thank you, Martin. Good to see that you have done some research. Maybe I can give you answers with a little something about me that you haven't yet learnt."

The gigglers in the class giggled. Inexplicable, of course.

Karen moved away from the lectern to the edge of the dais. She was quiet for a moment and then said, "For me, it was a combination of personal and academic interests, some of those going back to my early teen years. I have been asking questions about psychology since my early high school days; my Father said I started before then. I did not decide on my particular specialisation in psychology until my late 20s, so I had some time to figure out the reasons why. I just love studying people, how we think, feel and behave as we do. Perhaps the main reason I wanted to become a psychologist may be the one that brings you to this field of study in the first place. The human mind is complex, and psychologists learn how it reacts and responds in different situations. While this knowledge has practical applications in every human activity from parenting to politics, it is also a fascinating subject on its own."

"Why developmental psychology? That came about because I also studied education, and gained a doctorate in that too. Our psychological development 'from the cradle to the grave,' fascinated me right from the start of my studies in education. These days I am focused on research into specific aspects of psychology in adolescents and adults."

Karen paused briefly, scanned the wide-eyed freshmen, and then continued, "Now, let's move on. I am not your Tutor. I am your Professor. I'm not 'big-noting' myself, it just gives me a few privileges, one of those is that today I can sow a few seeds, and issue a few challenges." Was that a hint of anxiety drifting across the theatre? Maybe.

She issued her challenge. "Setting out on your adventures in psychology I want you to think about the psychology of precisely that. The adventure is your education. My challenge to you is this: Educators constantly seek to refine and reform systems of education, and as aspiring psychologists you would do well to ask, "What is education?" Your answers may provide you with insights that get to the heart of what matters for children, adolescents and adults alike."

"In my work as a developmental psychologist, I constantly strive to balance the goals of formal education with the goals of raising healthy, happy children who grow to become contributing members of families and society. Along with academic skills, the educational journey from kindergarten through college or university is a time when young people develop many interconnected abilities. As you go about your research, you will also discover common threads that unite the intellectual, social, emotional, and physical aspects of education. How can we best integrate

that with the wisdom of the ages to address today's most
pressing education challenges? For me, good education
facilitates the development of an internal compass that
guides us through life."

"It is important that you step back from divisive debates
on grades, standardized testing, and teacher evaluation -
and really look at the meaning of education. That is what
I did for my doctoral thesis in education. I researched the
answers to this straightforward, yet complex question.
Looking for wisdom from some of the greatest philosophers,
poets, educators, historians, theologians, politicians and
world leaders, I found answers that should not only remain
at the core of current education dialogue but also in the
psychology of it."

"By the end of your first year in psychology I want you to
write and hand to me an essay entitled 'What is Education?'
I want you to tell me the answers you found. Also, don't
reiterate my reasons, as yours for studying psychology. I
want you to think about and articulate your reasons, and
we can discuss those on another occasion."

"Thank you for attending. Have a happy productive year,
and remember that any questions you have for me, may be
submitted in writing to your Tutors who will ensure that
I get them." The class began to disperse. Karen pointed.
"Martin, please come to my office in fifteen minutes time."
Martin nodded affirmatively.

As the class dispersed Martin's friends lingered to
talk with him; about his impending ' interrogation' by the
professor. He then made his way to Karen's office, knocked
on the door, and entered when requested.

Martin was astounded by the size of the office; he
had never seen anything like it. It had three luxuriously
carpeted tiers, one step between each of them. The door
where he entered the office was on the lower tier. One entire
wall was glass overlooking a green garden of indigenous
trees and manicured lawns. A magnificent mahogany desk,
dressed in filigrees of veneer around an inlaid leather
writing place, was on the top tier by the glass wall. An
opened laptop computer was on the desk. The other two
walls surrounding the desk were lined with hundreds of

books on shelves. The second tier from the desk sided the glass wall, and the opposite wall was adorned with works of art; from various eras. The third tier also sided by the glass wall had a sunken 'conversation pit' with comfortable chairs arranged around a coffee table in the middle. Martin also noticed a projection screen on the wall above the conversation pit, and opposite the glass wall. The desk was illuminated by soft, warm lighting from the ceiling above it. The conversation pit was lit similarly. A seductively enticing fragrant scent of flowers lingered. Martin was in awe.

Karen approached him from her desk, saying, "Come in, Martin - please be seated." She directed him to the conversation pit. Martin sat down. Karen sat down, facing him across the small table between them.

"It's a nice office. Gemütlich, I like to think. I personally designed and funded it. Please don't think this reflects the spending habits of this university," Karen said, giving Martin's awe of it a moment to subside.

"Nice." Martin replied as his eyes scanned the room again before making eye contact with his professor. "Yes, very nice. I mean ..."

"That's ok, Martin." Karen interrupted him as his face blushed. "Let's get focused. I have been looking at your achievements to date. You performed at a consistently high academic level throughout your schooling. That may be predictable given your high IQ levels at each testing; very high indeed! Your record very favourably notes your creative ability also. Tell me, what do you think that means for you?"

Self-assured, Martin said, "May I enquire - why do you ask?"

Undeterred by his self-assurance, Karen responded, "Das ist sehr klug, Martin ... pardon the pun. When you have answered my question I will then answer yours. Do we have a deal?"

"Hmm ... deal. I hope you don't think I'm being too forward but I think I will enjoy having you as my psychology professor." Martin hoped he wasn't too cheeky.

"I'm sure you will, young man." Karen gently tugged his 'leash.'

With no trace of the awe that struck him earlier, Martin confidently answered Karen's question. "First, let me say that it's obvious that you know a lot about me; that I have done a great deal of study in psychology. It will not surprise you that my high IQ has intrigued me from the beginning, in particular I have wondered why I am creative, whereas others I know with high IQ aren't. I have learnt that psychologists have found that a high IQ alone does not guarantee creativity. Instead, personality traits that promote divergent thinking seem to be more important. Divergent thinking is found among people with personality traits such as nonconformity, curiosity, willingness to take risks, and persistence. I'm not boasting when I say that's me – with creativity thrown in."

"Good, very good – do go on." Karen urged him.

Martin stepped right in. "Yes, divergent thinking is a thought process or method used to generate creative ideas by exploring many possible solutions. It is often used in conjunction with its cognitive colleague, convergent thinking, which follows a particular set of logical steps to arrive at one solution, which in some cases is a 'correct' solution. By contrast, divergent thinking typically occurs in a spontaneous, free-flowing, 'non-linear' manner, such that many ideas are generated in an emergent cognitive fashion. Many possible solutions are explored in a short amount of time, and unexpected connections are drawn. After the process of divergent thinking has been completed, ideas and information are organized and structured using convergent thinking. Am I right?"

"Yes Martin, indeed you are!" Karen exclaimed with delight. "Now, before I tell you why I asked, can you tell me what it all means for you?"

Martin disengaged eye contact, scanned the room again, closed his eyes for a moment then upon opening them again he said, "Dr. Krause. It means that I am very unusual. It means that my high IQ and my creativity destines me for something of profound greatness that will be humbly manifested in a deep obligation and duty. That probably sounds far-fetched, even irrational but I have sensed this about myself since my childhood. Am I making any sense at all to you?" As he spoke his eyes were wanting to well with tears for his mental anguish.

Karen gently implored him, "Martin, please look directly into my eyes." He obliged. "No, it does not sound far-fetched, neither is it irrational and yes, it makes a lot of sense to me." She handed him a tissue.

Martin spluttered, as he dabbed his leaking eyes, "What? ... Why? ... How?"

Karen waited for him to dry his eyes then said, "Martin, you answered your question of me yourself. I know exactly how you feel. When I was young I felt the same way. You and I are of the same mould. I dealt with the apparent enigma by focussing on my studies and obtaining my doctorates, by submerging myself into my rewarding research in developmental psychology, and by maintaining my inner belief that 'my time' would come. Martin, if you are willing to trust me I earnestly encourage you to do what I have done, because I know that your time will come sooner than think."

"How do you know that?" Martin asked, now fully focussed in the dialogue.

"I know because ... my time has come, and as a result of that I also know that your time has also arrived." Karen's hands were apart, in open gesture.

"Dr. Krause. What are you talking about?" Martin's question was more like a plea.

Karen extended her hand gesture inviting Martin to place his hands in hers. Bewildered, Martin obliged. Karen said, "It is time Martin to lock firmly onto my eyes, and concentrate. I have something to share with you."

What followed happened so fast that in outward appearance nothing changed, save a glint in Martin's eyes that reflected profound understanding, trust, acceptance and relief. Inwardly everything had changed.

Martin smiled broadly. He couldn't contain himself. He stood up and danced around the office saying, "Thank you, thank you, thank you." He then embraced Karen. After a few moments he quickly released his embrace saying, "I'm so very sorry Dr. Krause ... I shouldn't have done that."

"Yes you should, Martin! It's quite ok." Karen quickly reassured him. She waited for him to calm down a little, re-established eye contact with him and said, "There is someone I want you to meet. Stand here with me, I will call him."

The office lights dimmed, the room seemed to darken even though daylight was still outside, and the air cooled a little. Martin felt a gentle draft that seemed to be freshening, then warming. The air fluctuations intrigued him. The draft began to swirl with an embracing vigour around the two of them. Martin was transfixed. In their midst the dimness gradually gave way to a kind of misty iridescent shimmer that glowed softly at first then brightened and coalesced into a human form.

Karen extended her hand in greeting. "Welcome Sekandar. I am pleased to introduce you to Martin." Martin promptly fainted and fell into Sekandar's waiting arms. Sekandar and Karen laughed, then together they eased him onto a nearby recliner. Sekandar gently stroked Martin's brow slowly bringing him back to consciousness.

As Martin's eyes opened Sekandar said, "It is a pleasure to meet you, Martin. I am Sekandar. Welcome, to the new paradigm."

"P ... pleased to meet you." Martin replied as his eyes cleared. Turning to Karen he suggested, "Maybe I should have chosen clinical psychology. I see a fantastic case study for a doctoral thesis right here, right now." She and Sekandar laughed heartily. Martin joined in.

Sekandar withdrew to the corner kitchenette in Karen's office and brewed coffee for each of them. He then joined Martin and Karen sitting by the coffee table in the conversation pit.

"Is coffee a regular drink on your world, Sekandar?" enquired Martin.

Sekandar accommodated the young questioner. "It soon will be. I like the occasional cup. I'm sure others there will too." Sekandar telepathically stoked the young mind and said, "Martin, I know you are now full of questions. Be patient. All will be revealed in the fullness of time. You are a very unusual human being, and it does mean that your high IQ and your creativity has destined you for something of profound greatness that will, as you accurately sensed, be humbly manifested in a deep obligation and duty way beyond anything you could possibly have imagined, until now."

"Meanwhile, focus on your studies, obtain your doctorates and submerge yourself in your research into the totality of mind that you will soon come to know as The Whole. Dr. Krause is your Tutor in that. You will also play an important role as Humankind prepares to join us in our ascendancy of the Galaxy." Martin's genius mind was already working, hard.

They finished their coffee then Sekandar turned to Karen, and fondly said, "It has been wonderful to spend these few precious moments with you. I will be with you again, soon. Take care of yourself, and your new protégé too." She almost swooned with his affection laden words - as she perceived them. Martin noticed. Sekandar placed a hand on a shoulder of each of them, and said, "Peace be with you." He stepped away from them. The movement of air that preceded his arrival returned, and in the iridescent shimmer that brightened the room again, he dematerialised. There was no sound. He was gone.

Martin said, "Dr. Krause, let me say that it's obvious that you know a lot more about me than I previously thought you did." Karen smiled.

Returning to the corridor the professor's new protégé Martin Klug was met by his freshmen friends who had been loitering - waiting for his return with news of his 'interrogation' at the hands of the professor.

"Well, what happened? How did it go?" They grilled him.

"Hmm ... not much ... went ok." That's all they got from their friend. Luckily his broad smile was concealed from them, because all they could see as he walked away was his back.

Media

Tomasina Nabia, Editor-in-Chief is not happy. "It's fake!" she screamed at the 'graduate cadet' reporter, as she held her hand horizontally across her forehead. "I've had it up here with fake news! Bring back the good old days when we reported what actually happened! My father was right when he said that reporters 'lost it when they started calling themselves journalists.' Fake news is subservient to the doctrine 'we know what you want to hear.' Well let me tell you something young lady, you don't know what they want to hear. Now get out there and bring me some real news!"

The cadet turned on her heels and slinked away, mumbling to herself. "She thinks she's a feminine avatar of Perry White."

"I heard that! Off you go, and come back when you have something of substance to show me." Turning about herself Tomasina muttered, "Where is my coffee?"

"That was a bit harsh, Tom." Suggested Rey Gibbs as he handed a cup of coffee to his 'colleague.' "Feeling a bit tense, are we?"

"Sorry about that Rey ... I didn't see you come in. You know, the young ones have had a whole lot of garbage preached at them in their university courses by tutors who have never even worked in a newsroom. Why did we ever go down this path? It was so much easier training kids off the street than having to retrain university graduates who think they know it all before they start," blurted Tom as she put down her coffee mug on her desk and dumped herself in the chair behind the desk.

Rey said, "I'm totally sympathetic my old friend. Unfortunately we have to work with what we are given. We don't make the rules anymore ... you know that."

Still agitated, Tom said, "Yes, of course. Remember the old saying 'bureaucrats never devour their young, they just keep procreating' - we are all victims of that, aren't we ... Enough of that. It's good to see you again. Take a seat. I don't see much of you these days, guess you're just as busy as me. So, what can I do for you Rey?"

Rey got straight to the point. "You can say yes to dinner tonight. I've something important to talk about with you. Here and now is not the place. Can you oblige me?"

Tom picked up her Handy, and said as she looked at it, "My other office ... Let me look at my calendar ... Hmm ... yes, yes I'm free. Where and when?"

Happy with that, Rey replied, "Grange St. Pauls, room 516 at 7:30. Inform the concierge that you are visiting."

"Good, I'll see you then." Rey stood up and left Tom's office promptly. With one hand to her chin and one finger perpendicular across her cheek in contemplative pose, Tom's eyes followed her friend as he left the newsroom.

Rey Gibbs, freelance contributing editor to a range of publications, isn't often in London. He started there as a cadet reporter. That was a long time ago but he likes to return to his old hunting ground. It was fortuitous that he happened to be back in London 'hunting' again, or rather researching an article for a rag back in the States. His old friend Tom Nabia is just perfect for his other task. She knows many people in the news media and is constantly in touch with them; not only in London but also in all the major centres around the world.

There was a knock at Rey's door; even after not having heard that particular knock for quite some time, it still sounded familiar. Rey opened the door. "Come in, Tom. Let me take your coat. Be seated, I'll be with you in a moment." Tom waited.

"So, what is this important matter you want to talk about?" asked Tom as Rey returned, handing her a brandy; he remembered that she liked that occasionally.

Rey deflected the question. "I'll come to that soon. First, tell me ... how are things with you ... apart from your frustration with young cadets?"

Tom sighed at first then perked up. "Well ... the job is going just fine ... and I've remarried. Did you know?" continued Tom, with a smile of contentment across her face.

"I heard that on the grapevine. I didn't catch his name?" Rey enquired.

"It's unlikely that you ever met Jack. He works in the office of the President of the UN Economic and Social Council." No secret with that news from Tom.

Inquisitive, Rey said, "The United Nations ... interesting ... maybe I'll meet him one day." Tom nodded approvingly. He sat down and said, "Our meal will be here soon, so that gives us time to talk about other matters. Journalism - I'd like you to tell me what you think of the state of the game, and then I will explain what's on my mind."

Tom was a bit broody. "Hmm... well I think the goal posts are moving around, and the playing field is anything but level. Nobody wants to play by the rules anymore. Those who buy our words, their numbers are diminishing exponentially anyway, are treated with contempt - not that there was ever any great affection for them all. Practitioners, i.e., journalists and reporters who exercise their personal conscience are systematically sidelined or discarded altogether."

"News is no longer comprehensive and proportional, as it should be. Genuinely significant and relevant issues tend to be swallowed up in the fetish for 'news bites.' Forums for public criticism and compromise are politically tainted. We have completely lost any sense of independently monitoring power, and we are no longer independent from those whom we cover. I always thought our professional discipline in essence was of verification, and that is now constantly threatened by political power brokers."

"Apart from all that everything is just dandy - any sense of loyalty to citizens at large is dead, and as for truth ... well that is the number one casualty. Come to think of it, it's all pretty violent really." Tom was wound up!

"Wow! I'm glad I pushed that button," Rey responded. Retrieving the brandy bottle from the bar, "Would you like another?" Tom responded with a short, sharp 'yes!' - An expulsion of steam might easily be imagined.

There was a knock at the door. "That's our dinner, Tom." It wasn't. His eyes still with Tom as he reached for the door to open it, Rey was taken by surprise when he turned to the open doorway to see Layne Bauer standing before him.

"Layne! What a surprise," Rey gasped, startled.

"Good evening Rey. Sorry I startled you. Is this an inconvenient time to visit?"

"No ... no ... come in. It's good to see you ... what can I say? Please let me introduce you to Tom... Tomasina Nabia... Tom this is Layne Bauer." Rey was untypically flustered. "Hmm ... that's not like me ... it's just that this is a surprise. I wasn't expecting you."

"That's okay, Rey." Layne said calmly as she turned to Tom. "Hi Tom, it's good to see you... Yes, we know each other," she spasmodically said as she turned back to Rey.

"You do?" enquired Rey.

"Yes, we do. We worked on a special feature for Time magazine. I was a rookie then. Anyway, I'm in London to talk with some people at the Brazilian Embassy ... making arrangements for me covering an upcoming festival of indigenous dance there. So, I thought I'd call by and say hello." Layne's 'explanation' was not entirely true. The 'Time magazine rookie' bit, and the 'festival' part was. The 'call by to say hello' was really a planned visit resulting from her recent consultation with Karen and Sekandar.

There was another knock at the door. Rey opened it he said, "Ah, dinner! Layne you don't mind if we ...?" He needn't have been concerned. The waiter explained as he entered that it is hotel policy to prepare more than would be expected, and that extra plates and cutlery etc., are always provided in the traymobile. That explained, the waiter departed.

While that was happening Sekandar had telepathically communicated with Rey briefing him with a strategy for Tom that he and Karen had devised with Layne - Rey agreed. Everything was now clearly understood. Rey deferred his originally intended continuance of his conversation with Tom, until they had finished dinner.

Conversation over dinner amounted to chit chat about their respective times together on various journalistic assignments and associated adventures around the world. When the three were satiated, Rey said, "Layne, Tom and

I were discussing the state of journalism today. She isn't happy with it. What are your thoughts?"

Layne suggested, "I guess it's reasonable to assume that I would agree with Tom. If she hasn't mentioned 'fake' news." Tom interrupted, "Of course, and your view?"

Layne opened up. "This is a bit of hobbyhorse of mine. I would define it this way... Fake news is false information masquerading as news, especially when the author knows it's a work of fiction. Of course, it's obvious that the term has been 'fiddled,' if you like to describe real news that is at odds with a personal opinion. That's not the same as fake news, but biased news and rejection of facts are related issues that are also important in terms of how we produce and mentally ingest information."

"You two would be more aware than me that the news media industry has changed drastically over the past generation or so, initially with the proliferation of cable news in the US and now with numerous online news sources. In most countries unlike the days when there were a few national TV networks and a handful of major national newspapers, there are now thousands of different producers of news appearing in social media feeds, each competing for the attention of the public who no longer expect to pay for a subscription. With revenues driven primarily by online advertising, the industry has become all about attracting viewers' clicks. The result of that is that news has been transformed from being objective to being subjective. You might say it has become entertaining - with impromptu opinions replacing genuine reporting; making it difficult for the public to determine what news sources are reliable."

"So-called 'confirmation bias' or CB is definitely a major driver of how we ingest information on television or online. I've heard psychologists say that CB is the product of wishful, rather than rational thinking. With so many options that are often acutely divided along political lines, many people tend to prefer sources that match what they already believe, casting aside those that conflict with their beliefs. Apparently other related psychological processes, like 'cognitive dissonance,' i.e., discomfort caused by holding conflicting ideas simultaneously are relevant."

"The generality of CB makes it relatively easy for the most people, including journalists to be misled by fake or biased news. We all want to see our core beliefs and hopes confirmed. I think it may be a mistake to imagine, for example, that something like political orientation per se dictates someone's gullibility." Rey and Tom nodded their agreement.

Layne wound up her little treatise saying, "It would seem that the challenge for the public, and particularly for journalists is to understand that fake and biased news and misinformation are present everywhere, and to be watchful in detecting and then avoiding it, while at the same time not yielding to denial of objective reality and then claiming that nothing can be trusted, everything is debatable or that facts don't exist at all."

"Wow! There's another button I'm glad I pushed. You two are in fine form tonight. Goodness me, if I can come up with something then maybe we can form a triumvirate and fix the world!" Rey excitedly responded to Layne's exposé. Approaching the bar he asked his associates, "Would you like a drink?" They each said 'yes' and Rey obliged with their respective choices. He then gestured for them to be seated. They acceded, and he sat down with them.

Layne took a sip of her drink, placed her glass on the coffee table before her, and said, "Rey, that really is a not such a flippant idea ... to form a triumvirate to fix the world."

Rey agreed, "Yes, I think you may be right." They both engaged their gaze upon Tom who had been engrossed in Layne's exposé and hadn't heard Rey's triumvirate idea.

"What? ... Sorry I didn't catch that. What did you say?" she spluttered, rejoining the trio. "Sorry, I was just contemplating Layne's exposé. It was very good."

Rey and Layne looked at each other, mutually focused in mind with their covert plan, then returned their gaze upon Tom and simultaneously said, "Let's form a triumvirate, to fix the world!"

At last, they secured Tom's undivided attention. As he engaged direct eye contact with her, Rey said, "We have something very special to share with you. Something that we know you want to know." Tom was transfixed, mesmerised. She felt herself being drawn into Rey's mind.

Externally there was no apparent deviation in Tom's demeanour. She was relaxed. The drink helped. Within, there was a profound change, and as Rey released the coupling of his mind with hers she said, "Oh, I see... I see."

"What do you see, Tom?" asked Layne.

Engaging with Layne's eyes Tom shook her head, negatively at first then affirmatively. "I see things ... differently ... somehow." Turning to Rey she asked, "What did you do to me Rey? How did you make me see ... to feel different? It's as though the world has been turned on its head, or is it just me? I'm feeling ... that I need an explanation."

Rey answered without equivocation, "Tom, I adjusted your genetic makeup by removing your innate human propensity to use violence to solve problems, replacing it with a propensity to solve problems co-operatively. It's ..."

"Wait, wait on. How? I mean, what are you talking about?" Tom interjected.

Rey replied, reassuringly. "Before the night is through, Layne and I will explain all the fundamentals of what has been done for you, and in the fullness of time you will learn much more about what it means for your life from now on. Be assured that it is all good. And, by the way would you tell us how you feel right now?"

"I feel ... I feel ... that I am not the person I was. It's ... it's a new me." She smiled.

Later that night two conversations occurred, one to one via the mobile 'phone network and the other between four telepathically.

Interlude

It had been a long day. The Summer holidays had come
and gone, the latest cohort of 'freshmen' had been settled
into their first year of psychology at the university, final
year graduates had been identified following final exams
and assessments; they were now looking forward to their
graduation day, and her protégé Martin is racing through
his tailored advanced coursework on his pathway to his
first doctorate.

Karen has brought Martin with her in her car to her
estate for the weekend. The brief respite from the hectic
weekly university schedules will allow them both some time
for relaxation, for discussion about his next units of study,
and to talk everything psychology, as might be expected.

They arrived at her country estate and entered between
the intricate stonework pillars supporting the wrought iron
arch over the gateway bearing the name Imago.

Martin said as they entered, "Imago, what a curious
name. It's Latin. Yes, 'imago' meaning 'image.' Don't
prompt me. I think I recall … ah yes, in psychoanalysis
the principle meaning of 'imago' is: an idealized image of
someone or something - a paradigm. I can see a connection
with you, but why?"

Karen interjected. "Martin, one day I'll tell you the whole
story, okay?"

"Okay." Martin replied and he muttered, "Hmm, Imago
… a curious coincidence."

Karen didn't react or respond to that. She drove on into
the long driveway majestically winding its way through
the series of heavily wooded undulations and manicured
grassed clearings to the front entrance of the estate house.
The estate was resplendent in the vibrant lushness of
summer growth. It was a beautiful, sunny, late afternoon.

Giles was waiting as Karen brought the car to a halt. He
approached the passenger's door. Opening it wide he said
as Martin alighted, "Welcome to Imago." Quickly moving to
the driver's door he opened it and said, "Welcome home Dr.

Krause." He closed the car door behind her then escorted her and her guest to the front door.

Martin was rather taken by this procedure. He had never before experienced anything like it, and he had no idea how or whether he should respond to the valet's courtesy.

Karen put his unease at ease. "Martin, I am pleased to introduce you to Giles, my personal valet. Giles is a member of our team."

Feeling more comfortable with the situation, Martin responded. "I am pleased to meet you Sir."

"No, no." Giles replied, "Please call me Giles, and I will call you Martin, in private conversation that is. We are both members of the same team."

"You mean …" he hesitated as he turned his eyes to Karen.

"Yes. Giles is a member of The Change team. Let's go inside," she said as Giles opened the front door. Karen entered. Giles gestured Martin to follow her. He followed them in, took Martin's luggage, issued him with Hausschue, informed them that he would be making coffee soon, and ushered them into the drawing room. He closed the door leaving Karen and Martin to themselves.

Just as he had been when he entered Karen's office at the university, once again Martin was astounded. He had never seen a drawing room like this. It too was much larger than he expected. The walls were lined with floor-to-ceiling book-laden bookcases, with hardly an empty space on any shelf; at least as far as his quick scan was able to detect. The floor was covered wall-to-wall in luxuriously ornate traditional English 'Axminster' carpet.

The furniture was exquisitely crafted, and the armchairs were upholstered in dark tan leather. There were a few coffee tables and classic green bankers' lamps on writing desks with accompanying chairs; obviously of modern ergonomic style but constructed to look like older forms. Even the ceiling was beautifully decorated with all white ornamentation, and classic warm-white LED illuminated pendant lamps hanging from chains appended to the high ceiling above. Velveteen red drapes, were tied back with tassel-ended golden braided ropes to allow the sunlight in from outside, succeeded in completing the creation of a scene that could easily have come straight out of a movie set. Martin stood there motionless, mouth agape.

Karen patiently waited for him to take it all in, then said, "Whenever you are visiting, you are most welcome to work here." She placed a hand on his back and gently prised him from his motionless. "Come, have a look at my books. Much of the resources you need for your studies are here."

Martin eased forward, past the reading desks and gradually approached the array of bookcases. He reached for a book that caught his eye, 'Psychohistory - Professor Dr. Karen Krause.' He withdrew it and began reading. Karen sat in one of the armchairs. With her hand to her chin and one finger vertically across her cheek in contemplative pose, she waited for the anticipated response from her protégé. He obliged.

Turning to face her Martin enquired, "I've heard of this. Did you ... are you?"

"Yes, I did. I am a member of the International Pscychohistorical Society," she said, filling in the blanks. Martin's eyes widened and it occurred to him that he wouldn't ask about that right now, because he might get the same response as with his enquiry about Imago.

There was a knock at the door. Giles entered, and announced, "Afternoon coffee is served!" He was carrying a tray with the coffee he had prepared. Milk, sugar and a selection of cake slices from the local Bäckerei were also on it. He placed the laden tray on the table before Karen, and she gestured for them both to sit with her. Martin remained standing, still with the book in hand.

Martin asked, "Four mugs? Are you expecting someone?" Then he felt a draft and his question was answered.

The warm-white lights of the drawing room dimmed, and the air cooled a little as the draft freshened, then warmed again. Martin had witnessed those atmospheric fluctuations before. Karen and Giles stood up. The draft began to swirl with that now familiar embracing vigour around the three of them. In their midst the dimness gradually gave way to a kind of misty iridescent shimmer that glowed softly at first then brightened and coalesced into the unmistakeable human form of Sekandar.

Karen stepped forward and kissed his cheek. "It's wonderful to see you again," she said as he gently returned a kiss to her cheek. Martin looked up at Giles. They both smiled.

"Likewise, Karen ... and you too Giles, and our young friend Martin," responded Sekandar, noticing the book in Martin's hand. "Well now, that's an interesting book you have Martin. Is it suggested reading for your studies?"

"Ah ... no ... maybe it should be." He and Sekandar turned their eyes to Karen. She nodded affirmatively. Martin was very pleased.

Karen quickly moved on from that prospective conversation, and turned her eyes to Sekandar seeking his approval as she said to Martin, "I wish to include you in our discussion." Martin looked at Sekandar, likewise seeking approval of Karen's inclusiveness.

"Yes certainly." Sekandar replied. "That's an excellent idea." That made Martin feel special.

Karen opened the dialogue, asking Sekandar, "Given the earlier inclusion of the modified algorithms, what is your assessment of our progress with the change?"

Sekandar began, "The change is progressing at an exponentially quickening pace. The latest analysis confirms the multiplying effect of our previously confirmed success of an additional capability given to the team, i.e., to transfer adjustments automatically, first from team members and then by and from those they have adjusted. I now expect the paradigm shift to be accomplished years ahead of the development team's initial calculations." Giles and Martin looked at each other again, with raised eyebrows in awe of Sekandar's revelation. Karen and Sekandar were smiling at each other. He then gestured for everyone to be seated. He too sat down, and as Karen had arranged the chairs in a close circle before his arrival he was able to establish eye contact with the three of them.

Addressing Giles he said, "Giles, I intimated to Karen that there is another purpose for your inclusion in the team. I will spend time with you soon to discuss the anticipated resistance to the change by some members of military establishments around the world. Please prepare yourself for that. Your knowledge and insight in that regard will be indispensable to the team." Giles nodded his ascent to Sekandar's imperative.

Addressing Martin, Sekandar said, "Martin, I commented about the book you were holding when I arrived. I would like you to focus now and tell me whether you sensed my intent."

Martin gazed into Sekandar's eyes and said, "Yes, yes ... I sensed you were being deliberately suggestive ... not just about the inclusion of the book ... I mean the subject of psychohistory, as suggested reading for my studies ... but ... I also sensed an ulterior motive." Martin sat back and squinted. "What is it?"

Sekandar's characteristic smile beamed. "Your powers of observation and perception are unusually acute. Yes, I do have an ulterior motive." Leaning closer to Martin, Sekandar engaged even closer with his eyes and said, "Martin, please tell me what my motive is."

Martin's eyes seemed to glow. He hesitated briefly. No, it was not a hesitation. He was reading. He was reading Sekandar's mind. "Your motive is to reveal my ability to read minds." With that statement he passed out and collapsed into Sekandar's waiting arms. Sekandar and Karen laughed, then together with Giles' assistance they eased him onto a nearby lounge. Sekandar gently stroked Martin's brow slowly bringing him back to consciousness; this was getting to be a regular occurrence.

As Martin's eyes slowly opened Sekandar said, "This is Sekandar. It is a pleasure to meet you again, Martin Klug. Welcome, to your new paradigm."

Giles was about to speak. Sekandar raised his hand, stopping him and confirming Giles' awe about to be expressed in his now muted question, he said. "Yes Giles, Martin's ability will be useful, and much more so than you currently perceive." Without uttering a sound, Giles inwardly reflected, "How great is the power of this species?" Sekandar replied, "It is the power of The Whole, Giles."

Martin, now fully restored to consciousness said, "Wow! Did I do that?"

Sekandar replied, "Yes you did, Martin. You used the natural mutation you were born with that enables you to read minds. The ability was already within you. It was your genuine willingness to try to read my mind that switched the gene fully on."

"What does this mean for me?" Martin nervously asked.

Supremely satisfied that he and Karen had chosen well her protégé, Sekandar affirmed, "Martin, it means that your long held awareness that you are a very unusual human being was entirely correct. Just as you earlier said to Karen, it means that your high IQ and your creativity destines you for something of profound greatness that will be manifested in a deep obligation and duty. It means that your dreams have not been fantasies, and they will henceforth be realised."

"How? .. What do you mean?" Martin's curiosity was aroused.

Sekandar explained, "First, your ability to read minds will improve with exercises that I will leave with you. You will continue your studies with Karen, and when your mental strength reaches a defined level of proficiency you will be invited to Terra Dyad to continue your education at the Terranian Institute for Education and at the Galactic Council."

"Invited, to what? No, no let me read your thoughts." Martin insisted.

"Certainly, Martin. Go ahead. The exercise will do you good." Sekandar responded.

Martin closed his eyes and concentrated, then realised he could see Sekandar's mind more clearly when he engaged direct eye contact with him. Martin started reading. He was about to recoil from what he saw in Sekandar's mind when he felt his mind being gently drawn back in. What he saw was not menacing. It was revealing. It was embracing. It was welcoming. It was enlightening. The work of Sekandar's real intent having been done, Martin felt his mind being gently released from Sekandar who waited for Martin's conscious reaction.

Martin stood up and said in a crisp disconnected voice. "The Whole ... it is ... everything ... it is beautiful," he said as his eyes glowed. When do we go? Ah yes ... when ... exercises ... studies ... Dr. Krause this is amazing!"

Karen and Giles stood and together with Sekandar and Martin they laid their arms around each other's shoulders and formed a huddle. In the huddle Sekandar said, "Martin, notice that it is only when your mental strength is strong enough that you will be going to Terra Dyad. You will not be obliged to accept the invitation. Indeed, you are at liberty to decline, even though you have expressed your eagerness to go right now. Continuing your education at the Institute and the Council will radically change your life. It will mean that you will leave behind your life here on Earth, your family, your friends, your professional prospects here, everything. We want you to think about that. Although your life on Terra Dyad would be an entirely life changing and life making experience, we want you to be sure that you make the right decision for yourself."

"Will I be able to visit Earth, to take my vacations here?" Martin enquired, with a mixture of concern and excitement twinkling in his eyes.

Sekandar was unequivocal. "Yes of course you can, but not as the Martin Klug you were yesterday, or even today. You will still be you. The difference will be the changes within you as a result of the fulfilment of your dream. Always remember that. Your destiny is one of profound greatness. Recall now what you saw with me when you entered my mind."

Martin recalled, and he understood. He picked up the book he had selected from Karen's collection, and looked at it. Closing his eyes he paused briefly then said, "Psychohistory." He continued, "The word psychohistory was coined by a famous writer of science fiction." He paused then said, "Intriguing ... that the concept described by the word, including the ability to read and to manipulate minds turned out to be real. Perhaps the writer knew something."

"Perhaps he did, Martin. Perhaps he did," annotated Sekandar as his characteristic smile beamed, again. Karen smiled with him. Martin drew back a bit, into thought.

Sekandar retrieved him from his thoughts when he said to all three, "I think it's time we had the Kaffee und Kuchen that Giles kindly prepared for us. We don't want to miss out on that. Is the coffee still warm, Giles?"

"Yes it is," replied Giles, who then set about pouring a mug for each of them. Everyone sat silently as they supped, contemplating Martin's transformation.

When they had finished their coffee and cake, Sekandar turned to Martin, and said, "By the way Martin, always use with discretion your ability to read minds. Everyone is entitled to their privacy. Don't ever violate that. Do you understand me?"

Martin unequivocally replied, "Yes, I do."

Karen stood up, and the others followed suit. "We have work to do." She said energetically, as she took Sekandar by the hand. Martin looked at Giles. They both smiled.

"Yes, indeed we do," acknowledged Sekandar, adding, "I will be in America with Rey, then Russia with Miri. They each may need my assistance. Then I will be with Yang Meixa in China. The rest of the team will do just fine with their respective engagements."

Karen enquired, "When will I see you again Sekandar?"

He stepped forward and kissed her cheek. "I will come to you when you call for me." Karen stepped forward and returned a kiss to his cheek. Martin looked at Giles. They both smiled.

Sekandar let go of her hand, took a step back and said, "Peace be with you all." He dematerialised, and was gone.

6

Amerigo

Hollywood

Tomasina Nabia, accompanied by Layne Bauer on their mission to the USA was thinking about their special assignment. She asked, "Layne, do you recall the old computer descriptor GIGO - garbage in, garbage out?" Layne didn't respond. Her fingers were caressing the keyboard of her laptop in a concerto of manipulation, and she hadn't yet reached the crescendo. Tom waited. Layne's concerto ended with her right hand raised in the manner of a concert pianist, her trailing fingers elegantly rising from the keyboard to meet her hand ahead of it.

"Did you say GIGO?" enquired Layne as she looked up at Tom.

"Garbage in, garbage out, the computer descriptor coined back in the late 1950s by George Fuechsel, an IBM programmer implying that bad input will result in bad output. While we all know the term is most frequently used in the context of software development, GIGO can also be used to refer to any decision-making where failure to make right decisions with precise, accurate data could lead to wrong, nonsensical results."

"Are you making a point about something, Tom?"

"Well yes, just that maybe our primordial ancestors somehow got 'the data' muddled up with a choice between their 'animal' instincts and their developing consciousness," Tom replied as she squinted.

"Wow Tom, that's deep. Hmm, thinking about it maybe they did. One thing's for sure, their muddleheaded decedents certainly got control of this country," Layne responded. They both laughed. "It's good that we're in the right place at the right time," she said as she closed her laptop. "We'd better get a move on, don't want to be late."

Layne had reflected for years upon her understanding of the Hollywood dictum of violence. She learned that generally speaking, movie violence in the most popular American genres is characterized by frequent intentional violent actions executed with high levels of force with a suppression of attending consequences. She knows that at least half the violent acts in Hollywood movies are of the lethal kind, and that explicit indication of injury in any degree was only rarely acknowledged and was systematically minimized.

What is more, she knows that the Hollywood narrative, regardless of genre, methodically disassociates cause from effect, violence from injury, and in effect creates impossible images of the human body. She is also aware that studies of the profiles of movie violence that result from the integration of these analytic categories conclude that they can be understood as the result of the distinctive narrative demands of different genres.

Being well-known journalists, Tom and Layne had been invited by a movie studio's PR department to attend a preview of another Hollywood 'bash 'em up, kill 'em' blockbuster. There couldn't have been a better 'coincidence' for them because two each from the top echelons of the NRA and the GOA would also be with them on the set where, prior to the preview screening in a nearby 'theatrette' they would first be introduced to the producer and the director.

"Welcome, gentlemen ... and ladies. Welcome to our studios, please come this way," said the attendant as they approached the specified set entrance. The obvious hesitation before he said 'ladies' didn't go unnoticed by Layne and Tom.

As they entered the building, Tom whispered to Layne, "One of these 'gentlemen' is a four star General. This will be interesting. I'll bet they're pals of the producer." Layne raised her eyebrows in response, relishing the obvious opportunity that was about to be delivered.

Layne was right. As a friend would, the General stepped forward and embraced the producer, "It's great to see you again, Frank. How're you doing? How's everything at the NRA?"

"Just fine thanks Dirk, just fine. Glad you could make it. This is gonna be one humdinger of a hit for the studio. You'll love it," declared the producer who then turned to the 'ladies.' "You must be ... Tom ... and Layne? Excuse me ... I wasn't expecting ..."

"Women?" Layne completed the sentence for him. He tilted his head and pouted. She rubbed his nose in his own patronising, chauvinistic folly. "Why not, Frank?" The General sniggered, quietly.

"Well ... no ... the names ... I just assumed ..." he spluttered as he dug himself a bigger hole, and so he moved on quickly, "Let me introduce you to our director."

"Good afternoon Layne, Tom. May I use your first names? Please call me Aaron. I've read quite a few of your articles ... by each of you ... impressive works. Let's not delay, we all have tight schedules." Flattery, palaver etc., there were lots of plausible descriptive possibilities applicable to his comments. "Hope you can stay for a minute or two following the preview. We'll have time then for questions, comments ... you know the routine." The director ushered them into the theatrette.

The preview was exactly what was expected, for everyone. The gun buddies loved it. Layne and Tom grimaced a lot and they were thankful the preview wasn't too long. When it concluded the visitors were ushered out of the theatrette and the producer offered drinks all 'round, which were gladly accepted by everyone, except Tom and Layne who declined.

"Ok, fire away. Only too pleased to answer your questions," said Frank, shooting straight from the hip, as would be expected from a gun-slinging producer of gratuitous violence.

The General fired first, of course. "Looks like a great movie, Frank. How did you get those scenes so realistic?" Dirk, his gun buddy sniggered again.

"We use a lot of computer generated animation these days Frank. We think we nailed the realism. Thanks for the compliment," Dirk gloated in the empty puffery.

"So, what did you think girls ... I mean ladies?" That was it for Tom and Layne. The producer had done his darnedest to rile 'the girls.' He was successful of course, and he noticed their reaction, a 'not happy Frank' look written on their faces.

Layne and Tom looked at each other. They wanted to play a bit more before they made their move. Addressing the producer and the director, Tom asked, "Gentlemen, how would you like us to write about your latest work?"

Thinking he would be able to write the script for the two journalists, smiling the director replied, "Well, we would hope that you will write positively about the engrossing storyline, the quality acting, the clever graphics and the realism of the film. Aren't they the elements you would normally focus on?"

Tom looked again at Layne. They were ready. Tom answered, "Yes Aaron, those are the elements we would normally focus on, but not with this film. In fact we would not and could not write positively about this film or indeed any film of this genre that you or any other studio in Hollywood has produced." Tom's statement was received like the best bait to a hungry shark. The gun buddies; the producer, the director, and the General took it, hook, line and sinker. Tom got the focussed attention she and Layne needed.

"Are you off your rocker?" demanded the producer almost screaming, as the others in support of him drew nearer to 'the girls.'

In unison, Layne and Tom said, "Yes of course we are. Look into our eyes, and it will be enlighteningly obvious to you that we are. Come, look closely." They obliged.

What followed happened so fast that in outward appearance nothing seemed to have changed. Inwardly everything had changed. The change was evident as a gleam in the eyes of the four that reflected a profound realisation that their love of violence was no more.

Layne and Tom each felt an overwhelming sense of relief that the deeply entrenched deliberate and blatant misinterpretation of the second amendment to the constitution of the USA by the US gun lobby, that has produced such devastating consequences for so many hundreds of thousands of individuals, will now be relegated to history. And, that the Hollywood dictum of violence had been quashed, gently of course.

It was time for the two invited journalists to leave, and allow the buddies to find their new lives. Layne turned to her confrère and said. "Thank you Tom for assisting me to effect the change in those four. That was easier than I anticipated. I can now see that Sekandar's mission will proceed quickly. Let's get out of here. We both have work to do."

Tom replied, "Yep, we sure do." Then as they left the building she added, "I really enjoyed that little episode. Not in any sense of gloating, rather as a means of serving."

Layne smiled. Later that day she telepathically communicated with Sekandar. "We're all done here. I am preparing to go to Brasil. Tom has to get back to her work, she has a paper to run. How is Rey getting on in Washington?"

Sekandar replied, "Well done, Layne. You and Tom handled the situation there with ease. As for Rey, he will be fine in Washington. I am watching over him, and I am sure he will not need my assistance. I will let you know how he goes."

Pentagon

The Pentagon, situated across the Potomac River from Washington, D.C., is the well-known symbol of the U.S. Department of Defense. Rey Gibbs, freelance contributing editor-at-large preferred to think of The Pentagon as HQ for the American war machine, or should that be war industry? In Rey's analysis it is not just a symbol. It represented the reality of the foundation this nation, firmly rooted in notions of making war. Pondering that he recalled a quote from a famous American writer: 'Violence is the last refuge of the incompetent,' and he knew that his reason for being in this place would soon be manifested in the greatest change The Pentagon would ever experience.

The only way a journalist can enter the Pentagon is by invitation from an authorised person on the inside. That he has. Rey is writing an article for one his affiliated magazines about the rehabilitation of soldiers returning home from 'active service' in war zones. The invitation, to be briefed about the latest and newly implemented rehab program, is from a senior naval officer. Such arrangements are not unfamiliar to Rey, he has been in military establishments on assignment in other countries, but this is his first time in HQ USA.

Upon arrival his person was searched, his credentials verified and then he was escorted to the office of his host; it was a long walk through the maze of corridors. The escort, a young non-commissioned officer knocked on the office door and entered, came to attention, saluted the host officer who was standing behind her desk, and said, "Mr Rey Gibbs, Ma'am." The host said, "Thank you. That is all." The escort, still standing at attention saluted again, turned about and closed the door behind him as he left.

"Welcome," the host officer said as she came 'round from behind her desk and extended a hand to shake. "I am Commander Rae van Graan. As one Rae to another Rey, please call me Rae ... and do take a seat." Rey shook her hand and sat down. The Commander returned to her seat behind the desk.

"I'm pleased to meet you, Rae. Thank you for the invitation. You have an interesting surname. Van Graan, it's of Afrikaans origin, yes?" enquired Rey.

Pleased, Rae clasped her hands and responded, "Yes it is. My husband is descended from an old Afrikaans family, and thank you for pronouncing it correctly. Here in the US some of my friends call me 'granny-van-rae.' They intend to be endearing, I'm sure. So, let's get on with the reason for your visit; our new rehab program."

Rey interrupted her. "Excuse me for diverging. I don't mean to be intrusive. I just have to ask. You look familiar. Have we met somewhere before?"

Rae released her as yet clasped hands, opened them simulating 'surrender' and replied, "Yes we have, Rey. I wasn't sure if you would recognise me. It's been a long time. My maiden name was Rogers. You, of course ... I know a great deal about you. No offence intended, it's protocol for anyone coming into the Pentagon. I think you'd appreciate that."

Ignoring Rae's disclosure about 'knowing a great deal' about himself, Rey clarified his knowledge of her. "Mizzou, that's where I remember you. Missouri University. Yes, you were studying journalism, and heading for your Master's degree. I recall that you started a year or two after me ... now I recall ... you were Roy Rogers ... no offence intended. Did you get your degree?"

"Yes, I was called Roy Rogers ... no offence is taken. And no, I didn't go past the first year into my Master's. I got a belated offer from the US Naval Academy, and as it is at Annapolis." She pointed. "Right there in Maryland. I accepted the offer, completed my course, graduated and landed this role a few years later. It turned out well. My parents live nearby, and I had already met my husband shortly before, on a home visit."

"Sounds pretty neat to me. Anyway, I'd better not diverge further. You were about to say ... about the rehab program." Rey deflected possible questions of himself, although he knew that didn't really matter. She already knew 'a great deal' about him but not everything.

"Yes. Let's get on with it. First, I have a portfolio for you to take with you, and I am happy to answer any questions you may have, but before we get to that my superior has requested that I introduce you. We'll do that now," she said as she stood, gesturing him to follow. She left him no choice, he followed.

The Pentagon is huge. It was quite a walk through the labyrinth of corridors to her superior's office. Rey walked beside the Commander, and all the while they were being escorted by same non-com who ushered him upon his entry. The escort must have been by her door, waiting in the corridor. Rey knew too that his every move was being watched and recorded. The trio arrived at their destination. Rey noted the sign on the door: Rear Admiral S. M. Matherson. The escort took his place by the door, and the

Commander entered with Rey in tow. They had entered the Admiral's outer office. Rae acknowledged the salute of the Admiral's receptionist, another young non-commissioned officer, who then engaged his intercom and announced the arrival of the duo. They entered as the door opened for them. This time the Commander gestured for Rey to enter first.

"Welcome Mr Gibbs, we have been expecting you," said the Admiral, as he opened the door. Rey scanned the other two officers who stood up to greet him, then shook the Admiral's hand presented for the purpose. Rey had not anticipated that he would meet a senior officer, but he was not perturbed because the situation obviously presented the perfect scenario for him to perform his task.

"Let me introduce you to my colleagues. This is General Walters and this is General Bradley. Let's be seated." Rey shook the Generals' hands respectively presented, and sat down on the chair indicated for him. The trio of big brass seated themselves; the Admiral behind his desk, and the Generals flanking him either side. The Commander sat in a chair beside Rey.

The Admiral came straight to the point. "We are aware that you have come to the Pentagon to be briefed by Commander van Graan on deployment of the new rehab program for personnel returning from active duty. Be assured, you will get the material you require for your article. Meanwhile, there is another matter concerning you. That is why you have been brought here. We want to ask you about that."

Rey responded with the obvious question, "And what would that matter be?"

The Admiral scowled. "Our intelligence people have been keeping us updated with a disturbing development that has been traced back to a group of which you are a member."

Rey again responded with the obvious question, "A disturbing development? Disturbing what?"

The Admiral's scowl intensified. "Are you a member of a group recently formed by Dr. Karen Krause, Professor of Psychology at the Free University in Berlin?"

"Yes, I am. Why do you ask?" answered Rey unequivocally.

Ignoring Rey's question, the Admiral pursued him "What is the purpose of the group, Mr Gibbs?" It was now an interrogation.

Rey was not perturbed. "This little scenario is getting to be a bit weird. Let me get this straight. Are you inferring that my association with Dr. Krause's group somehow connects me with 'disturbing developments' that you haven't yet defined?"

The Admiral wouldn't be deterred by such insolence. "Oh yes, this little scenario is indeed getting to be a bit weird. Now, let me get this straight for you Mr Gibbs. The inference to which you refer is quite rational. We know that you and Dr. Krause's group are responsible for serious disturbing developments, both here and elsewhere around the world. I repeat, Mr Gibbs … what is the purpose of your group?"

Unruffled, Rey calmly said, "Admiral, I am perfectly comfortable to explain the purpose of Dr. Krause's group. However before I do that, would you please do me the courtesy of elaborating. What exactly are the 'disturbing developments' that you are so keen to emphasise?"

The Admiral huffed, sat back in his chair, placed a finger vertically across his cheek, tapping it in obvious frustration, and his eyes turned to General Bradley. The General waited a contemplative moment then picked up the bidding. "This country is currently engaged in several military operations in various locations around the world. Our enlisted personnel are walking away en masse from their posts. Even their commanders are walking away, and they're saying that 'war is over.' These are very disturbing developments Mr Gibbs. Our soldiers are being left entirely exposed to our enemies who will surely attack them uninhibited when they detect the absence of any threat."

Rey also waited a moment; he detected an unseen presence in the room. Aware that the incorporeal Sekandar was with him he confidently moved to the end-game. "General Bradley, have your intelligence people detected any hint of your enemies mobilizing for such an attack in response to the abandonment of their posts?"

The General didn't expect that question. "Well ... no, not as yet ... but it will come."

Rey moved in with the clincher. "How can you be sure of that? Isn't it possible that your enemies have also laid down their arms, and are also saying war is over?"

Bradley turned to General Walters who squinted and scowled simultaneously. He said, "It is your group that is doing this, isn't it Mr Gibbs?"

"Yes it is, General." Turning to General Bradley and Admiral Matheson he said, "Yes it is gentlemen. I will now explain to you the purpose of Dr. Krause's group, and then my role in it ... if that's ok with you." Then to himself he said, "Now don't be smug Rey."

"F...g SOB," mumbled the Admiral.

That remark moved Rey to focus his words directly at the Admiral, the seething head of the triumvirate. He said, "One of your country's great philosophers once said: 'Peace cannot be achieved through violence it can only be attained through understanding.' Ralph Waldo Emerson was right, and I am fortunate to have been chosen to be a member of Dr. Krause's team who has the 'understanding' that is effecting a paradigm shift in underlying human assumptions of violence. The change is happening through an adjustment of our flawed human genome to reverse our propensity to use violence to solve our problems."

The Admiral's fuse was burning faster, and shorter. "What claptrap is this? Our intelligence knows that your group is but a handful of academics. How are you doing what you say you are?"

Scanning the group as he spoke Rey made his final move. "We each have been given the power to effect the change. Come closer, focus on my eyes and I will show you how it is done. This is for you too Rae." The four complied.

Again, what followed happened so fast that in outward appearance nothing seemed immediately to have changed. Inwardly everything had changed. The change was soon evident when the Admiral said, "Well I'll be a monkey's uncle!" Everyone laughed.

Although the realisation of what had been done surprised the Admiral it did not cause him to disbelieve. The American war machine (industry) would soon be relegated to history, along with the dictum of violence preached by the gun sellers and Hollywood. Worldwide, the effect would follow.

Rey sat in his car for a moment or two before driving away from the Pentagon. He thanked Sekandar for his 'invisible' support. Sekandar thanked Rey for a job well done.

Mesoamerica

"I'd recognise that voice anywhere," said Lilly Ruhr, as a person approaching her from behind sang, "Zip-a dee-doo-dah. ... Zip-a-dee-ay." She spun 'round and embraced the singer. "Stephanie Richelieu! What a surprise to see you, and you remembered our song!"

"My, oh my, what a wonderful day!" They both sang the next line, then hugged each other.

"Lilly ... Lilly Ruhr, gee it's good to see you. You look wonderful. How long has it been..? What brings you to Guatemala?" enquired excited Stephanie.

Linking arms with her friend, Lilly looked up at the hot Guatemalan sky and said, "Hey, let's not stand here in the sun. Let's find some shade ... a café ... if you have time."

"Sure thing ... I think I passed one ... back there ... come." Stephanie said as she took Lilly's hand and ran off with her. It didn't take long to find the place.

"This is nice, and the coffee is good. So much to catch up on. Where do we start? Of course, what brings you here?" Stephanie said excitedly.

"I'm meeting a colleague. I'd better keep an eye out," Lilly replied, leaning as she did to get a view of the sidewalk. "We have a little seminar to attend tonight," Lilly added expectantly.

"Oh ... um ... don't let me hold you up." Stephanie cut in, apologetically.

"No, no ... it's ok ... I think I see her ... there ... there she is." Lilly reassured her friend, as she stood up and waved vigorously, expecting her colleague to notice. She did, then quickly scampered to meet Lilly at the table.

The two met with a hug and a greeting kiss to the cheek. "I'm so glad you made it. I'd like you to meet my friend from our university days. Valentine, this is Stephanie."

"Hello Valentine, it's nice to meet you. So, you two are colleagues?" enquired an inquisitive Stephanie.

Looking at each other, together they said smiling, "Yes, we are."

Valentine, attempting to change the topic, said, "Lilly and Stephanie at university ... lots of tales there to tell, I'm sure."

Her attempt failed. Stephanie first answered Valentine's implied question then returned to her own earlier intended question. "Oh yes ... we were studying at French National School of Cognition in Bordeaux. They were good times but tell me, what's this 'little seminar' you're going to?"

No escape this time. Lilly said, "It's a seminar arranged by the Mexican Society of Ethnologists and Social Anthropologists. You can come along if you wish."

"Do either of you have a role in it?" asked Stephanie, ever the persistent enquirer.

Good news for Lilly and Valentine. The door had opened. "Yes, we do. We can tell you about that, if you would like to know."

"Well ... yes. I'm curious," said Stephanie. The enquirer walked right in.

Lilly smiled at Valentine, then at Stephanie. "Stephanie, do you remember the game we played at university, when we were supposed to be studying? I'm thinking of the one where we would see how long we could keep our eyes open without blinking; we kidded ourselves that it helped us remain sane under the workload ... ha, ha. Well, our role in the seminar is something like that."

"Really … sounds crazy. Show me what you mean." Stephanie's open invitation.

Evoking a youthful glee, Lilly said, "Ok, let's do it. You and I will go first. Remember, we have to concentrate."

Stephanie opened her eyes wide, and concentrated. Lilly did likewise, and she then acted. What followed happened so fast that in outward appearance nothing seemed immediately to have changed, and then Stephanie smiled. Inwardly everything had changed. She laughed, and said "Well, that was interesting. What happens next?"

Surprised by Stephanie's initial reaction to having been genetically changed, Lilly enquired, "Tell us how you feel?"

Now the effect started to show. "I feel … different … something … changed. What happened?" Stephanie was quite ok, just contemplative.

The three women had time. "We will explain that later. First, please tell us what brings you to Guatemala, Stephanie. We're busting to know," Valentine enquired.

"Oh, yes. My husband is here on business. I just came along 'for the ride.' I often do. And I've never seen this part of the world, so I thought why not? He'll be finishing up by about 5:00pm, and …"

Valentine cut her short, and asked, "Would you rather spend this evening with your husband? You don't have to come with us."

Apparently energised by her transformation, Stephanie declared, "That's ok, I want to come along I'll bring him with me … if that's ok. He always likes to be with me when he's not working. He'll be interested anyway."

"Sure. The more the merrier. By the way, what line of business is he in?" Lilly enquired.

"He's a business broker. He gets businesses in good order and then does deals with them everywhere. He knows people all over the world."

Lilly and Valentine who were totally unable to hide their delight, jumped to their feet and in a loud ecstatic whisper said together, "All over … the world …"

Stephanie, now well and truly tuned-in, declared, "Ok girls, let's go get 'em!"

In telepathic communication later that night Karen had a wonderful time listening to Lilly and Valentine tell her about the fun they were having, and the changes they had effected.

Eigenstate

The ten hour flight from Mexico City allowed for just enough time for Valentine and Lilly to have some shut-eye. After completing their 'work' effecting the change at the seminar in Guatemala City, together with Stephanie they had treated themselves to a few days of sightseeing, including Tikal, Lake Atilán - for a little historical research into the Mayan villages there, and they thoroughly spoiled themselves silly at the Xetulul Theme Park. The flight attendant had to stir the pair from their slumber. Their flight was about to land at São Paulo–Guarulhos International Airport.

Lilly was mildly wistful as she fastened her seat belt. "It's a shame we had to leave Steffi behind. We make a great trio. Ah well, she had to be there for her husband, and I guess we'll catch up again someday."

"We're sure to Lilly," Valentine reassured her friend. Then, infected by Lilly's hint of wistfulness she said, "Geez we had fun, didn't we." Any suggestion of sadness vanished. They smiled and gave each other a little hug. The plane began its final descent to a gentle touchdown on the runway.

Like Guatemala it was hot and humid here too; not too unusual for an afternoon in July. Valentine, the anthropologist and Lilly, the behavioural scientist had booked, before their recruitment into Karen's team, to attend the World Congress of the International Union of Anthropological and Ethnological Sciences at Florianópolis, Capital City of Santa Catarina. The concomitance was perfect. They had passed through customs, collected their luggage and were waiting for a representative of the Brazillian Association of Anthropology to meet them.

"Good afternoon ladies, I am Florian Ambrosio," said a young man showing his ID as he approached. Welcome to Brazil. I am your escort to Florianópolis. Please follow me. We have little time to board our flight." The duo obeyed. In transit to the domestic flight he was rather chatty. "In answer to the obvious question you may ask, no I am not named after Florianópolis, and I must apologise for the weather. These conditions are a little unusual for São Paulo. It's usually not quite so humid. We've had a few similar occurrences in the last couple of years; occasional little blasts of summer in winter. The climate scientists and meteorologists say it's the shape of things to come, as the planet's climate warms quicker. It will be much more pleasant on Catarina Island."

The trio passed through security uneventfully, showed their boarding passes and boarded the plane promptly because the last call had been made. They located their seats, a middle three, stowed their carryon luggage and sat down. He on an aisle. It had not occurred to either Lilly or Valentine to properly inspect the young man's ID, and so after a brief telepathy together Valentine, who was sitting next to him asked, "May I ask, what is your specialisation in anthropology?"

Raising a finger to his lips, as if to 'say' hush and this time clearly showing his ID, he replied, "No particular specialisation. I can elaborate when we are in Florianópolis." Eliciting concern on their faces they each comprehended what they saw. His ID was that of an operative of the Agência Brasileira de Inteligência - the Brazillian Inteligence Agency. He said, "It's ok, I will tell you everything later." The pair were cautious about saying anything more. Fortunately, the flight to Hercílio Luz Airport at Florianópolis was over in just over an hour.

Trying to look inconspicuous, Lilly and Valentine maintained their silence as they waited by the conveyor belt to collect their main luggage. Florian waited with them, and when all had been collected he ushered them to a waiting car.

Checking in at the Majestic Palace Hotel, Valentine turned away from the reception counter while Lilly completed the formalities. As she did so she thought she glimpsed a figure that looked very familiar. She turned back, with a shake of her head. Lilly noticed, and asked telepathically, "Is everything ok Val?"

"Yes, I think everything will be fine. He's here." Valentine replied, with a grin.

The porter escorted them to the lift and then to their room, with Florian following close behind. At the door to the room Lilly touched the key to the contact and opened the door. The porter entered, taking the luggage in. She tipped him, and he departed. As she was about to enter the suite, Florian said, "May I? We need to be sure." He entered ahead of them, apparently checked it out, returned to the entrance and said, "All clear." Lilly and Valentine entered.

"Good afternoon, Lilly ... Valentine. Did you have a good flight?" said Sekandar as he appeared before them, entering from an adjoining room.

Obviously unsurprised by Sekandar's presence, Valentine said, "Good afternoon, Sekandar. Yes, we did. The second leg of our trip was ... different. It's good to see you again. What brings you to Florianópolis?"

Sekandar withheld a response. Florian, obviously taken by surprise had not drawn his concealed weapon. It was useless anyway, Sekandar had seen to that. He spluttered as Sekandar neared him, "Where ... who ... what ... are you doing here?"

Gently stroking his mind Sekandar said, "Do not be afraid, Florian. I am Sekandar. I know who you are and that you have been assigned by your organisation to protect Lilly and Valentine from a potential threat. Be assured I am not that threat. I will give you something that will assist you in your assignment." Bewildered by this intervention Florian didn't even flinch when Sekandar placed his hands on his temples.

A few moments elapsed. Sekandar withdrew his hands and Florian said, "I need ... to sit down." Sekandar assisted him. Florian needed time to come to grips with ... everything.

Sekandar then said to Lilly and Valentine, "I'm glad you noticed me in the lobby. Thank you for your perception. Knowing that you did made my contact with Florian much easier. As well as effecting the change for him I made some mental adjustments in him that will strengthen your handling of the conference delegates at the Centrosul Convention Center tomorrow. He is a good man, and he will admirably fulfil his assignment to protect you."

"So, that's what brings you here," Valentine provided the answer to her question.

Sekandar smiled characteristically, and said, "Yes, and now I have to leave you two. Layne and Jorie may need my assistance. Farewell. Peace be with you." Sekandar stepped forward, kissed the cheeks of Valentine and Lilly in turn, then stepped away, and with the usual accompanying coalescent misty array of the colours of the white light spectrum he dematerialised, and was gone.

Poverty

Staff at the Diamond Convention Centre in Manaus, capital city of the Brazillian state of Amazonas, had been preparing for the event for months. The Centre was chosen as host venue for the International Festival of Indigenous Dance. Management of the Centre, which has its own nearby hotel, put every effort into preparations; even a late two month postponement did not deter them. The event attracted interest from many countries around the globe and International media attention.

Natália Rivero, Head of Cultural Affairs at the Itamaraty - the Brazilian Foreign Affairs Ministry, had been frantically rescheduling the festival of indigenous dance that was previously meant to be held in mid-Autumn. "Why is it so difficult to get people to do their jobs?" she said rhetorically to her aide. "Ah well, I think everything is in place despite the hiccups. I'm glad that most of the team's effort has been laudable. The festival is going well, and due to their efforts I'm sure it will be a great success."

Retrieving herself from her musing, she looked about as she ambled between function events. "Mr Jorie Barak! I'm so glad you made it. Come with me, there's no time to waste." She grabbed his hand and headed with him to one of the dance halls. "Do you recall that I said, when we were talking together at that function in Tel Aviv, that we would we have to refresh your dancing skills, get your feet moving again and your renew your rhythm? Well then, may I have this dance?"

He had no choice but to accept. He removed his jacket, placed it on a vacant chair, and said, "Certainly." As he did so she swirled him onto the dance floor and straight into a Samba. At first he couldn't recall the correct pattern of steps but that didn't matter, she led with ease. Jorie didn't know that Natália Rivero was a former national champion of Samba. He soon started to enjoy himself, and he felt that she was truly 'renewing' his rhythm ... making him feel ... relaxed ... comfortable.

Natália knew he was tiring and she gracefully swirled him off the dance floor and said, "There you go Jorie. I knew we'd get your rhythm back but let's not overdo it, you haven't danced in a while and I think you need to take a rest now. Let's find a nice quiet place." Once again Jorie complied as she took him by the hand. He retrieved his jacket on the way out and she led him to a room; she said it was set aside as her 'office' for the event.

This was no 'office' it was a luxury suite in the adjoining hotel. Jorie, although still catching his breath from the energetic Samba with Natália, felt uneasy. He gathered his wits.

Ostensibly to begin her planned seduction of him, Natália adopted an obviously sexy posture and said, "You are a handsome man Jorie Barak, reasonably fit and ... and now with renewed rhythm." She paused ... he waited ... "Tell me how did you got into politics. You seem to me to be rather young to be a politician."

Jorie wondered whether her seduction would be drawn out but decided anyway to respond to her statement. His experience suggested that by ignoring her statement and presenting one himself, she may be diverted from her intent to seduce and be compelled to respond with a question. "Politics has always interested me," he said. "Even as a boy I was captivated by the way the adults around me politicked in all sorts of situations."

He was right, she did. "Politicked? What a curious word. I don't think I've ever heard anyone use it. What do you mean?" Natália relinquished her sexy posture. Her 'intent to seduce' him having been dashed, but not vanquished perhaps.

Jorie sensed that and knew that he could now steer the conversation his way. He set about doing just that. "Natália, you are a senior civil servant. You associate with, interact with and have to deal with politicians every day. I don't really need to explain 'politicked' to you. You and I know that politicking is any activity that is done especially in order to win support or gain an advantage. We do it every day in most situations."

Acknowledging his point, and bringing forth her intuitive persona, Natália replied, "Yes, when you put it like that I guess we do. In this situation, with the two of us talking together, do you see an opportunity to be politicking?"

Jorie smiled. "Isn't that what I've been doing?

Natália wasn't fazed by his answer. Intuiting an ulterior intent to Jorie's rejoinder, she asked, "What is the real point you are wanting to make?"

"I will come to that. First, let me take you back to the function in Tel Aviv, where we were talking together. I recall that you said 'indigenous dance in particular' is one of your interests. I want to ask you whether you have done any analysis of the relationship between poverty and the preservation of indigenous dance, for want of a better term."

Looking a bit elvish she said, "For want of a better term? I'll talk to you later about that. Anyway, is there a particular reason why you ask?"

He with a dry smile then said, "Yes, there is. Natália, I'd like to introduce you to a friend who came with me to the festival. She is writing an article about the issue, and can better articulate what we mean."

Natália replied with obvious suspicion. "A journalist? I'm not sure I should be talking to her without approval from head office. They can be pretty touchy about media interviews."

Jorie reassured her. "It's ok Natália, she will have you vet whatever she writes. There will be nothing political in her article. It will be about the festival, and I know she is very impressed with what she has seen. I can vouch for her integrity. Believe me, from my position as a politician that's something rare in journalists. She is freelance anyway, and therefore she is not answerable to any media connection."

Musing at first, she then adamantly replied, "Hmm ... well ok, but you must be present when she interviews me, and it must be recorded for me to vet."

Jorie responded quickly. "I most certainly will be present. Thank you for trusting me. I will not let you down."

He took out his smartphone and called Layne; he made out that he was talking with her but actually called her telepathically; appearances can be important. "She will be with us shortly. She's been dancing too."

Layne arrived soon after. "Natália, this is Layne Bauer. Layne this is Natália Rivero, Head of Cultural Affairs at the Itamaraty and she is the festival organiser."

They exchanged pleasantries, Natália bid they all be seated, paused, switched on her recorder then said. "Welcome Layne, to the International Festival of Indigenous Dance. What is it about the festival that you will be writing about?"

Layne answered enthusiastically, "In my opinion this festival has to one of the best I have ever been to. The array of different cultures represented here is magnificent. The dancing has been very well presented and I particularly like the inclusiveness. Everyone is encouraged to participate, to get up on their feet and dance or learn to if they think they can't. That's great! I am really enjoying myself. I haven't had so much fun in years. I'll be writing about that, and more."

Clearly delighted with the tenor of Layne's impending report Natália threw out her hands in glee and said, "That is wonderful! I'm so pleased. Now, what would you like to ask me?"

Layne's maintained the smile on her face, that Natália's delight had elicited, and came straight to her point. "I expect that Jorie has mentioned our interest in the relationship between poverty and the preservation of indigenous dance, so I will elaborate. Jorie and I are members of a team that has a particular interest in issues around poverty and its relationship to violence. Members of our team see a definitive causal link between the two; that poverty is a product of violence, specifically resulting from indifference by prosperous and wealthy sectors of society to the pervasiveness of poverty. On the face of it preservation of indigenous dance seems to be predominately inherent in the ethos, the distinctive spirit if you will, of those groups in society who are in poverty. Would you agree with that assessment?"

Natália's reply was surprising. "Hmm ... You may be right ... in most cases ... but not all. I was born into a prosperous family, and was raised to believe that, if you are born poor it's not your mistake, but if you die poor it is your mistake. Let me say, I have no doubt there was more behind the precept than you might think. From my earliest association with kids in my social 'class' I was aware that my parents were not like theirs. My parents were not just saying it's not ok to be poor, they were really saying that it's not ok for anyone to believe that it is ok. This is why I am passionate about promoting cultural diversity. In my position I am able to get that very point across in every so-called strata of society, the poor included. The idea that it is ok to be poor has caused untold pain and misery, for the poor in particular but the wealthy have also suffered by not knowing that nobody needs to be poor. This is a psychological dilemma that is clearly evident in my country."

Jorie, not trying to hide his pleasure with her attitude, happily said, "That sounds like a mini treatise for an upcoming thesis!"

Natália responded instructively. "Indeed it does. Maybe I can name it 'Changing Apathy and Lethargy.' Just don't steal my topic, ok?"

Layne replied, "We will not steal your thesis title. In fact we can give you something that will assist you in writing it. Come closer, and concentrate on my eyes. You will see what I mean." Layne acted, and changed Natália's genome.

Natália leaned back into her chair, then stood up in her place, extended her hands wide and said, "I knew... I just knew there was something different about Jorie, and I sensed something about you ... and now ... I feel ... different. What exactly did you just give me?"

Layne and Jorie looked at each other, then Layne said, "I gave you an extra gift. Is it convenient to explain right now? You have a festival to oversee."

Natália replied, "Right now is fine. My team is running everything, and they will call me if they need me. Tell me now what you just did." She then winked at Jorie. "We have all night."

Later that night Layne had a fascinating telepathic conversation with Karen. They discussed Natália's transformation, and chuckled about Jorie's adventure; he had returned to the dance floor with Natália ... and then ...

Rossija

Piracy

"Captain, we have arrived at the location," the navigator informed the captain, who acknowledged with a nod. Captain Artem Semenov of the Military-Maritime Fleet of the Russian Federation was on supposed 'regular duties' in the North Atlantic with his boat, the latest generation Shchuka-B class submarine.

"Assume your positions," the Captain ordered with the tone of authority in his voice, and not too loud. Submariners seemed to come from all directions onto the bridge. They moved quickly and silently to their operational positions.

Captain Semenov had carried out this particular procedure quite a few times but he never took anything for granted, and also not with the one about to be undertaken. A delicate manoeuvre to position his boat precisely, required the utmost diligence. One little mistake could 'blow his cover' and alert his 'enemy.'

The first officer declared all stations ready, and the captain gave the order to proceed. Absolute silence was maintained as a robotic pod detached from its mother ship and descended slowly to the sea floor. The crew waited, patiently. The computer-controlled pod signalled arrival at its goal. Its exact position was reported to the captain. When that was verified the captain gave the order to proceed; a human safety protocol ensuring that possible mishaps at this stage were obviated. Silence was maintained as the captain and the pod's human 'overseer' watched the delicate procedure take place. Every similar procedure of this type had been completed without a hitch. This one was no different.

Captain Semenov's perfect record had been maintained. The pod returned to reattach to its mother ship, the captain gave the order for his boat to assume its usual operational depth, and then the order was given for the navigator to plot a course to home base. Mission accomplished; another communications cable had been successfully tapped.

The Tsar

Miri Tschekov had not been in Mother Russia for a few years, he preferred to work in the West, although his mathematics skills were often requested, or should that be 'required' back in Moscow. He was fully aware that such requirements entailed calculations that obviously had 'military' written all over them but he never played the espionage game; he had made his home in London, raised his family there and had managed to keep out of all that spy stuff. He also maintained a very highly respected reputation in academia, worldwide.

"This is ... interesting," said Sekandar as he surveyed the breakfast Miri had specially prepared for him. Kasha, butterbrots, fried eggs, tvorog on toast plus cereal with milk; and the almost obligatory cup of coffee, to top it off. "Don't look at me like that, Miri. I know what you're thinking, and no ... I don't need fattening up. We Terranians have a completely different metabolism to humans. I don't need all this food ... I'll eat this lot only because you have been so generous. Please don't do it again ... really."

Miri verbally uttered his thoughts, even though he knew Sekandar was reading every word before it came out. "Well ... I just thought ... we have a big day ahead of us ..."

Sekandar placed a hand on Miri's shoulder and reassured him. "It's OK Miri, you weren't expected to know about that. Now you do."

Looking ahead to their busy day, Miri said, "You know that the Russian regime, well actually the snoops at FSB plant listening devices everywhere, and I wouldn't be surprised if the SVR has an interest is us too. I can't be sure that this place doesn't have any, or that there won't be attempts to plant them on us or in the places where we will be today as well. I was thinking, are you mentally able to detect such devices?"

"Yes, I am, and yes I have detected them here. Don't be alarmed, Miri. I have provided the listeners with alternate conversations, in our voices. They will not suspect anything unusual."

Excited, Miri said, "Wow! How do you do that? We don't have any gear here to tap into their devices."

Sekandar pointed to his head. "Yes we do, Miri."

Not surprised by that, Miri added, "I'd love to see the algorithms for that."

Sekandar placed both hands on Miri's shoulders and said, "Be assured my mathematical friend, I will do that for you later ... it takes time to explain. I have no doubt you will find the process enlightening."

"Can't wait for that." Checking the time on his smartphone, Miri said "We'd better get a move on. People are waiting for us."

This is an auspicious day for Miri Tschekov. Nominated by the Moscow Mathematical Society he is to present himself at a State function where he will be bestowed with the Order of Honour for 'achievements in mathematics resulting in significant Russian technological advantage in the production of high-tech products,' so the citation read.

Miri in all honesty had no idea precisely what high-tech products benefited from his mathematics. Sekandar does, and that is why they will be attending. Many people will be assembled for the occasion, including politicians, academics, bureaucrats and representatives of the military. Sekandar was particularly pleased that the 'President' of the Russian Federation will be there.

The driver of an official car picked them up from their hotel and they were driven to the venue. On the way Sekandar scanned the driver's mind. It was the mind of a secret service agent and he took the opportunity to effect the change for him. Arriving at the venue the driver, whose forehead wore a frown said, "Thank you Sir. I will be here after the function, to take you back to your hotel."

Sekandar acknowledged him, and said, "Thank you. What is your name?"

His frown fading as Sekandar gently stroked his mind reassuringly, the driver replied, "I am Andrei ... Andrei Fedorov ... Sir."

"Thank Andrei for bringing us safely here. I am Sekandar, this is my colleague Miri. We will look forward to seeing you again, after the function. It will be safe for you to talk with us then." Andrei, looking a little bewildered, acknowledged with a timorous nod.

Alighting from the car Miri and Sekandar scaled the steps to the entry of the venue. An attendant met them, availed them of their coats and ushered them to their allotted seats.

Surveying the crowd, Miri said, "There are more people here than I anticipated, but where is the President?"

Sekandar smiled. "We will meet him soon, Miri."

Proceedings got underway and the procession proceeded. Miri was ushered to stand with others, in single file along an aisle by the auditorium wall, waiting for his turn to step up onto the stage. It was a lengthy queue but soon his turn arrived. As he stepped up Sekandar telepathically reassured him that everything would be ok.

He turned his head to acknowledge that and could not find Sekandar in the audience, even though he was sure he was looking in the right place. He then felt a freshening movement of air and surmised that Sekandar must have caused it. Indeed, Sekandar had vacated his seat, and had withdrawn from view of the audience. Miri deduced that he must have dematerialised; not from his seat because that would have attracted attention. Miri was right. Sekandar had assumed his incorporeal state.

The official who had been presenting the awards mid-stage, and had just presented the final military award, the Order for Naval Merit to Captain Artem Semenov, was vigorously beckoning Miri to approach him. Miri took his first step towards him, and then all the lighting in the auditorium flickered. Miri closed his eyes, anticipating that this might precede something more noticeable from Sekandar. Everyone else in the audience and the officials on the stage reflexively looked up at the lights. As they did so the lights flashed very brightly in synchronisation, just once.

The flash was so bright that it caused everyone to reel in response to its blinding effect. When Miri opened his eyes, he found himself looking directly at Sekandar who had resumed his seat. Sekandar winked at him. Miri realised what he had done. He returned a smile, and stepped forward to stand before the official who was still trying to regain his composure as he rubbed his eyes.

The official recited the citation headline, pinned the award medal to Miri's jacket, shook his hand, delivered the obligatory congratulations and Russian kiss, and then turned his eyes to the next recipient. Miri took the few paces to the stage steps, descended and proceeded down the aisle to resume his seat.

Miri didn't make it to his seat. A military officer, who hadn't witnessed Sekandar's 'theatre' entered the auditorium and approached him, down the aisle from the opposite direction. "This way Mr Tschekov," the officer said as he pointed to the exit. Miri sensed there was no point querying him, the urgency of the command was evident. He was escorted to the auditorium's vestibule where he was told to stand with Sekandar who was standing there, patiently waiting. He had similarly been detained, while Miri's award was being pinned.

Sekandar telepathically said to Miri, "Everything will be fine. We are about to go for a little ride, to meet the revered President of the Russian Federation."

The attendant who availed them of their coats as they entered the auditorium, returned them and ushered them outside. The icy air accompanying the breeze that met them when they left their hotel for Andrei Fedorov's waiting official car, was now calm. Gently falling snowflakes nestled on them as they were told to get into the waiting car. This was not Andrei's car. This was a big, black stretched 'limo,' and ostensibly menacing. The pair were 'accompanied' by two big men in dark grey suits; they sat opposite facing them, drilling them with their menacing stare.

It was a few kilometres drive to the Kremlin, and the snow was falling heavier as they arrived. Miri felt uncomfortable in the situation that seemed to be getting ever gloomier. Sekandar telepathically reassured him, "Everything will be fine." He then rhetorically asked, "By the way, have you ever met the President? He's a very interesting character."

"Dr. Miri Tschekov! At last I get to meet the great mathematician," said the President, condescendingly offering a hand to be shaken, then placing his other hand on Miri's back. "Come, I have a more congenial place where we can sit and talk. This gilded hall is so overpowering, it's not conducive to private conversations." Redirecting his just shaken hand, the President gestured for Sekandar to join them. "You too Mr Sekandar. An interesting family name you have. Do you have another name?"

Sekandar replied, "You will know me as Sekandar. That is my only name." He made himself clear. The President's eyes narrowed.

"Only one name. I have never heard of anyone with only one name. More of that later. First let me congratulate you Dr Tschekov. Your award is well earned. Your insightful contributions in mathematics are proving to be quite invaluable to us."

Miri wanted to ask, "How's that, Mr President?" but he didn't want to draw attention to himself. That might open a can of worms. Instead, he replied, "I am pleased that I have made myself useful." Never mind about the worms within, he squirmed inside anyway.

The President, not being able to see Miri's inner squirm, continued, "Hmm. I've heard that you are rather modest in your fame abroad, so I expected you to be just the same here at home. Let's have no secrets between us Dr Tschekov. Your mathematical genius has enabled us to secure our interests abroad, and to ensure that our country is safe. I personally want to thank you for that."

Miri, who was starting to understand what the fascination with his mathematics was really all about, briefly turned his eyes to Sekandar then back to the President, and said. "Thank you Mr President."

As an attendant entered the room wheeling a traymobile loaded with an assortment of bottled drinks, glasses, a coffee urn and mugs, the President stood up and said, "Excuse me gentlemen, I neglected to offer you something to drink." The attendant withdrew upon the President's acknowledging nod of thanks.

Drinks were taken. Everyone resumed their seats. The President focused his attention on Sekandar. "Well now Mr Sekandar, we have been intrigued by you. Why have you accompanied Dr Tschekov on his visit to Moscow? Are you a mathematician too?"

The President provided the perfect transition for Sekandar. It was almost like a musical segue; smooth and uninterrupted. "Yes, I am."

"Have you been working with Dr. Tschekov on his mathematics that have been of such important benefit to us?" The President was phishing.

Sekandar played along with the lead. "Yes, I have. We have learnt a lot through our professional and academic collaboration. The algorithms we have worked on have been particularly challenging. If you had an understanding of advanced mathematics you would appreciate that."

"Quite, quite so," the President responded awkwardly.

Sekandar continued. "I specialise in a particular branch of the mathematics of psychology. Its application is fundamental to psychohistory, which is the basis of my research."

"Fascinating. What is psychohistory?" The President nibbled the bait.

Sekandar tweaked the line. "An explanation would take quite some time, and require an acquisition of many concepts that you may find daunting."

"Mr Sekandar, don't underestimate my intellect. I didn't get to be where I am accidentally. Your synopsis of 'psychohistory' in words will suffice, for now."

"Very well." Sekandar stood up, and focussed his attention directly on the President. Miri was all ears; clearly enjoying Sekandar's imminent apparent subterfuge.

"Psychohistory has been defined as the branch of mathematics which deals with the reactions of human conglomerates to fixed social, economic and political stimuli. Implicit in all of the mathematical definitions is the assumption that the human conglomerate being dealt with is sufficiently large for valid statistical treatment. The necessary size of a conglomerate may be determined by a theorem. A further necessary assumption is that the human conglomerate is itself unaware of psychohistoric analysis in order that its reactions will be truly random. The basis of all valid psychohistory lies in the development of a plan. The laws of history may be seen as absolute as the known laws of physics. If the probabilities of errors are greater it is only because history does not deal with as many humans as physics does atoms, so that individual variations count for more ..."

The President raised his hands. "Ok, ok, daunting it is, and yet 'conglomerates' ... 'political stimuli' ... 'theorem' ... 'plan' ... How far advanced is this psychohistory?"

Sekandar responded emphatically. "As I speak, the discipline is at work." The President's eyes narrowed again. He stood up.

"At work? Where?" The President's voice delivered a definitive interrogation.

Sekandar made his move. "Right here, right now. I'm afraid your efforts to establish yourself as the Tsar returning to the bosom of Mother Russia end here and now."

The plainclothes man by the door drew his pistol, aiming it at Sekandar. Miri stood up, and said "Now see here ..." Sekandar motioned him to sit down again. He did, gingerly.

The President stepped forward, and standing very close to Sekandar he said. "Enlighten me Mr Sekandar. Precisely how do think you can do that?"

Sekandar moved a hand inside his jacket. The plainclothes man, who had maintained his aim, fired his pistol. Well no, he didn't. His pistol seized up and fell to the floor. He himself was frozen. His eyes glazed and he stood absolutely motionless. Sekandar and the President maintained eye contact.

Taunting Sekandar, the President snarled, "Is that the best you can do?"

Sekandar returned his volley. "No, this is the best I can do for you, personally."

Sekandar then walked straight into the President's mind, and took control of it. Certain adjustments needed to be made therein. He then effected the change to the Tsar's genome. Mother Russia would never be the same.

As they casually descended the steps from the overpowering gilded hall that so irked the President, Miri enquired of Sekandar, "Why did you go on with all that crazy psychohistory stuff? Was it really necessary?"

Sekandar calmly replied, as he placed his arm over Miri's shoulder, "Sometimes Miri, a perceived truth can be much more daunting than the real truth for a mind like his. The real truth is not necessarily the right trap to catch the wolf. The President was a man who believed he was the Tsar. When you review the words I used, you will understand that I appealed to that particular self. In the fullness of time and when he is ready for it, he will come to know the truth about The Whole."

Andrei Fedorov was standing by his official car and waiting for Sekandar and Miri. He hadn't been standing for long but it was snowing again, and the icy wind freshened. It was biting. He was glad to see his passengers appear on the steps. He opened the car door for them and closed it when they got in. He drove off and headed back to their hotel. After he rounded a corner or two he tilted his head and asked, "Sekandar, what did you do to me on the way to the auditorium? I feel different, changed."

Sekandar replied, "The night is young, Andrei. If you have time then come inside with us when we get back to the hotel. We can have a drink. Maybe Miri can rustle up something to eat, and we can talk."

Miri didn't hear that suggestion. He was muttering to himself, "Psychohistory?"

Yàzhou de

Zhonghuá

Enjoying his human experience, Sekandar was reclining on the sofa in an apartment in Beijing, and drinking a cup of coffee he had made for himself; he rather liked coffee, occasionally. He looked up and said to Yang, "When I was researching for this mission I came across a charming little ancient story that tells the origin of the words 'Europe' and 'Asia.' Maybe you know of it?"

"Hmm?" Yang Meixa muttered. She wasn't listening to him.

He told her the story anyway. "Apparently the land to the west of the road from Athens to its port Piraeus, was Asia and to east it was Europa. That seems unlikely, there are other stories, but the thought of that caused me to wonder about the various explanations for the Chinese name for Asia. Yàzhou de of course is just one of many."

Yang Meixa still wasn't listening. She was feeling retrospective as she stood by her hotel suite window and gazed out into the dense, suffocating smog outside. "Smog," she said, frowning. "It's the usual atmospheric condition here in Beijing. In fact it is the norm in many of China's big cities. I can't imagine having to live in this every day of my life. I came from a small village in an outer province, went to school in a town not far away from the village, I finished high school in that town and I didn't have to endure this when I went to university. I was lucky. Relatives of mine living in Australia sponsored my studies at a university there, before taking up my doctoral studies at Harvard. I am so grateful that they did that for me."

She shook her head in dismay, then turned to Sekandar. "I suppose you don't have anything like this on Terra Dyad, do you?"

He ignored her disinterest in his story about names, and replied, "Absolutely not Yang Meixa. Conditions like this have never existed there. For Terranians it is probably the most alien aspect of Earth. This is one of the consequences of the dominance of hierarchy. The competitive inevitability of that produced the capitalist system that produced unpleasant consequences like this," he said as he pointed to the smog that obliterated the sky denying its very existence. "That's an over simplification but essentially that is what happened. The co-operative path that we ventured down ultimately led us to what we call The Whole. Again, that is an oversimplification."

Yang cut in, "I can't wait to learn all about that."

Sekandar fed her expectancy, tempering it just a bit. "Wait you will have to but not for too much longer. The change is happening so quickly that you might perceive it as you would a viral outbreak."

She smiled. "Yes, I think so." Checking the time she said, "We'll have to leave for the meeting soon. We will be going by taxi, and that can be an adventure in Beijing. Maybe you might perceive that as an anti-body rushing along in a viral stream." They both laughed.

The meeting that they were about to attend was a follow-up from the last International Conference on Microbiology, Virology and Immunology. Attendees were only the principal representatives of the delegations that thronged the earlier main event. These individuals came from each country in Asia, including South East Asia, and from India, Indonesia and also from Australia.

"We were followed all the way from our hotel," Yang whispered to Sekandar as they alighted from their taxi upon its arrival at the meeting venue.

Sekandar responded telepathically, "Yes, we were. The occupants of three cars were engaged in a little game of tag the taxi, each car joining in from a different side road as one turned away. The occupants were secret service agents of course, as was our driver. And, by the way, talk with me telepathically from now on."

Yang Meixa acknowledged his request, and added, "I think it's the MSS. We must be of very special interest to them. The Ministry of State Security doesn't pay attention to the tiddlers, only to the big fish."

Sekandar confirmed her observation. "We certainly are of interest to certain individuals here. They know who we are. News travels fast, especially when those holding the reins of power in a state like this sense a potential threat. Fear not Yang Meixa, everything will be fine." The pair entered the venue, followed by security agents afoot.

Upon entering the hall Yang overheard a conversation between two of the delegates. Sekandar tuned in too. They picked up the conversation when one delegate said, "I don't understand why we spend all our time researching all these virological issues when the greatest viral threat to us is this country's fixation with their 'one road' dogma. The highest purpose of one road is that we, i.e., I mean the Chinese regime, cannot tolerate anyone getting in the way of its implementation, and woe betide anyone who does! The intensity of their incessant dogma strikes me as being not just arrogant but also threatening. I fear it will somehow lead to violent reactions."

The second delegate responded, suggesting, "Am I given to understand that you consider the regime's fixation to actually be a form of viral infection? It is, after all a manifestation of a mindset inculcated through an inherent desire for each and every member of the party to scramble their way up the hierarchy ladder to a position where they can, or at least where they assume they can wield more power?"

The first delegate replied, "Yes, now that you put it that way, I guess I am. The question arising is, how do we destroy the virus and preserve the individual at the same time?

Yang Meixa couldn't contain her delight when she heard the question. She stepped forward and said, "Excuse me. I just unintentionally overheard your interesting conversation. My name is Yang Meixa, I am a virologist. I agree with your diagnosis, and I think I have a cure for the condition that will deal with the virus and preserve the individuals as you would want."

Reading Yang's name tag, recognising her status in their profession and feeling quite comfortable with her eavesdrop, the second delegate responded. "What cure do you have in mind?"

Yang replied eagerly, "We can isolate the specific evolved gene in each individual, analogous as the pathogen in this case, which results in the incubation of the mindset that produces the condition. Then it is simply a matter of modifying the gene by removing the inherent propensity to behave that way; i.e., to use violence, to be violent."

Expressively bemused, the first delegate enquired, "Isolating the gene then modifying it? How do you propose to do that?"

Seeking his approval for her proposed next move, Yang Meixa turned to Sekandar who had been standing back a step away to her left. She flinched. He caught the look of genuine startlement that flashed across her face. He was being held by two grim-faced military-uniformed men, one of whom said to her and the two delegates, "You will all come with us. This way."

They had no choice. All four were hustled outside and bundled into a waiting van. The two delegates were protesting in the strongest terms. Inside the van yet more grim-faced men with weapons drawn ignored their protest. Sekandar gently silenced them and likewise soothed their minds. Telepathically he said to Yang Meixa, "Stay calm. Everything will be fine. Your opportunity to act will come soon. We are being taken for an audience with the General Secretary." He winked at her. She smiled. One of the 'heavies' noticed, and he scowled.

The everpresent smog effectively shrouded the hastening van, making it inconspicuous to any external eyes it passed that might have been interested. It was a long drive, darting left and right down side roads, ostensibly to muddle a sense of direction for the four hostages. Eventually they arrived at a rather austere looking building where they were bundled out of the van and hustled quickly inside. The two delegates quivered in fear as they stumbled into the foyer. Sekandar and Yang Meixa remained calm and alert.

The outward austerity of the building gave way to a lavish interior. A young woman approached the four, and in an obviously contrived convivial voice said as she motioned the direction with her hand, "This way, if you please. You will address the General Secretary as 'Your Excellency,' and you will not speak until you are requested to."

Large double doors opened slowly as they approached them, revealing a large room, ornately decorated in what could have been described as a colour red dominated tasteless mix of Chinese post-cultural revolution and neo-Chinese styles. A large similarly ornate desk seemed to be lost in the clutter of it all. The young woman motioned for the four to be seated on chairs in line and facing the desk. She addressed her leader. "Your Excellency." She then withdrew to stand near the now closed doors.

His Excellency, a stout grim-faced man wearing an abstemious lapel-less grey suit remained seated in his chair behind the desk, and not hiding his scorn through his fake grin he said, "Welcome to China, ladies and gentlemen. I can see that you have been having a wonderful time in our beautiful country." The two delegates grimaced in contempt. He picked up on that. His grin vanished. "Loose talk has brought you here. It does not augur well for you." The delegates became even more sullen.

He turned his attention to Yang Meixa. "You have been of interest to me for quite some time, since your secondary school days, in fact. Unusually bright students always attracted my attention. You have done well but that has been of no direct benefit to your homeland. That is unfortunate. So, you are now an Australian citizen. That is also of interest to me, and here in Beijing you have been planning to 'modify genes.' I'll come back to that but now I am intrigued by your friend"

Peering at Sekandar his eyes narrowed, and his voice slowed. "You. You are unidentified. What is your name?

Sekandar replied, "You will know me as Sekandar."

Squirming in his chair, the General Secretary snapped, "Sekandar who?"

"That is my name. I have no other." Sekandar calmly replied.

Clearly irritated, the General Secretary raised his voice a notch and demanded, "Well Sekandar, whoever you are you did not enter China through any authorised entry point. How did you enter the country?"

He did not answer. He telepathically signalled Yang Meixa. "This is your opportunity Yang. You know what to do." In that moment the General Secretary cocked his head as though he was trying to draw from Sekandar an answer to his question. He didn't get it. Instead, he got an interjection from Yang Meixa. "Your Excellency, let me explain."

The General Secretary snapped, "You have not been requested to speak!"

Yang ignored him and insistently repeated, "Your Excellency, let me explain."

Now totally exasperated, the General Secretary jumped to this feet and erupted. "What impudence! Very well, explain!" His eyes drilled her. That was exactly what she needed.

She returned the drill to his eyes. "Your Excellency, Sekandar and I are associates. We have come to Beijing on a special mission. As I intimated in my conversation, that your operatives overheard with these delegates to the meeting that we too were attending, we are isolating and modifying the specific gene in each individual, analogous as the pathogen in the language of virology, which results in the incubation of the mindset that produces adverse conditions. Conditions such as the unrestrained domination that you have. These conditions will lead to even more violent reactions than we have seen to date. The modification we are effecting will remove the inherent propensity within you and everyone else in China to use violence, or to be violent in any way."

The General Secretary had had enough! He wanted to pour venom upon her but it was too late. Yang Meixa had adjusted the targeted gene within him. He slumped back into his chair and cradled his head in his hands. He sobbed as he felt the unspent venom within his head subside.

In the interim Sekandar effected the change in the two meeting delegates, and in the young woman attendant, just as she was directing a headhigh kick at him. She missed and had crashed to the floor against his mentally directed inhibitive intervention. Hearing the thud as she hit the floor, Yang Meixa turned her attention from the General Secretary to the crumpled woman. Sekandar was kneeling by her saying, "Are you hurt?" He helped her to her feet. She shook her head indicating that she was ok.

Straightening her clothes, she asked, "Who *are* you?

With his characteristic smile Sekandar replied, "I am Sekandar, and this is Yang Meixa. Later, she will explain everything to you but first you need to attend to the General Secretary. He is not his old self, and he needs your assistance." She acknowledged, went to him and crouched beside him. His head was still cradled in his hands. She spoke, he looked at her. She comforted him. Bleary-eyed he stood up with her. They slowly made their way to the door, and left the room.

Yang had been tending the two delegates who had coped with the change better than the other two. The first delegate said, "The name Yang Meixa will be lauded among virologists. You have done something that we could only have dreamt. If you have time, you must tell us everything about this change that you have so skilfully effected."

Yang responded, "Rest assured I will. Now, let's get out of here." She linked arms with them, one on either side and they walked through the doorway to be met by the 'heavies' who had hustled them earlier.

She glanced at Sekandar who said, "It's ok Yang, these men will take us to wherever we wish." Amid the orderly flutter that had ensued during their audience with the General Secretary, he had effected the change in them too.

Yang took a deep breath, her first for a while. "Let's find somewhere to eat, I'm starving," she said as she and Sekandar were escorted, this time by friendly heavies to the waiting van. Climbing inside the van, they were joined by the young woman who had escorted them to the General Secretary.

"May I join you? The GS is resting. The change really knocked him. Don't worry, he'll be fine. My staff will watch over him until I return. She chuckled as she enthusiastically requested her inclusion, then said, "By the way, I am He Kexin. I know a special restaurant you will really like. The meal is on me. Well, it's really on my expense account."

"Sure, you're most welcome." Yang Meixa accepted her request, gladly. The van drove away sedately to He Kexin's 'special restaurant.' It was a pleasant evening for all, except perhaps for the GS who didn't feel much better until the following morning.

Nihon

Sumiko Kojima, political scientist is pensive. She verbally ruminates, "Apart from having to keep watch over the fanatical regime in North Korea, we in Japan have been concerned about China's 'one road' economic policy. On the one had we have had a lunatic, a pumped up little big shot, whose real intentions were anybody's guess, and on the other we had an oligarchy masquerading as a communist regime, dominated by people who think they can buy their way to economic hegemony by borrowing money that they will never be able to, and probably never intended to repay. They seemed to be blinded by their own dogma, i.e., the intent of 'one road' was that they wouldn't tolerate anyone getting 'in the road, if you get my drift.'"

"Well Sumi, why don't you have a good whinge?" Commented James Lynne, momentarily lifting his eyes from his mobile device. "Surely ..."

Sumiko hadn't finished. She cut in and continued, "Of course those were not our only problems. We are a nation with a declining population. If we kept going the way we were, we would have ended up losing any economic advantage that we may have had. Nihon was said to be the Land of the Rising Sun. Maybe we had gone past noon and had become the Land of the Setting Sun. We were on our way to a very dark night."

James switched off his device and engaged with her. "Interesting that you should have such concern for Japan. I mean, you are from the Nansei Archipelago. Okinawa, as I recall. Have the mainlanders ever cared about you islanders? I can't recall when I have ever seen you so pessimistic. It's not like the Sumi I knew during our post-grad years."

"I'm sorry James. You're right, it's not like me. I guess I'm just fed up with the failure of a long succession of politicians in my country to pull themselves out the systemic shortcomings of our political system. I just think they dropped the ball, and lost the will to change anything."

Concerned for his friend, James said, "This is an interesting mood you have created for yourself Sumi. You know that The Change will change everything."

Easing out of her gloominess, Sumi acknowledged James' concern. "Yes of course, I know it will James. I'm just sad that we couldn't have changed things without it. The ability has always been there but not the will."

"Hmm, I'll have to ..." There was a knock at their door. Surprised, James enquired, "Are we expecting visitors, Sumi?"

"Yes James, we are. Sorry, I didn't tell you." Expectantly Sumi moved quickly and opened the door. "Taka! You made it." The pair reciprocally bowed. James almost followed their lead but waited.

"Sumi! It's so good to see you. You look wonderful!" With excitement in her voice the familiar response gushed from the young woman in the doorway.

"Come in, come in." Taka entered, followed by another.

Taka's excitement continued. "Sorry Sumi, I didn't mention that I would bring my Father with me. I hope you don't mind. When I told him that I was catching up with you today, he asked to come along. He also studied political science and is keen to meet you. I've been telling tales out of school, as usual."

Surprised but delighted with a broad grin Sumi gladly acquiesced, "No, no, that's fine. Pleased to meet you ..." Taka hadn't yet introduced her father.

"The pleasure is all mine Sumiko. I've been wanting to talk with you anyway, and this seemed to be a good opportunity." said Taka's father, politely.

"Yes, yes ... as good as any ... I suppose," came Sumi's gawky response as she turned to James. "Forgive me, I neglected to introduce you to my colleague. This is James Lynne ... James, this is Takako Shusho ... and her father ...?"

"Jiro Shusho. It's a pleasure to meet you Mr Lynne," he said, then bowed.

James bowed, then extended a welcoming hand. "Plekased to meet you. No tiles for me. Just call me James. May I call you Jiro?"

"Certainly, James," Jiro replied.

Hardly able to contain her excitement upon seeing her friend Taka, Sumi cut in, "Come, please be seated. I will make us tea." Looking at Taka she added, "Would you like to ...?" Sumi nodded in the direction of the kitchen, bowed to the men then retreated with Taka.

Jiro accepted the offer. "Thank you. I would like tea," he said as the young women laughed their way into immediate reminiscing. It didn't matter that they hadn't heard him.

James opened the conversation with Jiro. "So, you are a political scientist too. You know, someone once said that the collective noun for a group of political scientists is a conspiracy. If that is so, then let us conspire." Jiro smiled. "Where did you study PS, Jiro?"

Jiro replied, "I was an undergraduate at Meiji University, then at the Graduate School for Law and Politics at the University of Tokyo. That was quite a few years ago. Where did you study, James?"

"I got interested in PS at College then went on to my first doctorate at Michigan University, and my second at the University of London; that's where I met Sumiko. These days I am a 'visiting fellow' at various universities around the world. Some have called me the original Travelling Wilbury. It's an unusual profession, PS that is, but I like it. And what profession did you choose, Jiro? "

Clearly comfortable in James' inviting presence, Jiro opened up. "Some of my old uni friends think I strayed from the PS brotherhood when I became a politician, but I like my profession. It's always challenging me to apply myself effectively and flexibly."

James' eyes lit up, realising that he might have an unexpected opening here. "Politics, eh. Are you currently in government or opposition?"

Feeling more at ease, Jiro opened up further. "We're in government, and hopefully so for a long time. Officially I am Assistant Minister to the Foreign Minister. It's a good job, tends not to attract much media attention."

"Interesting. Do you have a place in cabinet?" James enquired further.

"Oh yes. It tends to be a place of refuge ... after the chicaneries of the Kokkai ... the Diet ... the parliament. Hmm ... cabinet is where decisions ... deals are ratified, not where policy is developed ... or made. I think I can talk with you like that ... you will understand me."

Nodding his understanding, James sardonically added, "Yes, 'kokkai' sounds so close to 'cock-eyed,' and however you perceive that it is an apt analogy for cabinet rooms around the world."

Jiro laughed. "I have to agree with that."

Sumi and Taka now quiet, returned with the tea from the kitchen. They seated themselves opposite and facing the two men who were seated on the other side of the small low-profile table. According to custom they arranged the tea utensils, then waited until the men were ready, before continuing the procedure of serving the tea. Although this wasn't a tea ceremony as such, certain etiquette seemed appropriate.

Tea was served and sipped. Quiet was maintained for a few minutes then Jiro broke the silence. "Sumiko, I have read your articles on political systems and want to ask if it is ok with you that I appropriate some of your ideas into a policy paper I am preparing."

"Well ... um ... what in particular is it that interests you in my articles?" Sumi was chuffed.

Jiro explained, "There are elements of your ideas on representation that I feel could be useful for my purpose. We can talk privately about that if you feel it is not appropriate here and now. I just thought you wouldn't mind discussing this among like-minds, if I can put it that way."

"Here and now is fine," said Sumi, ok with that.

Jiro smiled and said, "Good. My paper's focus is on the structure of representation within the electorate. I like your idea of a more democratic representative system utilising multi-member electorates, making the system more inclusive."

"Oh that." Sumi laughed. "My idea is only a modification of similar systems currently in use in a few countries. Yes, you are most welcome to include my interpretations in your paper. Oh, and while we're on this subject James has an idea that I'm sure you will warm to." She carried Jiro's eyes until they engaged with James'.

Unknowing, Jiro's curiosity was perfectly positioning him mentally for James to take action. "Tell me about it, James. What is your idea?"

Engaging directly with Jiro's eyes he said, "I guess you could say it's directly related to you warming to the idea of a more inclusive system. The concept is predicated on a simple change that is effected like this." James acted. The change was effected for Jiro Shusho. James was pleased with himself that it was so easy. And it really was, easy.

Jiro blinked a few times, looked at his daughter who was smiling, then to Sumiko who was also smiling, then engaging again with James he said, "I see. Yes, that is certainly an idea that fits very neatly into the desire for a more inclusive representative democratic system. Thank you for giving it to me." Everyone laughed.

Jiro wasn't finished yet, and he asked, "Have any of you ever been to a Sumo match? They can get rather violent you know. I think we can have some fun there. Would you like to go to one? I easily can arrange prime seating. There are some privileges that come with being a Cabinet Minister." Sumi and Taka chuckled.

James was overjoyed with Jiro's amazing transformation. It was so smooth, so quick that as Jiro was inviting them to a sumo match, he had communicated the news telepathically to Karen and Sekandar. They were fascinated.

Gleefully James answered Jiro, "Yes, of course we would love to go with you." Jiro was already on his 'phone. A splendid night of change was thoroughly enjoyed by the four of them. And, Jiro couldn't wait for the next Cabinet meeting, and then the next session of the Kokkai.

Bharat

Valentine Plessis was happy to be back in India. Having been here several times over the past few years, the campus at Delhi University was becoming familiar to her. This time she is here to consult with her colleague and friend, about their upcoming trip to Africa.

She made her way along Chhatra Marg to the corner of University Road where the Central Library is located, just opposite the Art Faculty in the University Enclave. Her colleague had arranged to meet her there, in the foyer. Valentine walked through the main entrance and looked around but couldn't see her friend. So she seated herself on a circular bench nearby, and waited. Watching the people pass by as they came and went she wondered how many had been changed since her visit to her mother, and that amazing dinner at the Panchavati with her and her boyfriend the suave military officer Monsieur Jules Béraud.

As she was waiting, a man with a full head of immaculately groomed grey hair and smartly dressed in a very European styled pinstripe grey suit entered the foyer. He similarly looked around, as though he too was expecting to see a particular person. Unsuccessful in his perusal he sat down next to Valentine on the circular bench, and adjusted the bloom in his lapel.

Never backward in coming forward, Valentine enquired, "Waiting for someone too?"

He smiled and replied, "Yes, but she doesn't seem to be here yet." He looked at his watch; he was wearing a Rolex, no less. Valentine noticed. "Maybe I got the wrong time. Perhaps she …" He didn't finish his words. He rose smartly to his feet; Valentine noticed the beautiful shiny black brogues. He greeted his date with a kiss to her cheek as he held both her hands. Then, and only then as they moved to be beside each other did Valentine clearly see the woman. Surprised, Valentine involuntarily jumped to her feet. The woman noticed of course, and then came the embraces; warmly reciprocated, and with a kisses on both cheeks.

"Monique, it's so good to see you … and your, friend." Valentine casually greeted her friend, with an obvious query attached.

"My dear Valentine, it's wonderful to see you again too! And, this is Charles," Monique responded, noting the query but not reacting … yet.

Valentine acknowledged, offering her hand. "Pleased to meet you … Charles."

Taking her hand he lifted it to his lips and gently kissed it. "The pleasure is all mine, Valentine. Monique has told me so much about you, and it's all good I can assure you."

Valentine issued another non-verbal query. Monique didn't react to that and said, "Charles is interested in change management, and I knew I just had to introduce him to you."

Valentine wanted to but didn't get her response out. Monique could see that a bit of privacy might be required. "Come, let's not stand here talking. There's a nice café in the building, just 'round this corner." She hustled the two along. "Look, there's a nice little nook, it'll give us some privacy." Privacy it provided, and they settled in, ordered coffee and Valentine could now respond.

Oblique queries were getting a workout during this little non-verbal between friends. Valentine delivered another for Monique as she said to Charles, "And ... how did you ... acquire your interest in change management, Charles?"

Amused by the spiel between the two, Charles' chuckle remained internal as he attempted to end any perceived incertitude. "Well, to cut a long story short you could say it's all due to my daughter. It's her fault. At highschool she developed an interest in the subject. Observing that, my curiosity pulled me in, and the rest is history."

Hearing his explanation, Monique glanced sideways at Charles who didn't react but Valentine did. Not disguising her uncertainty about the relationship, Valentine almost choked as she spluttered, "Your daughter?"

Monique realised she needed to quench her friend's dubiety. "Valentine, Charles' daughter is my Sister-in-law. And to clear up any arrière pensée, Charles is the University Chancellor. I'm sure he won't mind me saying that he plays a ceremonial rather than an executive' role." Valentine responded with a shake of her head, both ways; as if to shake out all the confusion.

Charles responded to Monique's repartee. "Yes, that it is Valentine. It brings a certain degree of, let's say latitude that enables me to pursue academic interests that the Vice Chancellor can't, lest cries of 'conflict of interest' be wailed and demands proliferate that I be thrown into the eternal fires of damnation."

"That's rather poetic Charles. What academic interests does your 'latitude' afford you?" asked Valentine who had relaxed.

Feigning his wound, Charles responded, "Touché! Well, I am working on a rather large 'change management' project idea that I think will ultimately be fundamental to the survival of our species." Valentine's eyes widened as she turned to Monique, who eyes had reacted likewise.

"Let me explain. You may have heard general commentary such as: 'In India there are still too many young people who cannot be gainfully employed.' It's true. The problem is extant, and I have made eradication of the problem the focus of my project. Things must not stay as they are. Change must happen. The obvious question is: how do we effect change? And of course: how do we manage the change?' Tell me, is that too ambitious?"

Just as she speculated with the news headlines of her great deeds at the Panchavati, here too Valentine's imagination started to float away. A telepathic nudge from Sekandar brought her quickly back to reality, and she focused on the task at hand. "Certainly not, Charles! In fact I think your project is precisely what the world needs."

Overjoyed by Valentine's enthusiasm for his project, it was now Charles' turn to dream. "The world? I have been thinking India ... and then ... as you say ... the World."

A gentle nudge from Monique brought him back. "Let's start with India, Charles. This is a big problem to deal with. Maybe then we can look further afield."

Still dreaming of 'the big picture' Charles accepted her realism, and said, "Ok, let's imagine we can start here and now! How?"

Valentine drew close to him, and almost whispering she said, "Precisely Charles, let's imagine the 'how' of starting here and now. Concentrate on my eyes and together we can amplify our imagination." Charles was ready to try anything, so deep was his desire to realise his project. He concentrated. Her eyes were enticing his mind to draw even closer. He willingly let her take hold of his mind, and she acted. The change for Charles was an entirely natural transformation. He was on the pathway anyway, and just at the right moment Valentine appeared as his guide.

Valentine disengaged from Charles' eyes, and she drew herself away. She embraced her friend, saying, "Thank you my dear Monique for bringing Charles to me. You know very well that you could have effected the change for him. Why did you want me to do it?"

Monique smiled, and said, "I did say that 'I just had to introduce him to you.' Now I can also say that I just had to let you effect the change for him because you were so gentle when you did for me." They embraced again as a teardrop or two of joy welled in their eyes.

Charles stood up, adjusted his red and pink motif tie and his very European styled pinstripe grey suit, then with his hand he smoothed his immaculately groomed grey hair, all the way to the back of his head. He sat down again, and said, "Ladies, please excuse me. I have an appointment to arrange with the Vice Chancellor. Before I leave you I just wanted to say that things will not stay the same. Change will happen. I will start with the super-rich and deal with their absurd 'trickle down' dogma. They have been one of the main instigators creating the economic and social mess this country is in, and indeed the World. Of course there are other factors to deal with too. The inherent 'violence of subjugation,' as I call it, of the caste system here is just as culpable. I will deal with that too, thanks to what you have done for me. I don't know how I can possibly repay you."

Valentine interrupted him. She held both his hands and said, "Charles, you will not be alone in your endeavour. There is so much more for you to learn about the change that has been made in you. At this very moment the change is being effected in many hundreds of thousands of people around the World. Right here in India, Jules Béraud, a military officer, able to reach all levels of the establishment is making remarkable progress. And, my own Mother is reaching the poorest people in Delhi, through her own household staff." She drew Monique close and said, "My dear friend and colleague here has been changing staff and students here at the university. She brought you to me because she knew about your project and desperately wanted you to know, and now you do. It is wonderful to have you on board, and I know you will be absolutely delighted to learn, in the fullness of time, about The Whole, the source of The Change."

Charles squeezed her hands, released them and said, "I think I sense what that could be. Well, it is time to say adieu." All three arose and embraced each other. Charles, being Charles, took in turn the hand of Monique and Valentine and gently kissed them. "The pleasure has been mine." He walked away a few paces, turned and simultaneously all three waved and said adieu."

Valentine and Monica watched on as Charles disappeared from view. "Africa!" they said together as they turned to face each other, breaking out into laughter.

Valentine mused, "Hmm ... the 'purpose' of our meeting. It kind of got lost along the way eh? I am so glad it did. Now, what do think? Have we sorted everything for Arica already?"

Nodding her head affirmatively, Monique said, "Yes, I think so. Anything we have missed will come to mind anyway, and we can deal with that. You go ahead, and I will join you as soon as I can. I still have some stuff to finish here."

Valentine replied, "Ok. We'll stay in touch. Hope to see you soon." They embraced one last time and parted.

Indonesia & Pacific

James Lynne walked through the central square at Kota Tua on his way to a rendezvous at Café Batavia. He had been in Jakarta, and at Kota Tua previously. Back then he was on holiday and took the opportunity to experience the local culture; so different in this age than in earlier times but still offering hints of what once was. Some people still refer to this district of Jakarta as Old Batavia. It was the trading port for the Verenigde Oost-Indische Compagnie; the VOC as the Dutch called it. The English called it the Dutch East India Company.

162

As a political scientist he is aware there are those who say Indonesia is actually an empire. He thinks there is merit in that for there is no doubt that the impetus for its development came from the Javanese, following the demise of the VOC and the Dutch occupation. He thought over his extrospective awareness of the politicking during the 'reign' of the VOC long ago.

Easily finding the café, he entered. "Greetings James, and good afternoon," said Layne Bauer who was waiting for him, with Yang Meixa. "I thought this would be a nice a place for lunch, and it certainly seems to be."

"It's good to see you Layne, Yang. Yes, the food here is good, or at least it was good last time I was here. I knew the proprietor then. When did you arrive?"

Layne and Yang, looked at each other and laughed. Layne said, "Our flights must have landed at about the same time. We found each other at the baggage pick up. Anyway, right now I need food. I've never liked 'airline food,' and I didn't have much of it this time either. Where's the menu?" The three of them scanned the café for a waiter.

Yang added, "Me too. I could eat a ... look, here comes the waiter now."

A waiter rushed to their table. Gasping he pleaded, "Please accept apology for no menu on table ... velly busy ... no excuse ... solly."

James waved his angst away. "It's quite alright, we've been here only a short while."

Further calming was unnecessary because the waiter was tapped on his shoulder and waved away. "Is everything ok here?" asked the shoulder tapper, in a cultured voice.

James, who was facing the other way, spun 'round in his seat and said. "Well I never. It's Arie Mas. What a surprise to see you here." He turned back to the women and said, "Arie is the proprietor here."

Arie with his ever piercing eyes, responded, "Not anymore James, I sold the business to a Niece of mine, some years ago. I just like to eat here sometimes. And what a coincidence is this. What brings you back to Jakarta?"

Still showing his delight to see his old friend again, James replied, "We're here to attend a meeting of the ASEAN Regional Forum."

Arie extended his arms, wide. "This is extraordinary. Another coincidence. I just happen to be an advisor to the Forum, and I will be attending that meeting too. This is wonderful." He looked around the café, found the flustered waiter, called him over, whispered something to him, and waved him away again. With a big grin he said, "This meal is on the house. I still have some influence here you know." Directing his question to the women he asked, "May I join you?" There were those eyes again, piercingly, compelling.

Yang answered. "Why yes ... certainly. And ... will you be speaking at the Forum?"

"No, no. I'll be there observing, taking notes for some of the delegates... The Forum's Secretariat is here in Jakarta and that makes it easier for me to schedule following one-on-one meetings that may be required. It's what I do at these meetings. Living here makes my job a lot easier. It's only a part time contract and it keeps my mind active. And you three?"

Layne took the question, and said, "Delegates from the Pacific Islands Forum will be attending, and we saw this as a good opportunity to talk with representatives of both. We get two Fora for the price of one."

Genuinely wanting to know more, Arie said, "Sounds interesting. If I may ask, what will you be discussing?"

Reeling him in James said, "If you have a moment ... after we have eaten, we would like to tell you all about it. We have no doubt you will find it very useful in your capacity as an advisor."

"Yes, I can't wait. I can find a quieter private place too," said the compliant Arie, and the three conspirators smiled. The waiter returned with the meals.

When everyone was satiated Arie called the waiter over once more, indicated that they had finished, and asked the three to follow him as he headed for the street. "It's just a short walk ... this way ... I have an apartment here."

He said 'apartment' but really it was a luxurious penthouse in one of the newer buildings of the Kota Tua precinct, and not far from Café Batavia. Layne noticed the security personnel outside and inside the building. She enquired, as Arie ushered them to a lift, "Why the security people?"

"We can't afford to risk anything these days, Layne. It's better to be sure than sorry. Aha, here we are. Welcome! Please make yourselves at home," Arie replied as they entered, pointing to lounges arranged around a low table nearby.

He snapped his fingers, and a servant appeared. "We've just eaten but I think I should get you something to drink. Jakarta is a hot place, and you need to keep hydrated."

Just as he had done to the waiter in the café, Arie also spoke Bahasa Indonesia to the servant. Yang knew it is a standardised register of Malay, an Austronesian language that has been used as the 'lingua franca' in the multilingual Indonesian archipelago for centuries, and she found herself listening for any Chinese influence. She tended to do that everywhere.

The servant exited and returned very shortly after carrying a tray with a variety of what appeared to be iced drinks, and served them.

Arie couldn't contain himself any longer. "So, tell me all about it," came his request, so earnestly that it may well have been a command.

James didn't have to do much. It was those eyes of Arie. They engaged with James perfectly. Arie sat motionless. His eyes turned from piercing to sparkling.

James placed a hand on Arie's shoulder and asked, "How do you feel, my old friend?"

Arie blinked a few times, reengaged with James' eyes and said, "Why didn't you do this sooner, James?" Impatiently he then said, "Show me the rest of it. No time to waste, the Forum meets tomorrow. I can't wait for that." He laughed and added, "You must think I'm always impatient. That's the second time I've said that today. Anyway, whatever hotel booking you have for tonight I will cover, because you are now my guests."

With some gesturing encouragement from Yang and Layne, James tried to decline the offer. "Arie you don't have to ..."

Arie wasn't having any of that. Standing as his valet entered the room, he said, "My valet will show you your rooms. He will shortly retrieve your baggage. Meanwhile, relax and rest up for tonight you are my guests to dinner in my private room at Café Batavia. We are having dinner with some of the top brass."

Layne and Yang looked at each other, saying together, "Top brass?"

Arie's eyes were sparkling again. He knew he had aroused their interest. "Yes, generals etc. Some of them are old school pals. We get together sometimes."

Smiling his broadest smile thus far, Arie said, "I thought you'd like the idea. What's the non-violent English idiom for 'killing two birds with one stone?' "

Her eyes aglow with anticipation of the impending changed genomes, Layne suggested, "Could be 'one fell swoop' but that doesn't sound good either."

Everyone responded. "It'll do." Arie added, "Now, go get some rest."

Dreamtime

Dayspring

Sekandar stood at the Old Lighthouse Lookout Point at the Cape of Good Hope. It is situated at one of the southernmost landform on the African continent, and offers stunning views in all directions, on a clear day; and that it was this day. He looked out over the ocean, and was telepathically talking with Varia. It was a conversation that is difficult for a human mind to comprehend. She was able to see exactly what he saw, even though she was hundreds of light years away in her office on Terra Dyad.

She asked, "Have you ever been here before? I mean right here."

"Oh yes. It must be the 'human' boy in me. There is something enchanting and exciting at the same time about climbing to the top of a precipice like this, and I did climb this time. I didn't want to attract attention by materialising here. I just wanted the privacy with you. It is so beautiful here." He pointed again, "In that direction is Cape Aguhlas where two great oceans meet. I'll show you." He checked to confirm that in both locations nobody was nearby, and he dematerialised. Rematerialising at Cape Aguhlas he picked up the conversation. Pointing he said, "The Indian Ocean meets the Atlantic Ocean right there. Isn't that amazing?"

Varia replied, "It is beautiful. I love the way the currents swirl into such intricate different coloured patterns, merging but somehow remaining separate. We don't have anything quite that that on Terra Dyad. Thank you for sharing it with me." She paused a while, and pondered, "Sekandar, do you feel a familiarity with Earth, as though it is within a part of us?"

Varia 'saw' Sekandar's eyes gleam as he said, "Yes I do. I sense that our fascination with humans goes much deeper than we have perceived. We are kindred souls, together as parts of The Whole. Within, I know that embracing Humankind into our ascendancy of Kala-Ge is fundamental to our destiny. It is predetermined. It is a divine expression of love emanating from The Whole. Do you see that too?"

"Yes I do, and I see that it points to a common origin that is now being revealed. I know you know that too." She could 'see' that the revelation engendered the raw emotion in Sekandar that brought them together in their beginnings as a couple. She smiled, and said, "Show me more of this wonderful place now, before you have to move on."

He pointed to the west, then to the east. "South America is over there, and Australia is there." Looking southward he said, "And over there is Antarctica. I recall reading about this place in my earliest research of Earth. It has been poetically described as 'the end of the Earth.' It's easy to imagine the poet's thoughts, for this is the continent where Humankind originated, where the very first steps in a long journey were taken. There is a wondrous mystery in this. We are witnessing a new dawn for Humankind, and for Terranians." Together they dwelt a while in the intimacy of their knowledge.

Sekandar, looked to the sky and said, "Stay with me a while, and when the sun has set I will show you Kala-Ge as the humans see it." He sat himself on a bench by the nearby lookout. The hours passed far too quickly for them both. There was so much to talk about.

Varia related how everything was going at the Institute, and what Zane and Aedon had been doing in school and with their friends. And she had many questions to ask about Sekandar's experiences on Earth. She wanted to know about everything from foods that humans ate to fads in fashion, from teaching methods to theatre, and she even wanted to know what the weather is like. They could have stayed there talking all night!

Nightfall came. The sky was clear. The last flickering rays of sunlight retreated westward and the first twinkling stars appeared. Sekandar pointed to the heavens and said, "Look Varia, there is Jupiter. It is the largest planet in Earth's solar system. Up close it is magnificent." The darkened sky soon revealed Kala-Ge – The Milky Way. There was no need for Sekandar to point it out to Varia. Through his eyes she could see it, and as its luminosity intensified in the darkening sky she said with awe evident in her voice, "Oh Sekandar. It is so, so beautiful! Where is Terra Dyad?"

He pointed and said, "Right there."

She waved and said, "Can you see me?" They laughed.

Sekandar smiled characteristically and replied, "Yes, I can see you and you look just as beautiful as you did on the day we first met."

The tears of happiness welling in her eyes could not hide from her words in reply. "Oh Sekandar, I so wish I were there with you. Seeing Kala-Ge from there confirms for me the profound importance of your mission, and I am saddened that I can't share your experience in person."

Sekandar's words embraced her. "My dear Varia, when my mission is fulfilled I will be with you again, and maybe then we can plan a vacation to Earth. Just the two of us first, then later together with Zane and Aedon." Varia whimpered happily with that prospect, she didn't respond with words.

Bringing their conversation to a close, Sekandar said, "I must let you go. There is much to be done. I have yet to complete the dayspring, the new dawn for us all. Peace be with you my dear Varia. I love you."

She replied, "Ditto. Peace be with you Sekandar." They disengaged their conversation. Sekandar checked again to ensure that his dematerialisation would not be witnessed, and he was gone.

Awakening

Jorie Barak is confident and optimistic, he always is. His encounter with the mysterious Mr Shaka Ndaba at the function in Tel Aviv has brought him to Africa. This will be a moment of truth for the big man from KwaZulu-Natal.

Jorie arrived at Inkululeko, Shaka Ndaba's 'new town.' He was impressed. It was neat, tidy and aesthetically pleasing. The town was laid out with the appearance of being 'organic.' Even so it was obviously well thought out and prompted a feeling of functionality. It looked good, but was it too good? Jorie found himself with a niggling question that had stayed with him since that first encounter with the developer. What did he mean by 'spiritual infrastructure?' Sekandar had assured him that he would intervene if things turned awkward or threatening. That allayed any concern for Jorie, and he prepared himself to be alert. The taxi he had hailed at the airport in Durban, rounded the final bend in his trip and pulled up at the location provided. There the big man stood.

He didn't remain standing, he advanced toward the taxi and almost smothered the alighting Jorie with an unexpected 'handshake embrace,' followed by a booming, "Welcome to Inkululeko! It is so good to see you Mr Barak. I have been looking forward to this day. Come, let us walk together! My house is nearby." He set off at a brisk pace down the street, not hurriedly but not leisurely either. Jorie was unable to utter a word under the barrage of words assailing him; statements and questions one after another, never pausing for a response or answer. With a big hand resting on one shoulder Jorie managed to look behind the other way to see his luggage being ported, presumably by an aide. They soon arrived at the house, and as he was ushered inside, the big man stopped talking.

Again, Jorie was impressed with what he saw. It was a big house, all on one level. Approaching the house Jorie admired the architecture which was certainly modern but with an aesthetic design suggesting the Zulu heritage of its owner. Inside luxurious it was not but very well furnished, and tastefully too. The interior décor suggested a feeling of elegance without pretention. The quiet still atmosphere within was welcoming, an apparent contrast to the initial overbearing verbal welcome.

The front door was closed behind them when the luggage carrying aide had entered. Shaka led Jorie into what must have been the lounge room. He said in a gentler almost normal voice, "Please accept my apology for my exuberance. I tend to get a bit too excited sometimes. I haven't given you a moment to speak."

Ever polite, Jorie replied with his first spoken words since his arrival, "That's fine. Apologies are not required. I've just been taking it all in, and I simply want to thank you for inviting me, and for your enthusiastic welcome too."

His face clearly showing a sense of relief that his overbearing posture had been excused, Shaka responded, "Good. It is a pleasure to have you here. Please use my first name, Shaka. May I call you Jorie?"

"Yes of course," Jorie assented. Shaka showed his sparkling white teeth in a broad smile.

In a genuine gesture, Shaka said, "You have had a long journey. You will need to refresh yourself and relax. Kagiso will show you your room. Just call for him when you wish to join me. There is no rush. I will be in the garden."

Jorie accepted the gesture, and said, "Thank you. I appreciate that."

Kagiso ushered Jorie to his room. "Touch this contact Sir, should you require my assistance."

The shower, rest and change of clothes were 'no rush' refreshers for which Jorie was grateful. He ambled from his room looking for the garden. Kagiso, ever attendant unobtrusively appeared and said, "May I be of assistance, Sir."

"Thank you Kagiso. Would you show me the way to the garden?" enquired Jorie.

Kagiso responded politely, "Certainly, Sir. This way."

Aglow, the late winter afternoon sun typical of Natal was gently diffused by lush foliage above a small table where Shaka was looking very relaxed sitting in his chair.

He remained seated as he greeted his guest. "Good afternoon, Jorie. I see you are refreshed. Come, please be seated." He signalled Kagiso who retreated. "I rested a while too. I've been writing and reading at lot recently, and I guess my advancing years are catching up with me. Can't go hard at it as I could when I was younger."

Jorie sympathised. "Tell me about it. I often wish the years would not advance so quickly."

Shaka digressed. "I have been blessed with an unusual ability to 'read' the thoughts of others; without actually reading their minds. Am I right to have anticipated your niggling question about my 'spiritual infrastructure' comment."

Kagiso returned with a tray of aperitifs. Jorie waited for him to distribute the drinks before answering the question. "That's very interesting. Have you always had that ability?"

"I like that in you. You don't allow yourself to be fazed by my anticipation. Then again, I expected that. You are a seasoned politician, and I guess it is a required bravura in the dances of your profession."

"Required bravura, that was a beautiful poetic expression, Shaka," Jorie responded, showing off with a suave touch.

"My Mother would have said so too. So, was my anticipation of your question correct?" Shaka wanted sublime vindication.

Jorie satisfied him. "Yes it was, Shaka. Spiritual infrastructure, conjures in the mind a myriad of possibilities."

"Precisely! That is exactly the intent of the term. What possibilities does it conjure for you?" Shaka was getting excited.

"As you said, I am a politician. Responses to such unusual ideas inevitably educe thoughts of suspected intrigue, but I have not convinced myself that is the case with your intent. I think there is something else. Is there?" Jorie the politician was not about to be outdone.

Shaka's white teeth were on display again. "I like that in you too! Honest and perceptive, an unusual mix for a politician."

He paused, closed his eyes for a moment, opened them again and said, "Yes, there is something else Jorie. When I read your thoughts I feel an implied connection with you that I could not explain until recently. Let me explain. I felt a connection with a man in Australia, whom I have never met in person and yet he was connecting mentally with me. And now I have felt the same kind of connection with you. I could not explain this until I recalled the words of my Father. You see, I am descended from a line of what you might call royal connections with Zulu chiefs. That connection seems in this time in our lives to have a special relevance. It is something to do with things beyond just the physical person I am. It has a spiritual dimension that my Father knew well. Does any of this make sense to you?"

Making him feel comfortable with his smiling eyes in acceptance of Shaka's account, Jorie said, "Yes it does, Shaka. What were the words of your Father?"

"He said 'the change is coming.' I thought it was just a throw-away line when I first heard him say it. I was very young. But he said it several times as I grew into my adolescence and then I related it to the difficult political and economic times in which we lived. Do you know what 'the change is coming' means?"

Jorie drew his chair closer to Shaka. Leaning forward he extended his hands in an open expression of mutual understanding. Emotion was building in Shaka, a tear was welling and he dipped his head. Jorie said, "Shaka. Lift your head and look at me." He lifted his head slowly and peered into Jorie's welcoming eyes. "Your father's words were as a prophecy. The change he spoke of has come. I have brought it for you."

Bemused, Shaka entreated, "What is this change that you bring?"

Realising he hadn't effected the change properly, Jorie said, "It is a change that will ultimately fulfil your spiritual aspirations. I will give it to you shortly. Before I do I want you to know that the mental connection you had with the Australian was with Jiemba. He is an Australian aborigine, and an associate of mine. He will send you an invitation to join him in Australia. Your impending presence there is directly related to the fulfilment of your father's prophecy. There, all will be revealed. Now, stand up and look into my eyes."

Jorie was feeling pleased with his competency. He had effected the change for Shaka with ease. The big man was open and ready, even waiting for it. Sekandar's intervention was not needed. Shaka's smiling white teeth were now dazzling. Jorie squinted in the glare.

Shaka summoned Kagiso and said in his booming voice that had greeted Jorie's arrival, "We will have a feast tonight! It's time to celebrate!"

Kagiso smiled and said, "Yes Sir!" He retreated to the kitchen.

Shaka turned to Jorie and with genuine gratitude in his voice said, "Jorie Barak, thank you for being the divine herald of this good news." He laughed at his own comment then said, "No offence intended my friend. I mean, you being a Jew."

Jorie cut in, "That's quite alright. No offence is taken, for it is indeed good news. And, of course I am not divine." They both laughed.

Shaka couldn't help himself. He kept his sparkling white teeth grandly on display when he excitedly asked, "When should I expect the invitation to arrive from the Australian?"

"It will arrive soon. Jiemba wants to telepathically deliver his invitation to you 'personally.' He is not yet able to do so because your mind has not yet transmuted into the ability to telepathically communicate. That will happen for you in good time, and when it does he will deliver his invitation."

Shaka's eyes lit up, knowing that another of his anticipations was correct. "I knew it, I just knew it." Jorie smiled. Shaka added, "I am looking forward talking with Jiemba."

Jorie continued, "Meanwhile, we have much to talk about. I will give you the whole story behind what I have just done for you. Also, the change brings with it obligations and duties that will change some aspects of your infrastructure developments, and I have no doubt that your spiritual awakening will enhance those. May I say that your father would be happy to know that his prophecy is being fulfilled?"

Shaka looked upward, and said, "You certainly may. Perhaps my father knows that it has come to pass, and will be pleased with my spiritual awakening." Jorie nodded his concurrence.

The late winter Natal sun had long set, and the garden setting was bathed in soft yellow-blue lighting. The pair sat there contemplating the future. Kagiso appeared from the house and announced that dinner will be served. With their arms draped around each other's shoulders Shaka and Jorie ambled off to dinner, and a long night of talking.

Alcheringa

The transformation was not easy for the old elder of the Yolngu people from the Top End. Jiemba gently placed his hand on the old man's shoulder, and said, "This is the new dreaming you have heard about. How does it make you feel?"

The old man replied, "When I heard talk of this I thought it sounded like more white-man's lies but now I see what you mean. My people far away will say we must prepare Banumbirr, and that Jiemba will dance with Warriwul in a new dreaming. I must tell them to come." He started to walk away. "I will go walkabout, and tell them."

Jiemba stopped him, turned him 'round and said, "No need for walkabout, old man. They will know what you know because you know. That is another gift from Warriwul." He removed his hand from the old man's shoulder, and let him marvel at the thought of that.

The old man's bloodshot eyes started to well with tears of wonder. The tears didn't flow but caused his eyes to sparkle, reflecting the starlight. He gazed upward to the late winter night sky bejewelled with the stars of Warriwul – the Milky Way. He scanned the whole of the visible galaxy embracing the sky, then said with urgency, "Jiemba, we must prepare corroboree!"

Jiemba gently interrupted him. "We already have prepared. Come, it is tonight ... and there are very special visitors from far away I want you to meet. They will celebrate with us." He replaced his hand on the old man's shoulder, and they went walkabout, just a short way.

Winter nights in the Central West of New South Wales are often cloudless; this night was so, and with a new moon on the cusp of waxing again. It was just as it was on that night when Myaree met Sekandar here; apparently then for the second time, he had visited her previously without Jiemba's knowledge. He would soon know why. On dark nights like this the stars of The Milky Way are very bright to the naked eye, and for Jiemba it was ideal for 'consummating' the new Dreaming for his people.

The floodlit radio telescope seemed to be patiently waiting, pointing with open arms to Warriwul. Jiemba chose the location of Sekandar's earlier appearance there, as the place where the corroboree would take place. It now has a special meaning to his people; it will become a sacred site, for them and for all of Humankind.

He and the old man were first to arrive, and with the old man beside him he looked up to Warriwul and said, "Thank you." Together they gathered wood and made fire, the old way. With starlight and firelight dancing around them illuminating their faces, they waited for the others to arrive.

This corroboree would not be secret and therefore restricted to men, so next to arrive were the woman, with their children. They too had gathered wood for the fire, and had brought didgeridoos and music sticks. As they were settling cross-legged on the ground in a wide array which circled Jiemba's fire, the men appeared from the shadows.

Walking between the women they sat likewise on the ground. There were many assembled; not only representatives of the Wiradjuri also but from tribes from far and wide across Australia, Oceania and Africa. Similarly from the shadows came Jorie and Shaka who walked through the array to sit with Jiemba and the old man.

Shaka had never been to Australia before but he was aware that some contracts let for his development projects in Natal were awarded to firms here. Jorie, who was familiar with the place came with him from Natal and that made him feel at ease; not that he was ever ill at ease. The pair had earlier disembarked from the aircraft at Parkes airport, made their way to their hotel, refreshed themselves there then proceeded to meet Jiemba at the corroboree.

Myaree, Jiemba's mother stood up from the array of women and walked slowly to him then sat down on the ground beside her son. There were now five around the fire in the centre of the assembly; Jiemba, Myaree, Jorie, Shaka and the old man. Just as she had done on that earlier night by the telescope, Myaree again began to intone in her native Australian aboriginal dialect. Jiemba and the old man joined in.

Of course it was unintelligible to Jorie and Shaka but it was mesmerising in its effect. Their gradually chant faded to an end in silence. Jiemba, Myaree and the old man stood up and raised their arms to Warriwul. Jorie and Shaka reflexively stood with them. The group remained standing as silence enveloped them, and everyone else stood up too. The wonder and mystery that dwells with the awe-inspiring Milky Way held them in its spell, just as it had held the small group on that previous night

The air entertained a hint of coolness; a certain prelude familiar to three of the five around the central fire. A gentle breeze was freshening, and the old man sensed an imminent presence. The air warmed slightly and began to swirl with an embracing vigour around the huddle. In their midst the moon-less darkness gradually gave way to a kind of misty iridescent shimmer that glowed softly at first then brightened into the full spectrum of white light and coalesced into a human form.Their eyes opened wide, and the entire array of men, women and children stood up in startled amazement. Sekandar calmed their minds en masse and they settled back down.

Jiemba and Jorie simultaneously stepped forward to greet him, and Jiemba said, "Welcome to country, Sekandar." Sekandar telepathically acknowledged their greeting, then held out his hands to embrace Myaree who threw herself at him almost knocking him off his feet.

Sekandar held her close for a few moments then released her embrace, took both her hands in his and spoke to her in her own language. "Myaree, I bring greetings from Warriwul who has sent me to you again. This time, to tell you that tonight you will be with us all in country with him." Jiemba smiled. Myaree bowed her head, then retreated a pace or two backward to stand by her son.

Sekandar then turned to the old man. In his language he said, "Namarrgon, you are far from Gagudju. What has brought you here, such a long way from home?"

Displaying a broad set of white teeth accentuated by his dark brown face Namarrgon smiled with twinkling eyes, glanced across at Shaka then returned to engage with Sekandar's eyes and replied, "You know who I am. You and I are from Warriwul, and you know why I am here."

Sekandar characteristically smiled. "Your wisdom is great Namarrgon." He gestured Namarrgon to stand to his right side and turn to face him.

Sekandar then addressed all the people who had gathered. He projected his voice so that each person could hear him as though he was standing close, and therefore didn't need to shout. Lifting his head so that he was able to make eye contact as he surveyed the crowd, he spoke with a pellucid clarity of voice, "Most living descendants of the aborigines of Australia are unaware that some stories of the dreamtime are ancient descriptions of real phenomena involving real people." Drawing Namarrgon by his side Sekandar continued, "Namarrgon, elder of the Bininj tribe in the Top End, in the Northern Territory of Australia, is the current generational representation of the 'lightning man' of the dreamtime, and he bears his name. For many thousands of years he has signalled the arrival of the Wet Season in Gagudju; the time to pick bush tucker. Every generation of his tribe and their neighbouring tribes know to treat him with caution for his power is strong." Rippling across the crowd a nervous murmur was clearly audible.

Placing his right hand on Namarrgon's left shoulder, Sekandar then beckoned with his free left hand for Shaka to come near, stand to his left side and turn to face him. Placing his left hand on Shaka's right shoulder Sekandar continued, "Shaka is descended from a long line of Zulu chiefs. He has carried with him a prophecy simply stating that 'the change is coming.' The prophecy has been faithfully handed down from generation to generation. Each generation supposed that it had a currency of meaning peculiar to their time, not knowing what it really meant. They both will now know what it all means for them respectively."

Sekandar scanned the hundreds of souls watching him, and he continued. "This night we bear witness to the culmination of their traditional knowledge that began in the primordial past of Humankind. For Namarrgon, his primordial power which is so strong that he is able to bring the annual Wet Season to Gagudju, this moment affirms that for Humankind his descendants were and he is an integral part of Warriwul; The Whole. For Shaka the ancient prophecy fulfils the spiritual aspirations of himself and of his ancestors, which link back to the primordial origins of Humankind in Africa. The change has come and will soon embrace all of Humankind. This moment affirms that for Humankind he is also an integral part of The Whole"

Sekandar beckoned Myaree to come close, to take the right and left hands of Namarrgon and Shaka respectively in hers. She willingly complied, knowing that this would be a moment of revelation for everyone. He then drew Jiemba and Jorie in to stand behind and to either side of her, asking them to place their left and right hands on the right and left shoulders of Namarrgon and Shaka respectively.

The air entertained a hint of coolness. A gentle breeze was freshening. The air warmed slightly and began to swirl with an embracing vigour around the huddle. In their midst the moon-less starlit darkness gradually gave way to a misty iridescent shimmer that glowed softly at first then brightened into the full spectrum of white light and coalesced into a plume that connected the group with the dish of the telescope. An electric plasma stream from deep within the galaxy above momentarily surged into the dish acting as an antennae, causing it to glow as if white hot. The glow travelled along the connecting plume to the group, illuminating their bodies from within.

The internal illumination gradually subsided and dimmed to leave the group standing in the starlit darkness. The plasma stream retreated. Their eyes wide open, the entire array of men, women and children had stood up in startled amazement again. Sekandar calmed their minds en masse and held them standing in their places. Silence enveloped the whole assembly. It prevailed for a few minutes.

Sekandar took his hands from the shoulders of Namarrgon and Shaka and embraced them. Myaree, Jiemba and Jorie released their hands and joined the embrace. Their huddle remained for a moment or two before Sekandar released them. The others followed his lead.

Jorie was first to speak. Asking himself rhetorically, "Will they believe me when I tell them back in Tel Aviv about this event?"

Sekandar responded telepathically, "Yes Jorie, they will." Jorie nodded, acknowledging the reassurance.

Sekandar then spoke to Namarrgon and Shaka. "It is time to celebrate." As he spoke there was movement in the assembled array of people. Walking to the fore were members of Shaka's tribe, beating their drums and making music with their melodic voices. They stopped playing, turned and invited the others to join them. The impromptu musical improvisation enlivened everyone and Jiemba's corroboree danced into the night.

Aside, several conversations occurred. Dr. Joshua Barak, who had been all the while at his workstation in the telescope, emerged as he opened the entrance in its base. Jorie caught sight of him and went at once to greet his son. "Dad, wow! That is the best word to describe what I recorded."

Jorie responded, "Josh, you should have seen it from my position!" Their arms around each other's shoulders father and son returned to the telescope for some quiet time together.

Jiemba and Shaka knew there was at least one as yet unanswered question for Sekandar. They sought and found him in the boisterous celebration of the corroboree.

Exercising his keen ability to read the thoughts of others Shaka approached Sekandar and said, "I know you are wanting to tell us something important about Myaree and her connection not only with her son Jiemba but also with me. Is my anticipation correct?"

Sekandar replied, "Your anticipation is correct." He drew them aside to a quieter spot, gestured for them to sit on the ground with him, and he explained their relationship with Myaree. "Myaree's genetic makeup has a close connection with both of you; closer than you could have anticipated. By now you both would be aware that deciphering human genes is not a difficult task for me. This I know, you both carry elements of her genes. You both carry elements of her genes. You are half-brothers. She had fallen pregnant with two men. One from Africa and one from Australia."

Jiemba and Shaka looked at each other. Jiemba said, "Half-brothers? I know nothing of this. Nothing at all." Shaka affirmed the same ignorance, then enquired of Sekandar, "Do you know how this came about?"

Calming their minds Sekandar replied, "Yes I do. Let's do that another time. Right now you two need to get better acquainted, and there's a party going on here. Let's party first."

The pair acquiesced. The three of them re-joined the corroboree as Shaka questioned Sekandar about how his fellow tribesmen came to be.

From a distance Myaree watched her sons, and she smiled. The old man came and sat down beside her. Together they intoned in a whisper with Warriwul.

Interlude

Driver

"This looks a bit more luxurious than the other ground-cars here. Is that the word humans use to describe this type of ground-car?" Sekandar enquired as they approached Karen's car in the Tiefgarage at the university.

Karen elaborated. "It is a luxury car, a specially designed variant of the latest model. Some might say it is far too ostentatious, and wasteful in our world of scarce resources and endemic world poverty. They are probably right but I have always liked nice cars. This one is great to drive, and I love driving it. In any event obviation of the world's poverty problem is well in-hand in the wake of the change, and maybe that affords me some luxury."

"Maybe it does. It would be out of place on Terra Dyad. Everything there is electrically powered. As for ostentation, that description doesn't sit with you. You are not one to draw attention to yourself. I think 'style' is the way I would describe your acquired taste."

"Thank you," Karen graciously replied.

She uttered her command to open the car. There was a feint click and the driver's door opened. She turned to Sekandar and gestured for him to get in. He looked at her, smiled characteristically and got in. She went to the passenger's door, uttered another command, it opened and she got in. She looked at him, smiled and said, "You've been wanting to drive a car since your arrival, haven't you?"

"Yes, I have," he replied with enthusiasm, as the human boy' in him surfaced.

She placed her left hand on his right hand that had already found the steering wheel. "Well, today's the day. Let me explain how it operates."

Gently lifting her hand from the steering wheel, he lowered it to her lap and said, "May I explain how I sense that it operates?"

Anticipating his want to demonstrate his prowess, Karen responded, "I'm all ears."

Sekandar proceeded to describe in precise and accurate detail how the car operated and how it is driven. He turned his head to look at her and asked, "May I drive your car now?"

Accepting his adept description she said, "Go right ahead. You can use the navigator to direct you to Imago, and the computer to engage the safe driving features; that will make it easier for you on your first drive."

Karen was about to command the car to start but Sekandar had already uttered it; she raised her eyebrows, acknowledging that she could have anticipated that. Leaving the navigator and the driving features switched off, he exited the Tiefgarage with ease, found his way to the university grounds exit, then onto the road leading to the Autobahnzubringer. Having successfully made it this far, complying with the speed limits, he merged effortlessly with the traffic on the Autobahn and put his foot down.

"This is better than I thought it would be!" Sekandar gleefully said, glancing across to Karen who was looking a bit concerned. She looked at the speedo. 180! "How fast can this ground car go?" He asked as he depressed the accelerator further. 190!

Feeling a bit exasperated with his ardour to drive even faster Karen pleaded, "That's quite fast enough, Sekandar. You're not used to this, and you are a learner driver. Just a beginner. Slow down now, our exit is coming up." Acknowledging her angst Sekandar eased off the accelerator. The exit sign indicating '1000 m' came into view. Then '500 m' '200 m' and he further slowed the car and moved over into the exit lane.

At ease now that they were on the Landstraße leading to Imago, Karen placed her left hand on Sekandar's right leg. He glanced down at her hand there and smiled, characteristically. She said, "Are you aware that we have broken the law, you by driving without a permit and me by letting you?"

"Yes, I am. I took care of that." Karen thought it better not to ask how.

Suspecting the possibility of some more cheek from him, she added, "By the way, this car has an engine management chip that limits its top speed to 250 km/h."

Sekandar obliged her suspicion. "Yes I know. I took care of that too."

Karen thought to herself, "I have a delinquent boy in my car."

He thought responded, "Aren't you lucky." She slapped his leg. He smiled, again. She shook her head.

Imago

For the second time they arrived by car together at Karen's country estate and entered between the intricate stonework pillars supporting the wrought iron arch over the gateway bearing the name Imago. This time Sekandar was driving, with Karen his passenger. As he drove down the long driveway majestically winding its way through the series of heavily wooded undulations and manicured grassed clearings, she found herself paying particular attention to, and appreciating the variety of colours on display; in the foliage, the undergrowth, and in the scene itself. It pleased her.

Sekandar drove onward to the front entrance of the house where he slowly brought the car to a standstill in the driveway. He placed his right hand on Karen's left leg and said, "Thank you. I really enjoyed that. I hope I have an opportunity to drive your car again."

"Not without a permit," she firmly declared, leaving his hand where it lay. Pausing a moment in thought she added, "Don't get out yet." She gently lifted Sekandar's hand, placing it back on the steering wheel. "Drive 'round the back. You can garage the car and we can walk from there over to the marquee that Giles has erected in the garden. He will be expecting us."

Sekandar garaged the car, they both alighted, stepped outside away from the garage door. Karen was about to close the door with a remote control which she had retrieved from her bag when the door started to close. She slithered a sideways look at Sekandar who smiled, characteristically.

She took his hand in hers. He didn't resist, and they set off walking hand-in-hand together to meet Giles at the marquee. Before they got within view of Giles she stopped. Turning to face Sekandar she gazed into his eyes and said, "We both have partners, Sekandar. We will not take this further." She released her hand from his reluctantly, and they started walking again. Neither of them spoke another word, verbally that is. Sekandar telepathically reaffirmed his agreement with her.

"Guten Tag, Karen and Sekandar!" Giles greeted the pair fondly; remembering not to say 'Ma'am' he chuckled. They smiled as they greeted him likewise.

Karen said, "You have created a beautiful setting here Giles. Thank you." She noticed that Giles had prepared meal settings for five. "Are we expecting someone Giles?" With an 'over to you' look, Giles turned to Sekandar.

Sekandar responded. "Yes indeed we are. I have asked Amne and Guy to join us. We have something to discuss that involves us all. I hope that is ok with you?" Karen acceded with open hands and an affirmative nod. "I confirmed their availability earlier this morning. I was about to mention that to you and then we allowed ourselves to be diverted with your car." Sekandar received another sideways look from her.

Imagining something else for 'diverted with your car,' Giles exercised his valet composure and said, "Please be seated. I will fetch Amne and Guy, their taxi will be arriving about now. Excuse me." He departed. Karen and Sekandar sat down.

Karen placed her elbow on the table, rested her chin on her hand with one finger pointing upward across her cheek. She said, "So, this is the time when you will inform me about the 'very important purpose' for Giles that you mentioned earlier. How does it include Amne and Guy?"

Sensing a hint of apprehension in her, Sekandar calmed her mind then said, "Let's wait until we are all here. And, thank you for keeping your thoughts about this to yourself. That was more helpful than you would have thought. Let me also reassure you that Giles' task will not imperil him, nor you, and neither will Imago be put at risk. Ah, here they are." They arose to greet the trio. The usual pleasantries were exchanged. Giles ensured that everyone was seated. He served drinks as desired and sat himself down.

Sekandar dealt first with progress of the project. "In relation to our progress I think we can be pleased with ourselves. I think that's the appropriate human expression. The change is progressing in line with my calculations of the exponential effect of the implemented algorithms that I mentioned previously. However, it is important that we don't get ahead of ourselves." He paused there and said as he shook his head, "Goodness me, with these human figures of speech am I sounding too human for a Terranian?" The four burst out laughing.

Still chuckling, Amne said, "No, not too human but you might be sounding rather English old man." That brought on another burst of laughter. Mouthing 'old man,' Sekandar scanned the group seeking an explanation.

Guy helped him out. "It's not a derogatory comment, Sekandar. I will explain it for you later. Sekandar, we like your human figures of speech. Please continue on from …" Sekandar's quizzical facial expression abated and he continued.

"Thank you Guy. Yes, the paradigm shift will be accomplished well ahead of the original expectation. However, it is important that we remain focused on our mission, and be ever watchful for unwanted deviations, and for potential dangers." Ensuring he had their attention Sekandar then addressed Amne and Guy. "The latter concern is the reason why I have requested your presence today."

Sekandar explained, "I have identified three developing situations that are potentially dangerous, not to The Change but rather to those who have been changed. Amne and Guy, as you know there are extreme interpretations of your respective faiths that have produced adherents to those interpretations. So far some of those adherents have resisted attempts to be changed. These are interesting phenomena, which were anticipated by the mission development team on Terra Dyad." This was the sure and steady character that everyone associated with Sekandar.

Even so, Karen became more apprehensive. She asked, "What does this mean for Amne and Guy?"

Sekandar calmed her mind again. He continued. "Some individuals resistant to the change carry a mutation of the violence gene. Consequently they are motivating themselves to use violence to defend their positions. Knowing that the change is occurring around them, their belligerent mindset conduces them to plan the elimination of those whom they call 'the changed.'" Alarmed by this news Amne and Guy looked at each other, with dread written on their faces.

Sekandar held out his hands in prone position, and said, "Do not be alarmed. As I said this was expected. Anything expected can be taken into account when plans are formulated, and so it is with our mission." With supine hands he gestured for Amne and Guy to stand. They obliged. Sekandar placed a hand on the head of each. A few moments elapsed then he withdrew his hands.

Guy said, "Well, that feels different. What did you do?"

"I have given both of you the ability to directly seek out and adjust the mutant gene, and simultaneously to reverse the violent belligerent mindset in any carrier of the mutation who you encounter. Be assured that carriers are unable to detect that you are among 'the changed.' They rely on hearsay to identify their targets. You know already that I will be in perpetual telepathic surveillance of each of you to ensure your safety, and to intervene for that reason should your safety be compromised. You require no greater protection."

The duo's dread vanished, as did Karen's apprehension. Sekandar gestured for Giles to step forward. He spoke to the group. "On an earlier occasion I acknowledged Giles' effective security of Imago, and of each visiting team member. I pointed out that his demonstrated ability vindicated my inclusion of him on the change team. His contributions are exemplary." Giles, ever the dutiful servant remained quiet and still. He raised one corner of his mouth slightly, in a kind of half-smile in appreciation of the accolade.

Sekandar continued, "Giles will be with me from time to time as we deal with the few remaining pockets of resistance to the change. Of course they are there only because of erroneous perceptions grounded in various vested interests that have their roots going back many generations in human history. Giles' knowledge of the systems guarding those long-held interests will be invaluable to us both as we dismantle them and enlighten their protectors to the new paradigm for Humankind. His safety will be assured because I will be with him at all times during this important part of our mission. I will intervene should his safety be compromised. I might add that I expect to learn from him quite a few tricks of the trade in terms of intelligence activity and operations. As I intimated, Giles has maintained tight security here at Imago. He has ensured Karen's safety, and the safety of each visiting team member. He will now inform you of arrangements he has made during his absence. Giles."

Giles explained the arrangements. "Thank you Sekandar. Karen has approved the temporary appointment of Charles, my younger brother as her valet during my absence. He has always claimed that he is better qualified for this role than me. His claim is well justified, although a healthy sibling rivalry prevails that keeps us both at peak performance. We both have similar professional records, and he holds a similar appointment in England. He has arranged a stand-in thereby releasing him to stand-in for me here. Karen has exercised due diligence to verify all arrangements. My brother is totally trustworthy. Charles will also maintain the security measures as they are."

Sekandar added, "Thank you Giles. I feel that am will definitely be Giles' pupil in many matters. I should add that Giles took me to England to visit Charles. The similarities in character and mind are uncanny. He even accepted the change as readily as his younger brother! I'm sure everyone will like him, and we will meet him very soon. Giles, I'm sure you have a word to add."

"I do indeed. It's time for lunch! Excuse me, I will fetch it." Giles departed for the kitchen.

Karen said to Amne and Guy, "When we have finished lunch you are most welcome to explore the estate before you depart. I like to show it off. Hier gibt es viele schöne Ecken zum genießen."

Aided by Charles, Giles returned promptly, carrying lunch. They unpacked it; a buffet-style of various salads and an assortment of drinks. Once that was distributed among the group Charles became the centre of attention, conversation with him dominated. When everyone was satiated Giles and Charles returned to the house taking the 'remains' of the lunch with them. Karen took Amne and Guy on a tour of the estate gardens. Sekandar followed Giles and Charles.

In the house kitchen Charles, Giles and Sekandar dealt with the clean-up in the aftermath of lunch. When everything had been stowed, Charles said to Sekandar, "Thank you for assisting. May I ask how it goes with chores like this on Terra Dyad?"

Sekandar characteristically smiled with his reply. "Much the same as here, Charles. And, not just with chores. We

Terranians do everything co-operatively. I think 'many hands make light work,' is the English idiom that typifies our approach to every task, from clean-ups to the most complex physical and mental activities. In time you and Giles will experience that here on Earth as a result of the change. I encourage you to visit Terra Dyad to learn our methods applicable to your profession." The brothers accepted his latter comment as an invitation.

The trio discussed that and other things. Sekandar enjoyed the man-to-man moment; being human. Karen returned with Amne and Guy from their estate tour, then along with Sekandar, Giles and Charles she bid them farewell as they drove away from the front steps of the house. Giles and Charles busied themselves with estate management matters. Karen and Sekandar remained outside; time alone together again.

They walked for a while across the manicured lawns of the estate, then returned to Karen's study where they relaxed over a coffee together. She perused an academic journal. At first no words were spoken; their body language was anything but unspoken. Sekandar stood up, gently took Karen's hand, lightly squeezed it and in a playful manner asked, "Can I have another drive of your car now?"

With a measure of professorial authority in her voice she zapped, "No! I told you already, you can't drive my car again until you have a permit." Then, in her thoughts she said, "He really is like a delinquent boy!"

Again he thought responded, "Aren't you lucky." She slapped his behind. He thought responded, "Careful Karen, remember our agreement." She peered at him over her imaginary professorial spectacles.

7

Lessons

First Love

Ashlyn Krause entered her Mother's study, slumped into a chair before her desk and whimpered. "Ich habe keine Ahnung, wie schmerzhaft es für meinen Kleinen sein muss. Vieleicht was du jetzt brauchst, sind ein paar Streicheleinheiten." said Karen in motherly response to Ashlyn's perfect puppy dog pout.

Ashlyn tried in vain to snap her response but it just came out rather teary. "Sehr witzig Mutti. Du weißt nicht wie es weh tut. Ich liebe ihn."

"Oh, my dear Ashlyn. You know I really do know how it feels, I was once young too. A young woman's first love is never easy to cope with." Ashlyn forbade her Mother to call her a 'girl.' Oh no, she is a woman!

One welled tear spilled over and trickled down Ashlyn's cheek. "He's not my first. He's my second ... I mean he's my first real love, and anyway he doesn't know that!"

Providing her daughter with a woman-to-woman understanding look, Karen said, "Well then, you do have the expertise. So, are you going to tell him?"

Matter-of-fact Ashlyn declared, "No. I can't. He's not ready for me, and I have to wait. He doesn't yet know there will be no dilemma when the time is right, for either of us. Sometimes waiting is ... hard."

Smiling a frown Karen enquired, "Sounds like a rather complex situation. Do I know the man in question?" Turning her head away a bit, Ashlyn gave her Mother a 'well of course you do' sideways look. Twigging to her daughter's emphatic allusion, Karen said slowly and with sympathy, "I see. Is there anything I can do to make it easier for you?"

Leaning forward Ashlyn placed both her elbows on her Mother's desk, and curled her fisted hands under her chin. "I love you Mum, and I just want you to be here for me when ... when it's too hard to be waiting." She resumed her cross-armed pose in her chair. "Of course, nobody is to know anything. It's just between you and me. You understand that, don't you?"

"Yes of course, I will be available whenever you need me," Karen assured her, then asked, "Ashlyn, how do we keep this secret from Sekandar, and from ... him?"

Pointing to her head Ashlyn said, "No problem, I have a sign in here which says 'keep out!' I know, I just know Sekandar will respect that. As for him, well I don't mind if he finds out because every moment together counts, and I know if he did find out he would know that we have to wait."

Karen leant forward offering a hand for Ashlyn to take. She took it. Karen softly asked, "May I say his name?" Ashlyn jumped from her chair and raced around the desk to hug her Mother. Karen embraced her daughter as only a mother could, with Ashlyn sobbing in her arms. Gently prising her away Karen reassured her. "There is a lesson in this for you my dear Ashlyn. That is, we don't always get what we want when we want it. Sometimes we have to wait. Even though it just seems far too difficult to cope with at the time, when we are young waiting strengthens our character." Ashlyn's puppy dog pout returned.

"My dear Ashlyn. It may come as a surprise to you that I would say I know Martin well." Through her teary eyes Ashlyn glared at her Mother. Karen squeezed her daughter a bit tighter and continued, "Yes, I know it is Martin, and I would say that I know him just a bit better than you do yourself. He has been my protégé for quite some time now. He is a fine young man. Take it from me, I'm sure Martin will wait for you. Now, regain your composure young lady, we have to say goodbye to Sekandar and Giles. They are leaving soon. Let's go and wish them farewell." Ashlyn Krause, a 'strong woman,' composed herself and took her Mother's hand as they went to say goodbye.

Intimidation

Giles played Rugby at school in England. He later called it 'thuggery,' and its little brother Rugby League he called that 'thuggery fatigue;' both apt descriptions of those violent activities. This of course, was an interesting reinterpretation from a man who was trained in the art of covert espionage and warfare; both obvious manifestations of the inevitable consequences of the defective human gene. He was a young adult when he undertook that training. As a mature man he came to acknowledge that violence begets violence, it doesn't solve any problems. Then he met Sekandar. Everything is different now.

Giles and Sekandar had never attended an American Football game. It was as they expected, a feast of the use of violence to solve a problem; i.e., to score a touchdown. The term 'touchdown' was a rather quaint idea to Giles, noting that the only thing to touch down in the specified zone were the feet a player holding the ball, and not the ball itself. Aside from that, Giles was feeling uneasy as he watched the players crash into each other with the obvious intent of harming, if not maiming each other. Almost out loud he thought, "Violence has no place in sport! Violence is not sport!" Sekandar read his thought and mouthed a response agreeing with him. The half-time interval arrived and Sekandar said, "Let's find a place where we can discuss this situation."

The stadium was abuzz with the noise of the half-time entertainment and the crowd itself. Blending in with the natives they bought hot dogs and a beer each, and managed to find a quieter nook where they were able to sit and talk. Giles said, "This game is more violent than I expected, and that's saying something coming from a former Rugby player."

Sekandar replied, "Yes, it is violent but it was even worse during its formative years. The NFL deny it but the game evolved from variants of Rugby, and early on, players were killed on the field. Civic laws were enacted that prompted modifications."

A security guard in plain clothes approached them from a distance. Sekandar immediately detected his intent to question them. With a telepathically directed message for him to wait a while Sekandar halted his advance toward them. The guard scratched his head upon receipt of the message and turned away. Sekandar smiled. Giles noticed that.

Sekandar resumed his conversation with Giles. Pointing in the direction of the playing field he said, "This kind of human behaviour is totally alien to Terranians, no pun intended. Behind it lies the insidious intent of intimidation; i.e., to provoke the other guy to respond with violence, as a reaction to the fear of being harmed or maimed. It is the quandary of Humankind. It is interesting to observe that in this country laws have been enacted making intimidation or the threat of it a crime; 'knowingly putting another person in fear of bodily injury or harm,' is how the laws are defined. Interpretation of the laws state that 'threat to harm generally involves a perception of physical or mental damage.' This observation, of the obvious contradiction between enacted laws and behaviour, will help you understand why we had to intervene in human affairs. If we hadn't, Humankind would ultimately extinguish itself. We didn't want that. We want you all to join us in our peaceful ascendancy of the galaxy. It is your destiny."

"If the change is occurring exponentially, and everyone here will soon be changed, why are we here in this stadium? Is there a lesson in this?" Giles enquired, looking a bit puzzled by Sekandar's need for an iteration of his previously expounded oral exposition.

Sekandar replied, "Yes there is a lesson in this. We are here precisely for that reason." With a nod he pointed into the crowded stadium concourse. The security guard was again within sight and was making his way toward them through the crowd.

Sekandar gestured for Giles to remain seated. Nearing them Giles noticed that the person's uniform bore the insignia of a private security company and not of the County, State or Federal agencies. The guard stopped before them and as an opener he said, "How are you doing? Hey, I'd say you two are from out of town." He then addressed Giles first then Sekandar, "Yep, I'd say you are English, maybe German extract. And you ... you are an alien." Giles repressed a reflexive gulp and then remembered that anyone not a citizen in the USA was referred to as an 'alien.' Peering at Sekandar the guard said, "Wouldn't even try to guess where you come from. Where are you from man?"

Sekandar didn't answer as he always did to that question, rather he said, "Yes, I am an alien. You will know me as Sekandar, and this is my colleague Giles."

"Aha. Papers!" Giles reached into his coat pocket. The guard drew his gun. "Easy there. No funny business." Giles eased his hand in further, pulled out his passport and handed it over. Holding his gun in his right hand the guard took Giles' passport with his left hand, stowed it in a front-flapped outer pocket of his uniform, then to Sekandar he said, "And yours Sir."

Sekandar promptly replied, "I don't have one, Sir. And, I suggest you examine my colleague's passport and return it to him right away."

The guard whipped off his handcuffs from their belt clip, and in what seemed like a single well-rehearsed movement he grabbed Sekandar's right wrist and snapped a handcuff closed around it. Sekandar looked at the secured shackle. Giles looked at the secured shackle, then they both looked at the guard. The guard looked at Giles. Giles' 'look' said to the guard, "Not a good move Man." The guard looked at Sekandar. Sekandar's 'look' said to the guard, "He's right. That was not a good move. I suggest you give him back his passport."

The guard tilted his head and haughtily said, "Oh really ... and if I don't?" Sekandar and Giles stood up from the bench where they were seated together.

Sekandar said, "He's all yours Giles." That of course was a retrospective comment. Giles had, in what was a well-rehearsed movement, whipped the passport from the guard's pocket, the cufflink keys from their belt clip, and the gun from his right hand. The guard was transfixed, stunned by the performance. Well, he had little choice. As Giles pointed the guard's gun at him with one hand, he unlocked the handcuffs, removed them, handed them back to the guard with the other and put the handcuff keys into his own pocket. He then released the gun's magazine, and handed the gun back too.

Flabbergasted, the guard spluttered, "Who *are* you?"

Giles looked at Sekandar who said again, "He's all yours Giles." Giles placed a hand on the guard's shoulder and eased him down to sit on the bench beside him. Sekandar seated himself beside the guard who turned his head to look first at Sekandar then back to Giles.

Emptying the gun's magazine into his own pocket Giles said, "You won't be needing those anymore." Mouth agape, the guard watched as the rounds cascaded into Giles' pocket, and gingerly took in his trembling hand the empty magazine which Giles offered. "Give me your undivided attention and I will explain why." The guard complied and peered into Giles' eyes. Giles engaged.

Having effected the change in the guard, Giles disengaged. The guard turned to look at Sekandar, and said, "My Mother won't believe this. She just won't believe it. She'll wanna know what junk I'm on, and I ain't on any!" Giles laughed.

Sekandar replied, "That will be another surprise for you Dylan. She will believe it. Just tell her exactly the same as Giles told you. I'm sure she'll want to tell everyone she knows."

Dylan replied, "You say that like you know her. She sure will, she'll tell everyone in the neighbourhood. Of course she will. She's a goddam gossip!" The trio laughed.

Sekandar held his hands out, palms up before him, and asked, "Dylan, in your job you encounter many different situations that you have to deal with effectively. Is there for you a lesson learnt in your encounter with us?"

With his forefinger and thumb he stroked his chin. "I think so. Now I can see that any situation can be dealt with without the need to use violence. You demonstrated that when you dealt with our encounter by talking straight, man. You challenged me without threatening me, and your friend worked with that by using his amazing skill to disarm me." With his hands on his hips Dylan asked Giles, "Hey man where did you learn to do that? I wish I could be so fast."

Giles responded, "My friend, it's a long story. Maybe one day…"

"That'd be cool. Hey man, I gotta move on … I'm on duty. See you 'round." Looking back as he stepped away he said, in his security guard voice, "You two better move on. Hanging out too long here will get you noticed. I'd have to do something about that." He laughed and walked away.

Slavery

Lily read aloud, "Your salary is … your work hours are … you have four weeks annual leave … sick leave … other leave … these are your conditions of employment." She paused, and scratched her head. Looking over at Guy sitting opposite her she said, "They tell me where I am to be, when I can come and go, they tell me what for in no uncertain terms and to top it all off they put a price on my head." Lily Ruhr had wondered often about the concept of 'employment' and it's limiting hold on individuals. She shook her head, closed the 'Your Job' folder and plopped it down onto the coffee table. "This has to be defined as a form of slavery, and it is yet another manifestation of the violent nature of Humankind." She stood up and exclaimed in exasperation, "Surely there has to be a better way!"

"There is, Lily, or rather there was a better way but few were listening." Guy de Villiers said frowning as he looked up at her then back to the book in his hand. He read from it. "The Universal Declaration of Human Rights." He pointed to a page. "Article 23 Section 3 points the way; i.e., 'Everyone who works has the right to just and favourable remuneration ensuring for himself/herself and for his/her family an existence worthy of human dignity.' The problem has been the insidiousness of politicking on the convention which has successfully avoided due diligence as to its intent."

"Yes, I am well aware of that, Guy." She mused. "Of particular interest to me in my capacity as a behavioural scientist is the idea of a living wage. It is gaining momentum in intellectual circles as awareness of the effect of the technology revolution grows. You and I know that 'living wage' refers to a theoretical wage level that allows an individual to afford adequate shelter, food and the other necessities."

Lily sidled to the window, looked out, then turned to Guy and asked, "Do you mind if I elaborate?"

"Not at all. God ahead," replied Guy.

Lily went on. "Definitions of the idea vary but there is general agreement that a living wage should be substantial enough to ensure that no more than thirty percent of it gets spent on housing. The goal of a living wage is to allow employees to earn enough income for a satisfactory standard of living. I would add that any amount individuals can earn beyond their living wage is to be applauded and acknowledged as important enterprising contributions to an economy as a whole."

Guy said, "The idea has its critics, Lily."

"It certainly does," agreed Lily. "The idea of a living wage and what they claim are its effects on the economy, is hotly opposed by those with certain vested interest. Critics in that realm argue that implementing a living wage establishes a wage floor, which harms 'the economy' – meaning their pockets. They claim that companies reduce the number of employees hired if they have to pay increased wages, and that creates higher unemployment, resulting in a deadweight loss, as people who would work for less than a living wage no longer get offered employment. Their assertions are absurd and don't stack up in rational analyses of economic modelling."

"On the other hand supporters of a living wage, like me, argue that paying employees higher salaries benefits companies. Employees who earn a living wage are more satisfied, which helps to reduce staff turnover, and it also reduces expensive recruitment and training costs. Higher wages boost morale. Employees with high morale are generally more productive, allowing the companies to benefit from increased output from individuals."

"It's absolutely plausible," said Guy. "I prefer to think of the idea of a living wage as a 'universal basic income.' Maybe that makes it more a fundamental economic element than just an idea. Then of course there are the continuing arguments about 'trickle down' and 'trickle up' economics which is highlighted by growing inequality on one hand and the multiplier effect of savings on the other."

Lily looked at one of her palms, then the other. Guy reciprocated then said, "I've heard a lot about that. I'm not an economist, so it's all a bit hazy to me. What do you make of it?"

Lily replied, "Well, I'm not an economist either. I rely on interpretations of a couple of friends who are. They explained it to me like this. First let's take a look at what the two modes of economic thinking have as a logical consequence. Trickle-down economics is known as supply-side economics. The basic principle behind this system is that more money and tax breaks are given to the rich and therefore the money will flow to the bottom echelons of the economy. This sounds plausible given the way market forces operate and the nature of capitalism itself. History has shown however that its implementation has been flawed. More money goes to the top echelons and stays there rather than trickling to the bottom. This is primarily because of something called the propensity to save and consume. In economics, the propensity to consume is the amount of a person's disposable income they are likely to spend in the economy. Usually an average is taken, but there is a stark difference between that of the wealthiest individuals and the average of those at lower income levels. Those with less disposable income have a higher propensity to consume or spend and a lower propensity to save, meaning that the spending multiplier, or rather the rate at which the economy grows via spending, is greater in the lower levels than the higher incomes. Those who receive higher incomes save a greater portion of their income than spend it."

She took a deep breath and continued. "The contrary argument of trickle-up economics is based on the principle of giving more tax breaks and compensation to those at the lower income levels, thereby bringing an increase in income to the upper levels as well. This would be in the form of subsidies, tax credits for small businesses and other means. It would also promote local job growth and development and reduce the dependence on large-scale corporations to create jobs. It might even reduce the influence of large-scale corporations in national politics by reducing their importance in the economy. Those at the top don't lose in real economic terms while those at the bottom simultaneously gain and spend. More money will be spent and put into circulation, thereby greatly increasing the spending multiplier effect. This method would also significantly reduce inequality, which would increase both 'paper' and 'real' economic growth."

Lily paused and said, "Are you with me Guy?" He nodded. She continued, "Wrapping up the ideas, I understand that although trickle-down economics would work well with proper implementation, current legal systems are ill-equipped to handle it. Trickle-down economics failed because of the propensity of those with higher incomes to save. In order for it to work we would need to legally compel the wealthy to spend more on investment and on the populace; i.e., the workers. Instead of going into legal battles, it would be more efficient to focus on trickle-up economics because the market forces governing the propensity to spend and consume are much easier to work with from that angle."

Guy was impressed. He said, "You would have been a great economist! I like the logic of your argument. It confirms the view of my Father who said that a proper definition of capital in the capitalist system was often 'overlooked' by certain vested interests who emphasise that capital essentially is wealth in the form of money or property owned by a person or business of economic value. Whereas the true wealth in an economy is the human resource. 'Take people out of any economic model, and you don't have a model,' he would say. I guess you could say that 'trickle up' economics puts 'human capital' in its proper place as the essential assets available for use in the production of further assets."

"Precisely!" Lily declared. "I couldn't have put it better myself." They each resumed their seats, and with concern evident in her voice she said, "And then there is the issue of human trafficking, also something I have been looking into." Clenching her fists she bowed her head between them and said, "Guy why has it ever existed?"

Guy came 'round the coffee table, placed a hand on her shoulder and said, "Lily, there are many reasons. Let's talk about that when we have time. It's almost time for us to go. We are fortunate to have been invited to a business lunch, remember? Let's deal with that first."

Lily regained her composure, stood up and said, "Yes, of course. One thing at a time." Guy helped her take the remains of their lunch from the coffee table. Together they cleaned that lot up, got themselves together and departed for another adventure in what they giggled about as 'change management' – gene-change, that is.

Bullies

'Pensive.' Layne thought about the word. It's how she felt as she wrote her article for the magazine of an international anti-bullying initiative. Writing it evoked memories of her own pensiveness when she was targeted by a bully in her late teens. It was a difficult time. Mobile phones were new on the scene and all her friends had one. She was no exception, Layne Bauer didn't want to be the odd one out, oh no! In retrospect she knows that was the wrong attitude. Lessons learnt from her experience served her well, and she has written several articles about the issue. She settled down and started writing; sometimes she liked to write with her favourite fountain pen ... 'Bullying is a repeated act of ...'

Her Handy sounded an incoming call. She continued writing as her other hand felt for the phone nearby, '... someone misusing their power over someone ...' She glanced at the phone, and dropped her pen. "Karen! What a surprise to get a call from you. Are you ok? You usually call telepathically."

"Oh, I'm sorry I alarmed you Layne. Everything is fine. I was thinking of you and recalled your comment that you had been writing with your fountain pen. I thought why not go retro too, so I phoned you instead. I'm in town and I thought you might like me to drop in. I've been wondering how you are going, and it would be nice to catch up with you over a cuppa rather than over our usual telepathy."

"Yes of course! When can I expect you?" Layne replied.

Happy with the response, Karen said, "Should be at your door in about thirty. Is that ok?"

"That's ok. See you soon."

Layne watched as Karen's call disconnected, put down her phone where it was previously, and started writing again ... 'and making them feel powerless ...' She stopped writing, got up to switch on the coffee machine, returned to her desk, picked up her beloved fountain pen and started thinking about what she would write next.

She checked the ink level in her pen and started writing again. 'Bullying is a repeated act of someone misusing their power over someone and making them feel powerless. There are different types of bullying. These are social, physical and verbal bullying ...'

She slowly lifted her pen from the page, recalled the tips and wrote them down in dot points. '1. Don't respond. Don't retaliate. ...' She wrote down the points. Again she lifted her pen from the paper. Feeling satisfied with her words so far she said to herself, "Hmm that looks good." Gritting her teeth she added, "I'd better make sure I acknowledge my sources." There was a knock at her door.

Opening it she was greeted with a surprise. "Look who I bumped into!" Karen said as she embraced Layne, then stepped back to usher her find through the doorway. Layne gestured for them to enter; they already had anyway. "You don't mind if James joins us, do you?"

"Ah no, by all means." Layne acceded willingly. "What brings you both to London?" They replied simultaneously, "I..," and halted. Karen gestured for James to speak first.

James joyously shared his news. "I am in London enroute from Oxford where I have had the pleasure of addressing the 'old members' over dinner at Trinity College. The invitation was arranged by an old friend who is an alumni there. It was a great opportunity to catch up with her and with many others I know there. The change I effected for the alumni was met with enthusiastic approval."

"I say old man I didn't know you had connections at Oxford University. Can we say 'old man' in that context these days?" Layne playfully responded.

James replied, "Well, should I reply 'old girl' you may think that a bit odd but 'old man' is fine by me. Yes, I have maintained contact with Trinity. In fact I have been asked to speak at Trinity's North American Reunion too. It's always a good idea to maintain our contacts. One never knows where they will take us. Isn't that so Karen."

Karen responded. "Indeed it is, James. It seems to be the season for dinners and speeches. It was my pleasure to be invited to address the Alumni Reunion Dinner at Lancaster University. One of my recent graduating students surprised everyone when she took up her position as a Lecturer there, and she recommended me to the Alumni."

Karen crossed her arms. The fingers of her left hand found its way to her chin. She stroked her chin and continued, "You know, I suspect Sekandar's hand in these 'co-incidences.' He hasn't hinted but under my 'encouragement' he will reveal all." Karen's concluding suggestive remark educed chortles from Layne and James. Karen waved them away but that just confirmed the suggestion.

"Why are we standing here?" Layne queried. "Come, make yourselves comfortable and I'll brew the coffee."

James sat himself on the settee, made himself comfortable and shut his eyes. Karen sidled to Layne's desk, and seeing Layne's pen there she turned and asked, "I see you have indeed be using your beloved fountain pen."

Bringing the prepared coffee with her on a tray, Layne responded, "Yes. I'm writing an article on bullying, starting with peer pressure and including cyber bullying. Maybe then even to psychopathy. I'd like you to read it, and maybe you can give me some perspective as a psychologist."

Karen picked up Layne's article and read the first words of her article. She placed it back on the desk and speculated, "No doubt you intend to put your article in context with The Change?"

Layne replied, "Yes of course. Accentuation of the definitions to begin with will enable me then to emphasise the profound benefits brought by the change." She distributed the coffee mugs then said, "Karen, in terms of psychology what is psychopathy?

"Hmm ... this confirms Sekandar's 'co-incidences.'" Karen smiled. Layne did too. "My address at Lancaster was directed primarily at the psychologists among the Alumni; it would have resonated with the rest of them too. Layne, we could take days together talking about psychopathy. I'll give you an explanation that you will find useful." They each sipped their coffee and made themselves comfortable on the settee opposite James who had lapsed into a semi-slumber. He stirred when they sat down, opened his eyes and listened in.

Karen began, "Psychopathy is among the most difficult disorders to spot. The psychopath can appear normal, even charming. Underneath, he or she lacks conscience and empathy, making him or her manipulative, volatile and often but by no means always criminal. The psychopath is an object of popular fascination and clinical anguish: adult psychopathy is largely impervious to treatment, though programs are in place to treat callous, unemotional youths in hopes of preventing them from maturing into psychopaths. Psychopathy is a spectrum disorder and can be diagnosed only using a 'psychopathy checklist,' noting brain anatomy, genetics, and a person's environment may all contribute to the development of psychopathic traits."

She paused, turned her coffee mug, and continued, "The terms 'psychopath' and 'sociopath' are often used interchangeably, but in correct parlance sociopath refers to a person with antisocial tendencies that are ascribed to social or environmental factors, whereas psychopathic traits are more innate, though a chaotic or violent upbringing may tip the scales for those already predisposed to behave psychopathically. Both constructs are most closely represented in the Diagnostic and Statistical Manual of Mental Disorders as Antisocial Personality Disorder. I should add that the genetic change that we are effecting will obviate the propensity for humans to become psychopaths."

Layne responded, "That's very helpful, thanks Karen. Maybe I'll have to do more research to ensure that my article is accurate and relevant."

Karen smiled, then added, "I'll give you some links that will be helpful." They each sipped their coffee again and Karen continued, "Seeing as you mentioned 'peer pressure' I can also give you a perspective on that if you like."

"Yes please." Layne enthusiastically replied.

Karen began, "Great. Some time ago I wrote a paper about peer pressure; it formed part of some coursework for my students ... Peer Pressure and Bullying. There is a very fine difference in definition between these two terms. It was necessary to know the difference as each one could be dealt with differently. Peer pressure is when you are influenced by others to do something that you normally wouldn't do. This is because you either feel pressured to do so or have a need to fit in with your peers. Peer pressure can be positive or negative. Sometimes the child is surrounded by learners that have a positive influence on them, like studying or doing nice acts for others or volunteering. Other times it can be negative, like drinking alcohol or disobeying rules."

"As parents we needed to be aware of signs that our child might have been bullied or have struggled under peer pressure. We needed to have an open relationship with our child. For example, when Ashlyn was young I would ask her how the school day has been and what she did and who she hung out with. Doing that enabled me to be aware of any potential need for intervention. If I was concerned about her friends I invited them over for a play date to get to know them. As a general rule children that are being bullied will withdraw themselves from activities that they usually love. They can become quiet and hide away. When they start talking about not being worthwhile, then there is a serious cause for concern. Fortunately that didn't occur with Ashlyn but we both knew of kids who were adversely affected, and I was able to advise their parents; i.e., those few who came to me for advice, probably because they knew I am a psychologist."

"My advice usually included the obvious, i.e., it is important to let your child know that it is okay to say no. If you don't want to do something, say no. You don't always have to be liked and it can be worthwhile to find friends that share your beliefs. Peer pressure in many cases has to do with self-confidence. Children with high self-esteem are less likely to succumb to peer-pressure. Again, I have been fortunate to have had a child who always exhibited self-confidence."

"I also advised parents of Ashlyn's friends that they needed to be aware that their first instinct as a parent would probably be that they want to go to school and speak to the teachers or the child's parents of the bully. However sometimes that can make a situation worse and then the bullied child can be teased. It can work, but then there might be another bully down the line and what do you do then. Rather, I advised that it is better to teach their child skills to deal with bullies themselves. Teach the child that everyone is unique and special in their own way. If they are being teased about how they look and act, let them also laugh with the bully. As soon as a bully loses his or her power over someone they will stop. It is not 'fun' anymore. Obviously, there are situations which get worse and then it is necessary to seek further professional help."

"Giving my advice I also pointed out that growing up can be hard. It is vital that we have a transparent relationship with our children so that they have the freedom to speak to us parents about anything. It is also vital to make time for our children to ensure that we are aware of what our child is going through; be interested in their school and its activities. The more we as a parents know the more we will see the important signs, and issues can be addressed early on. With lots of love and care from us as parents, our children will get through it and come through the experience with stronger characters. Layne, obviously the approach I used would also have been appropriate in circumstances of cyber-bullying. And of course, now that the change is being effected, the propensity to bully will also be eliminated."

Layne had wiped away the odd welling tear as Karen's words evoked unhappy memories for her. She was ok though and she said, "Thank you for taking the time with me on these issues. I think my article will come out just fine."

Karen sidled closer to her, placed her arm around her and said, "I know it will Layne."

James, who had been listening intently to Karen's descriptions said, "Layne, we both know your article will be fine. You know, it often takes personal experience to really get a message across." Addressing Karen he said, "I have known more than a few politicians who could have benefited from your sage advice Karen. They, like children have also been targeted by bullies and psychopaths among their lot. Let's be happy, knowing that the anguish inflicted upon so many for so long will soon be something only read about in history books and not newspapers."

The trio finished their coffee then went on into the afternoon discussing their respective experiences in effecting the change.

Resistance

Kriegstreiber

Kal Kalinski warmed himself by the pot belly stove in the centre of the room, as he fiddled with one of the LED lamps he had brought along. Speaking to Sekandar positioned opposite him, perplexed he said, "I wasn't expecting this. How did this situation come about?"

Sekandar calmly replied, "It is not entirely unexpected, Kal. In fact we anticipated the possibility in our original calculations for this mission."

Wearing a pronounced scowl Kal asked, as he eyed Sekandar first then Giles, who had accompanied Sekandar and was also present. "So, what has happened?"

Sekandar explained. "We are dealing here with another mutation. This one has been engineered by some very clever geneticists working for a small group within the military. Although the group is small, the threat they pose is serious enough to warrant my personal intervention."

Seeking clarification Kal pushed for more information. "What is the threat?"

Giles stoked the recently kindled fire, inserted another piece of wood into the stove, and answered the question. "It is specific, Kal. Not only have they conspired to eliminate Sekandar but also among them are at least two who are exercising direct influence in commercial media. With that influence the group are planning a worldwide media blitz denouncing The Change as 'a dangerous hoax that must be dealt with' – that's how they put it."

Kal commented, "I guess that's not unexpected. The media and the advertising industry have a long history of creating illusions of 'reality.' No doubt they will be imagining their enjoyment in their planned moment of blitz, if you follow my jest."

Giles ignored the comment, and continued. "Simultaneously they plan to implement a mass reversal of the genetic change that we have effected. They fear their vested interests will be nullified. Retaining their unchanged mindset they are convinced there is a great deal at stake for them, and they have stated that they will 'use force as necessary' – again, their words. Their fears are real of course but they are not right in their belief that their plan will succeed."

Feeling he had somehow been duped by someone or somebodies in the military, Kal's pronounced scowl remained as he asked, "Why was I unable to detect anything about this? I had supposed I had penetrated the echelons of the top brass and had effected the change in them all."

Sekandar placed a reassuring hand on Kal's shoulder and said, "Yes, you did that very successfully. This group however had mentally hidden themselves from your reach. They succeeded in doing that but they were unable to hide themselves from my surveillance."

Adopting a defiant tone commensurate with his military training Kal continued with his questions. "Where are they hiding? What will you do to stop them?"

Giles answered Kal's first question. "We have located them together in a small forest house in the valley." He pointed to the East. "This gathering of them in one place is convenient for us because they are from Russia, China, Saudi Arabia and Israel; quite a divergent quintet. We would otherwise have had to deal with them separately. Sekandar ..."

Sekandar took Giles' cue and answered the second question. "I will rephrase your question, Kal. What will we do to stop them? Our strategy is dependent upon on our ability to work as a team; i.e., the four of us."

Kal sprang to attention, smartly clicked his heels together and said, "You can count on me Sir!" Realising there were three of them in the room, he said, "Four of us, you said. Who is the fourth person?"

Sekandar smiled characteristically and responded with his hand raised as he said, "Our fourth team member will be with us soon. Kal, I acknowledge that you mean to show me your respect by addressing me as 'Sir' but it is unnecessary. Hierarchies are an alien concept to me. We are a team, and each one of us is as important as the other."

Unperturbed, Kal replied, "I guess it will take a while to learn your alien ways."

Sekander again placed a reassuring hand on Kal's shoulder, easing any potential residual tension. They both smiled. Sekandar picked up a coffee mug and asked, "Anyone for coffee?"

No sooner had he asked when there was a knock at the door. Sekandar opened the door to Jorie Barak, who ushered in cold air and blown snow with him as he entered.

Seeing the mug in Sekandar's hand Jorie said, "I sure could do with a cuppa."

Sekandar stepped aside as Jorie entered, and said, "Coffee coming right up." Kal and Giles waved Jorie to join them in their huddle 'round the pot belly stove, and in turn shook his hand in greeting. Sekandar busied himself brewing coffee on the stove for all four.

Jorie rubbed his hands together, warming them over the stove; a very human thing to do that intrigued Sekandar. Jorie said, "I nearly didn't make it here. The deteriorating weather is bringing plenty of snow but the forecaster said it should clear through by the morning. We will be able to get underway after breakfast. The evening is ours gentlemen, and the problem before us is what we with do with the Kriegstreiber?"

Screwing up his nose Kal enquired, "The kreegs what?"

"Kriegstreiber. It's the German word for warmongers," explained Jorie. "Having had holocaust survivors in my family, it's inevitable for a word or two that has been passed down from them to slip into my own speech sometimes."

Almost spilling his coffee as he extended his arms Kal said, "I'm sure the 'fearless foursome' will deal with them." Turning his head to Sekandar he added, "Three of us have a background in military training, and ..."

Sekandar replied, "Your implied question is reasonable and welcome." Walking around the three huddled over the stove he said, "You are all now aware that Terranians don't use violence to solve any problem. We have other, effective means for solving problems. 'Military training' is an alien concept for us. It soon will be for your species too." Deftly changing the subject he said, "Jorie's comment, re our plan requires a response. Giles will now brief you."

Giles detailed the plan which was subsequently refined by the fearless foursome in the course of the evening before they unfurled their sleeping bags and got some sleep in their bivouac, a small hut in the Swiss Alps.

The snow storm had cleared in the early morning hours, enabling the team to set out on schedule on their mission to deal with the Kriegstreiber. Sekandar was preparing breakfast and a pot of fresh coffee well before the other three awoke. If not for the aroma of frying bacon, eggs and coffee they may well have slept longer.

"Good morning!" Sekandar greeted the three who stirred almost in unison.

Stretching as he yawned Kal looked up at Sekandar and said, "You're up early, and it looks like you must have been up for some time. Couldn't sleep eh?"

Sekandar smiled. "Although we can if we wish to, Terranians don't need much sleep." Kal returned a vaguely mystified look. "Now, let's eat. We will be underway by dawn." Sekandar served up breakfast which was wholeheartedly appreciated by his three patrons, and enjoyed by himself. He prided himself on a perfectly brewed cup of coffee too.

Meal utensils were cleaned, the fire in the pot belly stove was extinguished, sleeping bags were furled, rucksacks were packed and the LED lanterns were switched off and stowed in Kal's gear. Giles was back at the door of the hut after a quick reconnoitre of the vicinity. "All's clear," he announced as he entered.

Sekandar gathered the team close and said, "Throughout our sortie I will be in constant surveillance of our 'divergent quintet' and of you. If I detect a potentially dangerous situation for either of you I will influence your thoughts so that you will be able to take evasive action and come to no harm."

Giles said, "Ok, let's get underway." Having kitted themselves Kal's fearsome foursome set out down the mountain side and into the valley below. Their descent proceeded slowly at first as they trudged through the fresh snow that had fallen overnight. Descending further the going was easier through a conifer forest. It took about thirty minutes to reach the edge of a forest clearing. There they stopped to survey the surrounds. The forest house was on the far side.

Kal scanned the area with his telescopic field glasses. He stopped and scanned back to look closely at a camouflaged figure standing still several metres away from the house. "I

am looking at you and you are looking at me. What now?"
he whispered. The figure's field glasses were lowered. Kal
lowered his glasses, squinted and raised them again. He
said, "Aha, you are a woman." She raised her glasses again,
and smiled. Kal smiled in return. "Thank you ma'am, nice
to see you too. Oh, not so nice. You have a weapon, and
you have drawn it."

Looking first to his left then to his right Sekandar
said, "Yes she is a woman, her weapon is armed, and her
friends are approaching; they too are carrying weapons,
also armed. I anticipated this scenario as one of several
they have considered." Kal, Jorie and Giles instinctively
assumed defensive positions. They were not bearing arms;
Sekandar had requested that omission. He calmly said,
"Everyone remain still and quiet, I will deal with this."

Two from the left and two from right approached
quickly. They wore camouflaged battle fatigues. One of
them, wearing the insignia of a General stepped closer as
the others waited about ten metres away. "Gentlemen, we
have been expecting you." He singled out Sekandar, drew
very close to him and peered into his eyes. "So, you must
be the alien." Sekandar responded with his characteristic
smile, which induced a contemptuous grunt from the
General. The grunt was accompanied by a hand signal to
the waiting others who moved quickly to stand with readied
weapons before Kal, Jorie and Giles.

"You can wipe that smirk of your face, alien. Your
little game will soon be over." He slung his weapon over
his shoulder, crossed his hands behind his back, circled
Sekandar, re-engaged with his eyes then said, "Is it not the
perfect rhetorical sin of meaningless variation, that you
selfishly think you can come here and genetically modify us
involuntarily? Who do you think you are that you would be
so brazen?"

Giles thought to himself, "Meaningless variation. That's
an interesting hyperbole."

Sekandar smiled and calmly said, "You will know me as
Sekandar. Subsequent to The Whole aneling the strategy,
and with the imprimatur of the Galactic Council I came
to Earth with a mission; to effect a paradigm shift in

underlying human assumptions of violence. Our intent is entirely beneficent. The Change will enable Humankind to join us in our peaceful ascendancy of the Galaxy. Without it you cannot and will not." Sekandar made no move to take control of the General's mind, not yet.

The General disengaged his unblinking stare into Sekandar's eyes, and circled him once again. When he completed his circuit he brushed away Sekandar's reply. "Yeah, yeah, yeah. We've heard all that hogwash. We don't buy it, alien." He turned his back to Sekandar, took a pace away and gave an apparently rehearsed hand signal to his fellow rebels who acknowledged by taking a step closer to Kal, Jorie and Giles. The General turned about to face Sekandar.

Unflinching in his resolve to give the General an opportunity to concede, Sekandar calmly said, "General, why do you infer that we are talking about a deal that is for sale? There is no deal. It is do or do not."

The General took a pace closer. His hand moved over the weapon slung over his shoulder.

Unperturbed Sekander delivered the challenge that lit the fuse for the General, he asked, "Who do you think you are that you imagine you have an inviolable right to deny your species their evolutionary advancement?"

What happened next can only be described in slow motion. First, there was a bright flash that caused everyone except Sekandar to blink. In that blink of an eye the weapons fell from the rebels' hands, and the mutation that had been so skilfully engineered to repel attempts to effect The Change in each of them was re-engineered to permit it. Then the change was effected simultaneously in each of them, and Kal's fearsome foursome were doing their best to prevent them from collapsing onto the snow-covered ground beneath their feet.

Giles said, "Ok men, let's get them back to the house. It will be better for them to recuperate there where it is bound to be warm." In a demilitarised phalanx of arms slung around shoulders the troupe eventually made it to the house. Entering it they found Kal's 'smiling woman' sitting on a chair. She was holding her head in her hands and was muttering something that sounded like Mandarin. After he had assisted his fellow fearsome four to ensure the comfort of the others, Kal crouched beside her offering solace. In English she said, "Why did you smile?"

Kal replied, "Because you did." She smiled, and of course he smiled in return. They laughed. The others laughed.

She placed her hand on his hand and said, "I am Fen Hua. What is your name?"

Kal felt a gentle twinge in his mind causing him to recall Sekandar's words 'If I detect a potentially dangerous situation. I will influence your thoughts so that you will be able to take evasive action and come to no harm.' He looked over to Sekandar who returned his characteristic smile. He looked back at Fen Hua and said, "You are indeed a fragrant flower, Fen Hua. My name is Kal."

Everyone else in the little forest house raised their eyebrows in muted caution.

Dark Web

Springtime at Imago is glorious. From its earliest plantings there has been a deliberate adherence to replicating the assortment of plants found in the park at the famous Schloß Pillnitz by the banks of the Elbe at Dresden. The grounds at Imago however are not of the Baroque style there. Although carefully planned the estate grounds give the appearance of having been randomly planted. Visitors to Imago delight in wandering the walkways meandering through the estate.

Martin was happy to be there again. Karen had provided a little study nook in her library, where he could shut himself away and not be disturbed. He appreciated that. In fine warm weather he preferred to hide in a little grove enclosed all 'round by the close proximity of the hedge plants in a secluded corner of the estate. To keep his feet off the moist ground Giles had installed a small square of flooring and a thatched roof overhead to repel rain. It was supported by poles roughly hewn from trees on the estate.

Even if they passed nearby meandering visitors would not know it was there. That was just fine by Martin. For him it was the perfect place to have his laptop computer, and there to delve into the sinister depths of the dark web.

He studied the words on his screen that seemed to be drilling into his mind. 'Even a stopped clock is right twice a day. No-one is ever completely wrong.' His computer monitor had displayed the words for a good ten minutes. Much of what he had unearthed so far had been decipherable. Not that it was easy. Deciphering elaborate code never was. These two sentences however had him delving deeper into the mysteries of the Dark Web than he had ventured before.

Despite the risk of possible dangers, for the most astute minds the dark web is a mysterious place that befuddles most who choose to delve therein. Navigating it isn't easy. The place is as messy and chaotic as you would expect when everyone is anonymous, and a substantial minority are out to scam others. There's lots of illegal activity. It is a haven for hackers.

Martin had learnt that dark web sites look much like any other site but there are important differences. Lots of aspects had attracted his attention, such as the naming structure. Instead of ending in .com or .co, dark web sites have others. Top level domain suffixes designating an anonymous hidden service are reachable via the Tor network. Browsers with the appropriate proxy can reach these sites, but others can't. Martin had acquired several of those. Dark web sites also use a scrambled naming structure that creates Uniform Resource Locators that are often impossible to remember. That was no problem for him. Many sites are set up by scammers, who constantly move around to avoid the wrath of their victims. Those received his close scrutiny.

Even commerce sites that may have existed for a year or more can suddenly disappear if the owners decide to cash in and flee with the pledges of money they were holding on behalf of 'customers.' Martin had helped out a few of the more reputable sites, much to the dismay of hackers crawling around the edges just waiting for a slip up. On occasion he had also anonymously 'assisted' law enforcement officials who were getting better at finding and prosecuting owners of sites that sell illicit goods and services. The anonymous nature of the Tor network also makes it especially vulnerable to 'distributed denial of service' attacks. These also attracted Martin's scrutiny. Dark web search engines exist, but even the best are challenged to keep up with the constantly shifting 'landscape.' Martin noted the nature of those unremitting changes.

Martin is well aware of all that, and he is also aware that his mind is not like that of the astute minds of his generation. He is able to penetrate the depths of the dark web well beyond the reach of the best of them. He surfs the dark web for situational awareness, threat analysis and for just keeping an eye on what's going on. He stays informed of what's happening in the hacker underground. He knows what information is generically available and is cognisant of the digital assets that are being monetised by others. This gives him insight into what hackers are targeting.

Sekandar knows about everything that Martin is discovering and is often in contact with his mind as he surfs, and as he applies his rapidly developing knowledge of psychology and mathematics to his interrogation of the dark web. Karen's protégé is also his. He is grooming Martin for much greater things. Martin knows that.

He paused from his mental gymnastics and telepathically said to Sekandar, "Eureka! Those two sentences, 'Even a stopped clock is right twice a day. No-one is ever completely wrong.' They have occupied my mind incessantly, and I have now cracked the incredibly elaborate code behind it. It's clever but I have deciphered it. I've done it!"

"Yes, I noticed. Have you formulated a solution?" Sekandar enquired.

Martin replied, "Yes. Would you like to see me implement it?"

Sekandar replied, "Yes. When do you plan to act?"

Martin enthusiastically replied, "I'm ready now." As a mark of respect for his tutor he then asked, "Before I do, would you like to review my solution and implementation plan?"

Confident in Martin's ability Sekandar asked the obvious qualifier, "Is there an uncertainty?"

Convinced of his certainty, Martin replied, "No there is not. I have checked the maths and ran a series of models with Miri. We observed no discrepancies. I am also sure of the veracity of my code sets."

"In that case there is no need for me to review. Your mental processes indicate a remarkable degree of intellectual maturity, as does your collaborative inclusion with Miri and myself. I am impressed with your ability."

Martin was chuffed but also humbled by Sekandar's praise. He simply replied, "Thank you."

Sekandar then said, "Ok, let's see you do it."

What happened next is difficult to explain to a 'normal' human being. The elaborate code behind the sentences that had vexed Martin underwent a metamorphic transformation, so subtle that it left dumfounded the 'astute minds' that created and nurtured the original code. Martin's intervening tweaks were so intricate that they would never be able to detect the source.

The effect of his implemented solution was exponential. The exponent described by the mathematical notation multiplied the effect and all corners and levels of the dark web were no longer 'dark.' The surreptitious violence implicit in the intent of the labyrinth of illegal activity was irreversibly dismantled. What is more, it could not be recreated. The hackers' haven was no more. And it happened in the blink of an eye, at the hand of an anonymous hacker.

Martin stood up from his computer, raised his arms in a gesture of victory and declared aloud, "We have done it Sekandar. It is done!" He tried to look through the surrounding vegetation but couldn't see through it. He mentally scanned the vicinity, detected nobody within earshot and sighed relief.

Sekandar responded, "You did it Martin, you did."

Martin replied, "That's kind of you to say Sekandar. You and I know that it is not true." Delighted with their success Martin said, "I know what's next." Sekandar smiled characteristically.

Betrayer

Jules Béraud vented his discord. It was a variance that was eating away at him from within. Simone just happened to be in his line-of-fire. Showing his displeasure in his furrowed frown he said, "There's an old Latin saying 'Facilis descensus Averno,' meaning 'the descent to hell is easy.' The road to hell is paved with good intentions."

She snuggled closer, and with loving tenderness said, "Well let's get it all out of your head Jules. I think you need to do it now because our Valentine will be here shortly, and I don't want her to see you in such a state."

Cringing a little away from Simone's snuggle, Jules spluttered, "Why not? It's her fault, I mean she did this to me."

"Mon coeur, ce n'est pas gentil," she pouted as she snuggled in again.

"I'm sorry my dear Simone. I don't mean to be hurtful. I just don't feel quite right about this genetic change that the Sekandar has brought upon us all."

Pouting and snuggling a bit more, Simone said, "Hmm, promise me then that you will not upset her." Jules responded with his own 'hmm.'

Valentine returned, hung her coat, put on her house shoes, and greeted her Mother and Jules.

"I'm glad we are staying at this hotel. I know the owner. He just might call by and say hello, if he's here. I hope he does, he's a lovely man." Simone gave her daughter that 'oh, a lovely man is he?' look of expectation. Valentine waved away the suggestive hint.

Valentine noticed Jules' uneasiness but Simone intervened before she had a chance to enquire. "Maintenant, ne sois pas top á l'aise, ma chére Valentine.

There is a beautiful restaurant in this hotel and I have booked us a table. Come ..." She bundled up the pair, pushed them into the corridor and set off to dinner!

Simone was right at home in a beautiful restaurant in a five star hotel in Paris. It was not her daughter's preference but Valentine always did her best to please her Mother. Toujours sympathique, Jules just went along with it but Valentine could still see his unease. They seated themselves at the round table reserved for them. The waiter served them impeccably. Apéritifs were enjoyed, the meal was superb and Jules asked for the best wine – Champagne of course.

When the trio were satiated Valentine placed her elbow on the table, crossed her arms and earnestly asked Jules, "Are you ready to tell me now what it is that is occupying your military mind?"

Jules mirrored Valentine's posture and in a matter-of-fact manner replied, "Yes Valentine, I think I am." He sat back in his chair and said, "Facilis descensus Averno."

Valentine sat back too and replied, "What?"

"The old Latin saying 'Facilis descensus Averno' – the road to hell is easy. I was just talking with Simone about it. Do you know it?" Jules' posture was sober.

"Yes of course." Valentine answered prosaically. "It's from Virgil's Aeneid. I like the maxim. If it was coined by Virgil then I think he was very clever. It helped explain most of the problems that existed in the world, right up until The Change. Very few people have bad intentions. But most of the problems in the world were caused by good intentions. They may not have seemed good to us, but they seemed good to the ones taking the action. Good intentions alone were not enough to make their actions moral, nor ours. Then of course our defective gene influenced our actions. I think the maxim described the enigmatic nature of humans. So, what are you trying to say, Jules?"

He knew he couldn't contain the inner agitation stirring within. Shaking his head he responded gloomily, "I think that's where we're going, straight into hell."

Surprised by Jules' comment, Valentine enquired, "What an extraordinary thing to say. Why do you think that?"

Jules was having great difficulty articulating himself; clearly a reflection of his confused thoughts. "It's taken us off our natural evolutionary path ... and we've lost our professions ... and.it may be well intended... but it's just ..." He cut himself off with that and emphasised his prosaic persona. "It has to be denounced," he declared.

"Oh does it now. There I was saying to Charles, the Chancellor of Delhi University no less, that you had been ... let me see ... that you were 'able to reach all levels of the establishment ... and you are making remarkable progress.' Have I been deceived? No, don't answer that. I think I know what's going on here. I'm not a psychologist but I sense that I failed to properly effect the change in you, or maybe you couldn't be changed. Either or I think. So, I gather you see yourself as the betrayer. Am I right? "

Jules didn't answer. The opportunity to answer was taken away by Nikolei who had approached him from behind. He said, "Good evening Valentine. You look wonderful tonight, and I presume this lovely lady is your mother," he enquired as he kissed Simone's offered hand. "It's a pleasure to meet you Simone. Beauty runs in the family I see." Simone was flushed with delight to be so flattered by the 'lovely man' who had gained her immediate approval. Jules turned in his chair and pushed it out of the way as he stood to take the hand then offered in greeting from Nikolei. Holding Jules' hand he said, "It's a pleasure to meet you Jules. Valentine told me about you, all good I assure you."

Valentine who had vacated her chair greeted Nikolei with a kiss to his right cheek. Nikolei reciprocated. Simone was becoming rather jealous of Simone. "Please, join us," Valentine urged him. "We were discussing a quote from Virgil. I'd like your opinion." Jules wasn't sure if he should object to her intimation. He cleared his throat. Valentine briefly reiterated the issue of discussion then asked Nikolei, "What do you think?"

Nikolei perceived the problem. He comfortably seated himself between Valentine and Jules, and said emphatically as he looked at her, then him, "I think there are times when a woman has to do what a woman has to do."

Valentine, who had already been in contact with Sekandar to define a course of action, responded. "Yes I think you are right." She exchanged places with Nikolei to sit beside Jules, and said, "Jules, you are not the betrayer. Your misgivings about the change result only from an incomplete adjustment to the defective gene in you. I will now correct that." Simone, sitting on the other side, reached over the table and took his hand in hers. She squeezed, gently. Valentine said, "Look into my eyes, Jules." He obliged. Valentine acted.

Jules sat back in his chair and said, "Phew! That's a relief." Simone turned his head and kissed his forehead. He reciprocated. Nikolei and Simone smiled with satisfaction that a potentially dangerous situation had been dissolved.

"Anyone for a digestif? I surely need one!" exclaimed Jules.

Nikolei had already signalled the waiter who was now at the table, with the drinks to be served. Taking each drink in turn from the waiter's tray, Nikolei served his guests and thanked the waiter, who retrieved the tray nodded and withdrew. Nikolei said, "Jules, this evening is on the house. Well no, it's my shout. I don't want to fiddle the budget here, the manager would not be impressed." Everyone laughed. Nikolei stayed on with the trio as light-hearted banter went on into the night. Simone of course was in her element signalling to her daughter her absolute approval of the 'lovely man.' Valentine waved away at lot of signals that night.

Acceptance

Hackers

This was Ashlyn Krause's first visit to New York. The first thing she just had to do was to drag her Mum along to an Amazon Go. Of all the places to check out, why there? The Statue of Liberty, 5th Avenue, Times Square,

Rockefeller Center, etc., these didn't figure on her 'must see' list.

Up early, dressed and ready to go, Ashlyn urged her Mum, "It's so cool Mum. There's something there I want you to see. Come on, I'll show you."

Karen dipped her head slightly, and as though she wore spectacles she peered over them at her daughter, as only a mother can. "Ashlyn, it's only a supermarket. Why are you so insistent about going there?"

"Mum, it's not *only* a supermarket." Ashlyn asserted. "This is different ... and Martin is checking it out too." Ooops, that slipped out, but let's go with it! "Betcha he's waiting there for me ... right now."

Sliding her virtual specs back to the bridge of her nose, Karen supposed a minor victory. "Aha, I should have guessed, and have you 'arranged' any more 'surprises' for me?"

She wasn't about to let her Mum think she'd scored, and being rather matter-of-fact she said, "Oh yes, and Kitty will meet me there too."

"Will they now, young lady? What then have you conspired to do?" Karen enquired, returning the volley with a backhand down the line.

The frustration of youth couldn't hold back any longer. Moving into 'plead' mode Ashlyn pouted as the words slid out. "Come on Mum."

Just as Ashlyn had said, Martin Klug was waiting for her on the sidewalk at Amazon Go. "Hi Ash! Good morning Dr. Krause. You're going to love this," he added, as a kind of pre-emptive appeasement. "Kitty and Zed should be here ... here they are now."

"Hi guys! We made it ... ok, let's do it," Kitty said as she walked into the store with Zed. Then as an afterword she said, "Good morning Dr. Krause." She followed the gang inside.

Karen noticed the cameras everywhere, 'watching' them, and she whispered to Ashlyn, "I think we are being watched. Are our voices being recorded too?"

Ashlyn whispered back, "Yes, watched and recorded." Kitty and Zed had moved further into the store, and were taking a few items off the shelves, one by one and inspecting them. Ashlyn said to her Mother, "Watch carefully."

Apparently inexplicably the store's lighting flickered then died. So did the display cabinet lighting. In the darkness Zed reached into his jacket pocket, withdrew a small torch and switched it on. He raised his hands and clutching the torch in one palm he pointed both index fingers to the ceiling. "Everything is fine ... wait a moment. There, it's done!" He lowered his hands into an embrace with Kitty, and then high fives with Ashlyn and Martin. The lighting switched on again.

Karen cocked her head, looked over the rim of her virtual spectacles again, this time giving all four young scallywags 'that look,' then stepped directly to Zed, and said, "What did you just do?"

Looking very pleased with himself, and brimming with satisfaction, Zed replied, "Oh, simple ... I just ... modified their system."

Wanting specific clarification, Karen asked, "Modified their system? Whose system?"

Questioning the obvious, Zed said, "Why, Amazon of course."

"You hacked Amazon! How? Why?" Demanded Karen in a serious tone.

"It's not what you think. We didn't crack it, we hacked it. Do you know what means?" Zed responded emphatically querying her demand.

"I have an idea but please, do tell." Karen retorted, clearly not humoured.

Kitty positioned herself in front of Zed, who was not inclined to continue with the rally. He let her intervene, and he started looking at his smartphone. She explained what they had done, and clarified any misunderstanding for Karen, "Cracking a system means that you want to damage it. Hacking it is simply getting into it without any intent to cause damage. Zed found a way to get in, and we all helped him with a few modifications … to cover his tracks. We did this because we wanted to make their system secure from crackers, which we did. How did we do it? You don't wanna know."

Karen's response was partially conciliatory. "That sounds rather evasive, Kitty." She added addressing them all, "And I do want to know how you did it." Spectacles not needed this time.

Martin stepped up and said, "Dr. Krause. Come with us, and we will explain everything."

Reacting in frustration she turned about face. Standing there by the shop entrance was Zed's Father, Ezekiel Eisner with Miri Tschekov by his side. Karen interlinked her fingers and placed her hands on top of her head. "Ok, ok. This had better be very good." And she exited as Ezekiel and Miri parted, inviting her to lead on. The scallywags followed close behind.

The three members of The Change team with two of their offspring, one protégé, and one hacker sat facing each other in Karen's apartment in downtown Manhattan. Ashley prepared drinks as preferred and returned to the 'round table' debriefing.

Karen, the apparent outsider in the conspiracy, opened the conversation. "I could ask you all why you took it upon yourselves to leave me out of the loop on this, whatever it is that's really going on, but I won't. I expect you to inform me. I want to know everything, from the beginning."

Miri spoke first. "Karen, I am not the father of any of these … remarkable young people … and I guess that affords me the privilege of explaining the whole episode." Karen wanted to interrupt and question his use of the word 'remarkable' but Miri halted her with a raised hand. She complied and he continued, "Some time ago, Ezekiel got wind of something brewing." Kitty looked at Zed and mouthed 'got wind?' Miri smiled and continued, "… that a plan was being made to 'teach Amazon a programming lesson.' Ezekiel enlisted my assistance because he suspected that some very clever code would be required to pull it off. We agreed that it would be best not to blow their cover but rather to eavesdrop with some hacking of our own into their scheme; to assure ourselves that nothing malicious was planned. It wasn't. Indeed, we quickly found that the plan had a noble intent, and we agreed that there was no need to involve you."

Karen was now composed and listened with genuine interest. Ezekiel picked up the story, and said, "As we watched Zed developing code for his scheme we noticed that it was not just good, it was exceptional. He was incorporating advanced mathematics in his code. We discussed that observation, and continued our surveillance. We soon realised that the original plan was evolving into something much grander than the original plan. Before I go into that, there is something else. We found ourselves looking at something that, on the face of it, was unrelated. It was obvious that Zed himself was mentally scanning minds. We were also able to detect that he was also undergoing a mutation that would ultimately give him the ability to communicate telepathically."

The scallywags looked at each other with the obvious look of 'they knew all along?' Again with a smile Miri acknowledged the non-verbal, and continued, "Miri and I decided to contact Sekandar for advice. He encouraged us to continue with our surveillance of the program code development, and said the he would look after Zed's emerging telepathic ability. Because he perceived no threat to The Change, he agreed with our decision not to consult you but to ensure that we informed you at the close of the episode, which we are now doing."

Karen looked at Miri, then back to Ezekiel, and then to Zed. Establishing direct eye contact with Zed she spoke telepathically to him alone. The others heard nothing spoken, aloud or telepathic. With an empathetic 'feel' in her mental contact with the young man, she asked, "What do you think of your newfound ability, Zed?"

History will note the Zed Eisner coined the term 'mind to mind talk,' and with this his first real go at it he opened up at full throttle. "It's really cool. So far, I've only used it on the Amazon Go project. I found it easy to scan the minds of their people who showed up when the shop formally opened, just a few days ago. That gave me enough information to finalise my plan. I couldn't believe it ... the chief programmers were there ... and ... Oh, and I'm sorry I didn't think to change their gene codes. I was so focused on my plan ... I haven't even had a chance to see what else I can do with this 'mind to mind talk' ... but I guess you already knew all that ... and everything."

"Yes I did, Zed. I've known since you first contacted Ashlyn about the scheme." She paused, then said, "Zed, do you get the feeling that this 'telepathy thing' is a really big game-changer?"

Dreamily, Zed replied, "Yes ... I have ... had that feeling."

Karen moved to be beside him, placed her hand on his shoulder and said, "It is a profound game-changer, Zed. Our acceptance of it brings responsibility along for the ride." She gently disengaged their minds, and let him ponder the seriousness of the moment of change for him.

Knowing the others perceived that the two of them had been talking together telepathically, she elucidated. "I did not anticipate the emergence of Zed's ability to communicate telepathically. Sekandar did. What is more, he has informed me that it is a phenomenon that will gather momentum as The Change is implemented worldwide. As you know Martin is my protégé in psychology. The mutation phenomenon has been included in his studies, and Sekandar has briefed him about the ramifications. Martin will now elaborate for you."

Martin said, "Thank you Karen. Yes, it is now apparent that the mutation that occurred in Zed is also developing in everyone who has undergone the change in their genetic makeup. I myself have had the ability to read minds for quite some time, and you are aware that members The Change team have the ability. The mutation becomes evident first with an ability to read the individual minds of those in our proximity, and over time that will transmute into the ability to telepathically communicate. I have that ability too. Interestingly you will find that this fundamental change to who we are as individual human beings will feel like an entirely natural progression. I say 'progression' because that is what it is. Sekandar said that we are on a pathway leading us to take our place together with his species in our peaceful ascendancy of the Galaxy. The Change coupled with this mutation is preparing us for our journey along the pathway; a different pathway with the same destination for each of us. I know I'm already on mine, and I'm enjoying the journey. I wish you happy travels."

Ashlyn sidled next to Martin, Kitty sidled next to Zed, and they all linked hands. Ashlyn spoke for 'the gang' and with her trademark puppy dog pout she asked her mother, "Does this mean that we are to be 'forgiven' for hacking Amazon?"

Karen pulled out her imaginary reading spectacles, put them on the end of her nose, peered at the gang over the rim and said, "Let's leave that judgement with Sekandar. Right now, your team of conspirators can start thinking about tomorrow. It will be a big day, with all of us at the UN ... and there will no shenanigans! If you try, Sekandar will be on my side ... not yours.

Sceptic

Nikolei had spent the past week searching for Justin. Well not exclusively, he has been meeting with managers of his hotels here in New York. Nikolei had remembered Sekandar's words before he left him with Justin the concierge at the hotel in Berlin; where he had arranged his job as doorman: "Thank you.' Those two words will see you rise, in a few short years to be the owner of this hotel, and of the hotel chain itself. (It happened much quicker than that but that's another story.) When that happens remember to reward the concierge, your new employer, Justin Tyme." Justin's reward was his elevation to manager of the Berlin hotel.

Justin was happy in his job as manager and had no ambition to take an executive position in Nikolei's company, even though it had been offered. Even so Nikolei sensed an uneasiness in Justin, and had responded to the text message from him simply stating 'see you in NY.'

Standing on the sidewalk at kerbside before one of his hotels Nikolei looked to his left, to his right and then down to the text message displayed on his Handy. Just as he was thinking "where is he?" a text message arrived from Justin, as if in answer to his question. It was just six words: 'I am at The Ginger Man'. Nikolei knew the popular Midtown bar and so he hailed a cab.

Justin was waiting for him on the sidewalk. Unease was written on his face as Nikolei alighted from the cab. Nikolei noticed that of course, probably because he was expecting it. Justin managed a smile and said, "I'm so glad you made it. Let's go on inside." There were few people inside; 'lunch hour' had not started. Justin had reserved a table in a quiet corner. He indicated it, gestured Nikolei to be seated, and went to the bar to order drinks. Justin seated himself when he returned with them. He took a sip from his, placed the glass on the table and sighed deeply.

Sitting upright Nikolei placed his opened-palmed hands on the table, inviting his confidence. "What is it my friend. What's troubling you?"

Justin replied, "Is it that obvious?" He sighed again. Shaking his head he said, "I've heard about this 'change thing' and even met Sekandar back then in Berlin when you showed up. You know I'm not convinced. I mean where is this whole thing going? What does it all mean? I need to see something to convince me that what I hear is legitimate, some sort of evidence. Where can I get that?"

Nikolei sensed a familiar presence in the bar. Realising that Nikolei had not been changed, or that it hadn't been fully effected, he pointed to a person seated at the bar with his back to them and said, "Ask him. I'm sure he'll know where you can get the evidence you seek."

Justin's eyes followed Nikolei's pointed finger. The person turned around on his bar-side stool and in the American manner said, "Hello Justin, long time no see." Nikolei smiled.

Justin sprang to his feet and spluttered, "It's him. I mean how did you..? I didn't see you come in. How did you know?" He lurched forward and shook Sekandar's offered hand in greeting.

Wearing his characteristic smile Sekandar said, "I hope you're not losing your powers of observation Justin. Last time we met you didn't miss a trick." Justine responded with a nervous twitch as Sekandar took him by an arm, led him back to the table, gestured for him to sit down and he sat next to him. "So, it is evidence you are looking for?"

"Yes, but how did you..? Ah never mind." Justin sat there looking very sullen, and shook his lowered head repeatedly. Sekandar soothed his mind, helping him to settle.

He said, "Justin, I am here to annul your doubts. Take your time, there is no rush."

Sekandar turned to Nikolei and spoke to him telepathically. "Thank you for arranging this Nikolei, and it's good to see you again. You have 'made good' as the human saying goes. And, your thoughts on Nikolei, do you think he will be ok?"

Nikolei replied, "I have no doubt that he will be fine once he sees the bigger picture." Sekandar nodded, paused a moment then verbally said, "Nikolei, can you get me a mug of coffee please, long black no sugar? Nikolei said, "Leave it to me." He went to bar and placed the order.

Justin's unease was settling. Sekandar patiently waited in silence. Nikolei returned with the coffee. Sekandar nodded his thanks, took a sip and gently placed the mug on the table.

Sekandar brought Justin's eyes to meet his and said, "Justin, let me begin by assuring you that it is quite alright for any of us to be sceptical about anything, so long as our scepticism leads us to a thorough investigation. Do you agree?" Justin nodded. Sekandar continued, "You know how it is. When we were young our elders told us what to say, think, do and how to behave. Sometimes they told us who we can and can't love. It was easy to refuse to believe their sage advice without having had our own direct personal experience. We saw it as judgemental interference, and sometimes it was. And sometimes the advice was a soundly based declaration of something self-evident; i.e., something that can be assumed as the basis for argument. Do you see the logic?" Justin nodded.

"Now, think about this: some things can be explained logically and some can't be. Let's suppose that things that can't be explained by logic but can be by what is known as emotional intelligence. Let's call it EI. It is the ability to monitor not only our own emotions but also those of other people, to discriminate between different emotions and define them appropriately, and to use that to guide our thinking and behaviour. EI also reflects abilities to join intelligence, empathy and emotions to enhance thought and understanding of interpersonal dynamics. Do you see what I mean?" Sekandar waited.

Justin mused, but his eyes focused on each of Sekandar's eyes in return. He then said, "I've read papers on EI but what does this have to do with evidence as to where this change thing is taking us?"

Now that Justin's mind was working, Sekandar said, "Bear with me Justin. I will show you. Before opting for the intriguing choice of hotel management as your niche in the world, you studied psychology privately and therefore you are aware of what is known as the 'law of proximity' represented in what is termed a Gestalt. So, I want you to think of the 'the whole' evidence you seek as a Gestalt; i.e., a configuration or pattern of elements so unified as a whole in close proximity that it cannot be described merely as a sum of its parts. I am sure you know that this principle of organisation holds that things near to one another in space and time are perceived as belonging together as a unit. Do you see the simplicity of this abstract?"

"Yes, but it isn't a complete picture." answered Justin expectantly.

"Quite so. I am a Terranian and this explanation is at best an oversimplification but it gives you the basic idea of what The Whole is. Now, this is where we come to you and me." Sekandar's optic engagement with Justin intensified. He said, "At heart you and I are much more alike than you might realise. Am I right when I say that we both strive for justice, harmony, peace and a symbiotic proximity with everything?" Justin nodded his accord.

Sekandar nodded his acceptance of Justin's understanding, then disengaging his eyes from him he turned to look at Nikolei sitting opposite, then back to Justin. Sekandar's eyes gleamed as he said, "This is The Whole. I cannot put The Whole into words; for words alone will always be inadequate, so I will take you both on a short journey into it." He turned to Justin and said, "The journey will start in your minds. It will seem surreal at first even though it is real; you will come to know that as we journey. Along the way I will show you the evidence you seek. Should anyone later question your claim to what you will see, Nikolei will be your witness." Nikolei was relaxed with that. Justin was restive. Sekandar said, "Move in closer." They obliged, and he placed a hand each on their heads.

Justin's tension vanished immediately when he travelled with Sekandar and Nikolei into a place that he couldn't describe, except that it was 'welcoming.' It embraced him empathetically. And, he saw that it was embracing Nikolei and Sekandar likewise. It was the evidence he had been seeking. It made sense.

Sekandar gently stroked their minds as he gently brought them safely back from their journey, reconnected them with their familiar existence, and settled them back where they were at the table. He released his hands from their heads.

Justin looked at Sekandar, then at Nikolei and said, "It is welcoming. It is beautiful, and it explains everything. It embraced me and I felt as though I had come home."

Sekandar replied, "Yes Justin, it is welcoming. You, Nikolei, me, everyone and everything is welcome with The Whole. This is our home right there, right here and everywhere else. It is the home of everyone and everything." Justin smiled. Sekandar asked him, "Do you have the evidence you sought?"

His voice still reflecting the awe of his short journey with The Whole, he replied, "Oh yes, thank you for showing me. I'd like to go there again."

Sekandar replied, "You are there, Justin. You are. We are."

Primo Dictum

The two principal nay-sayers were about to do it again.
Not that they are alone in exercising their veto but they
have done it more often than the other three permanent
member states of the United Nations Security Council.
Indeed two member states have never used their veto.
The Council is in session. Presidency of the Council is
held by each of the members in turn for one month; not
just the five permanent but also the others. This month
the presidency is held by the representative of an African
nation. At this session another vetoed resolution was
expected. It didn't happen. Just as a vote was about to be
put, a draft in the chamber that had been apparent to some
members suddenly erupted into a gust of wind scattering
papers across the floor.

Sometimes, creating a 'scene' with Sekandar's
impressive arrival carried with it greater significance.
Scattering the members' papers heralded that. It was
evident that he liked the drama of a grand entrance;
the effect was always obviously intended to evoke awe
in witnesses, and it certainly conveyed his unequivocal
authority. Even though the change had been effected
almost universally, his arrival in this way at this particular
meeting dealt with several influential individuals
representing their countries, who had not yet been reached.
To Sekandar, the UN Security Council's prevalent inertia
to properly intervene in pervasive and pernicious violence
in the world, typified the dilemma for Humankind that had
now been solved. The Change changed everything.

Maintaining his incorporeal state, Sekandar
strengthened the draft which gradually became a breeze
that swirled with an embracing vigour around the Council
chamber as attendants scurried to retrieve more scattered
papers. The lighting slowly dimmed to a softness less
than semi-darkness, and a quiet stillness descended. The
darkened atmosphere gradually gave way to a kind of
misty iridescent shimmer that glowed softly at first then
brightened into the full spectrum of the colours of white
light which then coalesced into his human figure which

stood in their midst facing the President's bench. The lighting returned to its usual luminosity.

He stood still there circled by the round table of the Council, and waited patiently until the ebb and flow of murmurs subsided then ceased. His presence entranced the assembly, and everyone was filled with wonder; most of them had never before seen such an occurrence of his arrival. He scanned the as yet unchanged individuals and quickly effected the change for them.

Establishing eye contact with the President, and with authority and clarity of voice he spoke. "I am Sekandar. You know who I am. Subsequent to The Whole aneling the strategy, and with the imprimatur of the Galactic Council I came to Earth with a mission; to effect a paradigm shift in underlying human assumptions of violence. I am here to inform you that the change has been effected and to respectfully request your attendance, and the attendance of everyone attending this Council, at a Special Session of the General Assembly of the United Nations which I have requested. Before this session of the Security Council adjourns you will be informed as to the date and time for the General Assembly to convene for that session.

Without uttering another word, Sekandar turned full circle contacting in turn the eyes of everyone at the round table. He then looked upward as the iridescent shimmer briefly enveloped him as he dematerialised into it. The shimmer brightened as it flashed sharply into apparent nothingness. Sekandar had promulgated his Primo Dictum. He was ready for the next.

Secundum Dictum

The day of the Special Session at the General Assembly of the United Nations had arrived. Due to the large number of VIPs attending, additional security measures were taken in and around the UN precinct. Access to the premises was more restricted than usual, and was restricted to delegates and their staff; i.e., to staff members of the United Nations Secretariat, programs and agencies of the UN. Accredited media and affiliates were wearing a UN grounds pass. Other individuals invited to attend were each issued with a meeting-specific pass. Even though The Change is considered to be complete and threats of violence were not expected, security was as tight as always. The Secretariat had approved VIP passes for each member of the change team, plus one other person, to sit in the Hall of the General Assembly.

The UN Secretary-General attended this Special Session of the General Assembly, as did Heads of State of member nations. The President of the General Assembly opened proceedings and called for a minute of silent prayer or meditation; specified in protocol. When the minute had expired, a subtle movement of air was the first indication that this was going to be a very different session; just as had occurred in the Security Council earlier.

The draft began to strengthen and gradually became a breeze which began to swirl with an embracing vigour around everyone assembled in the auditorium. The lighting slowly dimmed to a softness less than semi-darkness, and a quietness descended. The semi-darkened atmosphere gradually gave way to a kind of misty iridescent shimmer that glowed softly at first then brightened into the full spectrum of the colours of white light which then coalesced into a human figure which stood beside the President's bench. The lighting returned to its usual luminosity.

The figure stood still there, and waited until the ebb and flow of murmurs subsided then ceased. His presence entranced the assembly, and everyone was filled with wonder; as with his earlier appearance at the Security Council most of them had never before seen such an occurrence.

Just as he did at the Security Council he spoke with authority and clarity of voice. "I am Sekandar. You know who I am, and yet you don't know me. I have come to Earth from far away. I am a Terranian. Terra Dyad, my home planet is in what you know as the Perseus Arm of the Galaxy that we know as Kala-G□, and you know as The Milky Way. Our planet has an atmosphere similar to Earth, and our star, Filo is about the same size as your star, Sol. My species is incorporeal, and as you have just witnessed we are able to assume any form that suits our purpose. You see me now as a human being, and that is our preferred corporeal form. You see me as an individual. That I am, and I am also part of what we call The Whole. My species has established hegemony of the galaxy, and as part of The Whole we are ascendant in it."

Sekandar had their undivided attention. He continued. "There is a unity at the very heart of the diversity of the Galaxy, and of the Universe which allows us to see The Whole in all things and to avow that everything belongs. The Whole is the actuating cause of the universe. The Whole is the universal being which is present everywhere and at the same time transcending all things created. This perception, which is to your minds akin to panentheism, is known to Humankind in various forms; in your monotheistic religions - Judaism, Christianity and Islam, and is also somewhat elemental in your philosophies like Gaianism and Pantheism."

Like a musical intermezzo a ripple of murmurs scurried back and forth across the auditorium. Hearing that, Sekandar responded with his characteristic smile and he continued. "Subsequent to The Whole aneling the strategy, and with the imprimatur of the Galactic Council I came to Earth with a mission; to effect a paradigm shift in underlying human assumptions of violence." Sekandar paused momentarily as he lifted his hands inviting Karen and her team to stand. "With the team headed by Professor Dr. Karen Krause. This was accomplished by effecting an adjustment to the gene in each individual human being; a gene that created the mindset inculcating the propensity of human beings to use violence to solve problems."

He lowered his hands inviting the team to be seated again then continued, "The change has been effected. It marks a paradigm shift in the evolution of Humankind. We welcome you into our ascendancy of the Galaxy. If the change had not occurred you would not have been welcome to join us, and your species would have withered to extinction."

The General-Secretary rose to his feet, to be at eye level with Sekandar. With an earnest but sincere expression on this face he asked, "Sekandar, in my travels around the world many people have asked me whether you have explained to me why you have intervened in human affairs at this time. Alas, I have been unable to give them a satisfactory answer. Can you tell us why?"

Sekandar acknowledged his sincerity, and replied, "Thank you for your question, and for raising this important issue. The answer to your question is this: It is not about me as an individual. I am part of The Whole. You will learn all about that in the fullness of time. I came to facilitate the change that would otherwise have taken many more generations. From the earliest awakening of humans as an intelligent species we have observed your development. Technological advancement of your species is on the verge of exponential development that will propel you beyond your solar system and out into the Galaxy. The change in your genetic makeup will ensure an inherently peaceful and co-operative disposition with each other and with those whom you encounter beyond. That is fundamentally important." The murmurs this time had a friendly fell about them.

Sekandar was now more direct in his remarks. "Before The Change, Humankind's genetic defect had on the one hand paradoxically rightly named individual violent behaviour, and on the other at the same time ignored or supported structural and systemic violence in all its manifestations, dealing with symptoms rather than the cause. Violence was embedded in your conscious complicity with systems that serve you as individuals at others' expense. That complicity created worldwide entitlement and privileges that were subconsciously unrecognised until The Change. The contemplative consciousness of The Whole sees this without being self-righteous. The Change has cleared away illusions, enabling Humankind to see that everything is integral to The Whole. Everything is of the same essence; sacrosanct in every endeavour."

Having remained on the one spot since his arrival, Sekandar now stepped forward. He spread his hands wide with palms up, and said. "The ultimate destiny of Humankind is out there, among the stars of our Galaxy. You have dreamt about your destiny since your emergence as an intelligent species. Your destiny is about to be realised. As I stated earlier, the effect of the change will enable Humankind to set out on a pathway that will lead you to take your place with us in our peaceful ascendancy of the Galaxy. We look forward to embracing you into that."

Sekandar said, "I will soon be returning home. I am leaving you with the members of the team that effected The Change." He lifted his hands again, inviting Karen and her team to stand once more as he announced them. "These are your pathway guides: Karen Krause, the team leader, and the members: Lilly Ruhr, Guy de Villiers, Amne Tahir, Miri Tschekov, Valentine Plessis, Ezekiel Eisner, Yang Meixa, James Lynne, Rey Gibbs, Layne Bauer, Jorie Barak, Jiemba and Giles. Heed their teaching."

Sekandar then turned to the President of the General Assembly, the Secretary-General of the United Nations, and the President of the Security Council. He bowed his head and said, "Thank you for permitting me to address the Assembly." They returned nods of acknowledgement.

He turned back to face the Assembly. Silence enveloped the auditorium. The draft that had ushered his arrival, returned and began again to strengthen. It gradually became a breeze which began to swirl with an embracing vigour around him. The lighting slowly dimmed to a softness less than semi-darkness, and quietness prevailed. The darkened atmosphere gradually gave way to a kind of misty iridescent shimmer that glowed softly around him. The shimmer coalesced, embracing him as it brightened into the full spectrum of the colours of white light, then vanished. He was gone.

The Assembly rose to their feet and the auditorium reverberated with applause as the lighting returned to its usual luminosity. The President stood and pronounced, "This Special Session of the General Assembly of the United Nations is closed." The Change Team were inundated with questions.

Exultation

Imago, Karen's estate has a long history witnessing the arrival and departure of many visitors since her Great-great-grandfather bought it and built his grand house there. The last three years have probably been the busiest. Since that late-autumn night following the first symposium, when the course of human history set out on the path to turn away from its violent, destructive past, individual members of the team have been visiting. Tonight the team will gather, all together for only the second time. Humankind is firmly on course to join with others in the peaceful ascendancy of the galaxy, and the team will be here to quietly celebrate their achievement, and to farewell Sekandar.

This evening will not be rushed. The team will be arriving soon. Karen stood on the snow-covered driveway before the house looking out across the landscape mystically illuminated by the full moon; just as it did on that earlier night. On this, a chillier early winter night she muses about everything that had transpired in such a short period. Just as on that afore night a snowflake landing on her cheek brought her back from her thoughts. The previously bright full moon above was now partially hidden from view by snow clouds that were gradually curtaining the sky; just as before. The stillness had given way to a chilly zephyr, freshening to a breeze. A first few fluttering snowflakes soon became more numerous, settling gently in her hair and on her shoulders. She turned to go inside and wait for the arrival of her team.

She halted her advance to the door. In front of her a misty iridescent shimmer glowed softly, then brightening it coalesced into the human form of Sekandar. With his characteristic smile he greeted her. "Good evening Karen."

Pleased to see him again she greeted him with a fresh smile. "Good evening Sekandar. All day I have been looking forward to seeing you." He smiled again. "And, by the way, is it a levity to ask if you had a good trip?"

He responded with an upsurge of emotion evident in his voice. "You are the cheeky one tonight." Karen embraced him, then gently kissed his lips; briefly. He held her then at arm's length and said. "Let us remember our agreement." She put a finger to his lips. He reciprocated with a finger to hers.

Stepping to the front door together, he said, "In answer to your question, Yes, I did have a good trip. While we're on the subject, and for your understanding, sometimes certain atmospheric and other spatial conditions must be taken into account. In due course you will learn about all that. When I choose to teleport myself in human form I am still the same person, just as you were when I teleported you, and I know whether or not the 'trip' is a good one."

They turned to face each other and he said, "Is that a satisfactory answer to your question Dr. Krause?" She winked at him. He received it without comment. She put a finger to his lips and offered him her hand. He took it. With her free hand she opened the door, they entered and proceeded thence to the drawing room, leaving those doors open.

Giles, happily playing the role of the valet, entered shortly after them. "Your guests will be arriving soon, Dr. Krause."

She responded in the proper manner. "Thank you Giles." She then resumed her conversation with Sekandar. "Will there be celebrations when you arrive back on Terra Dyad?"

"Yes Karen, I'm sure there will be, and the Galactic Council will send you a formal invitation to celebrate with us." His smile broadening, he added, "I like that human custom."

Agape at the prospect of travelling in space, Karen spluttered, "Karen Krause, travel to the other side of the Galaxy? I haven't even been in orbit around Earth. It's a trip of … how many … how far away … how could I do that … will I be travelling with you?"

Sekandar sought to persuade her. "Yes, you will be travelling with me. Let me assure you it is not as you may imagine. You will do it with ease. My ship is a state-of-the-art electro-magnetic space cruiser. It is very comfortable to travel in, and the trip to Terra Dyad will be quicker than you could ever imagine. From a psychology point of view I expect it will be a very interesting experience for you."

"Hmm, interesting indeed. When will we be leaving?" Karen nervously asked.

Sekandar suggested, "There is no rush, but I would like us to be on our way within a few days. If that's ok with you."

"Wait, I have to consider Peter," Karen appealed.

"Yes, of course," Sekandar replied. "We can talk further, later. Giles is about to ..."

Giles knocked, then upon Karen's acceptance he entered the room and said, "Dr. Krause, your guests have arrived." Again, Karen responded in the proper manner. "Thank you Giles."

Giles, obviously pleased that everyone's arrival was particularly punctual, opened the front door as one after another the team entered the house. He gathered coats and scarves from each person, and issued house shoes. Everyone was in animated discussion that gradually abated as they proceed to the drawing room. Karen welcomed each team member in a familiar manner; they know each other closely now. Giles offered drinks which some accepted. The valet's welcome done, Giles retired to the kitchen to supervise preparation of the meal, soon to be served.

In silence the assembled team stood in an informal array. All eyes turned to Sekandar and Karen. Karen said, "Thank you everyone for your punctuality," and as an aside, "By the way, you may have noticed that my valet was pleased with that. Being efficient himself he appreciates any reciprocation." The thanks, and her aside were acknowledged with hearty appreciative applause. "Before we dine I want to thank you all for effecting the change in so many, so quickly." She then turned to Sekandar.

Respect for Sekandar, the alien who had changed their lives forever, had grown during implementation of The Change. Whenever he spoke he received their undivided attention, and said, "My friends, it is done! You have effected the change." Everyone repeated, "It is done!"

He continued, "You are aware that the additional capability I gave you, i.e., to transfer adjustments automatically, accelerated the process. That is not to diminish the willingness each of you have admirably demonstrated to put yourselves in circumstances where you were able to undertake your task, always without considering your own welfare. That was entirely of your own doing. I played no role there, and didn't seek too. I am proud of you all."

Seeing that Giles had re-entered the room, Sekandar acknowledged his presence. Giles announced, "Dinner will be served." Everyone filed casually into the dining room and sat at the table. Giles' had invited his brother Charles join him, to assist him with his regular staff on this occasion. As a member of The Change team, Giles took his place at the table. Charles and the household staff served the first course.

Before they started eating Sekandar requested a moment of silence. He bowed his head and in a gentle tone devoutly said, "Let us remember our appreciation for the Universe, its power, beauty and mystery calling for our deepest reverence and wonder. And for our individual places in it, as integral elements of The Whole. We are truly thankful for this food, its bounty, and for our respective species the highest expressions of its creation. We are most thankful for the success of our mission to change the human paradigm of underlying assumptions of violence." Guy said, "Amen."

Smiling, he added, "I will be returning home again soon, and look forward to meeting each of you in the future when we can share another meal together. In the meantime, look after your families and each other." Lifting his head again he said, "Now, let's eat."

The meal proceeded silently at first, then with happy animated talk about their achievement. After the final meal course everyone made their way back to the drawing room where team members individually spoke with Sekandar; thanking him each in their own way for his intervention in the human journey.

When everyone had had their say, Sekandar acquired everyone's attention again, and said, "We come now to the question that is on your minds. What happens next? Recall what I said at our first meeting, and look in wonder as each of you realise the effect of the change. The correction of the anomaly has reversed the human mindset to pursue the propensity to use violence to solve problems. I came to facilitate the change that would otherwise have taken several more generations. Always remember that you did it; the ability to eventually do it always resided within you anyway. I merely encouraged it. The effect of the change is enabling Humankind to set out on a pathway that is leading you to take your place with us in our peaceful ascendancy of the Galaxy. We look forward to embracing you into that, very soon. You, i.e., Karen and the team, will know it first. Karen will come with me to Terra Dyad. There she will represent all of humanity in celebrations, and be prepared for her continuing leadership as humanity prepares to join us. She will then return to lead you as you take the next steps." Sekandar then turned to Karen.

Dr. Karen Krause, Professor of psychology always knew that she possessed natural leadership ability. She never imagined she would exercise it as she has with this project. She has warmed to it.

First, addressing Sekandar she said, "Sekandar, I know I speak for the team when I say that words may never properly thank you for your initiative. We do know however, that we will be ever grateful for you having chosen us to effect the change. It has been an enlightening and endowing experience. We also eagerly look forward to joining with you and all Terranians in the adventures awaiting us in the Galaxy." Sekandar nodded, graciously acknowledging her praise.

Giles signalled Charles and the household staff. They entered the room carrying trays of flutes and bottles of champagne. Everyone took a flute which was subsequently filled with champagne. Karen beseeched her team, "I wish to propose a toast." Raising her glass she toasted, "To Sekandar, initiator of the change." The team returned the declaration. "To Sekandar."

Turning to face her team assembled in an informal array around the drawing room, Karen continued, "There are so many accolades I have to shower upon you all. Your accomplishment has been made possible because of your energy and passion. There have been twists and turns on your journey, and hurdles to overcome. You handled obstacles and setbacks eloquently. Whenever you talked with me about the challenges you had to overcome, you inspired me to press on. Guy, Amne, Miri, Valentine, Ezekiel, Yang, James, Rey, Layne, Jorie, Jiemba, and Giles. Thank you. Finally, let's paint the picture of what your accomplishment might lead to. Many doors will open to us leading to new opportunities. Together, we have reached the top of the hill. Now we can see the mountain in the distance. Together, let's strive for our new future here on Earth and out there in the Galaxy." Karen concluded with applause. Everyone reciprocated.

Sekandar, standing beside Karen implored the team to draw near then said, "Giles would you please ask Charles to refill our glasses? I wish to propose a toast." Giles obliged.

Raising his glass Sekandar toasted, "To Humankind, resolutely on your path to join us in our ascendancy of the Galaxy." The Team returned the declaration. "To Humankind."

Sekandar continued, "We started here together and here together we will soon be parted. Parting is nothing compared to the delight of meeting again. We will meet again in the future. I don't know where, and I don't know when but I know we will meet again. A farewell is necessary before we can meet again, and meeting again after moments or lifetimes is certain for those who are friends. You are my friends. How fortunate I am to have so many wonderful memories of our collaboration that makes saying this goodbye so special."

The team noticed Sekandar's obvious emotion. He composed himself and added: "In all that has transpired since my arrival here on Earth, I see not only what has been done, I also see what remains to be done. Life is a journey, not a destination. Karen will return soon to lead you on that journey. Remember me and smile. I will know when you have done that, and I will return the compliment. Peace be with you."

The team returned the blessing, "Peace be with you, Sekandar."

Giles opened the drawing room doors and stood aside as the team gathered their coats, scarves and shoes. Karen shook the hand of each of her team members in turn as she wished them safe travels. Giles ushered everyone to their cars, then re-entered the house when the last one had driven away. Closing the door the valet turned 'round, finding Karen and Sekandar standing right there before him. Giles turned again and re-open the door. She and Sekandar stepped outside and onto the circular driveway by the front steps. Giles re-entered the house and closed the door behind him, leaving it unlocked. As he was doing so he said, "Good night, Sir."

Sekandar responded, "Good night, Giles. Peace be with you." Giles smiled, a knowing smile.

Sekandar took Karen's hands in his. His eyes turned skyward with her to look up at the full moon, now overhead in the clear stillness of the winter night sky that had 'opened' for them after the earlier snow. Karen's phone rang. Seeing the indicated caller she excused herself saying that it is an important call that can't wait. Answering the call she looked up at Sekandar then turned away as her head dropped ruminatively. She spoke few words.

Turning around again, with tears welling she said, "It's the hospital. Peter's condition has deteriorated. It is not looking good. I will have to go to him."

Reading her mind and understanding the urgency Sekandar drew her near and embraced her gently as he implored her, "Go to him Karen. You need each other now." Releasing their embrace he lowered his eyes, and holding her hands he raised his eyes and looked deeply into hers. "I will come to you when you call for me." She replied, "Thank you."

Sekandar let go her hands, took a backward pace and said, "Peace be with you, Karen." She replied, "Peace be with you Sekandar."

He dematerialised into the incorporeal; the shimmer a touch dimmer this time, and more softly coloured in the spectrum of white light which then faded to invisibility. There was no sound. He was gone.

Karen reflexively waved as she turned to re-enter the house. She 'phoned the hospital ward manager, informing her that she will be on her way sofort.

Departure

Sekandar wanted to go home before fulfilling his duties at the Galactic Council and he knew that would be unlikely given the profound, historical importance of his achievement. However, the Prime Narrator has persuaded his fellow Narrators to proceed with formalities in the extraordinary session of Council to be convened upon Sekandar's arrival, and to delay the following celebrations to give Sekandar and Varia time together. Sekandar had good reason to delay. There is an overriding importance. Varia is dying. Iskandar knows it, and he has not broken the news to Sekandar. Varia has requested that she must do that herself.

Returning alone to the Wald in Berlin, Sekandar felt a definite reluctance to leave Earth, and Karen would not be coming with him – this time. Although he knew there was no deadline for him to report to the Galactic Council, he was mindful that he shouldn't linger too long but he dismissed that thought and lingered.

Thinking back to his arrival when he stepped from the shuttle onto recently manicured green grass lightly strewn with fallen autumn leaves in various hues, he noticed that three years later the scene was for the most part unchanged. As he did then he marvelled at the scene before him and again he was overcome with a sense of serenity, akin to coming home. The fresh air, the aromas, the trees, the grass, all of it is so much like his home planet. The realisation that the similarity is uncanny caused him to ponder that.

It was time to leave. He signalled his cloaked orbiting space cruiser, to release his shuttle and send it to him. He is thankful that he didn't have to retrieve it until now; an emergency necessitating its retrieval during his time on Earth did not eventuate.

There was no sound of course as the pod detached itself from the interstellar ship, and it electro-magnetically descended, accelerating exponentially until it slowed again nearing its programmed location where it will meet him. A gentle rustling of leaves on nearby trees announced its return to the exact same location as its arrival just over three ago.

Sekandar was not hurried. He ambled towards the clearing in the grove of trees where his pod landed. He scanned the minds of the few people around, detecting the changed minds of each individual. A few people were strolling. A few were sitting on benches looking intently at their hand-held devices; communicators that are now well known to him. Here and there couples were cuddling, just as before. He thought again of Varia knowing that she would like it here; she likes serenity.

Nobody recognised him. He was anonymous in this situation. He is wearing the attire that he arrived in. His selection of attire throughout his time on Earth attracted no adverse comment and even a few compliments! Varia would have been pleased with that. He is carrying his bag of provisions that he had retrieved from the cloaked pod upon his arrival, and another with a few souvenirs; no doubt they would undergo examination before he arrives back on Terra Dyad. Reaching the shuttle he turned and looked about to ensure that nobody saw him entering it. Passing through the shuttle's cloak he vanished from view, and boarded his personal pod to prepare for lift-off.

The electro-magnetic motors started, and the shuttle ascended, accelerating exponentially until it slowed again nearing his orbiting interstellar ship. When he had transferred from the shuttle to the ship, Sekandar paused for some time. He looked down fondly upon the Earth, so many parsecs from his own, and he smiled, knowing his mission has been accomplished. His thoughts turned to Karen and her words "When will I see you again?" lingered as he looked down again to the Earth below. She telepathically replied "Soon, I hope."

Throughout his mission to Earth Sekandar had maintained constant telepathic communication with Karen and her team, and most importantly with Varia. She knows he is coming home, and she is eagerly anticipating his homecoming. She will have to wait a while longer.

Teleportation directly from Earth to Terra Dyad would be a much quicker way to return home but Sekandar wants to return in the same way that he departed; except that he will bypass the Interstellar Space Port and land his space cruiser directly. Even so, he will have time to gather his thoughts before his homecoming. He also has to finalise his report to the Galactic Council.

Sekandar's sleek state-of-the art personal space cruiser was subsequently positioned a safe distance from Earth in preparation for the first hyper-jump on his return trip to Terra Dyad. The trip was over in an inordinately short time as the ship negotiated a series of effortless jumps through hyperspace across the Galaxy, just as it did on the journey to Earth. The Interstellar Interchange Port orbiting Terra Dyad came into view. His ship bypassed it and settled into a low orbit around the planet. Activating its remaining flight plan it then electro-magnetically descended, seeking and finding its programmed path to its landing site. The landing was gentle and silent, and uncloaked of course. He arrived on the expansive lawns of the Galactic Council building. A wall of the ship turned translucent and a door formed. Sekandar stepped out and down onto the lawns of the Council precinct.

Now fully prepared for his return Sekandar had a minute or two to savour an appreciation of his home planet; a habit of his each time he returned from a mission. This time the admiration was particularly pertinent. He smiled characteristically as he thought too about what he had experienced on his mission to Earth, that most enigmatic world in the Orion Arm of the Galaxy. His thoughts were telepathically read by Varia who responded with a telepathic hug and a kiss accompanied by, "Welcome home Sekandar. See you soon."

He reciprocated and said, "Thank you, my dear Varia. I can't wait to hold you again." He could feel her release her mind reluctantly as she replied, "Ditto."

8

Galactic Council

Obtaining his bearings in the precinct of the Galactic Council he instinctively looked 'round about then up at the building; he remarked to himself, "Why do I always look up when I arrive here?"

He walked slowly across the lawns of the precinct and scaled the steps of the Council building. He stopped there and slowly turned full circle as he surveyed the city very much alive for him this time than at any time previously. Just as he experienced it before his departure for Earth the city 'organically' glistened under the brightness of this early summer morning. He smiled characteristically then entered the building, walking apace to the Prime Narrator's room.

Today he will be formally reporting to the Galactic Council the success of his mission. It is a formality, a remnant of protocol passed down from ancient times that enables him to articulate in essence the successful implementation of the plan and the successful result of his mission. The formality also enables the Council to express their gratitude and thanks, on behalf of The Whole.

Recognising him, the doors to the Prime Narrator's private rooms opened automatically as Sekandar confidently approached them. He walked through the doorway, smiled characteristically and with outstretched right hand he greeted him. "Good morning Prime Narrator."

As before no etiquette was needed; in the scheme of things they are equals. Iskandar responded, "Good morning Narrator Sekandar. Welcome to Terra Dyad, welcome home."

Iskandar embraced Sekandar then said, "Before we enter the Council chamber I want to personally congratulate you on the success of your mission. The way in which you carried out your mission was exemplary, and a superb representative example of the ideals of The Whole."

Sekandar bowed his head, acknowledging Iskandar's praise then responded, "Prime Narrator, you and I know that I was merely the prime enabler. My success is the success of The Whole."

Iskandar reciprocated a nod. "Yes it is. Let us make our way to the Chamber."

They left the Prime Narrator's room together, proceeding slowly to the Council Chamber just a short distance through those same hallowed halls of the Galactic Council building that they had briskly walked not long ago. This time Iskandar paused by several inscriptions on the walls, and engaged Sekandar in mutual explanation of them. They each knew these inscriptions verbatim; fundamental knowledge learnt on their paths to becoming Narrators. Written in their ancestral language they described the current understanding of the origin of their species and the acquisition of their incorporeal being; both of which were of continuing interest.

The two Narrators took all the time they needed to look around this place of governance that had been standing for almost a millennium. They had been within its walls on many occasions and knew it well. On this occasion they each found themselves being reflective of those times and of this place, and wondering no more about long unanswered questions about the precise planet of origin. That, at last had been solved. Sekandar in particular perceived it all differently now that he has returned from his mission. Iskandar read those thoughts and telepathically said, "Our ascendancy of the Galaxy is continuing, Sekandar. This day marks our formal acknowledgement of the greatest achievement of our species to ensure that."

They approached the doors of the Galactic Council Chamber. The huge doors opened as they approached, recognising them as with the doors to the Prime Narrator's room. They entered the large high-vaulted chamber, and the several hundred Narrators assembled rose to their feet in unison. Iskandar has requested that every Narrator attending this session of the Council is to assume human form, as an acknowledgement of Sekandar's revelation of the origin. Not a word was spoken, either audibly or telepathically.

Iskandar and Sekandar approached the steps to the central dais, mounted them then positioned themselves centrally upon the dais where they turned and stood together facing the assembled Narrators. Thunderous applause erupted as soon as they turned to face the audience. When the applause had subsided to distinct silence the Prime Narrator said, "This extraordinary meeting of the Galactic Council is now in session. Please be seated."

Iskandar waited for the audience to settle then began. "My fellow Narrators, there are three items of business in this session of the Galactic Council. Let us deal with the first. You will have noticed that the item is: Origin." There was a low-pitched buzz of expectant murmurings across the Chamber. Iskandar continued, "For millennia the precise location of the origin of our species has been a mystery. There has been much speculation, as we all know well. The mystery may be with us no more. Sekandar believes he has located the precise planet of the origin of our species. He will soon be able to confirm that Earth is that planet." A murmur rippled across the auditorium.

Iskandar continued, "In order that we can purposefully assist Sekandar with his effort to secure absolute verification, it is now time to incorporate every detail of his knowledge thus far into The Whole. Narrators of the Galactic Council please stand." In unison the assembled Narrators rose to their feet. Iskandar symbolically raised his hands, palms up and held out at chest height before him. Everyone followed his lead. The lighting in the Council Chamber was bright enough for everyone to be easily seen. There was a soft spotlight upon the two on the dais. All the lights dimmed further to a softness as all hands were raised. Just as with every incorporation of knowledge into The Whole, each individual Narrator dematerialised into the incorporeal, becoming a kind of misty iridescent shimmer, coloured in the full spectrum of white light that glowed softly then coalesced into a whole and slowly brightened slightly. There was no sound. The 'whole' remained so for two minutes exactly before separating into individual shimmers again, and then coalescing and rematerialising into individual human forms. Everyone returned to their places, and were standing as before. Iskandar said, "So be it." In unison everyone repeated, "So be it."

Facing the assembled Narrators, Iskandar said, "Narrators, please be seated. We will now deal with the second item of this session of the Galactic Council, The Change." Befitting his assumed human form he took a deep breath and said, "The Galactic Council was convened in a previous session to formally confer upon Sekandar his mission; to effect the paradigm shift in the propensity of human beings to use violence to solve their problems. The mission to Earth has been astonishingly successful. Humankind is now surely and securely on their journey to join us in our ascendancy of the Kala-Ge. And we rejoice in knowing that our primal origin may be one and the same. Our ascendancy of the Kala-Ge is now in its next phase because of the change." The Chamber again erupted into thunderous applause. Iskandar waited until the audience settled, then invited Sekandar to address the Council.

Sekandar stepped forward and addressed the full complement of this extraordinary meeting of the Galactic Council. "My fellow Narrators I have submitted the report of my mission; it is accessible in the mind of The Whole, along with my report on the origins of our species. We have all incorporated that. The paradigm shift in underlying human assumptions of violence, has been accomplished. Our ascendancy of the galaxy has a new reality. Our understanding of the origin of our species will complement our understanding of our incorporeal being. We will ensure that we all use our understanding, and all our knowledge and capabilities for the benefit of the 'Whole,' which now includes all of Humankind."

He stepped back a pace, Iskandar stepped forward and raised his right hand beseeching the Council to stand, which they did. In unison every Narrator said, "Congratulations Narrator Sekandar on your success. Peace be with you."

Facing the assembled Narrators, Iskandar said, "Narrators, please be seated. We will now deal with the third item of this session of the Galactic Council. This item is: Succession. My term as Prime Narrator will soon come to a close." Subdued murmurings of poignant resignation drifted across the Chamber. Everyone knows it is almost time for Iskandar to step down. Everyone would like him to stay on but they also know that customary successions in the role will always be respected.

The murmurings subsided, and the assembly allowed Iskandar to continue. "It is the custom of the Galactic Council to allow the incumbent Prime Narrator to choose the successor to that role ex officio, and for the Council to ratify the decision. You may be anticipating that I have chosen Sekandar to succeed me. I have not. Given his extraordinary contribution to The Whole it is right and proper for Sekandar to be free to pursue any new path in his life, of his choosing. It is my right as retiring Prime Narrator to release him from further commissions of the Council, except the verification of our primal origin. I now do so." Expressions of agreement with Iskandar's directive were accordant.

He continued, "I am not obliged to name my chosen successor at this session. When I have decided, I will inform you in telepathic consultation with The Whole. Council can then ratify my choice at the following session my when our incoming Prime Narrator will be installed. Now it is time for all of us to celebrate the new era in our ascendancy of the galaxy. Therefore this session of the Galactic Council is closed."

Everyone filed out of the chamber in no particular order, each going their own way in preparation for the celebrations; lavishly arranged for this momentous occasion. Iskandar and Sekandar walked out together. In the corridors that they had earlier ambled as they perused the wall inscriptions, Iskandar placed a hand on Sekandar's shoulder and said, "Please come with me to my rooms before you go to home to Varia. There is something I need to tell you." Still in awe over proceedings in the Council Chamber, Sekandar complied having no inkling of the tidings of which he was about to be smitten.

Iskandar did not dally. He walked quickly to his rooms with Sekandar, and gestured for him to be seated. "What is it you need to tell me Prime Narrator?" Sekandar enquired.

"Sekandar, Varia is dying."

"What? What are you talking about?" spluttered Sekandar, as he sprung to his feet.

"She requested that I refrain from telling you. In fact she requested that she must do that herself. I thought better of that and decided I should break the news with you now. I know her well enough to know that she will have anticipated that I would tell you before you see her. I know too that you will understand."

Sekandar was pacing back and forth in his anguish at this news, and said, "I must go to her, right now!" Iskandar stood up from his chair and implored Sekandar to listen, just a few moments longer.

"Well alright but make it quick!" Sekandar blurted.

"Yes of course, in a moment." Iskandar gestured for Sekandar to sit down again, then explained. "You will recall that I informed you before your departure that our security surveillance detected a series of unidentified signals emanating from a sector in the Galaxy just beyond our quadrant. The signals at various frequencies were aimed directly at Terra Dyad, and were repeated at irregular intervals. At that stage we didn't know if the signals were random or specific. Subsequently we identified the source and discerned a specific target." Iskandar drew near to Sekandar, and gently placed his hands on Sekandar's shoulders. "The signals appear to have been aimed at Varia."

Exasperation rising within him, Sekandar stood up again, and quizzed the Prime Narrator. "What? Why? ... Why didn't you inform me over the secure channel you gave me?"

Iskandar explained. "Varia requested that she must inform you herself. Being faithful to her request, and knowing there was no discernible direct inference to your mission there was no need to inform you earlier. I am informing you now because if Varia can't provide you with

an explanation as to why, who or what targeted her then
I know you will investigate. As yet Varia has not given us
any lead. In fact, on this matter alone she has shielded
her mind from telepathic interrogation. I must say we are
surprised she is able to do that."

There was no point being exasperated. Sekandar was
now confused. He slouched back into the chair. Somehow
he was able to ask of Iskandar, "What is her condition?
What is she dying of?"

Introducing an urgency into his voice Iskandar replied,
"It appears to be a previously unknown form of genetic
tampering made to look like a cancer-like invasion. We are
unable yet to decipher the altered elements of the gene
code." Seeing the anguish in Sekandar, Iskandar directed,
"Wait no longer here with me. Go to her now Sekandar. We
don't know how long she has to live."

Sekandar said no more, rose to his feet, turned and
left the room promptly. Iskandar contacted the hospital
telepathically, informing them of Sekandar's imminent
arrival there.

Watching him leave, Iskandar put his palms together in
prayerful posture and said, "Peace be with you Sekandar.
The Whole is with you."

Homecoming

This was a homecoming that Sekandar had no way
of anticipating. There had been absolutely no indication
of the crisis. Not from anyone, including Varia herself.
At the very moment he left the Prime Narrator's room
Sekandar dematerialised in the corridor of the Galactic
Council building, and teleported to the hospital. Not having
detected Varia's location in the hospital he rematerialised
at the hospital reception desk. He was directed immediately
to Varia's room, and proceeded there without delay. The
receptionist telepathically informed the attending doctor of
Sekandar's arrival.

The ward manager was watching out for Sekandar to
enter the ward. Upon entering Sekandar asked him, "When
was Varia's life expectancy last updated?"

Frowning, the ward manager replied, "Varia's doctor revised that about an hour ago. She may not survive another day."

Grimacing as he comprehended her answer, he closed his eyes then replied, "Thank you. May I please speak with Varia's doctor?"

"Certainly. The doctor will be with you soon," replied the manager.

As those words were spoken the doctor had entered the ward and she approached the waiting two. Taking Sekandar's hand the doctor entered Varia's room with him. Ushering him to the bedside she then withdrew with the ward manager to give Sekandar a few moments alone with his beloved.

Opened her eyes from slumber. "Sekandar! I'm so glad you made it," exclaimed Varia excitedly as Sekandar leant down to embrace her. Tears flowed profusely from them both.

What seemed like minutes passed before they gathered themselves and drew back to connect their tear-filled eyes with each other. Sekandar spoke first. "My dear Varia. What has happened to you? Why didn't you tell me sooner?"

Holding each other Varia responded, "First, I have to tell you that I knew about my condition days before your departure. It was distressingly difficult not to say anything to you, or give you any indication that something was wrong. Neither did I tell anybody else then. I couldn't say anything about this because the news would have disrupted your mission. You know that. I could only hope that you made it in time for me to explain everything. Now I can. Please understand that from my perspective."

A disconcerted Sekandar responded, "No, no. Arrangements could have been made for another Narrator to take my place. Everyone knows that family comes first."

Varia replied assuredly, "Sekandar, you know that is not entirely true. You know that The Whole comes first, and that is where your responsibility lies. It was your duty to enable the plan. Yours, and yours alone. You did your duty and The Whole will be forever thankful for that. Maybe in a less important circumstance things would have been different. Let's not dwell on that. I want to tell you what I think has happened to me." Sekandar fell silent and listened to Varia's explanation.

"Not long before we met all those years ago, I went to Carinus a planet in the Sagittarius spur. It is just outside our galactic quadrant. It was a personal visit to a friend who studied with me at university here on Terra Dyad. I knew her as Carrie. At our graduation ceremony she had invited me there for a kind of 'gap' holiday with her family, before I was due to take up my teaching appointment at the Terranian Institute for Education. We were university pals, you could say. We got on very well and often compared notes on our coursework. When I arrived on Carinus she showed me around her city, if you could call it that. It was more like a sprawling array of villages. It was nothing like anything here but intriguing just the same." Varia paused, momentarily closing her eyes. Breathing was obviously becoming more difficult.

As Sekandar waited for Varia to catch her breath, Varia's children and her Mother were ushered into the room by the doctor. Sekandar took one child under each arm. The children were in tears. They could sense that their Mother's life was nearing its end.

Varia continued, "I'll get to the point. Sekandar, there was something odd about Carrie's Mother. She was clearly uncomfortable with me being there. I learned later that she was a member of a mysterious religious sect that openly expressed disdain for the presence of Terranians. I thought that was very strange, given that our benevolence has been entirely beneficial to her people. "We will be rid of you!" she said. I didn't heed her comment, other than thinking that she was a bit crazy."

"The holiday was fine. Carrie's Father was friendly. Indeed, his demeanour was the opposite of her Mother. Then, as I was leaving their residence to come home, she said, "We will be rid of you, and you will be the first!" I had the presence of mind to scan hers. She clearly did not have the capability to read mine, and I was able to enter her mind easily. However, reading her mind was difficult because there were obstructions that prohibited deep penetration. I was unable to identify the obstructions, and there was scar tissue in her brain that might have indicated tampering." Varia paused again.

She mustered her remaining strength and continued, "Carrie, who saw me off at the Space Port on Carinus, assured me that she, and her Father too thought her Mother was insane. I know this is a strange story from long ago but despite that I have a feeling that Carrie's Mother is somehow connected to my terminal condition. Sekandar, I want you to find out. It may be important for The Whole." Sekandar, noticing Varia's bleariness said, "Yes of course Varia. I will find out, I promise you. Thank you for sharing your story with me. Now, no more words. You need to rest." Varia closed her eyes.

Mirum, the doctor and close friend of Varia, had been standing back with the children who were clutching her on either side. She stepped forward with them. Allowing her to come closer Sekandar released Varia's hands. The children transferred their clutch to their Father. Mirum read the monitors then said, "Sekandar, now is the time for you and the children to say whatever you need to. She was fading."

Sekandar took Varia's hands in his. She opened her bloodshot, weary eyes. "I love you to bits Sekandar. We have had a wonderful life together, and now you will have a new life. I want you to move on. You know you have so much more to accomplish. I have explained my condition to the children, and I have made arrangements with my Mother to help you care for them. We have raised them just right. They will turn out as fine young adults, and that will be sooner than you think."

Sekandar smiled, this time with tear-filled eyes making his expression intense with emotion. He brought her Mother and the children closer.

Her Mother said "I love you," then stepped back in tears. Her children whimpered, "We love you Mummy." They couldn't muster more words.

"I love you both to bits! My Zane and Aedon. I am going away, just as we talked about, and I won't be coming home again. Promise me that you will work hard in school. And, promise me that you will remember that it is not only your responsibility to contribute to The Whole, but it is also your duty. Most of all, promise me that you will watch over your Father."

With just enough composure the children said, with voices muffled in their embrace with their Mother, "We promise ... we promise Mummy."

Sekandar joined them, softly saying, "I'm sure Zane and Aedon will look after me very well." He whispered, "I love you to bits Varia. I love you with all my heart and all my soul."

He gently kissed her lips as she closed her eyes. She gently returned the kiss and whispered in his ear, "You will begin your new life. There is flame burning for you. Go to her soon. Peace be with you Sekandar."

He gently kissed her again. This time Varia couldn't respond. She lost consciousness, and slipped away. She had died.

Sekandar, his children, his Mother-in-law and Mirum, remained with Varia until the time came for her to be re-united with The Whole; this time unable ever to assume human form again. All the while with Varia in the hospital, everyone had assumed human form; the form their species prefers. And now the time had arrived for the inherently incorporeal Varia to relinquish her human form and dematerialise for the last time. To be integrated back into The Whole, from whence she came.

Sekandar raised his hands, palms up and held out at chest height before him. His children, his Mother-in-law and then Mirum followed his lead. The lighting in Varia's hospital room dimmed to a softness as all hands were raised. Each individual, including Varia dematerialised into the incorporeal, each becoming a kind of misty iridescent shimmer, coloured in the full spectrum of white light, that glowed softly then coalesced into a 'whole' and slowly brightened slightly. There was no sound. The 'whole' remained so for two minutes exactly before separating into individual shimmers again, and then coalescing and rematerialising into individual human forms, except Varia.

Sekandar said softly, "Farewell Varia, eternally with the Universe." In turn his two children, her mother and the doctor reiterated, "Farewell Mummy, eternally with the Universe ... Farewell Varia, eternally with the Universe." The group hug that followed ushered a gentle quietness, not just in the room but throughout the hospital. The Whole is reality.

Releasing the embrace, Sekandar said, "I will find the cause of this wrongdoing." The children clutched him firmly. Gently prying them from him he crouched to engage with their troubled minds.

Embracing their minds he said, "I am here for you. We need each other. We need time together. I will not leave you right now." The children continued to sob. Sekandar assured them further. "I want you to go home with Nana, and I will join you very soon." Sekandar gestured his Mother-in-law to take the children home with her.

"Don't be long Daddy, please," the children pleaded, as they departed with their Grandmother.

Sekandar said reassuringly, "I will be as quick as I can."

Turning then to Mirum he said, "Please ensure that you give me every scrap of information you have amassed about Varia's terminal condition."

Taking his hand again Mirum replied, "Yes of course, Sekandar. I anticipated your expectation. The entire log of data is accessible in The Whole. I have also established a real-time interface with our facility here, enabling you to have instant updates of our findings, and for you to add your findings and assessments." She added, "Sekandar, I would like to come with you to Carinus. Varia was my closest friend. I owe it to her to assist you in your investigation."

"Dear Mirum that is a worthy gesture. We will know whether your presence on Carinus is necessary when we have analysed all the data that becomes available to us. I will bear your want in mind. Your assistance otherwise will be invaluable. I appreciate that very much."

Stepping toward the ward doorway Sekandar said, "I must go now, my children need me. Of course, I will go to Carinus as soon as I can. I will keep my promise to Varia to find the cause of the wrong that was done to her. We will stay in touch, and I will see you before I go anywhere else."

Mirum responded, "Yes, of course. Peace be with you, Sekandar."

"Thank you Mirum. Peace be with you." Sekandar dematerialised as he walked through the ward doorway. He was gone.

Reunion

Paralía & Epitome

Varia's memorial service was three months ago. It seems like yesterday. Sekandar thought to himself, "Her untimely death was not right. It was so wrong. Perhaps it will always feel like that. I wonder how I will move on. She wanted me to, and I will ... I am."

His mournful thoughts resonated repeatedly in his mind. The memories will always be there. Nothing can take that away even though everything has changed. Sekandar has changed. He is not his former self. And so, here he is again at Paralía, and as he stands in human form in this particular spot by the front door to his house he introspectively contemplates everything about who he had been, who he has become.

Although it is not so long ago that he stood on the steps of the Galactic Council just before his departure for Earth, he remembered that he had then remained on that spot for a minute or two and had slowly turned full circle as he surveyed the city. It was very much alive for him then; an enchanting pulsating entity full of the wonder of his youth, the adventures of his early adulthood, the challenges and triumphs of his professional career, and most of all those wonderful years with Varia.

Just as they did then events of those times again flashed vividly through his mind as, this time in front of his house. He again turned full circle then stood very still, and looked up. "Everything has changed," he reminded himself. Recent events seemed like an eternity away. Perhaps they were. He knows now that not everything is necessarily as it appear to be. His species' ascendancy of the Galaxy has come to pass. His role in the culmination of that achievement would become irremissible reading for generations to come. Although some want to see him as a hero, he never wanted to be so described, and yet he is pleased that his exploits will be revered across the Galaxy. Staying a moment on that thought he smiled characteristically then slowly trod the path from his house to his waiting ground car.

Without delay he is driven away to fulfil an important rendezvous with someone whose identify is yet unknown to him. He senses no threat and is comfortable to oblige the request.

It was a long drive to his destination. The person who requested the rendezvous has instructed the ground car's computer to take the longest way possible, ensuring that he savoured the scenes along the way. His own earlier intuitive portent that his rendezvous would be momentous seemed to justify the extrospective tour. Just as of thirst, his growing need to know would soon be quenched.

The ground car came gently to a standstill before a building that he knows very well. Sekandar alights slowly, peering fondly at the building. It is the house at Epitome, the country estate of his childhood. "Why have I been brought here?" he thinks, quizzically.

Sekandar had been so preoccupied with all those other thoughts, of the day and of Varia that only now he noticed that he was unable to mentally scan for the presence of anyone else in his current surroundings. He tried to scan again, without result. That meant one thing. Someone is manipulating his mind. That someone must be in close proximity to effect that kind of mental interference. Still sensing no threat, the manipulation was 'friendly,' Sekandar strode the few paces to the front door, and knocked. At his knock the door opened slightly. He gently pushed it and it opened. He stepped inside. Darkness had already descended outside, and it was dark inside too. Nobody was within sight.

"Hello, is anyone home?" he asks. An answer is not forthcoming. Switching on the house lights with a mental 'wave', he moves from the entrance to the living room whereupon the mental interference falls away. There before him stands Iskandar.

"Dad!" Sekandar exclaims, as Iskandar steps forward to take Sekandar's hands that he had involuntarily thrust forward in his surprise.

He asks, "What brings you here Dad, and why the secrecy?"

Joyously Iskandar replies, "Welcome home, my son. A long time ago we made our home here in this house at Epitome. There are many wonderful memories here," he reflects fondly as his eyes scan the room. Pointing to the sofa therein he says, "Please, come and sit here with me."

Sekandar sat down as Iskandar continued, "Please excuse the secrecy. We have much to discuss, and very little time. I must not be long absent from my duties. I have shielded the entire vicinity, ensuring no detection from outside. It is important that nobody knows that you are here with me. Not because you are my son, there is another reason; a matter that I couldn't address at the Galactic Council."

"What could possibly be so secretively important?" Sekandar questioned his Father.

Iskandar replied, "There is a personal matter that we need to resolve, and I am sure the resolution I anticipate will be mutually pleasing. Before I come to that, first I want you to know I am ever available for you as you grieve for Varia. As you go through that there will be times when you will know that you need me. It was distressing for us all that you were confronted with her untimely death just at the moment when you must have been looking forward to celebrating your achievement with her. Assure me that you will seek my counsel, and my comfort whenever you need it."

"Of course I will Dad." Sekandar quietly assured his Father.

Iskandar continued, "You are aware that since you delivered your report to the Galactic Council, The Whole has been mentally sheltering you not only from the noise of general chatter but also from any attempt to communicate with you, other than for the regular routine of daily living. During the interval of 'silence' I intercepted several messages sent to you. One of them was clearly more important than any of the others; you will acknowledge that when you catch up with those. I contacted the sender of this particular message and explained the situation; that Varia had died and that we were temporarily shielding you from the outside world. The sender responded by accepting that then requested a meeting with you as soon as we felt you were ready to re-engage with the world. The Whole has left it to me to decide. I have decided and I will now introduce you to the sender."

Iskandar approached the living room doorway, requesting Sekandar to stand, be still and wait a moment. He then left the room and closed the door behind him. Sekandar could not resist an attempt to scan for another presence. He felt something that excited him. He stood still, facing the door. Iskandar opened the door, entered the room and stood to one side. Another person entered from the shadows of the now dimmed lighting in the hallway, the features of the person quickly became visible and identifiable. "Karen!" Sekandar called out her name, and openly expressing his unrestrained joy he leapt to her. They embraced each other closely, physically and mentally; the display of unbridled affection was obvious. As they embraced each other neither uttered words verbally. Standing by the door, Iskandar smiled; a familiar smile, with smiling eyes included.

A torrent of words now flowed from Sekandar who could barely contain himself. Releasing their embrace, the questions to Karen gushed, "How long have you been on Terra Dyad? How did you get here? How long will you be here? Did you bring anyone with you? Where are you staying? Did I say that you look wonderful?"

Karen raised her hand, gently touched his lips stopping the torrent of words with her fingers, and said, "Not so fast, Sekandar. First things first. I think your Father wants to say something." They turned to Iskandar who stepped forward embracing them both. Still facing them he stepped away.

Graciously he said, "I can see that I am not needed here right now. You have a lot of catching up to do and I have appointments to keep, 'matters of state', you understand. I think that is the appropriate 'human' idiom." They nodded affirmatively. "The shield will remain in place for now. I will inform you when it will be removed. I look forward to meeting again with you both soon. Peace be with you, Sekandar and Karen. Goodnight."

Sekandar, who had been holding Karen's hand all the while, momentarily released it. He stepped forward and embraced his Father once more, and said, "Thank you. This has been a wonderful surprise that I will always remember. Thank you for looking after me. I love you, Dad." Turning then to take back Karen's hand he said to his Father, "Peace be with you. Goodnight."

Iskandar stepped forward to Karen once more, kissed each of her cheeks, and whispered in her ear, "Welcome home." He smiled, waved, turned and left.

Lowering their hands after an au revoir a bientôt wave to Iskandar as he closed the door behind him, Sekandar and Karen turned to face each other and stare deeply into each other's eyes as they took each other's hands. The connection penetrated much deeper as they delved into each other's minds, into their beings. This is a moment they have longed for since that first evening together when they stood on the driveway at Imago. They knew this communion was not possible then, when they both had partners that they each would not betray. Recollecting that prior situation, and realising the current situation, they spoke aloud simultaneously saying, "Everything has changed."

Gesturing each other to sit, Karen gently pressed Sekandar's hands in hers and said, "My dear Sekandar, I have to apologise for not attending Varia's funeral. Iskandar contacted me, told me of his role as Prime Narrator, and revealed that he is your Father. He requested that due to my own circumstance I need not attend, and that in hindsight you would understand. He promised me that he would arrange for me to meet with you at this time, and also asked me not to tell you until now, that my partner Peter had died just a couple of days after Varia." In their mental embrace Karen informed Sekandar of Peter's untimely death.

Karen slightly tightened her grip on Sekandar's hands, and spoke verbally. "Unfortunately you didn't meet Peter; he was visiting his parents in Dresden when you arrived at Imago. You would have liked him. He was an oncologist, highly respected among his peers. Like you and Varia we too had been together since our teens; we met when we were studying at university. In time you will learn all about that. So, now you know that it has been a very difficult time for me, just as it has been for you." With a quivering voice she added, "I think we need to console each other."

With tears in his eyes Sekandar responded, "My dear Karen, please accept my sincere condolences on the death of Peter, and of course I apologise for being unavailable to console you earlier. Thank you for sharing your sad news with me, and for allowing my Father to shield me from that in the aftermath of Varia's death. I don't know how I found the strength to deal with that, on top of the excitement and celebrations of our achievement, arranged by the Galactic Council here on Terra Dyad. I felt that my Father had something to do with assisting me with that too." The verbal conversation ceased.

Resting their foreheads together Sekandar and Karen wept; it was time to grieve, and together to console each other. This too was time together they needed, otherwise. Their 'unspoken' conversation went on ... into the long nestling night.

Long fingers in varying shades of pink light, tentatively feeling their way, reached out across a clear sky into the dawning day. Draped in a sheer bathrobe revealing the beauty of her body against the penetrating subtle light Karen stood by the bedroom window looking first at Sekandar, asleep on the bed still warm with naked contentment, then outside onto this alien world; alien to her, yet embracing her with its strange familiarity. Sekandar's eyes opened, seeing her standing there. "You are awake … and you are so beautiful," he softly remarked.

Wistfully withdrawing her curious survey of the outside Karen let the robe slip from her shoulders, eased her naked body back into the bed next to his and kissed him. "Good morning Narrator Sekandar," she softly said with a smile as their bodies touched.

"Good morning Doctor Krause," Sekandar responded, with his characteristic smile. Lying on their sides facing each other they remained there looking into each other's eyes as they gently glided their fingers across each other's nakedness. They touched each other's eyes then looked deeply into each other.

Her eyes glistening with contentment, Karen said, "I want always to be with you, Sekandar."

Sekandar gently kissed her lips and then the tip of her nose. Re-engaging with her alluring eyes he said, "And I want always to be with you, Karen."

They both smiled then simultaneously said, "Are we ready for this so soon after the deaths of Varia and Peter?"

Karen affirmed, "You know we are Sekandar. We have read each other's thoughts."

"Yes we have," he replied. The long ensuing physical conversation was explicit.

The dawn had turned to day when they arose from the bed together. Holding hands, they embraced. Karen separated their embrace and said, "Well then Narrator Sekandar, you and I have work to do!"

"Indeed we do," acceded Sekandar. "I am going to Carinus. An important matter is waiting there for me to investigate. Mirum will be coming with me. She has ensured that all the information we require is readily available with The Whole, and the time is right to act now. We will get you back to Earth, so that you can prepare for your subsequent return to Terra Dyad for the next phase in your transmutation into your incorporeal entity. Now that that's sorted, let's have breakfast. I'm hungry."

"Not yet Mister," Karen said as she walked his naked body with hers into the shower.

They prepared breakfast together. Before they ate, Sekandar took Karen's hand, looked gently into her eyes and in a gentle tone he devoutly said, "Let us remember our appreciation for the Universe, its power, beauty and mystery calling for our deepest reverence and wonder. And for our individual places in it, as integral elements of The Whole. We are truly thankful for this food, its bounty. And for the highest expressions of its creation, including our love for each other."

Breakfast proceeded silently. Together they cleared away the breakfast utensils then each went about their final preparations before setting off into their day.

Sekandar stood with Karen by the front door of the old family residence.

Holding hands Sekandar and Karen admired the sky that carried a smattering of small cumulus clouds, not enough to inhibit the early morning warm rays of Terra Dyad's star. It was going to be another beautiful summer day. They held each other close. Widening their embrace and looking directly into each other's eyes, they simultaneously said, "Ich liebe dich." As the words were leaving their lips the expression of joy was obvious. Sekandar said, "Peace be with you Karen. Wait for me at Imago."

Karen reciprocated, "Peace be with you, Sekandar. Aufwiedersehen." Stepping away a pace or two he dematerialised into the incorporeal, and he was gone. Soon afterward she too dematerialised, and rematerialised at the Interstellar Interchange Port where she boarded his personal space cruiser. Sekandar assigned a Terranian pilot to take her back to Earth. She had work to do.

Translucence

Carinus

Mirum waited at the Terranian Legation, as Sekandar had requested. 'Legation' is a term humans would use to define a facility like it. It is not an adequate descriptor for a Terranian. It was just a particular building secured against any kind of probe, which one could find on every Terranian occupied planet beyond Terra Dyad, where Terranians would be secure in the event of perceived potentially threating situations. Sekandar had perceived such a situation on Carinus. It would be prudent for Mirum to wait there, and she did. She didn't just sit and wait, Terranians never did that, rather she occupied herself by reviewing the accumulated data within The Whole that she knew as The Carinus Case. Again, an inadequate descriptor but useful for humans. The Whole allowed only authenticated access to the data.

Mirum's review included observations upon her arrival on Carinus with Sekandar, their customary compliance with local protocol, and their customary transportation by ground car to their accommodation. Upon their arrival on Carinus she and Sekandar had observed an absence of minds that could access the data, except for one. That one mind was cause for Sekandar to ask Mirum to wait at the Legation where her mind would also be shielded from any form of probe.Sekandar had ventured out to locate Carrie's mother, the suspect individual. He was aided in his search by several factors including Varia's description, and Mirum's analysis of that.

Carinus had been terraformed many generations ago. Sometimes the transformation of a suitable planet resulted in a climate with mostly similar characteristics to that of Terra Dyad or Earth. It didn't work out quite so on Carinus due mainly to its elongated elliptical orbit about its slightly cooler star. Consequently, Sekandar had little time to physically find the person or being with that lone adept mind because the weather would soon change with the onset of the freezing Carinus winter.

The first gusts of cold air chilled his human form, and so Sekandar sought to warm himself in what had the outward appearance of a café. The inside was austere, there were no patrons other than himself, and the counter was unattended. He had been in similar situations and was prepared for any eventuality. He sat on a stool at the counter and scanned the premises for signs of lifeforms. As he did that a shimmer of red and blue light coalesced into a humanoid but not human form before him. Sekandar had not previously seen this lifeform. It sought to communicate telepathically with him, at first with difficulty and then in a language that he could understand. "I come in peace. You will know me as Novum. I see you are known as Sekandar, a noble name may I say."

Sensing no obvious danger Sekandar chose anyway to respond cautiously, "You are not of Kala-Ge. What are you of and why are you here?"

Observing Sekandar's caution, Novum replied, "I am of your nearest galactic neighbour. The name Andromeda is familiar to you; of course it is not the name we gave our galaxy. I have been sent to you to assist you in your quest to find the one of us who had come to Carinus."

Suspecting the obvious connection with his purpose on Carinus, Sekandar enquired, "Why do you seek 'the one,' and why have you been sent to assist me?"

Novum replied, "You know her as the mother of Carrie of Carinus. My assistance will facilitate a resolution."

Acknowledging that mutual understanding, Sekandar replied, "The one you seek is not Carrie's mother. Who is 'she'?"

Novum replied, "You are well informed Sekandar of Terra Dyad." He paused, clearly 'showing' a degree of concern. Sekandar felt it. "She is a fugitive mutant who adopted Carrie in her infancy. That was done for a particular purpose." He paused again then said, "May I continue our conversation verbally? I see you are adept at vocalised speech, and I would like to practise it in the language we are using."

The two were comfortable in each other's presence, and Sekandar replied, "Certainly."

Novum stated, "I see you are a special emissary of your species, sent to effect a change in the species that inhabit the planet you know as Earth. I also see that the purpose is to prepare that species to join you in your ascendancy of your galaxy. We applaud your species endeavour."

Pleased with the evident reciprocity of sentiments between them, Sekander said, "Thank you. I see that your species also assumes ascendancy of your galaxy, and that you too are with what we know as The Whole. I also see that your fugitive poses a universal threat, and that is why you have been sent to assist me."

Novum replied, "We concur. The purpose of Carrie's adoption by our 'fugitive is unknown to us at this stage, although we have good reason to assume a malicious intent. Working together we are sure to reveal that and then neutralise it along with the universal threat."

The café door slowly opened, bringing with it a gust of cold air. The door closed. The air settled. In the stillness a shimmer of red and blue light coalesced into an individual humanoid form, the same form as Novum. Taking a step toward the figure, Novum said as he established direct eye contact with it, "Well, well, Perfida has come to us."

Maintaining eye contact with Novum she pointed to Sekandar. "We will be rid of the Terranian, and you Novum Noesis will be next!"

Novum calmly responded, "Who are 'we?' I see no others."

"Your foolish games are over before they start, Novum Noesis!" She raised her arms laterally and uttered an unintelligible incantation. She didn't get far into it. Clutching her head she lunged forward and collapsed onto the floor in a writhing heap of acute mental and somatic discomfort.

Sekandar stepped forward to lend Novum a hand to help the stunned Perfida back to her feet. He retrieved a stool and together they seated her where she had stood just moments before when she uttered her incantation. They steadied her as Novum uttered a few words, unintelligible to Sekandar. He concluded with, "It is done." Sekandar understood that.

When Novum concluded his utterance, Sekandar said, "I see that the necessary changes have not damaged her, and my analysis of the data confirms that we have neutralised the threat."

Novum added, "I concur. Thanks to you Sekandar, our individual power combined was far too much for her. She had not fully accounted for it. I anticipated that. I see that you did too." He leant down and uttered a few unintelligible words to Perfida who was slowly recovering, then he looked up at Sekandar and said, "We must soon be on our way but I must wait until her metabolism has stabilised."

Wanting to resolve the most important matter for him, Sekandar said, "Certainly. That gives us time to define the nature of the attack, and precisely what killed Varia. We learnt quickly that it was a highly concentrated charge of plasma that must have been discharged from a fabricated source. The composition of the charge intrigued our team analysing its effect. We have also learnt that Varia's death resulted from a deformity previously unknown to us, of the sustentacular tissue surrounding and supporting neurons in her central nervous system. Why she was targeted is still a matter I still need to resolve."

Novum eased Sekandar's mind. "Of course, that is your principle reason for coming to Carinus. I can explain it for you now that I have scanned Perfida's brain to complete and confirm the data set. Her mutation was a singular anomaly which skewed her perception of what you and I both refer to as The Whole. That resulted in her belief that she was the universal power and anything contrary threatened her power and therefore had to be eliminated. As you have witnessed, her power was obviously not sufficient to be an overwhelming threat but it was developing and would have been much more dangerous if left unchecked. It was however strong enough for her to use her weapon to activate the nanobots she had implanted in Varia causing the deformity you identified."

Novum paused a moment before he continued. He said, "Perfida convinced herself that by testing her weapon on Varia, she could then deal with you. She knew that Varia's death would bring you here to Carinus where she believed you would be more vulnerable. You were her primary target. Perfida did not count on us finding her. Unfortunately we were found her too late to prevent her attack on Varia. Please forgive us."

Sekandar had seated himself on a stool by the café counter. He buried his head in his hands, a very human thing to do in the circumstance. Novum consoled his mind, and waited for him to lift his head again. When he had regained his Terranian composure Sekandar said, "Oh how I wish we had detected the menace sooner."

Novum said, "Yes, and so do we. Perfida had veiled herself long enough for her to come here, leaving us to believe that she must have hidden somewhere in Andromeda. Her ability to devise such an effective veil is now included in our understanding, which we share with you. We share with you all the data defining the weapon she created and used, and how to neutralise one if another is ever created again. I have recovered and neutralised the one she used. As it is with your species, we have no weapons. We also share with you our knowledge of inter-galactic travel, which will advance our joint purpose, to be as one with The Whole."

Sekandar replied, "Thank you." Forming his characteristic smile he then said, "Noesis? That is a word from an ancient language on Earth, meaning 'knowledge.' It implies a psychological result of perception, learning and reasoning. I assume you have been given your name 'New Knowledge' for a reason."

"I see that you and I will work well together in our future communication. You are perceptive. Yes, my name was given to me by the Galactic Assembly on Andromeda; a similar entity to your Galactic Council. It is a custom of my species to award a name for those of us who are chosen to undertake various missions across the galaxy. I am the first so chosen to venture the farthest. This was a very unusual case. I am honoured and humbled to have been chosen to undertake it, and to be known by my new name in this context."

Trying not to alliterate, Sekandar replied, "I see why you were chosen, Novum Noesis. You are able to transcend the transcendence of your species in the translucence of The Whole."

Novum replied, "I see the same with you, Sekandar." They both smiled. Novum said, "It is time for us to part. I bid you farewell. Peace be with you." Sekandar reciprocated likewise.

Novum took his now silent charge by her arm, and in a shimmer of red and blue light the Andromedans dematerialised and were gone. Sekandar contacted Mirum to inform her that all is well, that their mission on Carinus concluded satisfactorily and to inform her that her contribution to the efficacy of the required data was indispensable. He teleported himself to the Legation to pick up Mirum then they both teleported back home, to Terra Dyad.

Terra Dyad

To put it mildly, Martin Klug was excited about his imminent trip with Sekandar. He walked with him into a clearing at Imago, spread his arms and said, "I can't see anything, where is it?"

Sekandar stopped walking and said, "It's right here. Mind your ..." It was too late. Martin had taken a couple of steps further and he recoiled as the invisible cloak enveloping the ship repelled him. Sekandar steadied him and finished his warning, "... step. The ship is shielded by a forcefield." He stood there just a moment with Martin as he telepathically spoke to the ship indicating his presence then said, "Come, now we can enter." The seamless silvery skin of the ship shimmered briefly and as the outline of what looked like a door to Martin was evident. The door became transparent as Sekandar walked through it. He gestured for Martin to step inside.

Martin's excitement intensified, and his curiosity was aroused as his eyes darted about trying to take in all in.

'Wow! This is just so cool, so alien. My friends back home wouldn't believe that I am actually about to travel on a space ship to the other side of the galaxy. When we're in outer space can I have a drive of your spaceship?"

If Sekandar had been wearing spectacles he would have been eyeing Martin over them. "Maybe your tutor has been telling you tales about driving."

Not really being impudent, but maybe impertinent, Martin responded, "Your reputation precedes you Sekandar. Even my friends know about your 'driving.' If you can take control of a vehicle you have never had any prior knowledge of, I see no reason why I can't drive your spaceship."

"Sounds like a reasonable argument. I see no reason why you can't drive it. Just wait until we are clear of the solar system and she's all yours."

Martin was surprised by Sekandar's response. He replied, "Cool. Before then can you tell me something about this spaceship?"

"Yes of course, when we are clear of Earth's solar system I will 'show you around' – I think that is the expression you would use. Meanwhile, seat yourself and make yourself comfortable. We are about to ascend. You can watch the Earth on the viewer as we ascend."

The electro-magnetic motors started and the ship silently ascended from the clearing. Sekandar ensured that the ascent was slow enough for Martin to get the best possible view, first of Earth and then of its moon. Unlike his arrival where he chose to leave his space cruiser in orbit and descended to Earth in a personal pod, after reaching a point midway between the orbits of Earth and Mars, Sekandar took the ship at a vastly accelerated pace directly to its programmed co-ordinates just beyond the plane of Earth's solar system.

There he 'parked' the ship then turned to Martin who had his eyes fixed on the viewer, and said, "'Something about this spaceship' is what you asked. I will explain it in terms that you will understand. This is my personal interstellar space cruiser. You will have noticed that it is not large, it doesn't need to be. Even so it is about twenty metres long and five metres in girth, at the widest point. It is the latest 'state of the art' small personal electro-magnetic space cruiser; sleek, clad in shimmery silvery metal and fully automated; 'automated' meaning a perpetual telepathic link between me and the ship's computers, enabling communication regulating everything from plotting and navigating the ship's course to maintenance of the on-board environment, and constant contact with Terra Dyad, and with The Whole."

Martin's eyes glistened in awe. "That's impressive. Telepathic control." He perused the control station before him that consisted of nothing more than an array of Terranian symbols on a panel on the wall. Gazing at the panel he said telepathically, "So, you drive this ship with your mind alone?"

Sekandar answered telepathically, "Yes, and you can too." Martin turned his head to look at Sekandar who said, "Ok, she's all yours Martin – I think that's the expression you would use. Have a 'drive,' and take us home."

Martin sought clarification, "You mean ... to Terra Dyad?"

Sekandar smiled characteristically and answered, "That's what I mean. You will be in control – you are 'the driver,' and I will be in 'the driving instructor's seat' – Those are the expressions you would use, aren't they?" Martin nodded. Assuming certainty of his ability to take control of Sekandar's space cruiser he closed his eyes, focused his mind on the ship and took control of it, and it became an extension of him. He was now one with The Whole.

The trip to Terra Dyad proceeded effortlessly as the ship at first 'cruised' at sub-parsec speed and then negotiated a series of jumps through hyperspace across the Galaxy. The ship arrived from hyperspace at the outer reaches Terra Dyad's solar system. It was over in what seemed to Martin like an extraordinarily short time. Sekandar took back control of the ship from Martin and at sub-parsec speed he piloted it towards Terra Dyad where it settled into a low orbit around the planet. Martin resumed his gaze at the viewer which had automatically switched on following the last hyper-jump. Still in telepathic mode, Martin said, "This is your home planet. It looks a lot like Earth." He paused then said, "Terra, earth – dyad, two of the same kind. Now I understand." Sekandar smiled.

An object on the viewer caught Martin's attention. "What's that? No, no don't tell me ... let me ..." He paused then said, "That is an orbiting Interstellar Interchange Port. We're not going there. You will take the ship directly to the surface of the planet." Sekandar nodded. Martin smiled as he thought about what he had just experienced with his first inter-stellar trip through hyperspace in an 'alien' spacecraft and he reflected upon his awareness of his rapidly developing mental ability. He pondered too about another developing awareness, that all of this is explicitly and incontrovertibly connected with his destiny.

As the ship prepared itself for the final leg of their journey, Sekandar gently drew Martin's attention away from the viewer and said, "You will recall that when we first met I told you that you are a very unusual human being, and I confirmed that your inner knowing means that your high IQ and your creativity has destined you for something of profound greatness that will, as you accurately sensed, be humbly manifested in a deep obligation and duty way beyond anything you could possibly have imagined." Martin nodded his acknowledgement of that. Sekandar placed his hands on Martin's shoulders and said, "Martin Klug, you now know what that 'something' is."

Martin's persona assumed an air of mature humility. "Yes I do. I do," he said softly. His eyes gleamed with that inner knowing.

Sekandar removed his hands from Martin's shoulders, took his right hand and shook it firmly. "I think that is an appropriate human custom." They both laughed. The pair stood there for a few moments, right hand grasping right hand. Sekandar released his grip and said, "Before we land we have time to 'freshen up' and change our clothing into something suitable for our audience with the Prime Narrator, who is keenly looking forward to meeting you in person."

Sekandar's personal interstellar space cruiser continued on its orbit of the planet until the pair had readied themselves. Activating its remaining flight plan it then electro-magnetically descended slowly towards the layer of scattered cumulus clouds below, automatically seeking and finding its programmed path to its landing site. All the while Martin's eyes were glued to the viewer.

The landing was gentle and silent, and uncloaked of course. They had arrived on the expansive lawns of the Galactic Council building. The door formed in the wall where it was when they entered the ship back on Earth. Sekandar said, "After you. You are our special guest here on Terra Dyad." Martin walked through the door and stepped down onto the lawns of the Council precinct. He wasn't looking at the lawn. His eyes were busy soaking up the entire scene before him.

It was a cool late morning in early autumn. Turning full circle as he stepped slowly across the lawn a gentle variable breeze embraced Martin with a familiar hug. The Terranian thermal outfit wrapped him warmly. He felt himself being accepted by the serenity of the place. A few groups of three or four people were leisurely strolling about, some across the lawns some among the clusters of trees which for Martin completed the idyllic scene. Sekandar had walked ahead and stood waiting patiently for him atop the steps of the Galactic Council building. Martin ceased his slow rotation when he neared the steps of the building. Not taking his eyes away from it he said, "So, this is where it all happens." The moment his words left his lips he threw in a modifier. "Well, obviously not everything but that's an expression some humans might use." Sekandar smiled.

Martin scaled the steps to stand beside Sekandar who then turned him 'round to look out over the parkland and the city beyond. Sekandar said, "I have stood like this on this very spot many times and surveyed this city as we do now. For me it has always seemed like a necessary thing to do before entering the building of the Galactic Council. These few moments allow me to reflect on the mission ahead or the mission accomplished. Will you stand with me a while now and let your thoughts reflect upon the accomplishment that we have both been a part of." Martin didn't need to be asked, his thoughts were already filled with that and with his journey from freshman in Karen's class at Berlin University to his awareness, his knowing of what that 'something' he knew of in his youth really is.

Sekandar allowed Martin to take as much time as he needed for his thoughts, then said, "Come, the Prime Narrator awaits. By the way, on this first meeting he will appreciate you speaking verbally." They turned together and entered the building. Walking slowly through the hallowed halls Sekandar again allowed Martin all the time he needed to observe and wonder.

As they approached the Prime Narrator's private rooms the doors opened automatically, telepathically recognising them as they neared. They walked through the doorway and were greeted by the Prime Narrator who was waiting by his desk. He stepped forward and shook hands with each of his guests respectively. "Greetings Narrator Sekandar. Greetings Martin."

Addressing Martin he said, "Welcome to Terra Dyad. I am Iskandar, Prime Narrator of the Galactic Council. Other than on formal occasions please address me as Iskandar." Martin nodded his understanding. Iskandar added, "Did you have a good trip – I think that is the human expression, is it not?" Martin nodded again.

Exhibiting a mature stature beyond his years Martin replied, "Thank you Prime Narrator for your warm welcome, and yes I did have a good trip. Sekandar's personal interstellar space cruiser is an impressive vehicle, and he ensured my comfort admirably." Martin's rapidly developing maturity did not go unnoticed by the two Terranian Narrators.

With his arms extended wide before him and with palms upward Iskandar responded gladly, "Excellent!" Pointing to comfortable chairs he said, "Please be seated." To Martin they looked just like leather 'Chesterfield' lounge chairs. Addressing Martin Iskandar said, "Sekandar has brought you here for a very important reason. Are you aware of that?"

Supremely confident in his awareness Martin replied, "Yes, I am."

Martin noticed the characteristic familiarity of Iskandar's smile as he said, "I am pleased that you are." Seating himself next to Martin, conversationally he said, "I was just a few years older than you are now when I was requested to present myself to the Prime Narrator. I too was aware of the importance of that request. You have much more knowledge to acquire, and you need time to acquaint yourself with your new life here on Terra Dyad and here at the Galactic Council. Before we enter the Council Chamber I want to congratulate you on your dedication and mental proficiency as you have so far prepared yourself for your admission to the Galactic Council. In the very near future you will be the first human being to become Galactic Prime Narrator."

The profound gravity of the responsibility, obligation and duty that he would soon undertake was clearly written on Martin's face which spoke volumes of his willing acceptance of it.

They left the Prime Narrator's room immediately then proceeded at leisurely pace to the Council Chamber, just a short distance through the hallowed halls of the Galactic Council building. Time enough for Martin to look around this place of governance that had been standing for almost a millennium. This was the first time he was within its walls, and he was already aware that he would be walking here on many occasions in the future. On this first occasion he found himself wondering if he would perceive it all differently in the years to come. Iskandar read those thoughts and telepathically said to him, "All will be well, Martin."

The huge doors opened as they approached, recognising them as with the doors to the Prime Narrator's room. They entered the large high-vaulted chamber which was bathed in a soft yellow-blue light. Not a word was spoken, neither audibly nor telepathically as Iskandar, Sekandar and Martin approached the steps to the central dais. With Martin between the two Narrators all three mounted the steps then positioned themselves centrally upon the dais, where they turned and stood together facing the Chamber of empty seats.

Looking into the empty Council Chamber Iskandar closed his eyes for a moment or two, opened them then telepathically asked, "Martin, tell us what you see within."

Martin stood there looking upward into the soft yellow-blue light for a full minute before answering. As of fine silk the lighting in the Chamber gave off a shimmering reflection of the three of them. He closed his eyes for a moment or two, opened them then said, "Within, I see the translucence of The Whole which transcends the essence of us all, and of everything."

Iskandar said, "This is why you will be the next Galactic Prime Narrator. We have known this about you since you were very young."

Sekandar said, "You are able to transcend the transcendence of yourself in the translucence of The Whole. Your ability will facilitate the continuing development of your species and bring Humankind into ascendancy of the Galaxy with us."

Earth

There were three standing. Three were facing the wall. Moments before one had stood very close to the wall and recited prayers learnt in childhood. Standing some distance back now all three were silent in their contemplation. Each one respecting the variant relevance of the wall to each other. They were not hurried, and took their time. After a while the one standing between the other two placed a hand each on their backs and eased them away. All three remained silent until they had departed the scene; the Western Wall in Jerusalem.

Amne Tahir, Professor of Law, erstwhile collector of early Islamic artefacts, and member of a team of people who have set about changing the world, ushered his friends to a café nearby that was owned by a cousin. He took some time talking with his relative as he ordered coffee, then joined his friends at a table they found in a quiet corner of the café.

Jorie Barak, respected Israeli politician, erstwhile operative with the Israeli Special Forces, and member of that same team of world-changers, asked the man whom he now regards as a trusted friend, Guy de Villiers, Doctor of Divinity, erstwhile long distance runner, and member of that same team of world-changers, "My dear friend, what do you think has really changed as a result of The Change? What is different?"

Guy's reply was emphatic. "Everything is translucent. It always has been to me. The consequence of this is that I often found humans at their best and worst. Humankind is amazingly enigmatic; mysterious and difficult to interpret or understand. Perhaps that is our greatest strength as a species, or is it?" He stood up, walked to a window nearby then returned to his seat.

Feeling that their friend had more to say, Jorie and Amne waited. Guy took a deep breath and continued, "The essential problem for us is not between body and spirit; it is between part and whole. The problem is not that we have a body, the problem is that we think we are separate from others and from God. And we are not!"

Jorie responded, "I like that, Guy. Of course I would remind you that I am a Jew and like all good Jews I am 'programmed' to argue the point, and the counterpoint too. Your point may yet earn you an argument with me."

Jorie's remark caused Amne to feel inclined to bait him, and he thrust his worded epee. "Maybe that is one reason why your lot have found yourselves in so much trouble over millennia."

Jorie responded to Amne's thrusted epee. "Touché! I will reserve my judgement. We can come back to that later but first let's hear what else Guy has to say."

Guy closed his eyes and shook his head. "You two are incorrigible."

Amne stagily wiped his blade. "You may be right Guy, but do go on, please."

Guy did. "It is clear to me," he said, "that there is a fundamental unity at the heart of the diversity of the universe that resolves any conflict between that unity and the shared 'divine DNA' found in creation. This is an idea that is not mine alone. It is a logic in divinity which allows us to see 'the hidden wholeness' in all things and to confidently assert that 'everything belongs,' and that 'everything is sacred.' The distinction between natural and supernatural, sacred and profane, exists only as a mental construct."

Amne murmured, just a tad. Jorie shushed him.

Guy continued, "Far too easily throughout our human journey we have cited particular individual, private behaviour as wrongdoing while ignoring or even supporting structural and systemic wrongdoing such as corrupted hierarchy, corrupted government, corporate greed, modern slavery, war, abuse of the Earth ... and so on. Every form of wrongdoing has often been admired at the corporate level and shamed at the individual level. This left us utterly divided in our morality, dealing with symptoms instead of causes, shaming people while glorifying systems that are themselves selfish, greedy, lustful, ambitious, lazy, prideful, and deceitful."

Jorie murmured. Amne shushed him.

Guy raised a finger, and resumed his premise. "We can't have it both ways. Wrongdoing lurks powerfully in the shadows, in our conscious complicity with systems that serve us at others' expense. It has created largely unrecognized worldviews of entitlement and privilege."

Jorie responded. "That sounds rather like a polemic which invokes obvious questions in any mind that has not been changed, e.g., how can you make such naïve assertions like 'everything is sacred, and everything belongs?' What about manifestations of evil such as the holocaust, and in more recent times the madness which was ISIS, and the United States epidemic of mass shootings, and so on?"

Enjoying the rejoinder, Guy replied, "I agree that we can and should name wrongdoing for what it is. However, unless we first name the underlying goodness and coherence of reality, along with our own imperfection, we will criticise wrongdoing with self-righteousness that will only deepen the problem. The inference that follows is that only contemplative, singular consciousness is capable of seeing things like this without also being negative or self-righteous. Once we clear away the web of illusion we will be able to see that every created thing is still made of the same essence. There is no profane place, person, or creature. We can even find the sacred in human endeavours like sex, politics and religion. Everything is sacred. So in answer to your question Jorie, I believe The Change has cleared away the web of illusion."

Jorie was contemplative. Amne was pensive. Amne said, "Your observation is insightful, Guy. I think you are right. Guy's premise causes me to recall the notion of 'synergy. May I explain?" The other two nodded. "As you know, I am well versed in all religious texts. My 'expertise' if you will, is grounded in my knowledge of the law in all religious and international jurisdictions, and in religious doctrines."

Guy said, "I think I see where you are going with this. Please go on."

Smiling, Amne replied, "I thought you might Guy, and you too Jorie because of your upbringing in a family with a foot in both camps; excuse my use of the idiom. As I explain my premise, please correct me if you wish."

Jorie replied, "Respectfully of course, my friend. You probably know it better than me."

Pleased with the inclusiveness of his friends, Amne said, "Good, now let's go through it together." Guy and Jorie gladly nodded their assent.

Amne began with his premise. "There is a theological doctrine found in some religions called synergism. It holds that salvation results from the interaction of the human will and divine grace. I propose that in the context of The Change, synergy has a symbiotic potentiation with that doctrine; i.e., their realisation in real time and space is mutually beneficial. It is becoming more apparent to me that The Whole is the totality of being; and of course that may be perceived and interpreted in many different ways from religious perspectives. At the same time however it is indisputable that The Whole is an interconnected unity of which we are an inseparable part, even though in the past we have falsely imagined that we can separate ourselves from it. We have certainly tried to. Advent of The Change has confirmed that we are indivisibly united with The Whole. Further, it therefore also confirms that our perception, and our emotions have direct access to it. In that sense it is our ultimate reality. That is my premise, my assessment of what has really changed. There is more to it though, and this is where you two may assist me."

He paused, looked over his shoulder to sight his cousin, and said, "Before I continue, there is no religious impediment today to me eating something, and I could do with some sustenance. Would you two like something too?"

Rubbing his stomach, Jorie replied, "Yes, I would. What about you Guy?"

"Yes I would too," he replied, and added, "Thank you Amne for thinking of it."

Amne turned his eyes again to his cousin and raised a finger, bidding him to the table. As soon as he came Amne said, "Yousef, let me introduce my friends Jorie, and Guy."

They stood in their places and respectively said, "Pleased to meet you, Yousef."

In reply Yousef respectfully said, "Likewise. How may I be of assistance?"

Amne answered, "Your specialty for each of us would be good."

Yousef conveyed the request to his staff, and he returned shortly with the meals. The three friends relished Yousef's specialty which he provided more abundantly that usual, and they each thanked him for his thoughtful consideration. Fresh coffee was brought too.

Amne continued with his premise as they ate. "Unlike many of my brethren I tend to be wary of literal interpretations of holy texts. Most scholars have the same or a similar attitude. I have always believed that it is always better for me to express my point of view or my opinion about anything from my perspective and my perceptions rather than those of other commentators. It is obvious to me that the interpretation of every word in the sacred texts as literal truth misrepresents the inexplicit intent. In my mind the words are connotative; i.e., they have the power of implying or suggesting something in addition to what is explicit. I apply reasoning in drawing a conclusion or making a logical discernment on the basis of prior conclusions rather than on the basis of apparent direct observation."

Jorie said, "The inference of your reasonable reasoning has been the topic of much, shall we say 'discussion,' for countless generations of scholars, and commentators alike. No doubt that will all be very different in the aftermath of The Change. I wonder if I should be sad that the propensity for my brethren to argue will be no more."

Sympathetic for Jorie's 'loss,' Amne responded. "Maybe not. I am sure the use of constructive argument will still have a place for all of us. It enables us to examine and account for the advantages and disadvantages, the pros and cons of any matter requiring a solution or resolution."

"Precisely," declared Guy, who then looked rather sullen as he said, "Soon we will go our separate ways from this place, this holy city where so much has been given and taken. We can remind ourselves that it is symbolic of the apparent self-inflicted pain and punishment and anguish endured by Humankind for so long that was due to our propensity to seek to solve our problems by using violence, by being violent. I am reminded of words that were spoken a long time ago. Words that we failed to heed, appropriate within ourselves and act upon outwardly. Words such as 'love your enemies, bless those who curse you, pray for those who mistreat you. If someone strikes you on one cheek, turn to him the other also. And if someone takes your cloak, do not withhold your tunic as well. Give to everyone who asks you. If someone slaps you on your right cheek, turn to him the other also, and if someone forces you to go one mile, go with him two.'"

Guy paused. Tears welled in his eyes. Jorie and Amne placed their hands on his hands. They sat there a moment in mutual contemplation. Guy then said, "We are as children in our new cosmos, our 'new world' with The Whole. Let us always remember that."

A gentle draft was felt by the three. It strengthen and gradually became a breeze which began to swirl with an embracing vigour around everyone in the café. A familiar misty iridescent shimmer appeared. In that pertinent moment Guy, Amne and Jorie recognised the translucence of it. Glowing softly at first then brightening into the full spectrum of the colours of white light coalescing into the human form of Sekandar. Patrons in the café were awestruck. Sekandar soothed their minds and they settled back into their places.

"Greetings, my friends," he said as he stood by the table with these three of his 'world-changers' and said, "Gentlemen, may I walk a while with you before we part again?"

"Yes, let's do that!" replied Jorie as he responded, standing up with Amne and Guy. "Let me show you around. I know this city very well."

They thanked Yousef for his hospitality and fine food, and exited the café.

Leading them from the café Jorie literally bumped into a woman who was about to enter. She stumbled away and said, "Watch it mister!"

Jorie immediately helped her regain her footing and said, "Oh, I'm so sorry. I should have been watching were I was going."

Indignant, she abruptly responded, "Yes, you certainly should ..." and then they recognised each other. "Jorie, what a coincidence ... and Guy, Amne, Sekandar. Fancy meeting you here. What brings to Jerusalem?"

"It's a long story Meixa. Walk with us and I will relate it." Jorie replied. Yang Meixa walked with the quartet as Jorie related the story then enquired of her, "And, what brings you to Jerusalem?"

"That too is a long story, Jorie. If all four of you are free this evening we can talk about that over dinner. There are several fine Chinese restaurants here that I am connected with, and you will be my guests."

Agreeable to Meixa's surprise invitation, Jorie replied, "Sababa! What do you say, lads?"

"Sababa! Count me in," said Amne.

"Sounds good to me too. Haven't eaten Chinese in eons," said Guy.

Sekandar thought aloud. "Chinese food. I have yet to sample it. What is it like?"

Meixa hooked her arm in his and said, "You will love it Sekandar. I wouldn't be surprised if one day there will be a Chinese restaurant on Terra Dyad."

"Yes of course Meixa, I will be happy to join you for dinner. Terranians are not averse to sampling food from anywhere in the Galaxy, and who knows you may be right about a Chinese Restaurant appearing someday back home. Where and when will you expect us for dinner?"

Meixa smiled and handed Sekandar a leaflet bearing the name and address of the restaurant. "You are all welcome, and it will be my pleasure."

Sekandar then said to her, "Before you leave us, come with me." With her arm in his he took her, along with the others to within view of the Western Wall. There they stood looking at it. Sekandar settled their minds then said, "Let us together revere and celebrate the Universe, and rejoice in our acknowledgement that we are an integral part of it. Let us remember to cherish its magnificent beauty and diversity, and that all of us are equal centres of awareness of The Whole. Let us maintain an equal dignity and mutual respect for each other, mindful that we are indivisibly united. Let us also ever keep our minds open to our unending quest for deeper understanding."

They all stood there in silence for some time. Meixa broke the silence and said, "I have to leave you four now. I have things to do." She informed them of the place and time for dinner. The five separated; Meixa went her way and the four men when their way with Jorie on his guided tour.

Ascendancy

Imago

"Der Winter in Berlin kann sehr schön sein," said Giles as he entered Karen's study, closely followed by Ashlyn. They approached Karen, who was sitting alone in her study. With tray in hand he was carrying a coffee pot and four mugs. Giles placed the laden tray on her desk as Karen greeted Ashlyn with outstretched hands and a kiss.

Karen acknowledged, "Vielen Dank Giles. Na ja, der Winter ist hier schön auf dem Anwesen, wenn es schneit." Looking through her study window she smiled and reminisced, "It is so much nicer than gloomy cold rainy weather. This season is colder than usual, and snowier. I love it like this. It takes me back to my childhood when on snowy days such as this we played in the garden and made a snowman, and I did that later with Peter and Ashlyn." She paused. "Diese kostbaren Momente zusammen gemachte wunderbare Erinnerungen." Knowing that Peter could not be with them she paused again as the emotion welled.

Ashlyn, withholding her own welling tears, tried to comfort her Mother. "Ja Mutti, daran erinnere ich mich gern. Wir hatten so viel Spaß zusammen." They both smiled, hugged each other, then held each other at arm's length. Recalling those fond fun memories they laughed.

Karen, wiped her teary eyes, and resolutely declared, "Yes, and now my dear Ashlyn we can look forward with confidence to the future."

Giles drew up one of the two chairs facing Karen's desk and seated himself. He poured coffee for four, then taking a sip of his he looked up and enquired, "Will you stay here at Imago Karen or move to Terra Dyad to be with Sekandar?"

She didn't answer right away. She raised her mug to her lips and paused before taking a sip. Taking the mug with her she stood up and stepped to the window. Turning to face Giles she spoke softly, slowly. "Giles, Humankind will soon truly be part of The Whole. When that comes about we will have fulfilled our primordial dream of being at one with the Galaxy, with the Universe. We will then be able to come and go as we please or as the needs of The Whole prescribe. In that context wherever Sekandar is there am I also. Imago is my ancestral home, and I will be here as often as I can. I have a very strong spiritual connection here. That is important to me." She took another sip of her coffee, then asked Giles, "As a part of The Whole you too are free to do anything you wish. What do you wish to do now?"

Giles arose from his chair, and stood erect - as if to attention. With his familiar relaxed smile he spoke from his heart. "Karen, I have been your valet for many years. This is my profession, and I will be very pleased if you wish to keep me as your valet. You have mentioned in the past that you want to write much more about the subject of your profession. I sense that you will also want to write about The Change. To enable you to do that you will require an efficiently run household, and a properly maintained Estate. It would be an honour to do that for you." Bowing his head he added, "I am ever at your service Ma'am."

"Thank you Giles for your kind consideration. You are most welcome to stay on as my valet. You have served me with steadfast loyalty all these years. In fact I don't know how I could possibly replace you - you are irreplaceable. I know of nobody who could do your job as well as you."

"Thank you Ma'am." Giles replied, obviously pleased with the continuance of his much-loved profession.

"There is just one proviso to your continued employment with me Giles. In private you will call me Karen. When we have guests, those who are not members of The Change team, you may address me as Ma'am. Is that clear?"

"Certainly ... Karen," acceded Giles, obediently and then with a chuckle.

Karen waived away Giles' implied friendly jest. Smiling, she said to him, "He will be here soon..." Looking out at her snow covered estate, she continued, "I don't yet know when I will return but I will keep you informed." She was about to continue ... well, it didn't matter Sekandar had materialised before them.

"Good afternoon Giles, Ashlyn." Sekandar greeted them then came close to Karen, and whispered in her ear. "I've come to take you home." Karen momentarily masked her delight and, with her eyes pointing to the door, she said to Giles and Ashlyn, "That will be all for the moment, and thank you Giles for the coffee."

Giles, who lip-read Sekandar's whisper, complied saying, "Yes Ma'am ... I mean Karen ... Sekandar ... I wish both of you ... yes ..." Closing the door behind him, Giles waited to hear the result of Karen's 'mask' falling away. He then went about his duties.

Almost as excited as Karen, Ashlyn whispered in her ear Mother's ear, "I like him Mum, and I can see that you love him."

For some moments Karen warmly embraced her daughter, then waved her away saying, "I love you. I'll see you before I go." Ashlyn departed, reluctantly.

No sooner had the door closed behind her when Karen jumped to her feat, and in her unbridled excitement she said, "Yes, yes, yes. I've been waiting for you ... when do we ..?" Her question ... well, it didn't matter. Sekandar embraced her and kissed her; a full and gentle kiss.

Karen didn't want it to stop but he pried his lips from hers long enough to say, "Are you ready?" She replied, "Yes, I am," then she kissed him, firmly enough to say without words, "Ich liebe dich." Sekandar replied likewise, "Ich liebe dich, auch."

Freeing their kiss Sekandar said, "You'd better ask Giles and Ashlyn back in. We both know he would like to bid us farewell, in typical Giles style of course. And, you need a few moments with your daughter." With a light touch of a contact on her desk Karen called for Giles; it would be the last time for a while. She could have called him telepathically but somehow this was more appropriate. Giles was soon at the door, he knocked and entered, with Ashlyn almost clipping his heels.

Anticipating the reason for Karen's request, Giles addressed the pair. "Thank you for inviting me to bid you farewell. Be assured that Imago is secure and that I have ensured that everything is in readiness for your return, whenever that may. Thank you for having confidence in my professional judgement and for trusting me. I wish you safe travels."

Karen embraced him then kissed his cheek. "Thank you, my good and faithful servant. I look forward to returning to

Imago, and to get to work on my writing that we have talked about." Giles' eyes wanted to well a little tear but ever stoic his composure remained.

Sekandar placed his hands on Giles' shoulders, looked him in the eye and said, "I'll take care of her, Giles."

Giles, regained his composure and said, "Yes, I know you will."

Karen stood beside her faithful valet and she said, "Aufwiedersehn mein lieber wahrer Freund, bis wir uns wieder treffen. Friede sei mit dir."

Giles returned the farewell "Peace be with you both." He then stepped back to allow Ashlyn to say farewell to her mum. And Sekandar also. Ashlyn already envisioned him as her 'stepfather.'

"Goodbye, my dear Mum. I can't wait for your return, and when you do remember to bring Zane and Aedon with you. Promise me, please. It's just soo cool to have stepsiblings, and they'll love it here. We'll have soo much fun."

Karen lovingly reassured her daughter, "I cross my heart and promise you I'll bring them with me, just for a holiday ok?"

Twitching her nose she replied, "Oh well, I guess that's ok for now." She hugged Sekandar tight, and said, "Take care of my Mum and bring her safely home again, soon." She stepped back to stand next to Giles who put his arm around her.

The familiar iridescent shimmer of light returned and gently enveloped Karen and Sekandar. They dematerialised together, and were gone. Giles smiled and turned to look out at the snow covered estate. Ashlyn stood there with him, in quiet contemplation. The snowfall was getting heavier at Imago, and for Karen and Sekandar das Wetter anderswo war sehr unterschiedlich.

Epitome Again

The air was still. Sekandar strolled slowly from his Father's house into the small but tranquil garden, bordered with a variety of indigenous shrubs and trees framing a small manicured lawn. He paused briefly and glanced at Filo, the star that his home planet Terra Dyad orbits. The star was sinking slowly below the horizon, ushering another long summer twilight that he always enjoyed.

The warmth of the star that had warmly bathed his world in its light for another day, gradually gave way to a subtle cooling breeze; a mere zephyr drifting inland from the sea not too far away. Soon the first stars in the night sky will be visible. He knows every one of them; not only their names but also their properties and their respective places in the galaxy. Earth's star, Sol is not visible to the naked eye; it is far away in another quadrant.

He sat in his Father's swing-seat for two, and was pondering the future. He sat still for a minute or two without another thought then formed his characteristic smile when he returned to the moment; a smile with smiling eyes included. This is only his second evening at the old family residence with Karen, the first followed his Father's arranged rendezvous with her. And now, his Father has again arranged for them to be together here alone.

The twilight was fading as the last quivering rays of light were being swallowed by the encroaching darkness of night, and the first stars bravely flickered to life. As he watched the light disappear an earlier thought recurred, that the similarities between Earth and Terra Dyad are what attracted him to embrace his command of the mission to Earth. He is content, knowing now that those similarities hold no mystery but rather a majestic symbolism, typically emblematic of the Universe. Humankind is now with The Whole.

A few days ago he had taken Karen to the Galactic Council, where she successfully completed the final stages of her initiation into the incorporeal state of The Whole. He enjoyed witnessing her gracious acceptance of the privilege. An integral part of that process also formally united them as a couple. Generating much excitement in anticipation, the 'human' custom of their wedding and its accompanying celebration back on Earth was already planned. Ashlyn had conscripted the change team for that.

Karen spoke softly as she appeared from the house and sat next to Sekandar whose thoughts were elsewhere. "Sekandar, our meal is ready."

He eased back to the moment, stood up slowly with her, then stroked her auburn hair as he embraced her and kissed her gently. Holding her hand, together they took the few paces to the meal table set outside under the open sky.

They enjoyed the meal and the company of each other, talking about Sekandar's childhood memories in his Father's house, and Karen's childhood memories at Imago and in Australia with her Mother. When they were satiated and the chatter had subsided Karen put her hand in his and she whispered. "Tell me Narrator Sekandar, how did your species plan transpire, to pursue ascendancy of the Galaxy?"

Sekandar gave Karen a sideways look of familiar approval to her question, then looked up to the sky now twinkling with stars in random array, interspersed with an occasional brighter star, around the clusters of stars near the centre of the Galaxy.

"Kala-Ge." He said, maintaining his gaze into the night sky. He stood up. Karen joined him and followed his gaze, wondrously transfixed by the Galaxy. "Kala-Ge is an ancient Terranian synonym for 'home.' We Terranians have always perceived the Galaxy as our home. We have always known it."

Taking Karen's hand they sat down again. "Venturing out into Kala-Ge is as natural to us as going to the next room in the house would be for you. We never thought of it in terms of taking something that wasn't ours, and further to that, establishing hegemony of the Galaxy was discerned not only as a prequel to the ascendancy that we are now experiencing but as a prerequisite to it."

"We define ascendancy as a continuing process, and not just something achieved. For all intelligent species striving for ascendancy in all areas of life is a ceaseless and sometimes difficult journey. Good reputations can be both a propellant and a tether. The lesson is simple: when you have more to lose, you'll have a harder time ascending;

however you perceive that. The advantage that Terranians have is that the metamorphosis to our incorporeal state enabled us to appropriate a perception that we are not the masters of the Galaxy, nor of the Universe. In various forms Humankind has perceived likewise about themselves, albeit in an incomplete, inconsistent and spasmodic way. That is evident in various forms of human religious and philosophical development, although it has not been evident in human social development; the human genetic defect frustrated and impeded that."

"That is precisely the reason why we planned to effect the genetic change in humans. That is, to remove the propensity to use violence. It was a genetic proclivity causing humans to believe that their problems could be solved that way."

"Terranians held Humankind in high regard otherwise. Your species is amazingly enigmatic; mysterious and difficult to interpret or understand. Perhaps that is your greatest strength as a species. Yet it was inevitable that the genetic defect would have led you to your demise because of its cumulative, deleterious effect."

"The difference between our species is that unlike humans did before the change, we see ourselves as benevolent guardians of the Galaxy. That can easily be misinterpreted by humans, and other intelligent species in the Galaxy, as being paternalistic. We are not at all fazed by that. Our perception of this role brings with it responsibility, obligation and duty."

"Ethically we are constantly on guard with ourselves, to ensure that we maintain the best possible way forward in our continuing ascendancy. This bearing enables us to be perpetually effective in our guardianship of the Galaxy. It is the evolutionary process that transpired to pursue a plan for our ascendancy of the Galaxy. It may seem paradoxical but we believe that the enigmatic nature of Humankind will enhance the evolution of The Whole, now that the genetic defect has been removed."

Karen took his hand and gently squeezed it. She assertively said, "You are an acutely insightful and wise person Sekandar."

Sekandar engaged with her assertion. "That may be but my wisdom is not mine alone. It is a manifestation of the intellect of The Whole. Insight and wisdom are probably the most fundamental and distinctive expressions of the cognitive and intellectual character of my species that enabled Terranians to develop our galactic hegemony."

"Yes, I can see that," Karen warmly agreed as she smiled. "Wisdom is one of those essential qualities which is difficult to define, because it encompasses so much, but which people generally recognize when they encounter it. And it is encountered most obviously in the realm of decision-making. Psychologists tend to agree that wisdom involves an integration of knowledge, experience, and deep understanding that incorporates tolerance for the uncertainties of life as well as its ups and downs. In a wise person there is an awareness of how things play out over time, and it confers a sense of balance; and that has been evident with you right from the moment we met."

With his characteristic smile Sekandar responded, "Thank you, my dear Karen."

Her alluring dark blue eyes glowed as she looked into the sparkling hazel hue of his. "Allow me to continue with this. As a professional psychologist I have learnt that wisdom can be acquired only through experience, but by itself experience does not automatically confer wisdom. In my research I have looked into the social, emotional, and cognitive processes that transmute experience into wisdom. I found that wise people generally share an optimism that life's problems can be solved, and they experience a certain amount of calm in facing difficult decisions. Intelligence, if anyone could figure out exactly what it is, may be necessary for wisdom but it definitely isn't sufficient; an ability to see the big picture, a sense of proportion, and considerable introspection also contribute to its development. I see all of that in you Sekandar."

He replied, "Thank you again Karen. Mirrored differently of course, I see all of that in you too. That is one of the reasons why you were selected to head the team to effect The Change. It is also one reason why my Father chose Martin Klug to succeed him as Prime Narrator." Sekandar's eyes twinkled and with mischief in his voice he said, "Martin … Ashlyn … hmm …"

Karen responded by vigorously tickling Sekandar's ribcage as she 'commanded' him, "That's quite enough, Sekandar. Let them find their own way … qui sera, sera … ok!"

Readying himself for another tickling, Sekandar cheekily displayed his characteristic smile, now seemingly more human-like, and in a soft gentle voice he said, "Qui sera … sera." He got was coming to him.

The air was still. Each with a glass in hand of the finest red wine from Earth, Sekandar and Karen again sat quietly on the swing-seat for two in the small but tranquil garden of Epitome. They looked up into the crystal clear night sky now ablaze with the stars of Kala-Ge … The Milky Way. Sekandar placed his glass on the table beside the swing-seat, took Karen's glass from her hand and placed her glass beside his. He then gently took her hand in his and they stood up together. With both of them still gazing at the wondrous array of stars, Sekandar said, "I know every one of them; not only their names but also their properties and their respective places in the galaxy." He paused. "Sol, Earth's star is not visible to the naked eye from Terra Dyad; it is far away in another quadrant. To our ancient ancestors the fact of its existence didn't matter, nor did the existence of Filo matter to your ancients. Perhaps they were unable to perceive the eternal nature of it all."

He paused again. Engaging Karen's eyes, and with his eyes gleaming he said, "I love you … eternally … and right now I will show you our wonderful eternal galaxy."

Holding hands, Sekandar and Karen gradually turned into a kind of misty iridescent shimmer coloured in the full spectrum of white light that glowed softly then coalesced into a whole. The whole slowly brightened, and they dematerialised into the incorporeal …

There was no sound. They had gone … for now.

Acknowledgements

The kernel of Sekandar's Vector has been with me since my early teenage years; stowed away within my mind, and occasionally tantalising my imagination with brief sojourns to consciousness.

From time to time throughout her exemplary life of unconditional love with me, my wife of more than forty years encouraged me to write my book. I will always be grateful that she nurtured the seed. Although she is not with me anymore I know Barbara would be pleased that it is done.

There have been other people along the way, providing nutrients –

My questioning mind comes from my Father; I learnt from him to question statements and assertions, including my own.

My fascination with design comes from my Mother; albeit on a much grander scale with me than she could ever have imagined. I see Sekandar's Vector as a form of design.

My eldest Sister, Jenny always knew I was 'full of it,' and she has often encouraged me to tell the world. Thank you, 'my little big sister.'

My son Luke, who has become an avid reader himself, has encouraged me ever since I began writing my book. You are acquiring wisdom quicker than I did.

Dawn and Colin, both writers themselves and erstwhile mentors of mine have generously supported me with positive encouragement and helpful advice. Thank you for sharing your wisdom.

Cathy was meticulous with her critical early review of parts of Sekandar's Vector. Your contribution has been invaluable.

Bill made ready my novel for printing, and publishing. Your expertise and sage advice in formatting was indispensable. It saved me hours of work, and expense.

The cover for my book was designed by Aidan, at Baron Design. Thank you Aidan for taking on the task,

and for your creative work. Your future in Design is
assured.

The abiding friendship of my close friend Karen
has been the most important encouragement for me to
complete Sekandar's Vector. Your beautiful mind, your
true heart and the expressive energy and boundless drive
that you bring to your own life are deep and profound
inspirational motivators for me ... ild-e...

Thoughts:

"Violence is the last refuge of the incompetent"
Salvor Hardin, in Foundation
— Isaac Asimov

~

"Peace cannot be achieved through violence,
it can only be attained through understanding."
— Ralph Waldo Emerson

~

Paradidomi (παραδιδωμι)
'to give into the hands of another'

~

We are self-fulfilling prophecies.
We choose our own way through life,
otherwise it will be chosen for us.

Are these two axioms contradictory,
complementary, ambiguous or all three?

www.ingramcontent.com/pod-product-compliance
Lightning Source LLC
Chambersburg PA
CBHW071446110726
47908CB00003B/533